The Dragon Sw

Book 1 in the Danelaw Saga

by

Griff Hosker

i

The Dragon Sword

Published by Sword Books Ltd 2021

SWORD
BOOKS

Contents

Dedication

To Larry, one of my loyal readers who recently passed away. Of Norwegian descent, I hope he would approve of my story.

Prologue

I am Bersi son of Faramir and I am a warrior. My wife's brother, Sweyn Skull Taker is the hersir, but I command my own drekar. I had a dream, when I was young, of a sword. It was a dream which had reoccurred every month for the last year. When the hersir said we were to raid the church in Wessex then I saw the sword each night. It was not just a sword, it was that most magical of swords, a dragon sword. I had to find the sword and give it to my youngest son, Sven. He was my favourite for he was the youngest, but he had yet to raid with me. When my two elder sons had married, they had grown distant from me. I wondered if Sven thought I was not the hero that was his uncle, the hersir. I was determined that mine would be the first drekar to land and be the one who would find the sword. I knew it was there. I had seen it in my dreams. I saw a Saxon wielding the sword and that was wrong for a dragon sword had to be held by a great warrior and since King Alfred and King Aethelstan's deaths, we knew that there were no longer any great Saxon warriors. The Norns had spun and I would be the one to wrest the sword from the imposter. I would be the one to return it to our village, Agerhøne, and receive the acclamation of the clan but, more importantly, for my son Sven Bersisson who was destined for greatness; that I knew! I was not a great warrior but when I had practised with my youngest then I knew he was. He had a natural skill. The gods themselves had favoured him. His reactions were quick, and he knew how to do things without being taught. Perhaps that was why they had kept him in Agerhøne so that he could hone his skills. I was sad that he stayed with his mother and did not raid for I had been desperate for him to be at my side.

I had been in Ribe when I met a trader who had information about the legendary sword. I knew him vaguely for he had been a warrior with whom I had sailed but chose not the way of the blade but the way of the market. He said it was a dragon sword he had seen in a Saxon town as it had the remains of a dragon on the hilt. When I asked him where it was, he said that he had seen it on the belt of a Saxon who lived close to the River Fal in West Wessex. Dragon swords were rare and worn only by Danes or Norse. He said that the hilt was damaged and that it had a poor scabbard, but he knew it to be a dragon sword. It had cost me a gold piece to discover all but it was worth it. I kept the knowledge to myself and when my brother said that we should raid West Wessex then I knew that the Norns had spun. I had little enough to go on, but a Saxon with a

Dragon Sword would be a mighty warrior. It was when I knew we would raid the Saxon valley that I decided that I would be the first to step ashore and that I would be the one to face the warrior who would be one in the forefront of any fight on the Fal. I would win the sword. If he was a great warrior then he would have a mail byrnie and that too would be a gift for my son. Sven would become the great warrior I had never been. He would not have to live in the shadow of Sweyn Skull Taker. Even if I died in the attempt it would be worth it.

I persuaded the others on my ship and Thorkell who commanded another of our three drekar to let me lead. Thorkell must have had an idea what I intended for his drekar was so close to mine that we were almost touching. Perhaps he had known of the tale and wished the sword for himself. Such weapons draw men to them even more than gold. It was as we neared the Saxon shore that I knew this was a trap. We had raided smaller villages and Sweyn Skull Taker had kept closer to the coast as we headed for the Fal and I now knew that the Saxons had seen us and laid a trap. I knew it for I saw Saxon ships loom from the dark and I heard the noise of men from the beach. I heard the whistle of arrows as they showered us from the banks. Had Thorkell not kept quite so close to our stern then he might have escaped but he was so close to our steering board that he could not turn, and neither could we. We were doomed to die but Sweyn Skull Taker, our leader and hersir, and my nephew might have a chance of life! I turned to Olaf, my eldest, "This is a trap. We will land and fight ashore. Perhaps the noise of battle will alert the others."

My two sons, Olaf and Sveyn, were courageous and with sons at home with their wives, their blood would live on. We would not surrender! We kept rowing hard so that the drekar ground on to the beach and took two Saxons by surprise. They were crushed by the keel. It was my ship and my crew. I leapt from the prow with such a leap that I landed beyond the prow. I whipped my shield around as the first of the Saxons ran at me. I had good mail and a helmet with a face mask. I feared no one! I slashed diagonally at him and my sword bit into his neck.

"Agerhøne!" My two sons ran to my side and the three of us advanced. The noise we made would warn Thorkell and Sweyn. I hoped, when I shouted, that my cry would give them the chance to escape. We had expected just thirty or so villagers, but the Saxons had raised every farmer and warrior for miles around and there had to be more than one hundred men coming towards us. That they were a mob, and few were armoured made no matter. We would be overwhelmed. Already I heard cries as some of my men were slain jumping from the

4

drekar. Perhaps the ship's boys might swim to safety and escape. More of my men joined us.

Erik, whose brother Thrond sailed with Sweyn Skull Taker, joined us. He was grinning, "This will be an end to be told around the fires, eh Bersi? Thirty of us against more than a hundred warriors."

Olaf laughed, "Let us hope that we get to hear it then!"

"Enough talk, there are Saxons to be slain!" I turned to see who followed me. I saw that Thorkell had not escaped and the Saxon ships had him surrounded. He would take many with him, but he was doomed for the Saxons had fired his drekar. I saw that there were just twenty of us who were left to form the wedge and the Saxons had fallen back on the high ground. They were making a shield wall. Saxons do not use bows well, their first shower had alerted us and not harmed a single warrior, but their slingers sent stones to crack and crash into shields and helmets. They did not slow us at all. The slope was not a steep one and when we reached its foot I yelled, "Charge!" My sons and I ploughed into the shields. A spear gouged my face, but I ignored it and rammed my sword into the Saxon's throat. Olaf and Sweyn skewered their opponents and the three of us, backed by Erik and the others knocked down the men in the next two ranks. I turned to my left for I saw a thegn there and made for him. He had bodyguards with him, but they were not housecarls and I punched away the spear which came at me and brought my sword over to split the man's helmet and head. My men were dying behind me as they protected our backs from the Saxons there. Only four of us had any mail and we were at the fore. No longer the point of a spear the four of us fought side by side. Erik had the best protection on the left of Olaf, and it was my son Sweyn who was the first of us to die. With no protection on his right, even though he killed two of the thegn's guards an axeman hacked into his right arm, cutting it almost in two and driving his mail byrnie into his side. Even as he fell, dying, to the ground, he held on to his sword. I would see him in Valhalla.

His death enraged me, and I roared a challenge to the thegn and ran at him. I would kill him and take the dragon sword. I would die but it would be with the dragon sword in my hand! It was as I stabbed the bodyguard before him, and Erik had his head taken from his body that I saw that the thegn did not have a dragon sword. It was a good sword but not the one I sought. I resolved to take the thegn with me in any case. Suddenly Olaf pitched forward, and I saw a spear sticking out of his chest. He threw himself at the thegn. His sword hacked into the thegn's shoulder, but it was the Saxon spear which killed the thegn as my dying son, sword in hand, fell upon the Saxon, driving the spearhead deep into

5

him. The bodyguards began to hack at my son and even as I stabbed
one, I felt the sword enter my side. I felt a blow to the back of my head,
but my helmet held. I threw my shield at the men butchering my dead
son as I saw the sword emerge from my stomach. I whipped my sword
around and it connected with the head of the man who had stabbed me.
The sword bit deep into his skull as an axe hacked into my leg and I
could no longer stand. Falling, and knowing that I was dying, I gripped
my sword as I swept it around, cutting into the leg of a Saxon and then
the falling stopped, and blackness took me.

Chapter 1

My name is Sven Saxon Sword, and I became a warrior on the day my uncle returned from the raid which took my father and my brothers, leaving me with just a mother for my family. Back then I was known as Sven Bersisson and there is a saga as long as a dragon's tail to take me to the Saxon blade and my warrior name! I was both my mother and father's favourite. My mother because I was the youngest but my father because he believed I would be a great warrior one day. Whenever he could he would walk with me across the dunes and tell me of the raids and of his deeds. He knew how to tell a good story. Then when we practised with the wooden swords, he would tell of the shield wall and wedge. Sometimes his friend, Lodvir the Long, would join us and the two would spar. Lodvir was the better swordsman. Those were the best of days.

My uncle, my mother's brother, Sweyn Skull Taker, was the leader of our clan and he told me that I was an afterthought, a late baby. I was ten years younger than Sweyn who was my next brother. All my brothers were married and had children, but they were babes in arms. I should have gone to sea when I was ten; I wanted to go to sea, but my mother was ill that summer. She seemed to be ill every raiding season for the next four years and even though we moved in with my uncle in the huge clan longhouse, I was still denied the opportunity to go to sea and to raid. It was in my blood. My father, although disappointed, had asked me to practise every day and become a better warrior for one day, he told me, I would go to sea with him, Olaf and Sweyn. I obeyed him. My brothers' wives could have looked after my mother, but they all had very young children and I was the one destined to stay at home when I should have been a ship's boy on my father's drekar. They were also Saxons and did not seem to get on with my mother. I could never work out why.

We lived close to the town of Ribe, which is in Denmark, but we all spoke of going a-Viking. For the last three or four generations men from our village had been raiding the Saxons. They were an easy target. They had fine churches filled with gold and silver. Their land produced great quantities of food and their women were fertile. My brothers had married girls they had captured in the land on the south-east corner of the island which drew us there every summer. They made the best of weapons but the worst of warriors. True, we had suffered defeats, but they were few in number. That was the reason we were all shocked when just, *'Sea Serpent'* was rowed back to the village. The other two ships, my father's and Thorkell Squint Eye's were not following in its wake. This was unheard of. Three ships had left three weeks since and we had eagerly awaited their return. When only one ship was seen then the whole of the village turned out. I was the only boy left in the village who was older than ten. I had seen fourteen summers but because of my mother, I had not been to sea. My cousin Alf was still ill in the longhouse or else he would have sailed with his father. The others who waited were the old, the women and the very young. I stood with my mother and Agnetha, my uncle's wife. They both gripped my arms. The drekar was the biggest of the three and had twenty oars on each side. The other two had just twelve oars a side. I watched the dragon's head as it rose and fell approaching the dock we had built. The paint was faded. There would, normally, be just one raid left in the raiding season and then we would enjoy the rewards of the raids. We had taken enough already that we would not starve but the slow and steady progress of the drekar under reefed sails was ominous.

The four ship's boys leapt ashore and quickly secured the boat to the dock. As was customary the next ashore was my uncle, Sweyn. He was the only one in his crew with a full mail byrnie. He had taken it from a Saxon, some said it was a prince's. It was the most beautiful piece of armour I had ever seen. He also had the best sword in the village. It too was Saxon and he had taken it from the same Saxon. The Saxon had lost his head in the fight and it had given my uncle his name, Sweyn Skull Taker. The sword hung from his belt and he wore sealskin boots. He landed heavily on the dock as he jumped down. My uncle was a huge warrior. My father had told me that it would take four times as many wounds to kill him as any normal-sized warrior. I did not doubt it for a moment.

That day changed my life.

My uncle was a blunt man, and he wasted no words. He waved his left hand in the direction of the land of the Saxons, "Sven, your father is dead as are your brothers. Gunhild, I will become Sven's foster father until he becomes a man and can make his own choices." He nodded to the men trudging from the drekar. "We are tired and have had a hard row, let us eat!"

He began to head towards the longhouse. It was as though my father and my brothers were already forgotten. My mother, head bowed, followed. I was not satisfied, and I ran after him shouting, "My father and my brothers, you cannot dismiss them with just an airy wave of your hand! Why has your ship returned with nary a mark on her and the other two have not?"

He turned and there was anger in his eyes, "You are now my foster son and I would spare you the account. This is not for the whole stad to hear. Do not push me, boy, and let it lie!"

I was angry too and I squared up to him. It is laughable now for he was twice my size and I was not yet fully grown, "It was not just my family who perished. There are others here, many of them and their men were on the other two ships."

I saw his shoulders slump and he shook his head, "Perhaps I can change you and make you a better warrior than your father." He raised his head and looked me in the eyes. "You wish the truth?"

I nodded, "I do!" Inside I feared his words for there was something in his eyes which terrified me. I was not afraid of him, but his eyes bespoke some horror and I wondered if I had been rash.

"Then here it is, your father died because he was a fool. I liked Bersi. He could tell a good tale and was a skald beyond compare, but he had no judgement and we have lost good men because of that. We had gone to Wessex to raid. Their king, Aethelred, is weak and I had planned the raid well. We took one village and then another. I decided to sail up the river they call the Fal for it goes deep into their western lands and seek the church and monks who are like rich sheep waiting to be fleeced. I was the one who would have led for that was my way. Your father and Thorkell chose to go first before the appointed time and my crew were unready. It was a trap." He shrugged, "They must have been watching us and spread the word. For that, I take the blame, but the rest was down to your father and his quest for glory. They were ten lengths from us, and they headed up the narrower river to the settlement and church we had spied. A boat sped from one bank with a rope while the two ships, still rowing, were showered with arrows and rocks from the banks. Three Saxon ships appeared behind us." We had reached the longhouse and he sat down on the log outside.

His wife, Agnetha, brought him a horn of ale and put her hand on his shoulder. It was a sign of support.

"I saw the drekar afire and knew they were doomed. I saw the ones who had survived the arrows and the rocks pulled from the holed ships and they were butchered before we could even think of a way of getting to shore and then the Saxons came for us. I gave the order to turn and we fought our way out. I lost four warriors and shield brothers." He downed the ale and then said, "There, foster son, are you any happier now that you know how they died? Few died with a sword in their hand and the food and treasure we had taken were in the ships. We cannot raid again this year and food may be short. That is your legacy from your father. Now I have spoken enough!"

9

He stood and entered the longhouse. Most of the others joined them. My mother, tearful and looking as though part of her had died in Wessex shook her head, "That sounds like your father, Sven. I loved him dearly and it goes without saying that your brothers were also precious to me, but he had ambitions and he wanted to be the greatest warrior in the clan." She smiled sadly and added, "Perhaps the whole of Denmark. It was ambition killed your father. Come, let us go inside."

I shook my head and balled my fists, "No, mother!"

She nodded, "As you wish. The wolf is eating your heart and I can do nothing about that." She turned and went into the longhouse.

The warriors passed me as they headed, with their sea chests on their backs, into their own longhouses. Some went into the main longhouse. Suddenly a gnarled hand was placed upon my shoulder, "I will tell you more. Sweyn is right about your father but he was my friend, and you should have the whole truth."

I turned and looked up into the face of Lodvir the Long. I nodded, "I would like that for I cannot understand how these Saxon sheep trapped, captured and killed the crews of two drekar!"

He sat on the log and I joined him, "They were sheep, but they have learned to fight. They grow tired of paying Danegeld to our King. When we scouted the church, we saw that it was not a burgh like they have further east. It had neither wall nor ramparts and ditches. That should have been a warning. It was why Sweyn was cautious but your father and Thorkell saw it as an opportunity to reap a greater reward than any had taken on a raid. They left our camp six hours early and by the time Sweyn Skull Taker realised they were far up the river. The ships were set on fire and men had to leap into the water. That was how they captured so many men for a man cannot swim with a sword in his hand. When they landed, they would have been weaponless."

"You saw my father and brothers die?"

He shook his head, "Thorkell's ship was between us and your father's. We were lucky to escape for it was a well-made trap. Your father was not a fool, nor was Thorkell. All that I can think is that we were spied when we scouted out the church and they knew we were coming."

I thought about this, "Then had Sweyn Skull Taker led the ships he would have been sunk!"

Lodvir shook his head, "Your father left early, and it was dark when he rowed up the river. Without a burgh, we did not need to worry about landing in daylight. The plan had been to enter the narrow waters as dawn was breaking so that we could have edged up the river looking for dangers. Your father and Thorkell had every oar manned and the sails billowing. We had our sail furled." He turned to look at me, "You know that your father was my friend?" I nodded. "As much as I liked him, I have to agree with Sweyn, he was often a reckless man who acted impulsively. Your uncle is a planner." I began to become angry and tried to rise. Lodvir was a powerful man and he forced me to sit. "A man has to face his demons head-on, Sven. Today, whether you wished it or not, you became a man! The reason I say he was reckless is that Sweyn is a good chief who makes good decisions and while we may not have had the treasure other clans have taken from the Saxons until this raid, we had lost barely a handful of men. Your father wanted to be a Sweyn Forkbeard or an Olaf Tryggvason. He wanted a coat of mail for you like your uncle's."

I subsided and thought about his words. He waited patiently. Lodvir had no wife. She had died in childbirth and thus far he had not chosen another bride. He spread his seed in the thralls. He had spent much time with us in our longhouse, sometimes sleeping there. He knew my father. I had not seen the recklessness. I had just heard the stories of the raids and they had been told to me by father, the skald. As I thought about his words, savouring each one as though it was something to eat, words had been unpleasant while others had been bearable. I turned and said, "You said whether I wanted or not. What did you mean by that? I wanted to go to sea, but I had to stay at home!"

He shook his head, "Did you? Think about it, Sven; could you have pushed harder to go to sea? You were, you are, your mother's favourite and you enjoyed an easy life here in the village. You commanded your father's thralls and played with your wooden sword." His voice became lower, "Your father was not happy that you chose to stay with your mother."

"I did not!" Even as the lie spilt forth, I knew he was right and that led me to one conclusion. I was the reason my father and brothers were dead. He was trying to impress me. He always had. His stories of the raids were not the truth. The actions he attributed to himself were those of Sweyn Skull Taker. It all became clear. I remembered the looks on my brothers' faces. They had known. My father had tried to be Sweyn on the last raid. He had done so to impress me. I had killed the crews of two boats.

Lodvir was correct and my world did change that day. It was as though a weight descended upon my shoulders. I found I could not look others in the eye. I became silent and spent more time alone. I also determined to become as good a warrior as I could. The week after the drekar returned Sweyn held a Thing. All the men gathered outside the longhouse to speak of the future. Everyone offered their views. There was no criticism of my father or Thorkell. That was the past and the Norns, Urðr, Verðandi and Skuld, had woven that into the spell of the future already. We had to deal with the situation we had. As a clan we had a choice, we could leave the sea and become farmers only or we could return to the ocean and go a-Viking. It was clear from the arguments that only one or two wished to become farmers. That decided, the clan also took the path of vengeance. The men of Wessex who had trapped us would pay for their treacherous act. We would return in the next raiding season and wreak revenge upon them. That meant that every young man, including those three or four years younger than I would have to go to war and become warriors. Every eye in the village was on us, but especially me, as Sweyn told us that we would all have to train from dawn until dusk to replace the dead.

Lodvir was, unusually for such a warrior, kind to me. He took me to one side not long after the Thing and spoke to me, "You have used a sword, or a wooden one at least, but your hands would not last a week at sea. You have some strength but not enough to take an oar. The other new sailors will not be on the oars, you will, for they will be ship's boys."

"Then what can I do about it?" I resolved to be a better warrior than my father and, if the Gods allowed it, a better warrior than Sweyn Skull Taker. I would heed any advice that I could to make that happen.

He nodded for he saw the determination on my face. He pointed to the wood which lay four miles east of the village. "Rise each morning as the sun climbs to the horizon and run towards it with an axe. Hew as many trees and branches as you can and carry them back here. Do that every day and by the time we are ready for sea you will have hands which are calloused and toughened, and your back will be broader. The running will strengthen your legs for rowing needs strong legs."

I nodded and, as I thought about it, realised that I would not be able to carry much back. "Lodvir, I cannot carry much!"

He grinned, "Not at first but eventually you will and that will be a sign that you are growing stronger. Remember this will be in addition to all the other tasks you are given. We have a drekar to prepare for sea. We were damaged by the Saxon ships and besides the drekar needs the weed taking from the hull and pine tar applying. I do not think that you will have time for self-pity!"

I turned sharply. How had he known?

It was as though he could read my thoughts for he said, "That was your father's problem. He was my friend and, once, a shield brother, but he had a habit of blaming all his ills on others or the Norns. His favourite phrase was, 'it is *wyrd*!'"

12

I realised he was right.

He pointed to Sweyn Skull Taker who was practising with my cousins, his sons, Sweyn and Alf. Alf was of an age with me and had not yet gone to sea either. That was not out of choice. On the last raid, the fatal one, he had been due to sail, but the fever of the spots had struck and laid him low. He had recovered just a day or two after the three ships had sailed and I knew that he was bitter about missing the opportunity to go on his first raid. "Sweyn takes responsibility for his own actions. He does not blame bad luck."

And so I began a daily routine. I found a good tree the first morning but as my mother might have said, my eyes were bigger than my belly. I hewed it but the time it took to take all the branches meant that when I trailed into the village carrying half the trunk, it was mid-morning, and I was in trouble for we had begun work on the drekar. I saw Lodvir cock his head to one side and smile. He had known! The next morning I rose while it was still dark and ran without the axe. I retrieved some of the wood on that first trip and the rest by the second. When I returned, this time with my axe, the sun was rising and I chose a smaller tree which I hewed and even though it was heavy, carried the whole thing back. I would take the branches when I had finished work on the drekar. By the time the days had shortened, I could see the benefit of the work. My hands had passed the bloody stage and the new skin had hardened. I was now wearing my older brother's kyrtle for I had broadened, and I could make the run much faster.

After Samhain Lodvir came to speak to me. He had offered advice on a regular basis, how to keep the axe sharp, how to tie logs in bundles to make it easier to carry but this day he said, "When you go, on the morrow, look for an ash tree. There is a stand of them there. Choose one which is taller than you and as straight as you can manage. It is time we made you a spear."

Finding the ash shaft was not as easy as I had expected, and it was almost the winter solstice when I managed to find the perfect one. I was able to study the chief's. It needed to be sturdy but not too heavy and it had to be eight feet long. Once that was in my hands, I spent the short days when we had no work on the ship for the pine tar was drying, smoothing the wood. At the same time, I found the metal I would use for the head. We had poor Saxon swords and daggers my father and brothers had brought back from earlier raids and I chose the ones with the better metal. We had no weaponsmith as such, but we did have a workshop with a fire and an anvil. Our clan were all adept at metalwork and Lodvir promised that he would help me. There were always pieces of broken metal to be found but it had to be of the right quality and that

13

took me as long to source what I needed as did the ash. When, eventually, I had enough we went into the workshop with an already glowing fire as the icy wind from the land of the Rus chilled us to the very bone. We soon warmed up as the metal was first heated and then melted into the mould Lodvir had shown me how to make. It had a narrow point and then broadened. It would have been quicker had he done it, but he was keen that I learn, and I think it was another criticism of me. Being the youngest I had been both indulged and spoiled. Others, younger than I, knew how to do things I did not. When we left the head to cool, I was nervous. Until I could take a sword in battle this would be my only weapon and it had to be right. I was relieved when we took away the mould and the head was whole without a single crack or flaw. I spent three weeks polishing and sharpening it until it was ready to be fitted.

If I thought my work was done, then I was wrong. I had to find the wood for the shield. This was easier for my daily visits to the woods had shown me where to find all manner of trees and I was able to find the oak and the willow that were the best combination. It was not Lodvir who helped me to make the shield but one of our Saxon thralls, Egbert. Egbert had tried to escape not long after he had been taken ten years ago and my father had lopped off four of his toes as a punishment. He had been promised to lose more than his toes the next time and the thrall had accepted his fate. I liked him. I had been little when he had first come, and it had been I who taught him Danish while he taught me to speak Saxon. He had been a warrior and knew about shields. He had known about spears too but neither Lodvir nor any other warrior would have considered letting a slave near a weapon.

He had approved of my wood choices and helped me, after others had cut them into rounds, to work them until their edges were smooth and they were roughly the same size. "Master Sven, a poorly made shield is worse than no shield at all for a warrior relies on something which will let him down. Your people have better shields than mine and it was a poor shield which enabled your father to capture me. We will make you one which will be the best in Agerhøne. When shield walls clash weak shields are found wanting. You need three layers, at least. It makes the shield heavy, but you are strong." He smiled, "Stronger, anyway since first you began your runs and wood-cutting."

"Do we need to cut a hole for the boss?"

"Have you a boss that you can use?" A boss was a round piece of metal to fix in the centre of the shield enabling the user to punch with the shield. I shook my head. "Then for now we use three straps to hold it on your arm. When you have the metal it just takes a little time to cut a hole and fit the boss."

When the rounds were ready, we used good glue to stick them together, but Egbert showed his experience for he made sure that the grains of the three pieces of wood went in opposite directions. I was then made to leave the shield to dry for a month. I was impatient but, as Egbert pointed out, it would be another three months before we raided. All that he allowed me to do was to attach a piece of sheepskin to the arm side to provide some cushioning. Reluctantly, I left the shield.

My life after the death of my father was not all wood-cutting, hauling timber, repairing drekar and making weapons, it was also touched by violence. I had few friends and the ones I counted on as friends had died on the drekar with my father and brothers. They had been the ship's boys and young rowers. There were others my age and they had been on *'Sea Serpent'*. They were not my friends. The violence came from two boys, both a little younger than I whose father, Erik, had died on *'Sea Serpent'*. They blamed my father but as he was not alive to punish, they took their vengeance out on me. I suppose I could have blamed Lodvir for my beating as his insistence on my daily routine made my movements predictable. A week before I was to resume work on my shield, as I was coming back from the wood, laden with pine to be used on *'Sea Serpent's'* deck, they ambushed me. It was a good lesson for it showed me, when I reflected on it, how to spot an ambush. The cord they used to trip me was well hidden, but I had known something was odd before I tumbled to the ground, spilling my wood and dropping my axe.

Ulf and Erik were upon me in a flash and Ulf's foot connected with my ribs. I was just glad that it was his bare foot, or it might have caused more damage. Erik tried to kick me in the head, but I managed to twist around and take the kick on my upper arm. It still hurt but not as much as it might have done. Erik made the mistake of trying to repeat the kick, but I was ready and this time, as Ulf stamped on my back, I cupped my hands and threw Erik's foot in the air. He fell backwards and I rolled away from Ulf. I scrambled to my feet although the stamp on my spine had hurt. Instead of kicking, I used my height and strength. I punched Ulf hard in the face. It hurt my hand and his face erupted in blood. Erik had regained his feet and he smacked one of the branches I had cut into my already injured back. I punched Ulf again but this time in the stomach and he bent over double, gasping for air. Even as I turned to face Erik, he swung the branch at me but this time brought it across my face. I saw stars and began to tumble but I had the wit to reach out and I pulled the end of the branch towards me. He did not let go and we tumbled to the ground, our faces close together. He opened his mouth to bite my nose. I did not wish the name Sven No Nose and I brought my knee up hard between his legs. I connected with his groin and his scream was like a vixen in the night. As he rolled from me, I stood and grabbed the axe to threaten them.

"You pair of treacherous snakes, come at me again and one of you will die!"

Neither had the breath to answer and I became so angry that I walked over to Erik and raised the axe. A voice from behind me arrested my blow, "If you kill him then you will be guilty of murder and made an outlaw. Do you really want that?"

I turned and saw the chief, Sweyn Skull Taker, and his eldest son Sweyn Sweynson. I shook my head, "They ambushed me!" I pointed at Erik, "This one hit me from behind with a branch."

Sweyn nodded, "And they have both paid for that. You have acquitted yourself well, Sven and gone up in my estimation. Perhaps Lodvir's work has paid off. As for you two," Ulf and Erik had recovered their breath but that was all, "I know not what prompted this attack but whatever the reason, it ends here, or you shall not sail with me! Understand?"

They both nodded. I picked up the timber and held it close to me. I narrowed my eyes and made my voice as threatening as I could, "And if you try it again then bring a weapon and others for from this moment on I travel armed and I shall be watchful for cowards who strike in pairs and hide like bandits." I confess that my words did nothing to make peace. If anything they hated me more than ever but between the chief's threat and my attitude, they chose the path of peace, at least for a while.

Sweyn Sweynson said, "Here, cuz, let me take the wood."

Shaking my head I said, "Lodvir said it will make me stronger and I intend to be the strongest warrior on the *'Serpent'*!"

My cousin grinned, "Stronger than my father?"

I nodded, "I did not say anytime soon but my foster father is growing old and I have yet to fill out my body. I have time!"

I liked my cousin, Sweyn. He was five summers older than I was and a good warrior. At least from what others said he was a good warrior. That was the best way to judge until you went to war. He persuaded me to let him take the axe and when we entered the longhouse, having put the wood to season, he called over my mother to see to my hurts. My cousin Alf was there. He was the younger brother, just months younger than me and this vengeance raid would be his first voyage too. My mother tended to fuss even more now than she once had. I was her whole family, and I knew that when I went to sea it

16

would break her heart. I could do nothing about that. I tried to make her life easier. I smiled a lot and offered to do any little task she might need. I had lost my family too, but I was young. My mother was quite old, I had been a late child and I knew that she did not have many years left to her.

"What has happened?"

Sweyn smiled, "Aunt, it was just a squabble between boys. It happens but I do not think it will happen again."

I knew that it wouldn't. Sweyn Skull Taker would let it be known what punishment awaited any who hurt his stepson and I would ensure I had my seax with me. As mother tended and fussed over me, I worked out where I would carry the knife. It had been a spare my father had taken on a raid. Saxon seaxes were good weapons. With a slightly curved blade, they were of little use when using the point but if one slashed with them they could be deadly, but they had to be sharp. I had yet to take the seax and scabbard out. When my mother had finished then I would sharpen it.

Once she had cleaned the blood and taken the splinters from my head and face, she reluctantly let me go. I went to the chest with my father's and brothers' things. Their sea chests had been lost with their drekar, but they had all left spares, older weapons and war gear that they did not need. I first took my seax and laid it to one side. My father had given it to me, and it was a special weapon because of that. I had not opened the chest since their death, and I found all manner of treasures. Olaf had left a pair of sealskin boots. They were slightly too large, but I also found some oiled woollen socks and they made it a comfy fit. I would not use them until we sailed but they were a surprise and all the more welcome for that. I found my slingshot. I had not used it for some years. The attack spurred me to become as proficient as I once had been. I also found my brother Sweyn's dagger. This was shorter than the seax, but it had a bone handle and a straight blade with a point. I would put that in my new boots. I also found Olaf's leather helmet. He had worn it until a year ago when he had taken a helmet from a Frisian. They would do.

I was wary when both travelling to and returning from the woods the next day. I knew the trails in the woods well. I used two new routes, but no one tried anything. I had seen the two youths around the settlement and the dark looks they gave me told me that they had not forgotten and if anything the feud had been aggravated by the fact I fought back, and they had been punished by the chief. I put them from my mind once I returned to the work on my shield. Egbert had seen me wearing the seax and, indeed, when he had heard of the attack, he had

17

shown me how to sharpen it so that I could shave with it. When he began to put an edge on the blade I wondered if this was wise. What if he turned the blade on me? I laughed it away. There were many simpler ways to hurt me and escape would not take him far.

Now that the wood was glued, we attached the leather straps through which my arm would go and the longer carrying strap for my back. If I thought I was finished, then I was wrong. We headed over to the workshop where men made weapons. There was no fire. All the weapons for the raid had been made in the winter when the making of the weapons would give heat. Egbert had me search the floor for the tiny pieces of metal which had fallen from the hot iron. There was a surprisingly large number. He placed the pieces on the top of the shield and began to spread them out. When he was satisfied, he handed me a small hammer and asked me to embed them in the shield.

"Will they not fall off?" I could see the value of adding them.

He shook his head, "We are not yet done."

He returned to our old longhouse which was now occupied by our thralls. He brought out the tanned hide of the goat we had killed before Samhain. She had stopped giving milk and we had her young to rear. After spreading hot glue on the wood and the metal he tacked the skin around the front. He added a few more nails on the front and then smiled, "All done, Master. All you need now is a design."

I knew that was important and I said, "For now I will leave it blank. What colour can we stain it?"

"The easiest would be a dark red. We have old beetroot which is no good for eating and there are the blackberries which went rotten. I have still to throw them out."

The decision was made for me. I had no preference for red but it would do. We prepared the dye by boiling up a mash of beetroot and rotten blackberries. The smell was not pleasant, and we left it outside to cool. The next day we submerged the shield in the liquid and four days later when it was dry, we sealed it with pine tar. That took another week to dry and then I was ready for war which proved to be timely. Sweyn Skull Taker told us that we would be sailing in a week and we should prepare all that we needed. It was at that time that Alf fell ill. He would not be able to sail again and the absolute horror on his face told me that I was ready to go to war. I believe that had the ailment struck me then I would never have sailed. The Norns were spinning and I manage to avoid whatever Alf had.

My mother wept from the moment she heard until we pushed off. We had known this was coming and Lodvir helped Egbert and I make the chest from the first wood I had hewn from the woods. It was stained and varnished and ready to be filled with all that I would need. Despite her tears, my mother provided me with things I might need. She had baked a cake with honey and dried fruits. She told me it would last a month. Her tears had returned when she said she had made the same for my father and my brothers. She had used wool to weave me a kyrtle which she had oiled, and she had made me oiled woollen socks too. The sealskin cape was a surprise for I knew that they were valuable. It turned out it was my grandfather's. My father had kept it for sentimental reasons but Lodvir said that it was *wyrd*. I was meant to have it. I had a blanket for sleeping too. I packed my drinking horn as well as the wooden spoon I used and the knife which was not a weapon but something to slice meat from salted pork. With a good ale skin as well as a skin of my mother's special mead and a round of her cheese I was ready. Agnetha, my aunt, gave me some pickled herrings in a small pot. I felt like a man carrying my chest over my shoulder as I stepped aboard the drekar, her decks freshly cleaned and with the broken pieces of the gunwale replaced she was like a new ship.

My shield was across my back and I held my spear in my hand. When I looked aft, I was quickly put in my place. Thorstein the Lucky was the steersman and he stood with Sweyn Skull Taker. They were smiling and Thorstein said, "I did not know the ship's boys needed a shield, Captain."

"You are early, foster son, and that is no bad thing. "Where do you want him?"

They looked at each other, "Where can he do the least harm?"

The beating I had received from Ulf and Erik was nothing compared with their comments. I was placed at the bow where I would sit alone on the larboard side. I put my chest where I was told and laid my spear along the deck, securing it to the thwarts with rope.

"Hang your shield there!"

That was the moment I felt a warrior when I hung my red shield from the side of the drekar. I had changed from a youth to a man. I had no idea how I would fare in battle, but I had taken the first steps. As I sat there watching the rest of the crew board, I reflected that without my father's mistake I would be doing this with advice from my brothers and my father. As it was, I was alone. Lodvir had done his part and now I would be on my own. I would sink or I would swim. There would be no middle ground. I put my sealskin boots in my chest along with my seax. Until we reached Wessex, I would need neither of them.

Chapter 2

The youth who took the oar opposite me was roughly the same size as me, but he was younger. I did not know him for his family farmed outside the settlement. They raised pigs and I could smell them on Siggi, for that was his name. He appeared to be a little slow but I warmed to him when Ulf and Erik came aboard. They knew him and named him Siggi the Pig. The other ship's boys all laughed, and the name stuck. It mattered not that Griotard the Grim walked up behind them and slapped both on the back of the head so that they fell forward, the unfortunate Siggi was now burdened by a name he would not wish.

"Get to work you pair. Sven and Siggi will be working hard on this voyage while you pair will be playing at sailors!"

Griotard nodded at us and then walked down the centre of the drekar to ensure that the sea chests were all correctly positioned. We were at the narrow end of the drekar and would be the only new warriors rowing alone. The other new ones were closer to the stern and each rowed next to an experienced rower such as Lodvir, Griotard, Sigrid, Sweyn Sweynson and the like.

I turned to Siggi, "I am Sven Bersisson."

He looked at me and said dully, "I know. My brother was on his ship. It is why I am at sea. My father was lamed two seasons ago on a raid and one of the family has to go to sea."

I was unsure if there was criticism in his voice. As I later learned he spoke in a monotone most of the time. When we later spoke, he said it helped to keep the pigs calm.

"Do you not wish to go a-Viking?"

He shrugged, "I do not know these Saxons although if I can kill the men who butchered Snorri then that will help but I would rather be with the pigs." He put a finger to one nostril, stood, leaned over the side, and blew out of the other. He repeated it and sat down.

"There will be treasure, Siggi. That will help make your family's life easier."

He nodded and seemed to see me for the first time. "You wish to be a warrior, I can see that." He nodded towards his sword. "The sword is my father's, and I am not even sure I can use it properly. If you had a sword then you would know. That is the difference between us. When we raid, I shall stay close to you. I will try to watch your back but if there is fighting to do then I will be happy for you to do it." I liked his honesty and knew that he would do just what he said. He had that look of truth in his eyes.

"That is good." I smiled as I said it, but this was not what I had expected. I had expected everyone to be as excited as me. I looked down the deck and saw Sweyn Skull Taker and Lodvir looking at me. This was planned. I did not know the reason, but they had put me with dull Siggi for a purpose.

The last of the crew came aboard and I saw Thorstein the Lucky grumbling at them. Griotard the Grim ensured that they had correctly aligned their chests and that their shields were secured and nodded to Sweyn, our captain. He pointed to the ones who were before the mast and said, "Oars!"

They all went to the mast fish and each selected an oar. The ones who were between the mast and the steering board were the best warriors and oarsmen. When they had selected, Sweyn walked past the next five pairs of chests and said, "Oars."

That just left the six of us at the bow. I saw then that the two pairs before Siggi and I were fathers and sons. I knew them for they shared a longhouse. Eystein and his son were before Siggi and his brother Dreng and his son, Folki, were before me. When the others had chosen my foster father nodded to us and we rose to select our oar. By the time Siggi and I chose there were just two left and they were obviously the ones no one else wanted. I saw Ulf and Erik sniggering. Once more my pride took a beating. As I headed back to my chest, I reflected that if I had gone to sea with my father I would not have suffered as much humiliation.

My foster father had stayed at the bows. He did not address Eystein and Dreng but Siggi and I, "You two have the least experience and you will make mistakes. Hopefully, those mistakes will not cost us. Griotard has a knotted rope and it will eliminate your errors. Watch the rowers before you and copy them. If you make a mistake then raise your oar from the sea and then get into the rhythm again." He smiled at me, "This is part of your lessons, Sven. Bear it like a man and it will make you stronger. Lodvir has done his part and now it is up to you."

I nodded and held my oar vertically like Dreng. I waited for the next command, but my mind had worked out that Lodvir had been asked to do what he had done. I was the soft clay that my uncle wished to make into a warrior. I had thought the year of being ignored and left alone was some sort of punishment. It was not.

Griotard shouted, "Larboard oars, out!"

I saw now why my oar had been left until last. It was slightly warped! I pushed it out so that it was level with Dreng's and looked to

21

ensure that the blade faced the right way. He and his son had an easier task for two of them held their oar. The steerboard oars would push us from the quay. I could feel the breeze and knew it blew from the land, the east. We need not row for long, but I suspected that the captain would have us rowing until we tired. My father had told me that rowing made the different men onboard into one. As you rowed so you became part of the ship. I had not really understood that when I had been told but I had not been interested. Now I would find out if it was true or not.

The command was given to push us from the quay. Mothers, mine included wept and were comforted by other women. There was no cheering. That would be for when we returned. I could not see well for Siggi and the others were between me and the quay.

"Steerboard oars out!" The river was relatively calm and the drekar felt stable. Once we reached the sea then that would change. "Oars!"

I lifted the oar until I felt it touch the water.

"Pull!"

I can still remember that first moment as the blade pulled us through the water. I saw Dreng's head come back and I emulated him. My feet pushed on his and his son's chests. I lifted the oar and leaned forward and began the process again. There was no chant. It would have made little difference for I would not have known it. The Captain, Griotard and Thorstein were testing us. We had too many new men on board to do other. It was but a short way to the sea, less than half a mile but my back was complaining before we reached it. Carrying the logs and hewing the trees had given me muscles but I was using them in a different way.

As soon as we reached the sea Thorstein ordered the sails to be lowered and Griotard walked towards the bow. He stood behind us and I knew we were under scrutiny. I was determined not to make a mistake but as we hit waves and the bow came up, so my oar struck not water but fresh air. I saw now why Griotard was there. He snapped, "Keep your oars in the air until you can get back to join the others. Do not foul the oars of others." He smacked the knotted rope into his palm as a threat. I had been allowed one mistake!

The sail billowed and pushed the bow down into the water. I felt the sea beneath our keel and I glanced over at Siggi. I saw he was watching me. He nodded and I began to row once more. We must have pleased Griotard for he stayed just a short while before striding down towards the steering board. We seemed to be flying. The sail and the oars which dipped and pulled made me think we might see the land of the Saxons before the day was out. It was a foolish thought, but this was my first voyage. My back ached and burned but there seemed to be no sign of the Captain relenting. Then Griotard began to chant and the older crew took it up.

Bluetooth was a warrior strong
He used a spear stout and strong
Fighting Franks and slaying Norse
He steered the ship on a deadly course
Njörðr, Njörðr, push the dragon
Njörðr, Njörðr, push the dragon
The spear was sharp and the Norse did die
Through the air did Valkyries fly
A day of death and a day of blood
The warriors died as warriors should
Njörðr, Njörðr, push the dragon
Njörðr, Njörðr, push the dragon
When home they came with byrnies red
They toasted well our Danish dead
They sang their songs of warriors slain
And in that song, they lived again
Njörðr, Njörðr, push the dragon
Njörðr, Njörðr, push the dragon

The chant was repeated until all knew it. I learned later that the song was part of a longer work about Harald Bluetooth. We rowed, in my view, for too long. True, the work with the tree axe had hardened my hands and given me callouses and carrying the timber had strengthened and broadened my back but my hands were red raw because the saltwater aggravated them, and the muscles in my back burned as though Thor had placed his furnace behind me. When we were ordered to stop and to rise, as I stood, I could no longer see even a smudge on the horizon. We had completely left the land. I saw that we had changed course. We tramped to the mastfish and stacked our oars. I was pleased to see that Siggi and the sons of Dreng and Eystein looked equally drained. Lodvir stood by the ale barrel. I rushed back to my chest and took out my drinking horn. I knew that from now on I would need it around my neck. That way I could drink whenever I needed. I saw that the experienced rowers had done so, and I was at the back of the line waiting to have my drinking horn filled. Siggi had his drinking vessel with the white foam at the top and I held mine out for Lodvir.

He grinned at me and gestured at my hands, "And imagine what they would have been like had you not spent all those months working!"

Nodding, I greedily drank half of the horn and then realised that Lodvir had replaced the lid. I would not be given a refill. I would have to eke out the last half. "Why did we row for so long, Lodvir? The wind was in our favour."

He smiled enigmatically at me, "There are many lessons which you will be given, Sven. Some will be obvious whilst others will need you to think about them. You will have plenty of time to think for this voyage will take at least ten more days for we wish to avoid Aethelstan's ships." With that, he turned and headed for the steering board. It was clear to me now that the three senior warriors on this drekar were the hersir, Lodvir and Griotard. I also learned that nothing was done without planning. I headed back to the bow. The freshly painted serpent head was fearsome, and I knew why the sight of the prow of a dragonship inspired such fear in all. I sat with my back against the side of the drekar and with my feet against my chest. Siggi was doing the same whilst silently chewing some salted pork he must have brought from home. I was not hungry, but I had a thirst which one horn of ale would not quench.

I decided to see how long I could make it last and while I did, I gave thought to Lodvir's words. I looked at the crew. The older ones were throwing dice or playing other games of chance while the new ones, like Siggi and me were slumped against the side of the drekar. The ship's boys were adjusting sheets, stays and the sail. The Captain was exhausting the new crew and letting us know this new world we had entered. I made the ale last until noon and I wondered when we would be fed. My mother had told me to husband my supplies until I needed a memory of home or I was really hungry. She knew all about sea voyages. A husband, her three sons, not to mention her brother and her father, had prepared her well. I realised that I needed to make water. I stood and dropped my breeks.

"The other side, the steerboard." I turned and looked at Dreng, he smiled, "The wind is from larboard. A face full of piss would merely give others the chance to mock!"

I knew Dreng to be a kind man. My mother had told me so. As I relieved myself over the steerboard gunwale I saw that my foster father had deliberately placed Dreng and his brother Eystein for that reason. Sweyn Skull Taker said little to me in the time since he had become my foster father and I had thought he viewed me as a burden but perhaps he was taking his task seriously.

We ate in the early afternoon. The ship's boys had trailed lines astern and there was fresh fish which we ate raw and this augmented the fresh bread we had brought. Soon we would be eating stale bread but the first day it was soft and tasty. We drank water! The horn made the water taste a little like beer. Hopefully, when we raided Wessex, we would have fresh supplies again. We rowed again in the late afternoon, but it was not a long session. I began to see a plan behind it all. This time Griotard and Sweyn took an oar and we sang the Bluetooth song again. It was a statement that the two might be senior warriors, but they rowed too. When we finished, we were given another ale. This time I was not the last in the line. I was learning.

Although the sail was reefed a little when darkness came, we did not stop but carried on through the night. As I wrapped myself in my blanket, I saw that Thorstein the Lucky also wrapped himself in a blanket and Griotard took the helm. Ulf and Erik stood by him. They would be the watch. I took pleasure from the thought that they would lose sleep. I curled up between the thwarts and my chest. The gentle movement of the drekar and the exhaustion helped me to fall asleep quickly. I was awoken in the middle of the night by rain. It must have fallen on me for some time before I woke for my blanket was soaked and my kyrtle felt damp. I took the kirtle off and lay naked on the wet blanket before covering myself with my seal skin cape. I had to curl into a ball, but I was dry. I had learned another lesson.

The next day the drekar looked like the longhouse on the day the women did the washing. Blankets and clothes were laid out to dry. I wore the spare kyrtle my mother had packed for me. She had known what I had not and I thanked her. The days followed a regular pattern. We rowed twice a day although never as long as on that first day. I would speak to Siggi when we rested if only to hear the sound of my voice. I came to know him, and I learned that while he was not the quickest of men, he had a good heart. He had promised to watch my back and I knew that was more important than anything. After three days he shared his salted pork with me, and I gave him a small taste of my mother's mead. I had decided to drink that elixir sparingly but having eaten his pork I felt obliged to be hospitable in return.

We saw our first ship five days into the voyage. We had just turned west and, I guessed, we were off the coast of the island of the Saxons. The ship looked to be a larger version of a knarr and Dreng said it was a Saxon merchant who would, no doubt, head for the nearest port and give warning of a dragonship which was loose in the waters of Cent. Had we wished then I knew we could have caught the boat, but we had vengeance on our mind as well as treasure. We would sail west and only turn to the coast when Thorstein the Lucky deemed it right. However, the sight of the Saxon set us all to prepare for the raid. Every warrior had a whetstone, and I sharped my spearhead. It had already been sharpened but the sea, as well as the salty air, had dulled it. I realised that I needed something to cover it and protect it. If I found naught in Wessex, I would make a sheepskin sheath for it when I returned home. Siggi sharpened his sword. I could see by the way he handled it that he had little experience with the weapon. The advantage of a spear was that I had used one whilst hunting with my father and brothers in the woods where I had hewn trees. I knew how to hold it and I had sunk it into flesh, albeit that of a deer once and a wolf. I could also see that his shield had no internal padding. Egbert had helped me to make a good one and I thanked the lamed Saxon. I held my Hammer of Thor and closed my eyes, "Thor, watch over the thrall Egbert for he has served my family well."

The last two days of our voyage were hard for the winds and the weather changed. The wind turned to bring warmer but wetter weather from the south-west. The seas were wilder too and we had great crests to climb before plummeting into deep troughs. We were now heading north and west which meant we had some help from the wind, but we had to row for longer. It was then I learned how our sailors could row for such long periods. The oars which had been double manned were now single manned and the pace was slower. We used a different chant. It was not a saga but a chant about who we were. Our home and clan were called Agerhøne which means grey partridge and the chant was a play on that name.

We are the bird you cannot find
With feathers grey and black behind
Seek us if you can my friend
Our clan will beat you in the end.
Where is the bird? In the snake.
The serpent comes your gold to take.
We are the bird you cannot find
With feathers grey and black behind
Seek us if you can my friend
Our clan will beat you in the end.
Where is the bird? In the snake.
The serpent comes your gold to take.

It repeated itself endlessly. It was the sort of nonsense a child might make up, but we liked to play with words and as we rowed '***Sea Serpent*'** it seemed appropriate. It was also easy to learn and kept us going. The spare rowers relieved us and that was the hardest part of all. It was why we sang the song for we all had the rhythm and as one rower slipped out the other took over. It worked and none of us, even the new ones, missed a beat. We seemed to be getting nowhere as night fell although it was hard to judge distance when there was no land in sight. We hove to with a sea anchor and after cold fare and a horn of ale, we went to sleep. That was the night I shared one of my mother's honey cakes with Siggi. I know not how but it seemed to warm us and, surprisingly, I slept. I was helped by the fact that the strength of the wind lessened and the rise and fall was not as bad. We were not given long to sleep for the sun had barely risen when we were woken and put to the oars straightaway. The sail was unfurled, and we headed north by west once more. We rowed all day until Thorstein deemed that we could now turn, ship the oars for a while and sail north by east. When I went to make water, not long after the sun, had we been able to see it, had passed noon, I looked beyond the prow and saw a thin smudge. It was land. Our destination was in sight.

The ship's boys were sent up the mast to reef the sail. The violent pitching had ceased but it was still hazardous as it was a lively sea. I said, to Dreng, "Do we prepare for war?"

He shook his head, "We will not reach the coast until after dark and there we will step the mast before rowing up the fjord. Sweyn Skull Taker will not be taking any chances this trip."

Chapter 3

It was almost dusk when we passed the mouth of the river and we began to head east. Then we took to the oars and turned the drekar into the wind. We had the oars manned singly and I saw the reason as first the sail was taken down followed by the cross tree and then the mighty mast was unshipped and placed on the mastfish. It took until dark for that to be done and I felt weary already for it was hard keeping the drekar steady. Then, with the oars double manned we headed back to the mouth of the river. I saw that the Captain and Thorstein had planned well for the tide was on the turn and it was easier heading upstream into the wide fjord-like river. Night had fallen but I could tell that it was wide by the shadows I saw in the distance. We rowed steadily and silently. Sweyn Skull Taker walked up to the prow while Griotard stood by the mast fish. I did not know, at first, what my foster father was doing but when I saw Griotard gesturing to Thorstein I worked it out. He was directing the steersman. The daily rowing had helped to meld us into one crew. I no longer had to think about rowing. I just followed Dreng and his son as they leaned forward to pull back and then lean forward again. The saltwater had hardened my hands and while the scars were still ugly, they no longer pained me. The river was smoother than the sea and was also silent. The sound of the hull slicing through the water was the only one we could hear but I did detect, for we had not smelled it since we had left our home, woodsmoke. It told me that there were hidden homes close by.

Suddenly Griotard ordered, by hand signals, the steerboard oars to be raised. The larboard crew continued to row, and I knew that we were turning. Then the steerboard oars were lowered and I saw Siggi look at me to get the rhythm. That was the only time that our drekar did not sail smoothly and then we were as one, yet again. When Griotard signalled for us to slow I guessed that we were about to land and when a few moments later we were ordered to raise our oars it was confirmed. Six ship's boys leapt into the water, I heard their splashes as they landed in the shallows, and ran with ropes to secure us to the land. I stood, along with the others and marched down to the mastfish to replace my oar. The centre of the deck was crowded as men returned to their chests to don their war faces. I saw Thrond the Cruel smearing charcoal on his face while others used different colourings. My father had used the red cochineal and I knew this because once he had not cleaned it from his face when he had returned from a raid on the Pomeranians. He told me that in the firelight, at night, it frightened enemies. He told me how some Norse filed their teeth to add to the effect.

I reached my chest and took out my boots. I slipped one knife into the boot and then put my seax in my belt. I donned my leather helmet and then unfastened my spear. Siggi was already clambering over the side. I would not be the last to leave the drekar but there would be few behind me. I took my shield and slipped it over my back. It was hard enough to climb down a drekar with a spear. A shield would have made it impossible. The water was knee-deep, and I realised I should have donned my boots once I was on dry land. Griotard was impatiently waving to us to hurry to the path where the others were gathering, and I dared not stop to empty the water which sloshed in them. I hurried to join them and saw a stump of a tree. There were men behind me, and I sat on the tree, rolled back and was showered by the river water from my boots. I saw Lodvir smile in the dark. Half of the veteran warriors had open helmets while the rest either had one with a face mask or a nasal. Even Siggi had a helmet but my father's and brothers' were not there to be passed down. I would have to earn mine and to do that I needed to kill. Many Danes had become Christians. We were still pagans but even Christian Danes were unworried about killing Saxons, Frisians, Pomeranians, and Franks. We were warriors and that was what warriors did; they fought, and they killed or they themselves would be killed.

I stood as Griotard and the tardy ones arrived. Only Thorstein and the boys would guard the drekar. When we had enjoyed three drekar we had the luxury of leaving older warriors to guard the boats too. My father's reckless actions had put the whole clan in danger. What had he been thinking when he had recklessly raced to his death? Sweyn Skull Taker drew his sword and raised it to signal us forward. The plan had been told to us while we had sailed west. There was a large village and what the Saxons called an abbey. Sweyn would lead half of us to take the church while Griotard and Lodvir would take the village. I was to be with Griotard. His was the more dangerous part for the villagers would have weapons with which to defend themselves. My cousin, Sweyn, had explained that this was part of my initiation as my foster father could not be seen to be giving me special treatment. He would be with Griotard too. Siggi was with those raiding the church and so he could not watch my back.

We waited at the edge of the large village. It was bigger than Agerhøne. I took my shield from my back and slipped it over my arm. The others headed up the hill to the church we could see in the distance. The whiff of perfumed air drifted down. Dreng had explained that to

29

me. The Christian priests liked to use something called incense to make their churches smell sweeter. The containers they used would often be made of silver; they were valuable.

It was bad luck that we were spotted. A man emerged from a house perhaps eighty paces from us. He was probably going to make water. Just as the smells around us were different so our smell was too, and I saw him sniff the air. A mixture of seawater, raw fish and sweat must have drifted to his nostrils and turning he spied us and shouted. Thanks to Egbert I knew what he said. "Vikings!"

Griotard shouted, "Skjalborg!" We had to make a shield wall! Again this had been spoken of on the voyage. Eight of us had spears while the rest had swords and axes. The eight of us, led by Lodvir the Long, would form a block, five men at the fore and three of us including me, in the second rank. We would lock shields and advance down the centre of the village while the others raided the houses. My task was to hold my spear, as yet unnamed, between the two warriors before me and keep my shield in their backs. The shouts from the houses as our men entered drowned out any orders issued by Lodvir. He was the centre of the wall and as the tallest warrior in the clan, stood higher than those who flanked him. He made a natural rallying point. I pushed my spear between the shields of Leif and Lars, two brothers and held my shield in Leif's back. I had not practised this, and I just followed the instructions I had been given and hoped I did not let anyone down. If I did then the results could be fatal.

The village, we later learned, was called Lanndege and we had not known its layout. The lord of the settlement had a large hall, and it was on the far side of the village. Its shadow dominated the place. So it was that while Griotard and the others had little opposition, we could see, as we advanced through the village that men were organising at the far side. Lodvir shouted, his voice strident enough to be heard, "We hold, whatever they throw at us. Sweyn Skull Taker and the others will reinforce us once the church is taken and the priests slain!"

The screams of the Saxon men dying gave me hope but the sight in the distance of some men in mail filled me with dread. I did not even have leather to protect my body. The five men before me all had leather byrnies. Lodvir's even had some metal studs and he had a good helmet. Almost any weapon coming for my head would be fatal. I kept pace with my cousin Sweyn, who was next to me. I envied him his leather. He was in the centre behind Lodvir. On the far side, Dreng's son, Folki, protected his right. This was not because he was the son of the chief but if Lodvir fell then Sweyn would become the centre of our line. Folki and I were young and expendable.

"Stop!" We halted just forty paces from the Saxon warriors.

I saw why we had stopped, the Saxons had formed their own shield wall, but it was twice the size of ours! They lumbered towards us as Griotard and the others cleared our end of the village. It made sense to me even though I could see that it put the eight of us in more danger. The Saxons could take as long as they liked to reach us for the longer they took the greater the likelihood of help. The leader of the Saxons had a long sword and a helmet with a face mask and some sort of bird on the top. I saw that their shields were slightly smaller than ours.

Lodvir's voice was both commanding and comforting, "Remember, especially you new warriors, that you wait for my command before you punch with your spears. Let the Saxons wet themselves and strike too early!"

I learned that day the difference between a Saxon and a Viking warrior. We wanted to fight. They fought because they had to. I was a little afraid, as the Saxons approached, but I was more afraid of failure. I did not want to soil my breeks and I did not want to run away. I would stand and fight come what may! Four other Saxons had short byrnies and the only long one was worn by the leader, someone said they were called thegn. I wondered how Lodvir and the other four ahead of me could be so calm. I could hear my heart pounding in my ears!

Once again, it was Egbert's lessons and language which helped me. I heard the thegn shout, "Charge!" And I braced my shield into Lars' back as the Saxons sped up. It was a mistake for they did not keep as one and even I, a novice, saw gaps in their shield wall. The thegn had his sword raised. He would clatter it down on to Lodvir's head. They seemed to be so close and I wondered why no command had been given. Just the head of my spear, which had yet to taste blood, poked out before Lars' shield.

The command, when it came, made me jump but I reacted instantly, "Punch!" I rammed my spear forward with all the effort I could manage, and I felt it hit metal. I pushed harder, twisting it as Lodvir had taught me. I felt something snap and then I found something soft. A spear came for my head and it knocked my leather helmet from my head whilst scoring a red line along my scalp. I felt the blood drip. I pulled back my spear and this time, when I lunged, I did so upwards and to my right. That was whence the spear which had hit me had come. I know not if I was lucky or some hand guided me, but I saw my spearhead strike the Saxon under the chin. This was not metal, but flesh and the whetstone had done its work. It went up into the warrior's head and I pushed harder. He was wearing an open-faced helmet and I saw the light and life leave his eyes.

31

Suddenly I heard a roar behind me, "Agerhøne!" and a weight crashed into my back. Had I been a weaker man then I might have tumbled but the journey to the woods and back each day had given me legs which looked like young oaks. The eight of us were propelled forward and I found myself trampling on the face of the Saxon I had killed. I saw Lodvir's spear haft raised as he rammed it down hard. When I stepped over the body of the thegn then I knew who the victim had been. I did not know what to do. The breaking of an enemy shield wall had not been discussed and so I followed Leif and Lars as we pushed the Saxons before us. More were knocked off their feet and speared for I saw their bodies as we almost ran towards the thegn's hall. I saw a helmeted face below me, and I just rammed my spear down. I did not know if he had been dead or alive but something in me said that this was not a time for doubt. His scream as I withdrew the spear told me that he had been alive.

It was Sweyn Skull Taker who gave the next command, "Shield wall break!" We had been told what to do when this command was given. We were to unlock our shields and kill any Saxon who remained alive. This was a vengeance raid and there would be no quarter given.

The Saxons broke and were hurtling back to their hall. I was young and unencumbered by mail of any description. I just ran and I found myself ahead of Lodvir and my cousin Sweyn. After hauling logs for almost a year carrying just a spear and a shield seemed like nothing. I speared my first Saxon in the top of his unprotected thigh. He wore a leather byrnie, but his breeks afforded no protection from my broad-headed spear. It sank in easily and blood spurted and arched. I twisted and pulled making the leg collapse beneath him.

The blood told me it was a mortal wound and with victory in my head, I ran harder. It almost proved to be my undoing, although as I look back, I know that it was the Norns spinning. A warrior with a leather byrnie stood before me and his mere presence stopped me from running over the small bridge across the ditch which guarded the hall. His shield, sword and helmet marked him as a warrior and not just a farmer with a weapon. I was running too fast to stop, and he swung his sword at my shield. I completely missed with my spear thrust which went over his shoulder. His sword almost jarred my shield arm when he struck, but my thrust made me overbalance and we fell, not onto the bridge but into the water-filled ditch. When we hit, the force of the landing knocked the spear from my hand and if I had not made such good leather braces for the shield, I would have lost that too. As it was, I knocked the wind from the Saxon, but he had a sword, and I was weaponless. He had a full beard flecked with grey, which told me he was a veteran, as well as a broken scarred nose, and he spat at me for our faces were close. All other noises were in the distance. I knew that fighting continued but my battle, my struggle for life was in the water-filled ditch with this Saxon who seemed ready to end my short life.

"Danish dog! Today you will die!"

I suppose a more experienced warrior would have had some witty reply, but I was scared that my first battle might be my last and then I remembered the knife in my boot. I kept my weight on my left arm and the shield while I drew the dagger. His left hand was still attached to his shield and as I raised the blade, he saw what I intended, and he tried to pull his shield up. I shifted my weight a little as I tried to bring the knife up. It had slipped down, and I had to scrabble after it. I saw him move his head back to butt me. I grabbed the hilt of the blade and pulled it up. He wore a mail coif as well as a helmet and all that I could do was go for the exposed eye I could see. I was helped by the fact that his head was moving forward to butt me with his nasal. I drove the dagger up into the orb and then the soft matter that was his brain. I kept pushing even though he had stopped moving.

I felt a hand touch my shoulder and I whirled around. It was Siggi and he was grinning, "You are alive, oar brother! I think we have won!" He put an arm out to pull me from the ditch. I slipped my dagger into my boot and let him raise me. I was shaking. It was not fear but the sheer joy of being alive and excitement at what I had done. I had fought to the death with a veteran and won. I retrieved my spear and then laid down my shield. Others had entered the hall and the screams from the women told me that men were still wreaking vengeance. My appetite was sated and now I sought the rewards.

I nodded back up the path to where we had first fought. "There is a warrior I killed up there. He will have a hole in his byrnie and a smashed face. You may have his helmet and sword. This is a better one. The byrnie is mine!"

He nodded, "I have yet to kill! The priests died without a fight!"

I pulled the coif and helmet from the body. I unfastened the baldric and took the belt and the scabbard from the Saxon and then I prised his dead fingers from his sword. I started to unfasten the fastenings on the leather armour. I saw as I glanced around that the sun was beginning to lighten the sky. I heard Griotard and Sweyn shouting orders, but none appeared to include me. I kept at my task. When I had the leather armour, I saw a silver cross around the man's neck. Here was a find indeed and I pulled it from his neck and slipped it into my boot. I stood and slipped my shield around my back before strapping on my new sword. The sheath looked a little tattier than I had expected for the sword was well made. I suddenly remembered that the man would have a seax and I bent down to retrieve it.

Siggi came towards me. He had the sword and helmet, which was dented. "Where is the mail byrnie?"

"Thrond took it. He said he had killed the man."

I did not like Thrond. His brother had been on my father's ship. He was Erik's uncle, and I am sure he had put the boys up to the attack. I knew that I would have to let the matter lie, for the moment. I had earned the mail, but it was not worth a fight. I had a leather one and that would have to do.

"No matter. I have done well!"

"You both live!"

I turned and saw a bloody Lodvir carrying the helmet and mail of the thegn, "Aye, Lodvir and I thank you for your lessons. I think that today they saved my life!"

"That is for sure and I know not what possessed you to charge like a berserker with neither helmet nor mail. I see that you now have both and you Siggi, have a better helmet."

Siggi was an honest youth, "It was Sven killed the owner, but he let me have them."

Lodvir nodded, "You have learned well, Sven, and you think about your oar brothers. Perhaps there is hope for you. Take your treasures to the ship and then return. You will not need your spear nor your shields. We have work to do!"

We were not the first to reach the drekar, now bathed in the early morning sunlight. I laid my treasures across my chest. I retained the sword for I would look like a warrior.

Thorstein the Lucky nodded approvingly, he had been a friend of my father, "You are now blooded, Sven. That is good. Your treasures will be safe. I shall watch them." I think the words were a warning for Ulf and Erik. He said to them, "Lift the deck. We will have a treasure to load!" The deck close to the mast fish could be lifted. The ship's boys, especially the smaller ones, would be tasked with crawling beneath the deck to load our treasure.

As we headed back, I saw the Saxon women, weeping and wailing, carrying the treasures from the church. It had been a rich church. Some carried the vestments of the priests while others carried the gold and silver plate as well as candles and candlesticks. Dreng and Folki prodded them with their spears to keep them moving. When we reached the village, we saw that the dead Saxon warriors had all been stripped of their weapons and from the church came the smell of burning. Having been emptied, the wooden building was being fired. That told us that we would be leaving soon for the fire would bring warriors from miles around and the attack on my father's ship told us that there might be hundreds rather than dozens.

Sweyn Skull Taker had taken off his helmet and he nodded towards me, "You did well, foster son." He pointed to a couple of milk cows, "The two of you take these to the drekar. Secure them at the bow." He was smiling as he told me, and I groaned inside. The voyage home would be a smelly one as we would have the two cows closely tethered. The cows moved when we prodded them with two broken spear hafts. The heads had already been taken. No metal was ever wasted. Others were driving some goats and a few sheep towards the ship. Barrels were rolled down towards the river. We had done well. There would have been coins in the thegns hall. If we were lucky then some might make their way to our purses. It all depended upon the generosity of the chief, our hersir, Sweyn. He made such decisions. It took us longer than the rest to negotiate the path. Thankfully the two cows emptied the contents of their bowels and their bladders before we had to drive them aboard. Hopefully, after just consuming water on the voyage home it would be largely their pee we would have to clean. Siggi knew animals and he coaxed them aboard up the gangplank which creaked ominously as they were led to the deck and thence the bow. We did not get to go back to the village for we saw flames rising as it was burned. We had not found where they had buried our dead, but they had been punished. They might be able to rebuild but it was more than likely, so Dreng told me later, that they would simply abandon the village and start again.

Thorstein said after Siggi had securely fastened the animals, "You two, help the others to raise the mast. There is no need to hide any longer."

By the time, the mast was in place and the cross tree hauled up, the deck had been replaced and the twenty slaves herded close to the mast fish. We had almost no room now. Animals, booty and slaves filled it all. While the sail was fastened to the cross tree Griotard came to speak to Siggi and me. "You will not need to row on the way home."

I nodded but knew that something was coming, "That is kind, Griotard the Grim, but I am sure there is a price to be paid."

He laughed. That in itself was a rare event, "You are as clever as your father was, "Aye, the two of you should move your chests to the larboard side of the drekar. You will both be watching and tending the animals. Use ropes to make a pen to keep them close to the bow."

Siggi did not seem to mind. Raising pigs was even smellier than cows. By the time the sail was raised, and we cast loose from the shore it was late afternoon and we had almost completed the rope pen. There was always plenty of old rope on a drekar. The ones which had broken in the storm had been replaced and we used those as well as the spares. I cleaned my spear and said, to no one in particular although I suppose it was aimed at Siggi, "I have no name yet for my sword for it has not spoken to me, but the spear shall be Saxon Slayer!"

He nodded absent-mindedly for he was examining the cows, "As good a name as any."

When the cows began to low it was Siggi who knew what to do. "They need to be milked!" As we left the burning village to head to the sea it was the happiest I had seen Siggi. He was right. He was no warrior. I, on the other hand, had never felt so alive! I wished that I had not had to look after my mother for then I could have learned to be a warrior by watching my father and brothers. Now I would have to watch others. Perhaps this was meant to be; *wyrd*.

Chapter 4

I could see from the huddle of warriors gathered by the steering board that all was not well. It was not the two dead men whose bodies were in shrouds waiting to be buried, it was something else. When we had sailed up the narrow river it had been in the dark and now, I saw just how narrow it was. The current and the wind meant we could use the sails. Soon we would enter the bay-like fjord, but I remembered how my father and Thorkell Squint Eye had been trapped at that very spot. As Siggi happily milked the second cow I said, "We may have to use our weapons once more, my friend."

His face fell, "But we have escaped!"

"When we reach the sea then we will have escaped. Have you a bow?"

He shook his head, "Just a sling!"

"And I have one. I will fetch them. I do not intend to suffer the same fate as my father and my brothers."

Griotard came down the boat. He shouted at the wailing women to be silent as he passed. Terrified, they obeyed. He spoke to the men he passed, and they stood. Lodvir came along a little further and spoke to those of us by the bow. "Sweyn has decided that we prepare to fight our way out if we have to. The burning village and the church will tell the whole land that the Danes have returned. Until we reach the sea we prepare to fight. Slings and bows will be needed." He saw our two in my hand and grinned, "Like your father!"

I had received two such comparisons and as much as it made me feel good there was also a warning. My father had had a fatal flaw which had killed not only him but his crew and Thorkell's too. I would have to look at every decision I made and weigh it up or else I risked treading the same path and, perhaps, suffer the same fate. I was learning that I was my own man, and I would shape, as much as the Norns allowed, my own destiny. I had a small bag of stones and I tied the pouch to my belt. I was desperate to don the helmet and perhaps the coif, but I was aware that might invite ridicule. I would wait until we were back in Agerhøne before I did that. I was guided by the fact that none of those who had taken some of the prized mail byrnies had donned them. That could wait.

I knew this would be a slow dusk. The clouds we had enjoyed earlier had now disappeared and the sun hung low in the sky. It would descend slowly. When we burst from the narrow river into the wider

37

expanse of water, I felt like cheering, but I did not. I merely fastened my sling to my belt and took a swig from the stale ale in my ale skin. I could afford to finish the old ale for we had Saxon beer now. We would not be rationed. I tipped my head back and drank deeply. I was hungry too but that would have to wait. From what I had been told we would have to carefully place our cargo, barrels, humans and animals before we reached the sea. It was as I lowered the skin that I saw them, there were two Saxon ships, and they were heading for us. I wondered how and then, as I looked aft to the steering board, I saw to the east the pall of smoke from the burning village and the church. Had we made a sign to say Vikings are here we could not have been clearer.

The two ships had been seen by all and the men with bows each nocked an arrow. I laid the empty ale skin in my chest and took the sling from my belt and selected a round pebble from my pouch. I was not as good as some with a sling, I knew that but I was not the worst and, as my actions at the village had shown, I was far from being the worst new warrior.

Dreng said, "Now is the time for your new helmet, Sven."

I saw that the others had all donned their helmets. I took out mine. It had a nasal and had been damaged. I guessed that was in our fight. I would have to repair it. I placed it on my head. It was a little too large. That could be remedied when we reached home but as a temporary measure, I took it off and placed two socks from my chest on the top of my head. When I replaced the helmet my vision was no longer obscured. In the time it had taken me to do so the two ships had drawn closer. It told me that our drekar was more heavily laden. We could have used the oars, but I think our captain thought we had the beating of the two of them. They outnumbered us but as we had shown in the village, that meant nothing. Their plan was clear. One would sail across our bows while the other would come at the steering board. When Lodvir led half a dozen well-armed warriors to the bows that was confirmed. Sweyn was taking no chances that the eight of us at the bow would be overwhelmed.

Lodvir had a good bow and I watched him choose a good arrow from the arrow bag he carried. He smiled when he saw the helmet, "You came of age this day, Sven. Your father and brothers are toasting you in Valhalla." I nodded. "Do not waste your stones. Wait until you know that you can hit them and if they board then you must use your new sword."

"Will they board?"

"They will try for we have captives, and they will attempt to save them. Thorstein is not just lucky he is skilled. He will use his guile to outwit them."

The wind was helping the leading Saxon which was attempting to cross our bows, more than it was serving us and we were converging. Lodvir was correct about Thorstein for he turned 'Sea Serpent' towards the Saxon. Although it seemed like a foolish action for we slowed it was pure genius for the Saxon had to adjust their course or risk flying past our bows. Thorstein resumed our course so that the Saxon was just forty paces from us. That was well within arrow range and Lodvir and the other archers began to shower the Saxon ship with arrows. I had been told not to waste my stones, but I knew that I could hit the ship. I whirled the slingshot above my head as the Saxon continued to close with us. When stones and arrows flew from the Saxon ship then I knew I had the range and I released. I had no way of knowing if I had hit the man at which I had aimed because the Saxons ducked down behind their gunwale when they had released their arrows or their stones. We continued to close with them, and I wondered if Thorstein had misjudged the moment. The arrows from our steering board began to hit the Saxon. I whirled and flung for all that I was worth. When the arrow clanked off my helmet, I thanked Dreng for his advice. It made me see stars briefly and I knew that the helmet would be dented but I was unhurt. and I threw the next stone even harder. We were close enough now to hear the cries as men were hit. The screams of the Saxon women added to the cacophony. They were begging the Saxons to save them. It was when we closed to within ten feet that three women on our ship attempted to jump aboard the Saxon. It was too far for even an agile ship's boy, but it must have looked tantalisingly close. The women had no guards for all our crew were fighting. One woman almost made it but her head cracked against the side of the Saxon. The other two fell into the water and the Saxon captain turned away to avoid crushing them. It was foolish for they would drown anyway.

Thorstein put us over to widen the gap. The second Saxon had been attempting to close with us while we were engaged with their consort. Thorstein's move would take us across their bows. I knew he was skilful, but he took us within twenty feet of her stubby prow and as we passed every archer and slinger sent their missiles down the length of the boat. This time I was able to see men as they fell and then when we had passed the ship Thorstein turned again and resumed our original course. We were now ahead of both of them.

"Crew, to your oars. Sven and Siggi, guard the women!"

I put the sling in the stone pouch and drew my sword. There had been twenty slaves when we had set off. Fourteen women and six children. I had seen three women leap over the side but when I counted, I saw that there were just nine women. Another two must have leapt over for some reason. Siggi joined me and I said, as the oars were run out, "Do not try to escape. My sword is sharp, and a lamed slave can still work!" I was not sure that I could hurt a woman or a child, but my voice must have made them believe that I meant it for they all cowered and shrank closer to the mast fish.

It was the first chant we had learned and not only did Siggi and I sing along with the others, but we also stamped our feet on the deck to keep time. I had seen the captain and Thorstein do the same.

> *Bluetooth was a warrior strong*
> *He used a spear stout and strong*
> *Fighting Franks and slaying Norse*
> *He steered the ship on a deadly course*
> *Njörðr, Njörðr, push the dragon*
> *Njörðr, Njörðr, push the dragon*
> *The spear was sharp and the Norse did die*
> *Through the air did Valkyries fly*
> *A day of death and a day of blood*
> *The warriors died as warriors should*
> *Njörðr, Njörðr, push the dragon*
> *Njörðr, Njörðr, push the dragon*
> *When home they came with byrnies red*
> *They toasted well our Danish dead*
> *They sang their songs of warriors slain*
> *And in that song, they lived again*
> *Njörðr, Njörðr, push the dragon*
> *Njörðr, Njörðr, push the dragon*

The hard work on the voyage paid off and as I looked astern, I saw the Saxon ships were falling further and further behind. Ahead of us, I saw the open sea. The crew did not have to row for long as the Saxons gave up.

"Oars in! Reef the sail! I want the cargo balanced before we venture forth!"

I wondered how my foster father could keep all these things in his head. We had won battles and yet he was already planning ahead. The crew stacked their oars, and the experienced ones went about their business. It was the new ones like Folki and Eidel Eysteinsson who looked lost. I turned to Siggi, "Come, we have animals to tend to." One of the women was glaring at me. She held her arms around two children who looked to be less than five summers old. I said, "What happened to the warriors who raided you last year?"

She gave me a triumphant look, "Those who did not drown were either burned on their boat or had their heads taken!"

I nodded, "Then they died like warriors and will be in Valhalla!"

She made the sign of the cross and then grabbed the wooden cross around her neck, "Pagan!"

I reached down and tore the wooden cross from around her neck before slinging it overboard. It was a petty thing to do but I was young, and I wanted vengeance for my family. I know now that I should not have asked the question, but I wanted answers. I learned something. Do not ask questions unless you are prepared to live with the consequences. For the next few nights, I found it difficult to sleep. What had been the actual fate of my family? From what Lodvir had said the Saxons liked to decapitate corpses but to be burned alive in a dying drekar was not a fate for a warrior.

The animals had been upset by the action but Siggi knew just how to calm them. We also started the monotonous clearing of the decks. The sheep and the goats were relatively easy to clean. The shovel we had sufficed but the cows necessitated buckets of seawater. Then we had to use some of our precious water to let them drink. Siggi and had to go around each animal with a bucket to allow them to drink. One benefit was that they came to trust us. Siggi was better with them than I was. He would sing to them and talk to them as though they were humans. They responded well to him. I decided that I could never be a farmer.

To celebrate our victory and the fact that we were both alive I shared some of my mead. We had long eaten the last of his pork but as we had taken honey cakes and bread from the village and they would need to be eaten quickly, it was almost a feast.

"Do you wish to go to sea again, Siggi?" I guessed the answer, but it was important to know. I needed to discover if Siggi would be a shield brother as well as an oar brother.

"No Sven. I came because my father said I owed it to Agerhøne. I did not enjoy the raid. I was fearful that I would die. I think your foster father knew that for I was just asked to guard the door of the church when they slew the priests. My sword was not needed. I just followed the others." He smiled, "You were in your element. I could see you with your spear and you seemed fearless. You are a warrior."

41

I nodded, "I felt alive and invincible. I will be sorry if I do not sail with you again."

He stroked the goat which had nuzzled up to him, "It is *wyrd*, Sven. You will go to sea again and wear a byrnie. You will come back with slaves and booty. I will be content looking after the pigs and, perhaps, some of these animals."

I learned much from Siggi. None of it helped me to become a better warrior but I think I became a better man. He was kind and gentle and he had a way with animals which was almost magical. He became the friend who remained at home while I went to war. When I spoke with him, I saw a different life and that was important.

As I sat down, I took out the blade to examine it. I had held it but when I had taken it then it had been dark and when I had guarded the women I had not looked at it. Now I could see that it was not an ordinary blade. Words were etched on it as well as a dragon. The hilt had an intricately worked design on it which looked like a dragon. There had been something on the pommel. Normally swords had a round or oval piece of metal, but the jagged metal told me that whatever had been there had been broken for some reason. Why would a Christian Saxon wield such a pagan weapon? As I held the sword it seemed to speak with me. I shuddered for it felt as though someone was walking on my grave. I sheathed it. I would not take it from its tattered scabbard again until I was on dry land.

The first day at sea we buried the two men who had died. Their families, when we reached Agerhøne, would be given their share of the profits and they would also be cared for by the village. As with me, men would become the foster fathers to the young.

The voyage home was faster than the voyage out. Sweyn Skull Taker had planned the raid well for we picked up the winds which always came at that time of year. They were warm winds from the south and west. We did not need to row, and we sailed with a lively wind and little rain. The rain helped us to keep the animals watered. The tending of the animals also kept us occupied while the others found the voyage back less enjoyable. The rest of the warriors had less room and there were squabbles and a few fistfights. Griotard ended them all with his fists! When we saw the coast ahead then we knew we were not far from Agerhøne. We lost two more of the slaves before we reached home. No one knew if they had fallen overboard or if they had chosen to take their own lives. Griotard the Grim was not pleased and I took perverse pleasure in the beating with the knotted rope that he gave to Erik who had been on watch over them. He had obviously been asleep!

We were seen from afar and the whole village awaited us. I knew that this trip would have been harder for them all to endure. Had we failed to return then the village would have died. This time there was not silence but cheers although I saw the women and children looking along the drekar to spot the faces of their loved one. My mother had a cloth to her eyes. I waved at her and she waved back. I had survived. While we were secured to the quay, I packed my chest. It was heavier than when I had left. Siggi and I were still in charge of the animals and we untied our rope pen while the others followed Sweyn Skull Taker and disembarked. When there were just the ship's boys, Thorstein and the animals Siggi took them off one by one. There was no discussion about this for we both knew that Siggi was the best suited for the task. I stayed with the others. When the first cow was led down the gangplank the other became fretful. I started to sing one of the nonsense songs which Siggi had used whilst stroking her ear. She became calmer. We left the goats until last and we led the two of them down the gangplank.

Sweyn had returned to the empty quay. He said to the two of us, "You looked after them well for none died. As a reward, you two may choose the first animals."

I shook my head, "Let Siggi have two for he did all the work."

I saw a look of pride on my foster father's face and he nodded, "Choose, Siggi."

He picked the two cows and turned to me, "Thank you, oar brother. We may not fight together again but you will always be in my thoughts." His family joined him, and they took their animals away.

I hefted my chest on my back and took my spear. Sweyn said, "He will not sail again?"

I shook my head, "You knew, did you not, that he was no warrior?"

"Aye, you can tell with some men. My heart tells me that you are the opposite and wish to go to war once more."

I nodded, "I felt alive when we fought, even though I was close to death. Now I have a helmet and a sword as well as a mail hood not to mention a leather byrnie, I will be better able to fight."

We were approaching the hall, "You should have had a mail shirt!" I turned in shock. How had he known? I had not spoken of it. "Had you come to me I would have made Thrond return it to you for Lodvir knew that you had killed the Saxon and it was yours by right."

I put down my chest outside the longhouse. I would empty it there and dry out the wet items and sort out what needed washing. "Had you done that, foster father, then there might have been bad feelings in the clan. Thrond and his family do not like me as it is."

"You are wise, Sven, and perhaps this is for the best. You are too young for a mail shirt."

"Too young?"

He nodded, "In battle, enemies seek those who wear such shirts for they are thought to be worthy opponents. You were lucky in that first battle, but other enemies will be harder to fight. We will not sail for a month. You need to practise. Your cousin Sweyn will help you for he needs someone to hone his own skills and now you had better go inside and see your mother."

My mother had left with the other women when they had seen us safely returned. She would be with them preparing the food. I left my chest with the lid open and went into the longhouse. The only lights were from the two cooking fires and I saw my mother. I strode up to her and, seeing me she held out her arms. There had been a time when she had seemed huge to a young boy growing up. Now she seemed to have shrunk and she disappeared in my arms. I felt her sobs as she wept.

"I am home, mother, and I am safe. Your husband and your sons have been avenged."

She pulled away, "I care not about that, Sven. I would not lose you."

"I thought I was lucky in the battle, but I think someone was watching over me. Fear not for me, mother."

She shook her head and went back to the pot, "I am a mother and that is what I do. Sort out the clothes which need washing and which you wish to discard."

I looked at my treasures, as the afternoon sun began to set. The helmet was, as I expected, dented in a number of places. I would be able to beat them out. The leather byrnie had also been damaged a little, but I would repair it by adding metal studs. On the way home Dreng had suggested that I make a virtue out of a fault. I liked Dreng and Eystein. They were good warriors, but they had a kind side. I now knew why I had been placed at the bow. My foster father was protecting me.

Chapter 5

One change I noticed, after our return, was the increased respect I
enjoyed from most of the men in the clan. Thrond and his family apart,
the settlement seemed genuinely pleased that I had done so well. That
was also reflected in the treasure I received. I had a bag of coins which,
whilst not a huge amount was the largest purse I had ever seen before.
Of course, unless we went into Heiða-býr or Ribe then I would not be
able to spend it! I gave half to my mother who tried to give it back to
me. As Sweyn my cousin told me, I would, in all likelihood see the
money returned to me in any case. Now that we had stood together in a
shield wall, we were closer and that closeness increased as we practised.

What became clear to me was that the shield wall we had used was
not the one the clan would use if we fought in a battle. The other
younger warriors who neither farmed nor fished, gathered each day at
the beach to either learn new skills or practise existing ones. It was
there, when there were ten of us, that I learned how to fight with a
proper shield wall. Lodvir the Long took us and he carefully allocated
our positions. The front five locked shields and the five behind, that
included me, placed our shields at an angle above their heads. I could
now see that we were like a hedgehog. Our spears were the spikes, and
we would be able to withstand many men trying to break us. Then
Lodvir showed us the technique to break a shield wall. He ran at us,
armoured in his new mail byrnie and leapt in the air to crash into the
wall. He broke it but that was largely because we were not expecting it,
but I still saw how effective it could be. On another day he joined our
shield wall to show how to make a wedge. He was the tip and with our
shields above us, we were able to advance quite quickly. He taught us to
use a chant for that would help us keep in step.

We only had Lodvir for a week and then he spent time with
Thorstein, Sweyn Skull Taker and Griotard the Grim, planning our next
raid. When I was not practising, I repaired the helmet and my shield.
The latter had been cut in the battle and needed to be repaired. It was
not pretty but Egbert showed me how to use nails and more goatskin to
add strength to the shield. We painted it once more. He was interested
in the sword for there was writing upon the blade. I could speak Saxon
but not read it. Egbert must have been an educated man for he was able
to read it.

"It is not Saxon, master, it is Latin!"
"Latin? Your priests speak that."

He nodded, "From what you told me about the man from whom you took it he was not a noble. He must have taken this weapon from someone else; it is not a common warrior's sword. The inscription says, '*Melchior made me*'. Melchior was one of the wise men and a weapon smith was either given that name or took it to give himself a reputation. It would have cost gold to have it made and a man does not buy such a good sword if he just wears a leather byrnie. There is a tale behind this blade, and it is well made." Running his fingers along the flat of the blade he said, "This is an ancient blade and as well made a sword as I have ever seen. I wonder how your Saxon came by it?" He nodded towards the scabbard. "The scabbard was not made for this sword. If he took the sword in battle or was given it then he would have had the scabbard. You should make a better one. I can help you."

He was right for I had noticed that the blade was loose in the scabbard. Had it been made for it then it would have been tight. We began to work on the scabbard, but it was not ready by the time we went on our next raid. We had done well in Wessex, along the Fal, and the slaves were useful, but we had not taken enough cereal. It was harvest time in the land of the Franks to the south of us and they grew fine wheat there. This time there was no Thing. There was no vengeance involved. Griotard came to ask me if I would join the raid. I accepted of course but it meant we would have a smaller crew. When we rowed it would be harder for me. I had ceased my daily run and woodcutting. I hoped that would not prove to be a mistake.

The crew who would sail her were summoned to the drekar to clean her and to replace damaged and worn ropes. It was then I saw that Erik had moved from being a ship's boy to a rower. He would be fighting alongside me, and I did not know how I felt about that. I put that from my mind as I filled my sea chest. I had learned from my first voyage. I now had a padded head protector as well as two full changes of clothes. I had oiled a cloak which I had been given after the Saxon raid. It would keep me dry for the sealskin cape was not large enough to make a shelter for me. My weapons were all sharpened and this time I had a sheath fitted inside my boots; I would not have to scrabble around for it this time. I also took a hat made of beaver fur.

The day before we left Siggi turned up. He was not raiding but he had a sack which he handed to me. He smiled, shyly, "It is just salted meat and a round of cheese. The cows we took make good cheese. We have salted and brined it so that it will last until you return. We wrapped it in nettles. It gives it a good flavour."

"Thank you, my friend. I know why you are not coming with us, but I shall miss you."

He nodded, "And I will miss you too for you made me laugh a lot, but I would miss the animals and my family more. I will fight for the clan but not to get grain or take slaves."

"I understand." We then chatted about the raid. Siggi had been affected as much as I had but in a different way. The cows were a different variety from the ones we raised, and he and his father were keen to use Ketil's bull to see what their offspring would be like. That was the difference between us. I had no interest in animals, except to eat them!

There were fewer people to see us off this time. We had a smaller crew. The oars were single manned and the two Siggi and I had used at the bow were empty. Many of the seasoned warriors did not come with us. Neither Dreng nor Eystein took part but Folki did and he had the larboard oar while I had the steerboard one. Once again, I was closer to the bow and before us were Lars and Leif. They were my shield brothers and before them were Sweyn and my other cousin, Alf. This was Alf's first voyage although he was the same age as me. I knew how he felt. A veteran warrior was measured by the battle rings he wore, his wounds and his name. Only four warriors had a worthy name. It was not something you decided yourself. You had to do something to earn it. In Griotard's case, he had killed three Saxons on a raid in Cent and because he had not smiled, even after he had taken their heads, he was called the Grim. As we rowed out to sea, I knew that I was dreaming of the day I would be given my name.

Poor Alf suffered. At least Siggi and I had shared the same experience, but the only other virgin rower was Erik and he had been a ship's boy. Once more the first row was a long one and when we put the oars away, I saw that his hands were red raw. His big brother gave him tough love. He made him put his hands in saltwater and I knew that would hurt. He then bound them tightly in cloth impregnated with seal oil. When we went to the ale barrel, he could barely hold his horn. No one laughed at the son of the chief, but I saw Lodvir smile sympathetically as he doled out the ale.

We went back to our chests but sat with our backs to the gunwales to enjoy the sun on our faces. We were all new warriors and although Sweyn had been on five other raids he had never raided the Franks. We knew that Göngu-Hrólfr Rognvaldson had carved out an empire for himself to the south of the land of the Franks and we did not wish to earn the enmity of the clan they called Normans. For that reason, we would be sailing up the river the Franks called the Somme. We learned all of this through Sweyn and his brother. They had been party to the planning.

Young Alf, now that he was no longer rowing, was exuberant, "Lodvir says that there is an abbey too and it is a rich one endowed by a Frankish Emperor it is said."

His brother snorted in derision, "Look at how many men we have on board. We took a small wooden monastery in Wessex. This will be a stone one and the Franks have horsemen. I do not think that we will raid the abbey. Perhaps if we joined with other ships we might." He looked at me and chose his words carefully, "The raid when your father died was supposed to be practice for the raid on the Frankish abbey. We will raid it but not yet."

Once more my father's fatal flaw had hurt the clan and made me even more determined to make up for it.

We were really three crews, four if you counted those by the steering board and the boys. There were the young ones, by the bow, then there were the older, veterans. The third were the ones who were with Thrond. Not all were of the same mind as he was, but we were all different. I did not mind for the ones who were at the bow were my shield brothers and, generally, the younger warriors. That was another difference from my first voyage. Here I was able to chat with the others. Siggi had not been one for chatter and even when we returned, after the raid, he preferred to speak of the animals and his home. I was able to talk of the only battle I had been in. I realised as we spoke that I could now see the battle from the viewpoints of others. Sweyn had been in the second rank with me but the battle he had seen was slightly different to mine. Even Lars and Leif who had been before me had enjoyed a different perspective and when the wall had broken, and we had charged then it was different for all of us. They told me that they thought I was dead when I went into the ditch. When they hurried on to the hall, they were intent upon revenge for my death. Inside the hall was a different war.

"Spears are of little use inside a building. You need a sword or a seax." Lars had been one of the first to enter the hall and his spear had been hacked in two by a Saxon sword.

I nodded, "So each man's battle is unique?"

Lars smiled, "It is why men make up the stories to tell around the fires. The older warriors do as we do and speak of their battle and they are all woven together to make one."

I shuddered and touched the hammer of Thor around my neck. Agnetha, my aunt, was a volva. She had woven a piece of cloth for me before I had left and sewn it into my beaver hat. It was a spell to keep me safe. Were our sagas spells too?

We had to row again in the afternoon for we would need to get some sea room to avoid the islands of Frisia. There were channels there, but they could be treacherous and the Frisians, whilst supposedly allies, were treacherous enough to ambush a stranded ship. We did not row long and, as the sun set, we stacked the oars, and the sails were reefed. The weather had been benign, but I took no chances and when I made my bed, I created a nest of the sealskin cape and the oiled cloak. Alf smiled at me, "Cousin, are you a bird?"

Sweyn shook his head, "On the last voyage he and Siggi were soaked in a storm and he has learned from it. I do not think we will be given a wetting, but it does no harm to be prepared, does it, Sven?"

"I would rather look foolish and be dry than to be seen as tough and wet!"

I slept well for it was a gentle motion which the drekar enjoyed and when I emerged, I smiled. The air was damp. There had been what we called a sea fret, a low mist which hung in the air. Sweyn and Alf were bedraggled, their hair dripping, and I donned my beaver hat as I stood. I smiled, "So cuz, what think you now of Sven's nest?" I slipped the sealskin cape around my shoulders and placed the oiled cloak over my chest to keep it dry and to make a seat if we had to row.

Sweyn had the good grace to give me an apologetic bow, "You have something of the galdramenn in you, Sven and next time we might emulate your home."

I made water and then collected my morning ale and food. The sea fret lasted barely an hour and then the sun rose and dried out the drekar. We put on sail and with the wind coming from the south-west were able to use the wind and not the oars. The day's sailing was easy, and we made a good pace. We rowed once more but that was just to help the new men. Alf and Sweyn copied me as we slept. We woke to a fresh day. Our course took us between the land of Cent and the Flemish coast so that we could see them both. This was a busy waterway and we spied ships. There seemed to be an unwritten rule that ships were safe in this channel. Certainly, none took flight when they spied our dragon prow and we saw similar ships sailing north. Perhaps they had been raiders to Wessex. From what Sweyn told us the power of Wessex was on the wane. More of our people had settled to the east of Wessex and Mercia. They raided but on foot and horse rather than a ship. I could see advantages to that. Jorvik was a Danish city in the heart of what had been the Kingdom of Deira. Dreng had spoken on the last voyage of perhaps settling in the land that was known as Danelaw. As the afternoon wore on and we left the coast of Cent behind us to the north I wondered about travelling thence myself. My only real tie to Agerhøne was my mother. I had no land there. I suppose my shield brothers were a tie but if I wished to be a warrior then I would have to leave. My uncle only raided two or three times a year. The Great Army of more than a hundred years ago had gone to Mercia and fought for three years winning the greatest treasures and defeating army after army. Guthrum the Great was still spoken of in hushed terms.

Lodvir came down the drekar to give us our instructions. We would reach the river after dark and step the mast in the estuary. We would then row up the river. Abbeville was ten miles upstream, and we would not go near to it. We would land five miles along the river, turn the ship around and then raid. There would be two raiding parties: one north of the river and one south. I would be with Lodvir and Griotard south of the river. Sweyn and Alf would be north with my foster father. The aim was to get as far from the river as we could without being seen and then work our way back. They would ensure the greatest haul. I was disappointed not to be with my foster father and cousins but when I saw that Thrond and Erik were with Sweyn the Skull Taker then I understood. I was being looked after again.

I spent the rest of the afternoon preparing for the raid. I donned my boots and then the repaired leather byrnie. I had done my best to clean all the dead Saxon's blood from it, but I had not been totally successful. I took my sword and scabbard from my chest. Egbert was still working on my new one. I also ate from my supplies. I drank some mead and ate some of the cheese and salted meat Siggi had given to me. I remembered Wessex and how I had been starving. Finally, I ate two of my mother's honey cakes. By then the sun had almost set behind us and we stepped the mast whilst facing south. We then turned the drekar with the oars and headed towards the Frankish river. Griotard stood just behind us with Tostig, one of the new ship's boys. He was seated on the prow and the two of them would guide the drekar down the river. We would not be rowing fast. It would be a steady passage making as little noise and risking as few of the hazards on the river as we could. The ones who wore mail would have an uncomfortable row.

It was almost an hour before we were close enough to see the banks of the river. Sweyn Skull Taker had chosen this river as there were no defences or towns at the mouth. We could slip in unnoticed. I sniffed the air as we headed upstream. The smells were subtly different from Wessex and home. We had rowed a mile before I detected the smell of woodsmoke. Perhaps my hands had hardened, or it may have been that we had less rowing, but I had no discomfort in my hands. Alf's were still bandaged and the look on his face suggested that he was still in pain. I hoped we would not have to do much fighting for I doubted that he would be in any condition to do so.

Chapter 6

I do not know how the landing place was decided. Perhaps Thorstein the Lucky lived up to his name but when the signal was given to raise our oars the riverbanks looked no different to the ones of the last two miles. Sweyn Skull Taker and his men quickly donned their helmets and took their shields while the ship's boys held us to the bank. They slipped ashore. It was not done as quietly as we might have liked for more men now had mail. We had been told to leave our spears behind. As Griotard had told us, if we needed a shield wall, then we had lost for we hoped not to encounter warriors in large numbers. As they disappeared the boys came back aboard, and we took to our oars to turn us around and face downstream. We sculled our way to the other bank and while the boys fastened us, we stacked our oars. I returned to my chest and donned my skull protector and helmet. We had repaired the leather strap and I fastened it securely. I lifted my shield and, after fastening it over my back, clambered to the gunwale. I leapt to the grass-covered bank.

Lodvir waved us forward and he led. Griotard was at the rear and I fell in behind Lars and Leif. We ran along the path which Lodvir found, at a steady pace. Metal jingled and leather creaked. There was an occasional dull sound as metal hit wood but as we had not smelled any woodsmoke then it was unlikely that any would have heard us. This was farmland we ran through. The path took us across some fields with winter cereals already growing and through the others which had already been harvested. There were small orchards and copses too and then we spied our first farmhouse. There was a glow which told us they had lit their fire and were awake. Lodvir led us away from it so that any farm dogs would not be alerted. We ran through some winter barley which was just ankle-high. There was a hedge at the end, and we clambered over it to find a road. We paused, not to take a breath for we were not tired but so that Lodvir and Griotard could confer, albeit in a whispered tone.

They chose to go right, and we ran down the stone made road. Animal dung told us that horses or draught animals used it and that was a good sign. We were seeking a large farm and we found one not long after the smell of burning wood drifted to us. It was, however, walled. Lodvir stopped and pointed to Lars, Leif and me. Three other warriors took their shields from their backs. I saw what we were to do. Six men would hold the three shields and we three would jump on the shields as they were raised. We would climb over the wall and open the gate. It was Lodvir and Olaf who held the shield I would use. I ran and leapt on to the war side, the side without the strap for it was flatter. I was boosted high and I easily grasped the top of the moss-covered wall. Swinging my leg up I straddled the wall the better to see the interior. I spied the glow from a bread oven and now that I was closer, I could smell the bread. That meant a baker was awake. I spied a large hall and a handful of wattle and daub huts. I saw what looked like a stable and a granary although as they were darkened shapes it was hard to be certain. There was a lord who lived here and he had serfs and slaves. It also meant he had oathsworn. I slipped my leg over as Leif and Lars also dropped to the ground.

Lars pointed to the gate and then me. I nodded and ran. The gate was unguarded and, when I reached it, I hefted the bar. It was heavy and I wondered if it was too heavy to move silently. The months of hewing and carrying logs made it a simpler task than I had expected. Even as I lifted the bar and placed it to the side, I heard a dog bark. Its bark was cut short by a yelp. I eased the gates open and the rest of the warband ran in. I swung my shield around and drew my sword. The dying dog had alerted those who were inside.

The time for silence was over and Lodvir shouted, "To the hall! Lars and Leif clear the huts. Sven, find the horses."

I was disappointed for mine was the least dangerous of the tasks, but I obeyed and headed towards the stable. The smell of horse dung told me where they were. I do not know why the second dog had not barked before but as I neared the stable a huge snarling beast raced towards me. I had no time to think and I hacked my sword sideways at the furry body. This was the first time I had used my sword in anger and I know now that I did not use it as well as I might. The Norns were spinning for had this been a warrior with a weapon then I might have been dead. I mistimed the swing and did not catch the animal cleanly. I knocked it from its flight, but its claws still raked my arm. The leather byrnie afforded protection. Cursing my mistake I swung the sword a second time and hacked through the dog's neck. The sword was sharp and the blow clean. Behind me, I could hear the shouts from the hall and the clash of metal on metal. I went to the stable door and opened it. There was darkness inside, but I could smell animals and I heard a whinny and the lowing of cows. They were using the stable as a byre too and that suggested draught animals. As my eyes became accustomed to the dark, I saw the shape of two large oxen and three small horses. I had done what I had been asked and I left. It was then I spied a second building attached to this one and there was no door. I peered in and saw a wagon and two handcarts. A scream from behind me made me turn and run towards the hall.

"Sven, stop him!"

I looked towards the sound of Lars' voice and saw a Frank with a spear running towards the stable. I hurried to intercept him. The man had a helmet and a small shield. His spear was shorter than the one I had left on the drekar. He looked to be older than I was. My mind took in such factors for older meant more experienced. I gripped my shield tighter as I tried to work out when we would collide. I had been asked to stop him and stop him I would. I ran so that he was to my left for that was where his weapon was. The Frank had to eliminate me before he could reach the stable and, I assume, get a horse and ride for help. The mistake with the dog helped me to concentrate and I held the sword so that I would use the edge more cleanly. His spear was longer than my sword and I was ready, as we closed together, for his strike. He knew how to use a spear and it was a good hit but my sword was already scything in an arc. I had taken in that he held his shield high and so my swing was lower. The blow to my shield was hard but the collision made us both stop. My sword swung and I felt it hit something soft. It was Egbert who had told me how to use the sword and I obeyed his instruction.

'Draw the sword back and forth when you find flesh Master Sven!'

I did so and heard a shout of pain and then my blade ground against bone. The Frank's leg collapsed, and I pulled back my sword to use the point. He had no mail, and his tunic did not cover his neck. I skewered him and he fell to the ground his lifeblood pumping away. This was not the time to collect booty and I ran towards Lars and Leif who were still battling close to the huts. I saw that six bodies were lying there. Three had weapons. Lars had his cheek laid open.

They nodded a welcome and Leif said, "You two watch here in case another is hidden within."

He disappeared inside the huts and Lars said, "You killed your first man with your sword, Sven, you are a warrior."

I felt myself swell with pride. I saw the blood dripping, "Your face, does it need attention?"

Almost absent-mindedly he wiped the back of his hand to wipe the blood away, "It is not deep. The Frank with the spear was lucky!"

Leif emerged from the last hut which was the largest. He was driving a dozen women and children before him. They were wailing and weeping. The noise from the hall had drowned out their cries. Lars said, "I will watch them. You two see if the others need help! I can handle these." I saw the terror on the faces of the Frankish women as they watched the blood dripping from Lars' face. They would not move!

The sound of fighting was abating as we ran to the door of the hall. Two dead Franks lay in widening pools of blood but inside the door, I saw the body of Faramir who had been gutted. The interior was dark, and I hesitated. It saved my life for two Franks, both youths but with swords in their hands burst from a room to our right. The stab from the Frankish sword was partly taken on my leather byrnie. It grated against some of the studs Egbert had fitted. I punched with the side of the shield and the Frank who had tried to kill me reeled and I lunged with my sword. I struck a rib and so I angled the sword up and drove it all the way through his body. It came out on his shoulder. Leif's opponent also lay dead.

Leif shouted, "The outside is secure!"

I heard one last scream and Lodvir shouted, "The hall is taken! Find the granary and see if there are wagons."

I shouted, "I know where both are!" Turning to Leif I said, "Follow me."

Dawn was breaking and the crows were already gathering in the trees anticipating a feed. I opened the gates to the stable cum byre and said, "There is a wagon with two carts around the side."

Leif cupped his hands, "Lars, fetch the captives. They can work!"

We manhandled the wagon and the carts into the yard and while Lars put the harness on the oxen and attached to the wagon, Leif and I moved the women, children and old men to the granary. When I opened the doors, I saw that the granary was half-filled. We found some sacks and had them filled while we waited for Lars to fetch the wagon. Lodvir joined us with some of the men. The rest were with Griotard, ransacking the hall.

He pointed to one of the carts, "Bergil, put a horse into the shafts and then take it to Griotard we will load it with the treasure and weapons as well as Faramir's body."

"Aye, Lodvir."

Bergil the Brawny was well named for he was huge and very strong.

Lars led the pair of oxen and the wagon over. They were not the largest oxen I had ever seen but they would do the job. Once the sacks were filled, we set the women and old men to shovelling the grain into the wagon. We did not take it all but that was not kindness. It would have taken too long and we had a limited amount of time before news of our raid was spread. We piled the grain sacks on top of the wheat. When the last cart was hitched to the horse we set off.

I asked, "Will we not fire the hall?"

Griotard shook his head, "We wish to surprise the first farm we saw. The last time was a vengeance raid. Here we are feeding our families for the winter."

Lodvir turned to me and Leif, "You two had the least fighting and being young, should be fresh. You will come with me and we shall scout." With that, he turned and started to lope off. Slinging my shield over my back and sheathing my sword I followed him. Leif was ahead of me and we ran back down the road. It was easier in daylight but, equally, more dangerous. Ominously, from the north, I spied smoke. There were three spires. Without turning, Lodvir said, "They are beacons. The Franks know we are here."

When we found the hedge and the ankle-high field of barley Lodvir did not hesitate but led us through. The farmer and his family had been alerted by the smoke and they were loading a small wagon which had a horse in the traces.

"Draw your weapons. We stop them from leaving. Griotard will not be far behind us."

I drew my sword. I had yet to name it. Melchior seemed too Christian a name. Until I did the blade, good as it was, would never be what I wished it to be. One handed I lifted my shield over my head and tried to slip my arm in the braces. The shout from ahead told me that we had been spotted and that urgency helped me to slide my arm through the last two. There were six men ahead and the same number of women. The children screamed as the men grabbed weapons. It was hard to know how this would turn out; six men fighting for their families against one great warrior, a young one and a novice!

Lodvir raised his sword and gave a blood-curdling scream. Leif and I tried to emulate him, but I fear mine came out as a nervous squeak. I saw that none of the Franks wore mail but three of the men had helmets and they drew swords. They jumped from the wagon to approach us. One turned and said something to one of the others who took the reins. The other two younger men held fire-hardened spears and they advanced towards us. Lodvir was terrifying. He hurled himself at the three Franks who wore helmets. He seemed fearless and that inspired me. I ran to his left while Leif ran to his right. It meant that Leif and I could be outflanked but we had to protect Lodvir. It was our duty.

I took the blow from the Frankish sword on my shield. The man was strong but the padding we had put on the shield absorbed the impact. The fire-hardened spear was rammed towards me and I was forced to look away as the wood smashed into my helmet, making my ears ring. I rammed my sword blindly towards the swordsman. I saw the Frank who had been in the centre, lying on the ground as Lodvir slew

56

him. My sword had found flesh, but I knew not where. As I pulled my sword back for a second strike, I saw the sword raised to strike my shoulder. When I raised my shield, I felt a sudden pain in my side as the fire-hardened spear struck my hip. The point broke on my hip bone. I took the sword on my shield and rammed the engraved blade up into the Frank's jaw. As the wooden spear was torn from me, I felt the blood drip and I became angry. The Frankish youth who had stabbed me was younger than I was, and I turned on him as he thrust his broken spear at me a second time. It hit my shield and I brought my sword down to hack through his upper arm. As he started to fall, I backhanded him across the other arm and while he was still falling, I gave such a mighty swing that the blow hacked through his head. He lay on the ground and I raised my sword.

Lodvir's hand arrested my swing, "Enough, he is dead, and you are wounded."

I gritted my teeth, "It is nothing!"

He tore the tunic from the dead Frank and said, "Hold this against the blood. Leif, stop the wagon!"

I heard a roar as Griotard led the rest of our men to come to our aid. Lodvir took the leather belt from the Frankish farmer and fastened it so tightly around my waist and hip that I thought I could not breathe. Griotard looked at the dead men and my wound and nodded, "Good. Now go with the wheat to the drekar. Thorstein will tend to you while we finish here."

There were two others who had wounds from the hall: Lars and Sigismund. Lars put his arm down to help me to the seat of the wagon. "A good raid thus far, we have lost only Faramir!"

I pointed to the smoke to the north of us, "But they know where we are!"

When we reached the river the drekar was on the opposite side of the river. They were loading that which Sweyn Skull Taker and his men had captured. I saw no wagons and the men appeared to be loading barrels and chests. Alf and Sweyn were on the other side and I waved, just to show them that I was still alive. The wound was hurting. Lars saw me wince and handed me a skin of something. "Here drink this. It will ease the pain."

"What is it?"

"Wine. The Franks prefer it. Drink for it is stronger than ale." I swallowed some and almost spat it out for it had a sour taste. Lars nodded for me to continue and I did. Surprisingly, it did ease the pain a little. "Pour some on the wound, it will help."

I did as he told me, and it worked for the pain was numbed a little.

I saw the drekar begin to scull across from us; the mast and the cross tree were in place as well as the sail. Some of the shields along the side now had arrows sticking from them. Lars shouted, as the bow came close, "We have wheat and weapons as well as Faramir. Sven here has a bad wound." He smiled, "Mine is just more obvious."

I saw my foster father and what looked like a rare look of concern. He shouted, "Get the wounded aboard and then unload the wagon and cart. Butcher the oxen."

Men leapt over the side as the ship's boys tied up the ship. As I was helped up the quickly fitted gangplank my cousin Sweyn said, "Were you pursued?"

I shook my head, "We raided two farms and the men there died. And you?"

"We found a small village with a church. We battled and one man escaped. We had just collected what we could when horsemen came. Beorn and Bersi died. They died well but…"

I nodded as I was deposited at the steering board. "Take care, cuz!"

Thorstein turned to the ship's boy and said, "Take off his byrnie."

I saw that it was Ulf who was the ship's boy. He was not gentle as he pulled it. Thorstein saw it and cuffed him about the back of the head, "By his wounds, Sven is a warrior! You are a barnacle to be scraped off the bottom of the ship! Go and put Sven's shield on the gunwale and then load the booty!" As a chastened Ulf slunk off Thorstein shook his head, "That one will never make a warrior. Perhaps if his father had not died… you cannot live in the past for there lies madness." He tutted when he saw the wound, "A fire-hardened spear?" I nodded, "Nasty! There will be splinters and they can poison. I will do the best I can, but time is against us. With the Franks north of the river raised against us, we may have to battle to reach the sea." He handed me a stick, "Place this in your mouth for this will hurt." He took a pair of pointed metal pliers. I remembered that they were used to pull out bent nails. I knew what was coming. They would pull out the wooden splinters.

Swinging my sword around to my front, I gripped the hilt and hoped that the Saxon made blade would bring me some comfort. I nodded and I felt Thorstein pull. I thought I would bite through the piece of wood. More blood spurted and I saw that some splinters came out with the blood. Thorstein grunted in satisfaction. All the while I watched the grain and other treasures being loaded. When I saw butchered meat coming aboard then I knew that the oxen had been slaughtered.

Sweyn Skull Taker loomed over us and smiled, "How is he, Thorstein?"

"It is a bad wound, hersir."

58

My foster father nodded, "You will have to tend to him later. The Franks are coming, and we have almost loaded the drekar."

Thorstein nodded and poured some vinegar on the wound. The pain was as bad as when he had pulled the largest splinter. He then took a handful of rosemary-infused honey from his pot and smeared it on the wound. He hurriedly tied a bandage and then handed me a mead skin. "That is all I can do for a while. Sit here at the stern and have a good swallow of mead. If the Norns allow us to make the sea I will finish my work."

"Thank you, Thorstein, do not worry about me."

He stood, "Prepare for sea." He turned to me, "You are a good boy! I can see a warrior in you!"

Another compliment made me feel better immediately and I drank a good swallow of the mead. After the wine, I began to feel a little light-headed, but the pain was abating. The crew climbed aboard. I saw smiles and waves from most but Erik and Thrond scowled. They must have hoped I would die. We were at least four men light as we headed back down the river. There were three dead, and I could not row. I was going to take off my helmet and then I realised that I might have to fight for we were not at sea. The sea was our friend. My foster father had made a blót before we had left and Njörðr would, I hope, look favourably on us. We had not killed any Norse or Danes and the Franks were Christians!

I think I must have dozed off for a while for when I woke the crew was rowing and the sail was billowing but stones were clattering into the shields and the sides of the drekar. I saw arrows sticking from the mast. The noise must have woken me. A stone hit my helmet. I was glad that I had left it on. The ship's boys were slinging stones back at the Franks but there were few of them as some were needed to sail the drekar. I saw that Thorstein was living up to his name. His helmet had been struck by a stone and the steerboard had arrows in it, but he was unharmed.

He saw me looking at him, "Stay close to me, Sven! Let us hope that my luck rubs off on you!"

Even the hersir was needed at the oars and I had never seen *'Sea Serpent'* move so quickly. Being on a calm river helped but I think the crew all knew that our lives depended upon it. I could just make out clear water ahead and that meant the sea. If we could make the sea, then we would be safe. As the banks receded so the stones and arrows diminished and then stopped. Thorstein sent the ship's boys to adjust the sails and, with his eye on the sea, he smiled.

The Norns were spinning. It was as we negotiated the tidal race at the mouth of the river that the Frankish boats attacked us from all sides. Their signal fires must have alerted those who lived close to the mouth for a half dozen fishing boats and two small ships, filled with armed men used the incoming tide to race towards us. Thorstein was lucky but he was not a miracle worker. As soon as the boys shouted the danger he aimed *'Sea Serpent'* at a fishing boat on the steerboard side. That took us away from some but closer to the others. Fighting the tide our men could not relinquish our oars and the boys were busy in the rigging. I heard the Saxon boat slam into our steerboard. This was potentially a disaster. If they could either cut the withies or kill Thorstein then the drekar was lost. I still had my sword in my hands, and I stood. The drink and the wound made me a little woozy but when I saw the grappling hook bite into the gunwale I did not hesitate. In two strides I was there, and I hacked through one rope. Two more hooks followed and even as I cut one a Frankish warrior began to clamber over the gunwale. I swung hard with my sword and the blade bit into the man's shoulder. It also tore open my dressing and I felt the blood flow. It was my life or the ship's, and I did not hesitate. I cut through the last grappling hook, but a Frank had managed to climb over the side and was behind me.

"Sven, brace!"

As I turned, I widened my stance and saw the puddle of my blood forming on the deck. Thorstein put the drekar to steerboard and we crashed into an enemy ship. The collision made the Frank, who held a two-handed axe stumble a little. He was bare-chested, and I rammed the tip of my sword into his gut. The blade grated off the bone and I twisted as I pulled it and his guts from his body.

Griotard roared to the crew, "Row! We have a ship to save! Row!"

There was no chant, but the rowers worked as one and they strained and heaved on the oars. We flew over the white-capped water and Thorstein put the drekar towards the larboard so that we struck another Frank. I looked around for another enemy, but my eyes would not focus, and darkness took me.

Chapter 7

I found myself floating and, in the darkness, I wondered if the ship had sunk and I was in the sea. The last two collisions had been hard, and we could have sprung a strake. I did not feel wet. I felt nothing. Then it came to me, I was dead, and the thought filled my head that at least I had died with my sword in my hand. If that was true, why was I not in Valhalla? A dread filled me. I had died with my sword in my hand and yet I was not in Odin's mead hall; Valhalla was a myth, and this was all that there was. I would float around in inky blackness for all time.

It was then I saw the warrior. He was a greybeard, but his plaited beard and hair told me that he was a Dane and more, he wielded my sword. I saw the writing. When he saw me, he nodded and held the sword by the blade. I reached out for the hilt and his voice mouthed something…

"Sven, come back. Sven, open your eyes!"

It was Sweyn Skull Taker's voice. Had he died too? I forced myself to open my eyes. but they seemed to want to remain closed. When I did open them, I saw the sky, although it was darkening towards sunset and I could see Lodvir and Alf looking down at me.

Alf shouted, "He lives! He is alive!"

I heard a cheer and I tried to sit up. Thorstein's voice commanded, "Do not rise, Sven, or you will undo the work we have done!"

I lay back, closed my eyes, and tried to talk. My voice came out as a croak. A skin was put to my lips and I tasted mead which warmed me throughout. "We escaped or are we prisoners?"

I opened my eyes as Sweyn Skull Taker said, his voice as warm as the mead I had drunk, "We escaped Sven Saxon Sword, for your bravery saved the ship and the clan!" He put his mouth to my ear, "You have redeemed your father's foolishness. He can rest now in Valhalla."

I took in the words he had said and asked, "Sven Saxon Sword? I am named?"

Alf grinned, "Aye, cousin, for it was you and your sword which kept the Franks from Thorstein, and he was able to save the ship. His luck almost deserted him and had you not risen like a wraith from your deathbed then we might have ended up on the rocks like two of the Franks."

Thorstein's voice came again, "Let him sleep for I wish to tend him myself. You have done a good job, Sweyn Skull Taker, but I am the healer and there was too much blood for my liking. We need to find a beach and tend to the hero and the drekar."

The words made me smile and I closed my eyes, happy to obey. This time my dream was of clashing steel and screams. Houses burned and men died. The grey-bearded warrior did not return.

When I woke it was dark and we were ashore for my hand felt sand. There was a fire, and I could hear the voices of the rest of the crew. I tried to raise myself but my side felt stiff and Alf said, "He wakes," hands helped me to sit upright. I detected the smell of burned hair and flesh.

My cousin Sweyn fetched me a horn of ale and Thorstein knelt next to me and sniffed, "They call me lucky but you, Sven Saxon Sword, had all the luck today. When you fought and burst your wound the blood washed out the tiny fragments of wood in your side. I could never have found them, and they would have rotted within you. You would have died. Your courage saved the ship and also saved you. *Wyrd*. You can move about a little for I burned the wound." My last dream made more sense now. The burning had been when they had cauterized the wound.

"The ship is safe?"

My foster father looked down and handed me some cooked beef, "Aye, despite Thorstein's efforts to sink us. We have made temporary repairs to the hull, but it will take a month to restore her."

"Then we have done raiding this year?"

Sweyn Skull Taker laughed, "He touched Death and now sounds disappointed that he cannot face it again! We have no need to raid, Sven Saxon Sword, for our hold is full and we have food aplenty. We took some weapons and gold from the Franks and you, as the hero of the battle, have your share. Eat, drink and rest."

Thorstein nodded, "Aye, there is no need to row on the way home for we have wind from the south-west to take us to our families and there will be a great celebration. I would not have wished to be the one to tell your mother that I had lost her last son!"

The older warriors left us and Sweyn and Alf sat by me. My cousin Sweyn shook his head, "Two voyages and you are named! More, Thorstein said that your heroism deserves a saga. Surely the Norns favour you."

I shook my head, "What else could I do? I did not choose to stand and fight, but all were rowing and I knew what would happen if Thorstein was hurt."

"And that is what makes you a warrior. You are well named." He gestured towards the sword. "I wonder if I had been the one to have fought that Saxon and taken his sword would the weapon have changed me?"

"Changed me, Sweyn? I am not changed."

Alf laughed, "Aye, you are cousin. I was not on that raid but when you stepped from the drekar I saw a different Sven to the one who sailed on the vengeance raid. You strode down the gangplank and looked more like a man than a youth."

Sweyn leaned in, "Lodvir thinks that the sword is a special one. While you slept, he looked at the blade and said it was an old sword and while it was made by a Saxon, he does not think that it was made for a Saxon."

"But I took it from a Saxon!" Even as I said it, I remembered Egbert's words. I lifted the sword and scabbard. There was a story here, but would I ever discover it? I ran my hand over the roughened, damaged pommel and corded hilt. It ought to have a name. All such swords did but none came to me.

It was Sweyn who saw my look, "Cousin, do not try to make a name come. You will find one. One night when you dream and look into the darkness the name will creep, like a fox in winter and when you awake the name will be the footprints in your mind."

I laughed, "Are you now a skald?"

"Perhaps for you, it seems, are to be the hero of the family."

By the time we reached our home, I was used to the itching and the stiffness. Thorstein told me that they would both disappear, and the ugly scar would simply be a reminder of how close to death I had been. I was accorded the honour of being the second one off the drekar. I tried to mask the wound, but mothers know these things and her smile changed to a frown as I embraced her. "You were wounded!"

There was little point in arguing, "Aye, but it is healing, and I am not like Lars with a maimed face." She looked up as my shield brother walked down the gangplank. His scar was red and angry. He had been lucky too for the end of the scar was close to his eye. Warriors could fight with just one eye, but it was a weakness few desired!

Alf and Sweyn carried my chest, shield, and spear. The families of the dead wept but the rest rejoiced as the sides of beef, wheat, barley and oats were brought ashore. The gold and silver we had taken would be divided later but a man cannot eat gold! We had food for the winter, and we would not need to raid again.

My aunt was a volva and when she entered the hall with my foster father she said, "Now that you have a name, Sven Saxon Sword, I will weave a spell for the scabbard the Saxon makes for you but before I do, I would like to hold it. Perhaps it will tell me its story,"

I unbuckled the baldric and handed the belt, scabbard, and sword to her. She went to her chamber. She and Sweyn had a curtain around their sleeping chamber. They needed privacy and she needed to work her magic where eyes could not spy on her.

My mother poured some of her mead and sat next to me. "Tell me all and leave nothing out!" My mother was a kind lady but when she put steel in her voice then you obeyed. I told her all but I tried to make it seem less dangerous than it actually was. Sweyn and Alf did not help by chipping in with details which seemed to make my act even more heroic, not to mention reckless! I watched as she shook her head, "I will wash your clothes. You will need a new tunic."

We ate and we drank. Some of the young women, too old to be called children and not yet women hung around us, ostensibly cleaning or fetching food and drink but Sweyn and I knew that they were on the lookout for a man, a husband, and my exploits made me someone who was desirable. I knew there was one caught Sweyn's eye for he spoke to her, "Bergljót, do you wish to fetch a warrior another ale?"

She laughed, "I do not know;" with an impish look on her face she turned to me, "Sven Saxon Sword, do you wish another ale?"

Sweyn coloured and my cousin, his sister, Sigbrith laughed too, "Brother, you will need to perform some great deed before you will be accorded the fame of our cousin. He has just returned and yet everyone in Agerhøne is talking of him!"

Sweyn shrugged, "The Norns spin and next time it will be I who is given the chance to be a hero!"

I smiled, "Cousin, I was just in the right place at the right time. Had I not been wounded then I would have been on an oar."

Alf, who was a thoughtful youth said, "And now we would all be dead."

We looked at each other and knew that he was right. When I had been stabbed in the side, I had thought that it was bad luck but now I thought differently. It was meant to be so that I could be given the chance to be a hero. Had I stayed where I had been laid, on the deck, I doubt that anyone would have blamed me but that would have meant that Thorstein would have died!

It was good to be in the longhouse and I wondered if that was because I had not let anyone down and there were no scowling glances. Thrond, Ulf and Erik were in their own home, here I was amongst friends. I had faced death and survived. I had wondered if I might flinch or simply fail. I had not. Sweyn Skull Taker was the last to enter the hall and he came over to take a horn of ale proffered by his son.

He raised it to me, "Foster son!"

I raised mine in reply, "Foster father!" There were unspoken words in the looks we exchanged.

"Let us go outside for it is time for the division of the spoils of war."

It went without saying that the grain would go into our granaries and the beef salted down for all to use. The weapons which had been taken by warriors would go to them. I had killed men and some of the weapons would be mine. It was the coins which would be shared by all. Skull Taker was flanked by Griotard and Lodvir. Leif and Lars fetched a table and when it was placed in the open area before the longhouse Thorstein and his son, Einar brought out the chests with the treasure we had taken. Although the raid south of the river had yielded modest amounts of coins and booty, the church and the halls to the north had been a rich vein of loot.

My foster father emptied the chest, and the eight equal piles he made were impressive. First, he took his share; He took two of the piles. He did not take as much as other chiefs, but I saw some of the warriors looking less than happy. He then divided the rest into seven equal piles. He gave one to Lodvir, one to Thorstein and one to Griotard. He said, "This one," he moved a pile to the side, "is for the families who lost warriors." It was a generous amount for only three had died. He took another pile, "This is for the warriors who were wounded." He looked at me, "Some counselled me to give a whole share to Sven Saxon Sword." I saw anger fill Thrond's face. "But that would not be right, and I do not think my foster son wishes it, do you?"

I shook my head, embarrassed at the attention, "No, Chief Sweyn for I did nothing that deserved extra reward. I served the clan." When I saw his face, I knew I had said the right thing. Had this been a test?

"The last two piles are for the other warriors. One for those north of the river and the other for those south." He pointed to the weapons which had been taken. "When the warriors who earned them have taken their weapons then the sons of the men who died can have their pick of the rest."

I saw the sword which was mine by right. It was not a bad blade but it was not as good as the one I had and so I left both it and the two daggers which were mine by right. Again I saw that my decision met with the approval of the other senior warriors.

"We feast this night on Frankish ox, wine and ham!"

I went with the other wounded warriors. Lars had already divided up the pile. I knew that it was far more than Leif was given and I felt guilty. I put the coins in my purse. I would give it to my mother for safekeeping.

Sweyn put his arm around my shoulder, "Bergljót was casting her eyes at you, cousin."

I shook my head, "I think she was just teasing you. It is you she has her eye upon, besides, I am not ready to take a woman yet."

He laughed, "No man is ever ready. It is like using a sword. You need to practise!"

Sweyn was a good-looking young man and all the village girls were attracted to him. He had enjoyed dalliances with many of them. He was too sensible to spread his seed for he was the son of the chief. It did not do to alienate warriors and their families. Thanks to the loss of two ships and their crews we were now a small clan.

"Then you practise away. I will go and change for I wish to enjoy the oxen and the mead. It will help me sleep!"

I returned to the hall and gave the purse to my mother. She smiled, "I will keep this safe for you. I have the money your brothers and your father brought back. I do not need it but one day you might. Perhaps you could buy a knarr and become a trader."

I looked into her eyes which pleaded with me to do as she had suggested. I had to be honest with her for there was little point in building up her hopes. I shook my head, "I am a warrior and not a merchant. The voyage and the wound showed me that. I have little experience, mother, and yet I acquitted myself well. Fear not, I do not think we shall raid again this year."

She smiled, "I pray to the Allfather that you will not."

Just then Agnetha came from her chamber and she handed me the baldric, sword, and scabbard. She sat at the long table and placed them upon it. She smiled at me, "We shall wait until your foster father is here for he should hear what I have to say."

I was intrigued but my mother frowned, "It is not cursed is it? My family has suffered enough."

Agnetha was much younger than my mother and she smiled, "I told you before, Gunhild, Bersi was not cursed. Sweyn made a blót before he sailed, and the spirits did not speak of a curse." She stopped short of saying it was a flaw in my father and I was grateful for that.

He came over to us as Agnetha waved at him. He saw the sword on the table and said, "The Saxon sword."

She shook her head, "It was made for a Viking, but it was made by a Saxon."

Sweyn gave a patronising smile, "Warriors know weapons and volvas know how to weave!"

Agnetha's smiled was a cold one, "Have you examined it, my love?"

He shook his head, "Sven told me of the inscription. No Viking would have that made for him."

"Look at the blade, the cord and the pommel and then tell me again it was not made for a Viking. I do not know if it was a Dane, a Norse or a Rus but I know signs."

I confess that I did not know what she meant. I had studied the blade endlessly when I had sharpened it and I could see nothing that made it a Viking sword.

As soon as Sweyn held the sword I saw his eyes widen. I had thought that it was just me and the thrill of holding the sword was the same for every warrior when he wielded his first sword. "I am sorry, Agnetha, you are right. This feels like a Viking weapon. He looked at the inscription and the writing. He followed his finger up to the hilt. I had thought that the hilt looked like my father's weapon but when Sweyn examined the cord which was wound around the hilt his eyes widened and then he stopped when his finger reached the pommel and the slightly jagged piece of metal. Egbert had said we could smooth it down, but it might take a long time. I had not been bothered as it was so tiny that I barely noticed it and unless you looked closely for it then you could not see it.

"What is it foster father? I see nothing save a cord which has colours in it. That is unusual but why would that mark it as a weapon not made for a Saxon?"

"The colours represent a snake and the broken piece at the top would have been its head. This would have marked it as Viking. It is a dragon sword. I have heard of them but never seen one. They were popular almost a hundred years ago and were made for great leaders. Most had them buried with them or when they died, their swords were killed."

"Killed?"

"Heated and then bent over an anvil so that they could not be used again. The fact that a Saxon took this and used it as his own is interesting. How did a Saxon manage to do that? I am sorry that I did not look closely at it when you first had it and that I questioned you, my love."

She smiled as he kissed her hand, "You are right I do not know weapons, but the sword spoke to me. It said it was a dragon sword."

I recoiled. Was the sword possessed?

Agnetha smiled, "I was a long time studying this and I went into a trance. The spirit of the sword and its owner spoke to me."

I said, eagerly, "Then you know who it was made for?"

"No, just that he was a great warrior but..."

Sweyn was intrigued, "But what?"

She shrugged, "I know not how to explain this to someone who does not converse with the dead... the spirits lost interest in him. They speak of a great warrior and then... nothing. I am intrigued, Sven. You must discover the real story behind this, and you must guard the sword well, although it has powers as you discovered when you were attacked. Your thrall Egbert has done the right thing. By making a scabbard for it then the sword will regain more power and my spell will add to that strength."

Alf said, "It will be some time before he needs to use it, mother, for the ship is damaged and will need to be repaired. We will not raid again this year."

Agnetha looked at her husband who nodded, "We destroyed two Frankish ships, but we paid a price."

My cousin Sweyn said, "Could we not spend our money? I would like to use mine to buy a better sword. It might not be a dragon sword but," he tapped the pommel of his own sword, "this one showed its weaknesses in Frankia. It was hit by an axe head and is no longer true. At the very least I might buy a good blank and work on it. Ribe has good weaponsmiths."

Sweyn Skull Taker looked at his son thoughtfully, "The king holds court at Heiða-býr and I have yet to pay him our tribute. I think we might visit Heiða-býr and then the three of you can spend some of your money. Ribe is all very well but the best Danish weaponsmiths are at Heiða-býr! What say you?"

It was the best of news. Sweyn was right we had no decent weaponsmith in Agerhøne and while I did not need a weapon then I might buy some mail. I did not have enough for a full byrnie but a vest might be within my budget.

Chapter 8

We enjoyed a great feast, and I drank too much or, perhaps, I was still weak from the wound. Whatever the reason I think I passed out and when I woke there was a pail near to my head and it was full of vomit. My mother gave me a weary smile when I woke, "My brother, your foster father, brought you to bed. If nothing else, my son, your heroic act has made you closer and my brother forget your father's faults."

Had I not felt so ill then I would have comforted her for she wept but more of the Frankish ox and the red wine I had mixed with ale decided they had spent long enough in my gut!

Egbert brought me the scabbard and I slid the Saxon Blade into it. It was a tight fit but that was what I had wanted. He had placed the spell from Agnetha on the inside next to the sheepskin. He was a Christian and had not been happy about it, but he was also a thrall and did what he was ordered. The skin which covered it was unadorned. I ran my fingers over it and Egbert said, "I did not know what you wished upon it, Master Sven."

I nodded, "And until yesterday neither did I but since I spoke with Agnetha I do. I would have a red dragon. Can that be done?"

He stroked his beard. "We have beetroot and that can be used to make the red. Would that do?"

I shook my head, "I would have it look as though it was shining and have green eyes!"

"The green we can do but the shining?"

"Let us begin with what we can do and then I will give thought to the shining!"

My wound meant that I was not needed to repair the drekar and Egbert and I enjoyed four days making the dye and painting it on the scabbard. It was when Alf asked me to go to the anvil and workshop that I had my idea. The warriors who had returned from the raid had been repairing their armour and weapons. Alf now had a helmet which, although damaged, was serviceable and he asked me to help him repair it. Mine needed a little attention too. The stones the Franks had sent at us had caused a few small dents. I knocked mine out and used it as a lesson for Alf. His required more work and it was while he was hammering out a deep dent that I spied, on the floor, the tiny fragments of metal which had come from weapons being sharpened. I started to pick them up.

Alf stopped his hammering and laughed, "Cousin, we have thralls who can clean the floor!"

I shook my head, "I am not cleaning the floor, I am collecting the treasure."

There were a surprisingly large number of them. When we had finished and I returned to Egbert I said, "I collected these. How can we fix them to the scabbard?"

"We have glue, but they might fall off. Perhaps some pine tar might hold them in."

We heated the glue and painted the dragon with it. Then we began the painstaking work of fitting the metal. There was one larger piece and I used that for the eye. Then we picked out the dragon's back until we reached the chape of the scabbard. Taking a hammer I gently beat the metal into the still soft glue and when it was done, left it to dry. The next day I took the scabbard to the drekar where they were using pine tar to seal the strakes they had replaced. No one minded when the hero of Frankia painted some on his new scabbard. I forced myself to leave the scabbard for as long as possible before I placed my blade into it. We then worked on my shield. I now had a design to go against the red. We painted the scabbard on the shield and then copied the red dragon. It looked effective but we would now put the shining metal to make it even more dramatic. That too was sealed and left to dry.

Although I saw Sweyn Skull Taker every day, he was generally busy with the drekar but when the bulk of the work had been done, he sent for me and his two sons. Lodvir and Griotard were with him. Unusually the two best warriors in the clan did not look happy. I said nothing for I was in austere company.

He ignored the two senior warriors and addressed us, "We will leave for The Heiða-býr in two days. You will need your sleeping blankets. As we will visit the king you should take your best tunics as well as your helmets. We will be taking a chest of tribute for the king."

Griotard the Grim snorted, "And instead of taking us he will be taking you three striplings!"

I saw my cousin Sweyn colour and then he smiled and said, "I am not insulted, Griotard the Grim. Feel free to disparage us while we sit here!"

My foster father waved an irritated hand, "Peace! We have been through this, Griotard. Our clan has changed. We lost two crews. The younger warriors need to be nurtured." He looked at us, "You three are my sons. Up to now, I have kept you apart from me but that is to change. I need a hearth weru, shields who will fight at my side when we go to war. All three of you are young and need experience. Hence

Griotard's concerns, Sweyn, but I believe that what Sven did in Frankia is a sign. The three of you get on and three is a special number. The Saxon Blade has come to us for a purpose. Our fortune is changing. You three will now become oathsworn. You are my sons but now you will swear to protect me!"

We all know what it was we were swearing. I was ready to swear there and then but my mother had just passed and heard the words. Her hands went to her mouth and she fled.

Sweyn said, "Do not decide yet. You can say no." He nodded at Lodvir and Griotard, "That will please these two. Tomorrow morning, if you are willing then we will make the blood oath and you shall become hearth weru!".

I knew what my decision would be, but I had to speak to my mother. I caught up with her close to our old longhouse. "Mother, this is meant to be. You would wish me to do this if my other father was alive would you not? This is your brother."

"Yes, but you are my son. I know it is meant to be but do not ask me to be happy about it."

I took her in my arms and held her tightly. I could not change, and neither could she. I walked her back to the longhouse. She was lonely and I could do nothing about that. She had outlived her husband and her sons. The wives of my brothers should have been a comfort to her but they were Saxons. They lived close to other Saxon thralls who had been freed. They brought her grandchildren when they had to but that was all. Others did not approve of the choice of hearth weru but for different reasons than my mother. Hearth weru would be rewarded by the chief. Thrond and those who thought like him objected to that, but they could not argue with the decision. Hearth weru warriors were always the leader's choice.

That evening Lodvir explained the ceremony to me. After he had done so he said, "I did not object to your appointment out of envy or spite. You know that is not my way." I nodded. "It is just that Sweyn Skull Taker is an exceptional chief and the three of you have to protect him. You will be carrying treasure and while Denmark is not as wild as the lands to the west of us there are still brigands."

I held up the sword, "I believe that this was sent to us for a purpose, and I do not think that the spirits, gods or Norns who sent it would wish it to fall into the hands of brigands."

"Perhaps, but I will be happier when the four of you are back at home!"

The next morning we rose before dawn to be ready for the ceremony. When we reached the mound there was just Lodvir, Griotard,

Agnetha, Sweyn Skull Taker and the three of us. Others may have wished to be there but this was a personal choice and only those invited by the hersir could attend. Someone had already cut the turf square at the top of the mound. It was laid soil side up. Agnetha, Lodvir and Griotard stood to one side while we were placed around the square. The hersir held a dagger. I had not seen it before but I knew that it was used for all our important rituals.

"You three warriors have all chosen to come here of your own free will?"

We chorused, "Aye, Sweyn Skull Taker."

"And that the oath you make is binding, even beyond death?"

"Aye, Sweyn Skull Taker."

He took the knife and handed it to Agnetha who sliced a long cut in his right hand. He held it over the turf so that any blood dripped into the soil. She then sliced her son, Sweyn's palm. He and his father shook hands. The blood continued to drip. Next, she came to me and sliced open my palm. I felt no pain. I shook hands and was aware that my hand was slick with blood. Finally, she did the same to Alf.

When that was done Sweyn said, to his father, "I am Sweyn Sweynson and I swear to protect Sweyn Skull Taker even if it means my life."

"I am Sven Saxon Sword and I swear to protect Sweyn Skull Taker even if it means my life."

"I am Alf Sweynson and I swear to protect Sweyn Skull Taker even if it means my life."

Agnetha laid a piece of woven spell on the soil and placed the turf back. Sweyn Skull Taker put his arms around Alf and Sweyn and stepped on to the turf. I put my arms around Sweyn and Alf and they around me and their father. We moved around the turf clockwise, stamping as we did so.

Sweyn Skull Taker stopped, lifted his head and smiled, "And now we are one!" I saw that it had all been timed to perfection. The sun rose in the east and bathed us all in light.

The journey was just seventy miles for Heiða-býr lay to the south of us and was the greatest city in Denmark save for Roskilde. All roads led to it as well as all waterways. The portage was just ten miles in length, along the corduroy road which meant a ship could avoid the dangerous waters between Denmark and Norway. A ship could sail from our sea in the east all the way to the west. The seas to the east were also close by and so Heiða-býr was chosen by the kings of Denmark to enable them to control two seas. King Sweyn Forkbeard was an ambitious king and he wanted to rule even more. He wanted Norway to be his. We learned all of this from Sweyn Skull Taker as we rode the four ponies down the King's Road. The three of us were far more nervous than my foster father. He was unconcerned about the dangers of the road.

On the first night, as we camped in a pleasant dell with a wood and a stream, he explained, "There may well be bandits and brigands but who would take on four mailed and armed men? There are others who are easier prey to be had." Sweyn, my cousin, did not look convinced while Alf and I accepted the logic of the statement. "My son, why do men become bandits and brigands?"

He shook his head, "I had not given it any thought."

"I have. They are men who no longer have oar or shield brothers. They are not farmers." He gestured to me, "Siggi chose not the way of the sword but the way of the plough. There are always oars to be had for those who farmed and failed but a bandit uses a sword and steals. That very fact means that they are not as skilled with a weapon as a warrior. If they were then they would still have a berth and sail the seas." He lay back, as the pot bubbled with the hunter's stew we were making. "No, I shall not fear attack despite Lodvir's dire predictions. Rouse me when the stew is ready."

That was another role for hearth weru. We would make sure that the hersir was fed before we were. We would only eat when he had eaten. We had made a good camp; the animals were tethered, and our weapons were close to hand. One advantage Alf and I had, having been at home longer than Sweyn, was that as young men with growing appetites, we had stayed close to the kitchen and watched the thralls preparing the food. Although we were younger than Sweyn, when it came to the preparation of food, he was the fetcher and the carrier and we two were the cooks.

Sweyn was woken, not by a shake of the arm but the smells which rose from the pot. We had found wild garlic as well as thyme and those smells, along with the ham we had fried in a skillet were enough to rouse him. He filled his wooden bowl and said, "Eat! My eyes know the size of my own belly. This will suffice. You have done well with your first meal."

We drank ale while we ate and then took out the skin of Agnetha's mead. Every alewife knew how to make mead but, unlike ale, each one made one which had a different taste. I liked my mother's but Agnetha's had a red tinge, like blood, and I liked it too. We did not guzzle the mead but savoured it.

"Foster son, show me the scabbard you and the Saxon made." I handed it to him. When dried and varnished it looked even better and I was pleased with the effect, especially the dragon's scales. Sweyn ran

73

his fingers over it and nodded approvingly. "It is good that the Saxon thrall helped you to make the scabbard for the blade was made by a Saxon."

My cousin, Sweyn, said, "But how did a Saxon get hold of a dragon sword? I cannot understand that. They make good swords, but the man Sven killed was just a warrior who did not even own a mail byrnie. Surely a dragon sword had to be owned by a great warrior. I could see how a mighty warrior might defeat a Viking and take his sword but not a Saxon from a little village in Wessex."

The hersir handed me back the weapon and poured some more mead. "The Norns spin, my son. I know that you are a skald and want the story but sometimes the spell hides the truth from us. The sword was clearly sent to Sven for a reason. Was it weregeld for the loss of his father and brothers?" He shrugged, "I know not but I do know this, the fate of the clan, as well as Sven's, is bound up in the sword and now that it has a scabbard which suits it then its power can only grow. However, Sven, the dragon on the scabbard will attract attention and you should be ready for that. If you wished to hide in a shield wall you cannot for the scabbard will draw every eye, sword and spear to you."

"I do not want to hide."

Sweyn emptied his horn and nodded, "Then you need to practise to become a great warrior for many men will seek the dragon sword!"

That night I found it hard to sleep for I had not thought of the fame the sword would bring me. A warrior does not choose his own name. My foster father had a name which made him sound like a wild warrior and he was anything but. He happened to take one head and the rest of the warband gave him the name. I was now stuck with my name; it would certainly arouse curiosity. I knew what my foster father meant. Some men would try to pick a fight with me just to try to win the sword. It was at that moment, as I was finally drifting off to sleep that I saw that Sweyn, my foster father, had been looking out for me. As hearth weru I could not be challenged to fight for whoever did so would be challenging the hersir!

As we headed down the road the next day my foster father gave us good counsel. "King Sweyn, like his father King Harald, is a Christian. Keep your Hammers of Thor out of sight. The king does not demand that we all follow the White Christ, but he does not like paganism flaunted before him. If you need to use the name of Odin, then whisper it."

Alf was a curious youth, "How can a warrior be a Christian, father? Are they not supposed to turn the other cheek?"

Sweyn laughed, "Aye, they are supposed to, but I think we are more pragmatic than those priests we slew in Wessex! And his Christianity did not stop him from seizing the throne from his father and driving him into exile, where he died. Make no mistake, King Sweyn Forkbeard is a ruthless man, and you should not underestimate him."

Hoiða býr was everything I had expected. Although made of wood it was a huge city with ditches, ramparts, and mighty gates. The first gate was the hardest to negotiate for mailed warriors questioned Sweyn Skull Taker at length. There I saw a curious guard stare at my dragon. It was a foretaste of the scrutiny I could expect. After our village, it seemed vast and it took us some time to wend our way through the narrow streets to the fortress in the centre. Here King Sweyn Forkbeard's power was clearly in evidence. The walls had sentries and the gate had a drawbridge. It was only later that I deduced it was rarely raised and that, too, was further evidence of King Forkbeard's power as it meant there had been no threat to his authority. We had passed his mighty churches on the way through the city and I saw a cross prominently displayed on the roof of the Great Hall.

There was a steward who also acted as military adviser to the king and I could see that he had been a warrior. He had lost two fingers on his left hand. He seemed to know my foster father for the greybeard smiled when he grasped his forearm, "Sweyn Skull Taker! It has been too many years!"

"Aye, Karl Three Fingers. These are my sons and foster son. They are my hearth weru."

The steward looked us up and down, "They are young. Are they blooded?"

He nodded, "Aye, and Sven Saxon Sword here could have eight battle rings if he chose."

"Then there is more to all of them than meets the eye." It was almost an insult, but Sweyn Skull Taker had warned us about this and told on the way, that we needed skin as thick as a mail shirt. None of us reacted. "And what brings you here? You were not summoned." This was an interrogation for King Sweyn was mindful of those who sought his throne.

"I am here to give King Sweyn the tribute he is due from our raids in Frankia and Wessex."

The steward looked relieved, "Then I will take you to the warrior hall and fetch you when it is time to eat."

It was a huge warrior hall and bigger than the hersir's longhouse. There were warriors within when we arrived but barely enough to quarter fill it. We found sleeping mats which looked clean and we

75

placed our gear there. A younger warrior wandered over, "I am Einar of Heiða-býr welcome to the warrior hall. My father is one of King Sweyn's hearth weru and I walk these walls. I have not seen you before."

I was new to all of this but even I could see that the young warrior was challenging Sweyn Skull Taker. I saw, at that moment, he had ambition.

Sweyn folded his cloak and said, without turning, "Not that it is any of your business, but I am Sweyn Skull Taker of Agerhøne, and I am a hersir. These are my hearth weru."

He was young and he laughed. Sweyn and I heeded Sweyn Skull Taker's warning and said nothing, but I saw Alf colour. The young man sneered, "They are younger than I am! They could not defend you against my sisters!"

Alf reacted, "We have all killed men in battle, have you?"

It was Einar of Heiða-býr's turn to colour, "The next time we go to war then I shall, never fear!" he turned on his heel and stormed off.

Sweyn turned to his son, "I told you not to react. We have made an enemy now."

Alf was still angry, "We do not need him. He is a youth like us, but he has never fought."

His elder brother said, "Father is right. This is his home, and he will have friends. There may not be many of them, but they will side with him and the others will have a poor impression of us before we even speak."

Alf saw the wisdom in his brother's words and nodding, subsided.

Karl came for us once the sun had set in the west. There had been ale in the warrior hall, but no food and I was starving as we made our way to the feasting hall. We wore no mail, but we had our swords hanging from our belts. Other warriors made their way with us to the hall. Even before you entered you were impressed. The wooden beams which supported the roof and flanked the door had been carved with dragons. The king might now be a Christian, but the hall had pagan roots and that was reassuring. The double doors were guarded by two warriors in mail byrnies and they pulled them open for us. We were greeted by a wall of warmth and the smell of woodsmoke, ale and sweat. It was a place of men. There were two hearths, one at each end of the room and the short table at which the king sat was flanked by two long tables. Karl led us to the end of one of the longer tables. It was close to the end of the king's table. I saw Forkbeard watching us as we approached. He was well named, and his plaited forks gave him a frightening aspect, but I also saw his eyes. They were calculating eyes and he studied us closely. My cousin Sweyn carried the chest with the tribute, and I had seen the king's eyes flicker towards it.

We did not sit, and Sweyn Skull Taker had briefed us while we awaited the summons. We bowed and the hersir said, "King Sweyn, the warriors of Agerhøne have raided Wessex and Frankia; accept this tribute as a token of our fealty!"

Sweyn walked forward and placed the chest on the table. The king nodded to the warrior to his right who opened the chest. He peered inside and nodded. The chest was closed, and the warrior took it away. Sweyn returned to us and King Sweyn Forkbeard nodded, "Sit." He stood and raised his drinking horn, "Hersir Sweyn Skull Taker of Agerhøne!"

Although there were still tardy warriors entering the ones who were there raised their horns and shouted, "Hersir Sweyn Skull Taker of Agerhøne!"

At first, my chest swelled with pride and it was only later that I realised it was not the acclamation I had thought. He had not waited for the hall to be filled and he had not given the hersir anything but the most cursory of acknowledgements.

There was a priest to the left of the king, and he stood. We remained standing as every warrior stood. The priest intoned words I did not understand. I guessed they were in Latin. When he had finished half of the warriors said a word I did not recognise, and many made the sign of the cross. We did not and the king noticed for I saw him watching us. He sat as did the priest and that was the sign that the feast was about to begin. We sat and were, seemingly, ignored. My foster father kept an impassive face as thralls, Wends and Pomeranians in the main, brought us food and filled the drinking horns we had taken into the hall. The food was plentiful and delicious. This was a king's table and he wished us to be impressed. The ale was good but there was no mead and I wondered at that. When we had a feast or entertained guests then that most precious of liquor was fetched out. It was easier to make ale you merely needed grain. For mead you needed honey and we had the best honey for close to our home were wild herbs and wildflowers which made the mead the finest of drinks.

We had heeded the hersir's warning and said little. Sweyn Skull Taker spoke easily with the warriors close by him. Agerhøne was too far from Heiða-býr for us to know too many of the warriors we met. When we fought with others it was the men led by the Jarl of Ribe, Harald Longstride. Despite the food and the impressive hall, I was not comfortable and when men began drifting away and we were able to follow Sweyn Skull Taker from the hall I was glad.

Back in the warrior hall, we prepared for sleep. As hearth weru, we ensured that the hersir was in his bed before we took off our swords, boots, breeks, and tunics. Others drifted in and I saw Einar of Heiða-býr enter as I turned on my side to sleep. He gave us a hard stare. Alf had done us no favours.

The sun had been up but briefly, and I had made water already when Karl Three Fingers came for us. "King Sweyn would speak with you, hersir."

We dressed quickly and followed the steward to the feasting hall. The hall looked less impressive when we entered. There was the stale smell of spilt ale, the food which had been left and the vomit which thralls were clearing up. I had smelled it in the warrior hall when I had woken. There were some warriors who did not know when to say enough. I had done so once and sworn that I would never do so again. The king had his son, whom I later learned was called Cnut, and the bearded warrior with the battle bands next to him. This time we were allowed to sit opposite to the king. He smiled, "I see you bring your hearth weru, Sweyn Skull Taker. Do you fear for your life or is it that these are your sons?"

My foster father smiled, "They are my sons, King Sweyn, and who better to be hearth weru for they are bound twice by blood now?"

He nodded and turned to his son, "You see Cnut, even the lowliest of my lords are wise." The boy no more than five or six summers nodded sagely. "You are not a Christian, Sweyn?"

My foster father shook his head, "We follow the old ways in Agerhøne, King Sweyn."

"So you still kill priests."

"Not in Denmark!"

The king laughed, "Good for I should hate to have to banish you for such murder. You lost two ships, I believe?" The hersir nodded, "Perhaps that was a punishment from God, eh?"

Sweyn Skull Taker said, "If so then his priests paid the price for we slaughtered all of them and you are richer for we brought you the tribute from that church."

It was a clever move by my foster father. If the king felt strongly about the killings, then he could refuse the tribute. The king nodded, "Just so. Know that I will have need of your ship soon. Do not waste any more of your warriors."

"You make war then, King Sweyn Forkbeard?"

"I have ambition, aye. You are a small part of my kingdom but like the other hersir who wish to live in Denmark, there is a price to pay and that is obedience to my commands."

I saw my foster father bristle. He had counselled calm but the king, to my mind, was trying to intimidate him.

"King Sweyn, I have never disobeyed a command which you have issued."

The king took a piece of fried meat, chewed, and then swallowed it, "Just so long as it continues but we would prefer it if you did not raid churches."

There was a pause, "And is that a command?"

The king smiled, "No, just a request."

My foster father smiled, "Which I will attempt to do but sometimes the prize is too great."

"Very well, you can return to your home then and await my command to gather your warriors." It was as I stood that the king spied my scabbard. "Your hearth weru appears to have grand ideas, hersir. He has a dragon scabbard?"

Sweyn Skull Taker nodded, "It is not grand ideas for the blade is a dragon sword."

For the first time, I saw the king not in control of himself, "A youth with a dragon sword. Sit and tell me all." He pointed to me, "You...?"

"Sven Saxon Sword."

"Put the sword on the table so that I may examine it and you had better tell the tale!"

I did as I was asked but I was annoyed. I had shown it to many people, but I did not like the king and did not wish him to touch it, but he was the king. I laid it before him and told him, simply, the tale.

When I had finished, he nodded and said, "There is a tale here. Would you care to give the sword to me, Sven Saxon Sword, for it is a sword for a King?"

I felt the other three stiffen and I knew that their eyes were upon me. I looked at young Cnut and he was smiling. I saw his fingers playing with the hilt of the sword, where the head of the dragon must have been. I knew that if I gave the sword to the king, he would give it to his son. I might be given some reward, but I would not have the sword. "I am sorry, King Sweyn Forkbeard, but I cannot do so. The Norns have spun and they wished to give the sword to me. I dare not risk their wrath!"

His face contorted with anger and his voice was cold when he spoke, "The Norns! A pagan tradition! There are no such creatures!" Even though we had been told not to touch them all of us, including Sweyn, touched our hammers of Thor. Even the king's bodyguards, ostensibly Christians, did the same. I even saw what might have been fear on Forkbeard's face as he realised what he had said. He waved a hand, "Keep it, for it will do you little good."

As I replaced the sword in the scabbard Cnut said, "Thank you, Sven Saxon Sword, for allowing me to touch the sword. I like the dragon design."

Before we left, we visited the market and the weaponsmiths. Agnetha had asked for those things that could not be made in our village while the weaponsmiths yielded blank spearheads and short swords. The hersir spent the coins we had taken wisely for he wished the clan to be stronger. Sweyn bought himself a better helmet which, like mine, had a nasal. He had tried on mine and liked it rather than those which had a face mask for the eyes. Alf bought himself a long dagger. He just wanted to buy something, like his brother had. I kept my coins in my purse for I was happy with my weapons and, after looking at the prices, realised that I did not have enough yet for a mail byrnie. That would have to wait.

The first part of the journey was in silence because, I think, none of us wished to say something which might be overheard by one of King Sweyn's men. It was only as we found a place to camp that Sweyn Skull Taker spoke, "You managed to say the right thing, Sven, but I wonder at the wisdom, now, of the scabbard. It draws attention to you."

"Then I will use the old scabbard, but the sword will not like it."

"In that case just use the scabbard at Agerhøne and when we go to war or to raid. Next time we go to visit the King we leave the sword at home."

I nodded for I did not want Forkbeard to have it.

Chapter 9

We did not need a Thing to discuss what the King had said but my foster father told Griotard, Thorstein and Lodvir. They did not like Forkbeard any more than I did. Griotard was particularly disparaging, "Anyone who drives his father away to die in exile is not a man to be trusted. What are his ambitions? To rule the world?"

The hersir shook his head, "If I were to make a guess then I would say that the King of Norway, Olaf Tryggvason should watch his back."

Lodvir asked, "You know something?"

The hersir nodded, "When I spoke with Karl Three Fingers, he said that Eirik Hákonarson, Jarl of Lade, is a frequent visitor as is the King of Sweden, Olof Skötkonung. As treacherous a threesome have yet to be born."

Thorstein held his hammer of Thor tightly, "And it is a trinity too. That is powerful."

My cousin Sweyn said, "But King Sweyn said he was a Christian and did not believe in the Norns."

Griotard laughed, it was so rare an event that I was taken by surprise, "Then he is doomed for no one disparages the Norns without it comes back to hurt them."

We had not been away for long, but Sweyn Skull Taker cared more about our village than the king and his ambitions. "The drekar is healed? She can sail?"

"She is as good as new, hersir, and we have strengthened her bow in case you wish to ram any other vessels." Thorstein the Lucky's voice had a hint of humour to it. Unlike King Sweyn our hersir was able to take humour for he knew the village was soundly behind him. King Sweyn feared that another might try to take his throne.

"We do not need to raid again this season, and I would make the crew stronger. We will draw her from the water. By Einmánuður I would have every boy who is older than twelve summers to take an oar, wield a spear and fight in a shield wall. You will have to use the younger boys, Thorstein, to crew the ship."

He nodded and as he picked a piece of salted beef from his teeth said, "The boys will not be a problem. They enjoy scurrying up the sheets and stays, not to mention balancing on cross trees and gunwales but twelve-year-olds in a shield wall?"

I saw that Griotard looked equally concerned but Lodvir's voice supported the hersir, "Alf and Sven here showed us that young warriors can acquit themselves well and we have the two as inspiration for others. All the boys in the village speak of Sven Saxon Sword. It may have been the Norns or luck which sent the sword to him but the boys all dream of winning a dragon sword. Even Alf has a sword made by the Saxons. It will be a winter of hard work and training but the routine I set Sven seems to have worked." He chuckled, "And as Ulf will be one of the new warriors we are training, then that will be interesting in itself."

Sweyn Skull Taker nodded, "And we are better equipped. On Sven's first raid, I was the only one who was armoured. Now we have more warriors who wear mail. We have more helmets and the purchases I made from the weaponsmith means that the young warriors can be armed. It is how we teach them to fight which is important. I know we were lucky when we were on the vengeance raid." He spread his hands, "I made a mistake. I should have used the newer warriors to take the church. I did not expect the thegn to have so many men. The shield wall almost broke."

Lodvir shook his head, "That was meant to be. Had you been there then who knows where the dragon sword would be? I am now convinced that the sword sought out Sven here." He paused and weighed his words, "His father and his brothers were slaughtered not far from where we fought. I am no volva and do not understand the spirit world but a handful of us, with just one experienced warrior, held a Saxon shield wall until Griotard and the others came to our aid. Do not think what might have been, hersir, it is better to look at what was!"

And so, as Tvímánuður came to a close and with the few crops we grew harvested, young warriors were initiated into the clan. As with me, Lodvir insisted that they all begin to run and to hew logs from the wood I had used. This time he was more specific and had them hew the smaller branches. That was for many reasons; most were younger than I had been and not as strong but, more importantly, we did not wish to destroy the whole wood. They had to be ready for shield wall training by the third hour of the day. I had not had any such training and neither had Alf. As the hearth weru of the hersir, we were used to modelling for the trainees. While the hersir watched and observed each new warrior Lodvir had the three of us demonstrate how to use a shield and a spear. The other warriors were not needed for it was the same as when I had made my spear. The rough wood had to be smoothed before the metal head could be fitted and then the spear needed to be balanced. We were smoothing the rough edges from the young warriors.

By the end of Haustmánuður, they had learned enough for the other warriors to join us once a week while we practised as a warband. For the first two sessions, the three of us stood with the hersir to watch. Griotard and Lodvir shouted and ranted at those who did not obey quickly enough. There were injuries and wounds for the young warriors were learning and some earned scars long before we even went to war. Sweyn Skull Taker was also looking at his older warriors to determine who could be at the dangerous end of our most potent weapon, the wedge. The two brothers, Lars and Leif, were just a little older than I had been. Both had married since our last raid for they were both much richer. They had managed to acquire some mail and rather than using it as a short byrnie they had attached pieces to their leather byrnies. Both had good helmets and had taken Saxon swords. Most importantly, they had continued to grow and were now amongst the biggest warriors. Their father, Lars, had been the biggest warrior in the clan. Sailing with Thorkell Squint Eye he had perished in Wessex. The two young warriors were perfect to join Alf in the third rank. Lodvir and Griotard were in the fourth rank. I felt honoured that along with my cousin, Sweyn, I was in the second rank behind the hersir.

It was Gormánuður when we used the wedge formation for the first time. We used the beach. It was there that Thrond made the mistake of challenging Sweyn Skull Taker. Now that Ulf had joined us there were six warriors from Thrond's family in the warband. He had the mail shirt which was mine by right and it was he who questioned having three such young warriors at the front.

"Hersir, the tip of the wedge is the most important part of the formation. If they fall then you will be isolated and might die. Put stronger warriors around you!"

Sweyn had nodded, "Would that not suit you, Thrond the Cruel? Do you not aspire to be hersir?"

The words were delivered with a smile but Thrond looked as though he had been physically struck.

Griotard snorted, "Over my dead body!"

Sweyn Skull Taker gave Griotard a warning look and said, "My son Sweyn, and Sven Saxon Sword have both earned the right to be at the fore. It was the two of them who broke the enemy line when we raided the Wessex village and it is my life, Thrond the Cruel. I am content and that is why they were chosen as hearth weru." He took off his mail coif so that all could see his face. "Let me say this once and then it is over, "I chose my hearth weru as is my right. They are family and as such, I trust them more than any other warrior. They have sworn a blood oath. I know, more than any, the danger I put them in, but I know my sons and I know their strengths and weaknesses." He paused, "If any warrior doubts my ability to lead the clan then there are two choices, challenge me for the leadership of the clan or leave." There was silence as I knew there would be. The clan supported my foster father and Thrond, as I had seen in the two raids, was never at the forefront of a fight. "Then as there are no dissenters we will carry on with the training."

It took four sessions before we were able to move from the two-deep shield wall into a wedge and another two before we could move back without accidents. The wisdom of having Lodvir and Griotard in the fourth rank became clear when we moved back into the shield wall for it made the centre of our wall like stone. All the new warriors were in the second rank and my foster father alternated them in the second rank with stronger, older warriors. By Mörsugur the snows and ice had come and training for the clan stopped. Alf, Sweyn and I continued to train. Unlike Lars and Lief we were not yet fully grown, and we ran along the beach carrying logs above our heads to strengthen our backs and arms. Thrond's family mocked us; others told us that, but we did not care. While they caroused and wassailed, we ate well and trained. The only day we did not was on the day of the winter solstice but, even then, we did not overdo it.

It was that night when Sweyn became betrothed. He was older and I know, for we shared all our most intimate thoughts, that his loins itched. Bergljót had long since given up on me or perhaps it had been a ploy to win the son of the hersir. Sigbrith told her brother than Bergljót knew once I wielded the new sword that I would be a warrior with a reputation. She wanted a husband and as Sweyn would be the next hersir he was a safer choice than me. Since we had returned from Heiða-býr they had been courting. Sweyn had bought her a silver hammer of Thor from the market there and he had given it to her. The solstice was a time for betrothals for it was a special day. As the son of the hersir, this would not be simply a handfast marriage and so the date was set for the first day of Þorri. Agnetha chose the date after she and the other volvas wove and determined that it was the most propitious date.

We still trained each day but as the wedding day approached Sweyn spent longer speaking to his brother and me about his hopes and fears for the future. It was more about the hopes than anything else. "I want to father more warriors for the clan. You two should do the same. We are the best of the young men and we need to breed strong warriors."

I laughed, "You sound like Siggi talking about a new boar! It is not just about mating. My mother still grieves for my father and she will do so until the end of her life. I want a woman like that, and I have yet to find her. When I do then I will know. Besides, I wish to become a better warrior. I have been lucky up to now but our father is right, Sweyn, men will try to kill us harder than any other of our warriors for we are hearth weru! He will fight in the most dangerous part of any battle and we will be there at his side! I will choose a bride but not yet."

He nodded and Alf said, "I want a girl who is not from this village. Sweyn has got the only one, apart from my sister, who does not have a face like the backside of one of Siggi's pigs!" Although it was not true, we all laughed.

The day before the wedding the hersir held a meeting with Lodvir, Thorstein, and Griotard. As his hearth weru and his sons, we were there. The night would be given over to carousing, for that was traditional amongst the warriors before a man wed. Lodvir, who had been married once but his wife had died in childbirth laughed, "Aye, that is to make him incapable on his wedding day of raising anything more than a smile!"

Sweyn blushed and we all laughed although I am not sure that either Alf or I actually understood it. "We will decide where we raid. The king has not forbidden us to avoid churches, but I think he would prefer it if it was not an ally."

Griotard said, "And we do not wish to raid the Norse for they are as piss poor as the Scots."

"And I would not like to steer around the island to the west of us with a crew which is just half-trained." Thorstein was a realist.

We were hearth weru and none of us ventured an opinion for we did not know enough anyway.

Lodvir was the thinker, "We have too many young warriors to risk a numerous enemy."

Griotard snorted, "We are warriors! We fear no one!"

"And, my friend, what of the day when King Sweyn asks us to go to war with him? What if we have lost so many warriors that we cannot crew a ship? We are using youths on this raid who should not actually go to war. The next ones will be those who are Thorstein's ship's boys! They cannot even hold a shield."

Sweyn Skull Taker had been silent for that was his way. He was happy for his advisers to argue while he weighed up the different choices we had. "You are all right and if we are to bring back both treasure and food whilst having the shortest voyage then we sail due west to the river to the north of Hwitebi. That abbey has been emptied of treasure but when we were at Heiða-býr a warrior told me there are places which rear animals. Some of the folk who live there have Danish blood, but they are now Christian and have rich churches. He had raided Gighesbore and they brought good thralls with Viking blood as well as animals, iron, and grain. He said there were two other places which could be reached from the river there, Herterpol and Norton. They both have rich churches for they have close connections with Dun Holm which houses the bones of a saint. I think that the river draws us there."

The four of them drank their ale and I knew that they were each thinking of reasons to raid and reasons not to. It was Thorstein the Lucky who came up with the deciding reason. "I too have heard of this river, it is called, by the Saxons, the Tees, and on its north bank are many seals. There was a time when there were many close to here too. We need seal skins as well as the oil and the meat preserves well. If nothing else, it would help to blood the young warriors for a seal is easier to kill than a warrior but there is still danger."

That led to a long discussion about the merits of the river and Sweyn Skull Taker, who was not afraid to make a decision said that, at Einmánuður, we would raid to the north of the river. We would land at the sands there and raid Norton. We would then be able if we chose to raid Herterpol too. I did not care where we raided. I had practised every day with Sweyn, and Alf and I knew I was better with a sword than both of them. There was no surprise that I was better than Alf but Sweyn was older, stronger and had been on more raids. I put it down to the sword. We did not practise with our war weapons. We used the shorter, older swords but I could see the Saxon Sword and the scabbard. Somehow that made me a better swordsman. I had still to name the weapon. I was unworried. When it was ready to be named then it would tell me. My spear had demanded the name Saxon Slayer and that was good. I would practise alone with the Saxon Sword until it gave me a name. I found it balanced well in my hand. I always practised alone using a shield. That was Lodvir's advice for he had told me that I should feel as though the sword and shield were extensions of me. Sometimes I would have Egbert blindfold me. Alf laughed when he saw me fighting that way. I had my reasons. If it was dark, and often it was when we raided, then your eyes might deceive you. Fighting blindfold helped you to learn to use your other senses. At first, it was hard, but I gradually learned to use smell and touch to help me. I never minded looking foolish just so long as I could improve.

After the meeting was over, we prepared for the feast to send Sweyn to the world of a married man. He and Bergljót would still live in the longhouse but, like the hersir, his father, they would have a curtain hung from the roof for privacy. Alf and I made fun of Sweyn as he combed his hair and then plaited it. He did the same with his beard and moustache. Neither Alf nor I had hair long enough but that did not stop us mocking Sweyn. It was what warriors did. All the men of the village were at the feast. I drank sparingly. Alf and I had promised to look out for Sweyn if he had too much to drink. He did not. We enjoyed the evening which was filled with songs of the past and warriors long dead. There were tales of Odin and Freyja and the afterlife field of Fólkvangr. It was a good tale to tell as it was a tale of love and a warrior. The last tale which was sung was the song of Ragnarök and the great battles. It was at that point that Sweyn decided to retire. It was the right moment. Sweyn Skull Taker, Griotard, Lodvir, and Thorstein had gone to bed after Fólkvangr.

It was Thrond who began the fight, "You cannot go to bed yet, Sweyn Sweynson for we are not done yet."

Sweyn smiled, "Thrond, I will be wed tomorrow, and I have enjoyed the feast. I thank you all."

Thrond was far too drunk and he shouted, "I say you shall not, boy!" He lurched towards Sweyn and Alf and I stepped before him.

"Thrond, this is Sweyn's night and he can choose when he wishes to retire. Erik, Ulf, take your kinsmen to bed."

The two of them were also drunk but not drunk enough to take either Thrond or the three of us. They just sat there looking foolish. Thrond looked at them and then me, "Offspring of a fool, out of my way!" He threw a punch at me. I saw it coming for he was really drunk, and I just stepped away from him. He overbalanced and his head smashed into the bench. I saw teeth fly from his mouth and blood followed. He rolled on to his back and I saw that he had passed out. I turned him on his side in case he vomited. I had heard tales of men drowning on their own vomit. That was no way for a warrior to die.

Alf said, "Ulf, Erik, take your kinsman back to your longhouse. We will say no more of this." There were just a dozen warriors left in the hall and Thrond was the most senior. They nodded and we escorted Sweyn to the place the three of us slept. We made water in the pot which the thralls would empty and use to clean the clothes before they were washed and then we lay down. We listened as Thrond the Cruel was taken outside. He had barely left the longhouse when we heard him being sick.

"Thank you, brothers."

I said, quietly, "It was me with whom he was picking a fight."

"We are blood brothers. He picks a fight with one of us then he does so with us all!"

I woke first and I heard the thralls clearing the table. I made water in the vessel and realised that the thralls had emptied it during the night. I was heading for the jug of ale on the table when Sweyn Skull Taker emerged from his chamber. "You and my sons handled Thrond the Cruel well last night."

"You saw?"

He nodded, "The shouts awoke me, and I peered out. You all did the right thing. Thrond is a problem. If we had more men to raid, I would send him hence, but he and his family give us seven warriors."

"I am sorry, foster father, for he appears to blame me for the loss of his family."

"He always hated your father and that was because others in his family preferred him to Thrond. His brother Erik wanted to sail with Bersi! It is the Norns and they have spun a spell so complex that none can unspin it. My wife has tried. We have to live with it. But you showed that the clan is at the heart of all that you do. I believe the sword changed you and your future. Now let us get the warrior ready for his wedding."

Most Danes would simply have a handfasted marriage where the couple would join hands before the clan and announce their intention to be man and wife. Sweyn was the eldest son of a hersir and, as such, the volvas of the clan would spin and the woven spell would be bound around their hands. Bergljót had spring flowers in her hair and, as the son of the hersir, Sweyn wore his sword. It was as the whole clan was gathered that I saw Thrond was missing. His wife was there, and his two children as were Erik and Ulf but Thrond was not. I saw that Sweyn Skull Taker noticed the absence too as did Lodvir and Griotard. I believed that it made the ceremony better, but I knew there would have to be retribution as his absence would be deemed to be an insult to the hersir. The ceremony passed, the couple kissed and then retired to their flower-strewn bed. Everyone else remained outside and thralls brought drink and the pig which Sweyn Skull Taker had bought from Siggi's father. It had been cooked overnight.

Siggi came over to see me. Without the rowing and the training for war, I saw that Siggi was putting on weight. He was still the same oar brother and he came over to clasp my arm. "The pig is Thor! He was an old pig and had ceased fathering piglets before I went on the raid. My father gave the hersir a good price, but he will be tasty. The layers of fat will give it a good flavour. I will go and fetch us some of the crackling."

I smiled as my friend left. He might speak one or two words about war, but he would wax lyrical about a pig. He returned with a wooden platter covered in the crispy crackling. He proffered the plate, and I took a piece and crunched it, "You are right. It is delicious!"

He nodded and bit a huge piece which dripped fat down his golden beard, "The secret is to soak the skin in seawater but dry it off before cooking and I use my father's sword to score the skin."

"I thought the thralls prepared the food!"

He snorted, "It was our pig and I wished Thor to be treated well. I supervised the cooking. It will be so tender that you will not need a knife!"

He was right and I ate with my friend. I had seen little of him since the raid and it was good to speak with someone who was not a warrior. Without warriors, farmers like Siggi would be robbed and probably killed but without farmers, the warriors' existence would be so much poorer. Alf joined us and Siggi hurried off to find a plate of food.

"Thrond is not here!"

"Aye, Alf, and perhaps that is for the best."

Alf shook his head, "Father is angry. He does not show it, but he is."

Just then Siggi returned and I enjoyed the whole conversation about the best way to cook pig again. I did not mind for I liked Siggi's passion. With Alf involved the conversation turned to the raid and Siggi was able to show polite interest because whilst he would not be involved in the raid, he would enjoy the benefits. Pig fat was good for cooking, but seal oil could be used for cooking and for lighting too. The candles we would take from their churches would also give us light. The seal skins we would bring back enabled all of us to work outdoors in any weather.

"If you are able to get some young slaves then my father would buy them." The rule was that the slaves not wanted by the men who captured them would be sold at a low price to those who did not raid. The ones who remained would be sold at the Ribe slave auction.

"What do you seek?"

"It matters not so long as they are under the age of ten. Those are easier to mould. Older ones are set in their ways. If you could find a female. then that would suit me. We live far enough from the village that I do not get to enjoy their company very often. A man has needs, eh Sven?"

Alf laughed, "Not yet. Sven here wishes to be a great warrior. He would have tales told about him."

I felt uncomfortable for he was right. I wanted to be the hero who scalds made up songs and sagas about. The food was good, and the ale and mead flowed well. Men would not become as drunk for their wives and daughters were there, watching them. I just enjoyed the company of Siggi and Alf. We were young men and we simply talked. Had you asked me an hour later what we had spoken about then I would have had no idea but as Alf and I bade Siggi farewell and he trod an uneven path to this home, I felt happy. Happier in fact than at any time since my father and brothers had died. I could not think why but, as I lay down to sleep, I put it down to their spirits being happy and that made me happy. I had no more unpleasant dreams about my family. The world changed the day that Sweyn married.

Chapter 10

Sweyn and Bergljót displayed their blood-stained bedsheet for the clan to see and all were happy. It took a day to clean up after the festivities, but Sweyn Skull Taker was not yet ready to help us. He waved over Alf and me, "Arm yourselves. I need my hearth weru!"

Any lingering hints of drunkenness ended as we donned helmets and byrnies and strapped on swords. We said not a word but hurried after the hersir as he headed for the longhouse of Thrond and his family. Thrond was outside and his face showed the effects of the fall. He had not only lost teeth but broken his nose and blackened his eye. He made a half-hearted attempt at a bow as he stood. Sweyn Skull Taker was a good man and leader, but he wasted no time on preliminaries.

"Thrond the Cruel, you have insulted me by failing to attend my son's wedding. What is your excuse?"

He did the wrong thing. He jabbed a finger at me and shouted, "He attacked me without provocation at the feast for Sweyn. I demand that he be punished."

I saw Ulf and Erik to the side and their heads were lowered. The last thing they needed was to be embroiled in this pack of lies which oozed from Thrond's mouth.

"You lie!" It was Sweyn Skull Taker who spoke.

Thrond shook his head and I saw that it pained him, "If he told you that then he is the liar and proves that he is a nithing."

Silence reigned until Sweyn said, coldly and calmly, "My foster son did not need to tell me anything for your rantings and ravings woke me. I saw the whole thing. You tried to strike him. You missed and fell over a bench. Now, who is the nithing?" Thrond glowered belligerently at me. "So, Thrond the Cruel will you answer me? Why did you dishonour me by failing to attend the wedding?"

"Because you are a bad leader, and all your family are equally bad. I do not wish to follow you. You rule nothing for Agerhøne is a speck of dirt on the backside of the King of Denmark and there are other places where a warrior like me can use his sword!"

I saw his wife put her hand to her mouth for she knew what that meant. The hersir said, "Lady, I am unsure if your husband is drunk or the knock has driven the senses from him. When he is ready to apologise to my family and to me, I will hear his words. He has until the sun sets."

She nodded and kissed the back of the hersir's hand, "Thank you, lord. I will speak to him."

We turned and headed back to the longhouse. Lodvir and Griotard along with other warriors had seen us make the long walk to the longhouse and were waiting for us when we returned. Sweyn gave an honest account of what had happened.

Griotard spat, "Then he is banished! It is a simple enough law."

My foster father nodded, "Aye, but does it mean his whole family goes? Thrond is the bad apple but some of the others might be made into warriors. We will see and I want no provocation."

By noon it was clear what the answer would be. Thrond and his younger brother Karl packed a pony with their war gear, mounted two other ponies and headed north to Ribe. His wife Ada came over to us with her sons, Ulf, and Erik. I saw that she was tearful and had been knocked about, presumably by Thrond, but she was also defiant. "My husband has left. He wished us all to leave and there were words." I saw her put her hand to her eye where she had been beaten. "We are now divorced. I beg you to allow us to stay."

"Of course, and we shall care for your family. You are of our clan. I am sorry that Thrond was so bull-headed."

"He is well named, lord. Had this not happened I would still have divorced him for he is not a pleasant man!"

When we left, the following week, I know that even Sweyn Skull Taker was unsure of the crew he led. We were just two men short of the number we had intended to take, and it was not numbers, it was the effect Thrond's departure might have on those we did take. How would Thrond's family react? Since the death of his brother Thrond had been the head of the family. Agnetha did her best. She and the volvas had woven a new banner for us. On it was emblazoned a skull which told the world who led the raid. Hitherto we had just had our unique dragon prow but the red banner with the white skull, protected by the volva's spells seemed to make the drekar more powerful.

As we hung our shields from the side Alf commented on that, "You made a wise choice with your dragon on the red background. You, our father and the drekar now seem as one. That can only be a good thing!"

It had been luck, but I hoped it was right. As we took our places at the oars, for the first time closer to the steering board, I wondered if it had been just luck. Had Egbert and I been guided by some spirit? Whatever the reason as I leaned into the oar and we pulled away from the shore I felt more confident and the lifting of the weight of an enemy not being aboard also helped me. I now felt I rowed amongst friends. I shared an oar with Alf while Sweyn was with his father. Marriage had changed Sweyn; it was more than I had expected. He seemed far more mature and considered in his actions. He also appeared less close to Alf and to me. He had been married such a short time and I was astounded at the change. It made me fear marriage for I did not wish to change. One thing which remained the same was his love of words and singing. He had always enjoyed composing songs and sagas and now, as we headed out to sea, I knew that he was composing for while we chanted to get the rhythm, he did not join in and yet I knew he had the beat. It was when we ceased rowing and had our horn of ale from Lodvir that I asked him what he had been doing.

"You have good eyes, Sven, or perhaps you know me well. You are right, I was composing a chant for us to sing. The ones we use do not reflect who we are. There are no songs about my father, Lodvir or Griotard. You deserve a verse yourself."

I shook my head, "I have done nothing yet. Save the songs about me until I deserve them."

He nodded and lowered his voice, "I have been composing a song about my father taking the head and the mail. I have asked Griotard and Lodvir what they did. While you were all singing the song of Harald Bluetooth, I was using the beat to make a song about Sweyn Skull Taker."

He was also even more considerate towards the new members of the crew. He had always been kind to them but now he went out of his way to ensure that they were comfortable and that their hands were not too blistered. That may have been because marriage had made him realise that one day, he would be hersir, I know not. Bergljót's younger brother, Bergil, was one of the new crew and Sweyn made certain that he was not suffering too much.

Our voyage would be a short one, Thorstein estimated it at less than four hundred miles. That was just two days, perhaps three. It was, of course, a new one for us and we would be out of sight of land for most of it. The winds would not be in our favour heading almost due west but coming back, hopefully laden, we would make a swift voyage. There was, in addition, an excited mood on board. There were three reasons for this: we had many new crew, Thrond was not aboard and we were going somewhere new. We would be raiding men with both Danish and Saxon blood. Jorvik, which had been the Saxon Eoforwic was now the capital of a Danish land which the Saxons called Danelaw. Many men came from the land of the Danelaw to raid. Agerhøne was small, as Thrond had called it, '*a speck of dirt on the backside of the King of Denmark*'. We were small and that meant we were away from the main centres of Danes. We knew not who ruled in Danelaw. For all we knew it might be a kinsman of King Sweyn but we had not been forbidden to raid and so we would.

We rowed more regularly than on the previous raids and I knew that the new oarsmen were suffering. We had an hourglass which had been taken on the raid to Wessex and we used that, not only to measure our progress but also to regulate the changing of the oarsmen. We rowed for an hour and then had an hour off. Even I was tiring when we saw the sun setting ahead of us and Thorstein reefed the sail a little and after a meal and ale we curled up in our own nests. I had learned from my previous voyages. The drekar was wider where we now slept but Alf and I rigged my cloak so that it covered us both and we used his cloak as a bed. With our chests and the gunwale affording us protection too we were snug and as warm as could be expected in that sea which was almost as cold in summer as it was in winter. The second day was a repetition of the first and I saw Sweyn Sweynson tending to the hands of the new crew with the salve his mother had made.

This time Dreng and Eystein were with us. They and their sons were still at the prow and when we came together at the mastfish for some ale, we spoke. Dreng shook his head when he looked at me in my byrnie and with the Saxon sword hanging from my baldric. "You know, Sven, when we sailed that first time, I feared that it would be your only voyage and when you and your spear were placed in the shield wall, I thought you would soon be with your father and brothers in Valhalla. I am pleased I was wrong."

"Aye, Saxon Slayer stood me in good stead. We may need it on this voyage for the men we might have to fight have Viking blood in their veins."

He nodded and emptied his horn, "We can handle them for without Thrond the drekar feels, I know not how, but better. The crew are in good heart."

It was dawn the next day when we found ourselves in the estuary. Thorstein had shown all his skill and arrived when there was just enough light to see the river and yet allow us the time to step the mast. Once the mast was down and on the mastfish we took our oars and with every one manned and Sweyn Skull Taker at the prow, we headed up the river. I saw the sands to steerboard and even in the half-light of dawn spied the seals which basked there. Our drekar had such a shallow draught and was so unladen that it mattered not if the tide was high or low so long as we took the central channel and Sweyn Skull Taker took no risks. The river twisted and turned but we saw no settlements either to steerboard or larboard. I spied smoke to the south and the north, but it was a thin tendril in both cases and suggested that the settlements were too far away to spot us.

Norton, Thorstein had discovered, lay to the south of the marshy river and was on a higher piece of ground. Across the marsh was a tiny village which had been a Saxon stronghold in times past. Billingham was reported to have a stone tower in its church but from what we had heard was now a poor relative of Norton. If we had the time, then we might sack the church there. It took most of the day for us to edge up the river. We had to resort to changing the rowers and I wondered at the wisdom of this raid. It seemed a great deal of work without too much promise of a reward. It also struck me that although the ones who lived here had Danish blood, they had given up the sea for we saw no evidence of ships of any type.

Young Olaf Drengson was the lookout on the prow, and I discovered later that it was his sharp young eyes which spotted the smoke of Norton. Thorstein made the signal for the larboard rowers to stop and we steered towards the shore. I saw that, in the east, the light was going as the sun set in the west. We would not be fighting this day, but the night was a different matter.

We had approached from the east and saw, on the higher ground to the south, the village which lay less than a mile away. The undergrowth and the dark hid us. The boys jumped down and sank to their knees in the soft mud. I had yet to don my coif and my helmet and I sat on my chest and took off my boots. There was little point in covering them in mud. I used the thongs to tie them together and, after slinging my shield around my back I hung them around my neck. After donning and tying my helmet I picked up Saxon Slayer; I was ready. This time I would not simply jump over the side. I was hearth weru and I had to wait upon the hersir. He clambered down and we followed. The wisdom of jumping down barefoot was clear when Alf's boot was sucked from his left foot and he fell face down in the mud. Sweyn Skull Taker did not wait for his son but strode off to join Lodvir and Griotard who were using hand signals and organising scouts on the drier, higher ground. I found a deep puddle and I washed the worst of the mud from my feet before donning my boots. The hersir was just twenty paces from me by the time I had done so. We had to wait for the tardier and muddier ones to join us.

This time we had no idea of the layout of the village but the church dominated the village anyway and so we headed for the cross which topped the church and whose shadow could be seen, even in the gloom of dusk. Sweyn Skull Taker led and as Alf had been the last to join us, having had to recover his boot, Sweyn Sweynson and I flanked the hersir. I held Saxon Slayer in two hands. I found that easier than in one hand. Lars and Leif were at the fore as the two of them worked well together and were capable scouts. Lars turned and raised his spear; they had found a path. The path wound through trees and I saw, from the blossom, that some were apple trees while others were plums. It did not look like an orchard, but it seemed to me, as we headed up that it might have been a former orchard which had run wild for there were also many brambles and wild raspberries growing there.

Griotard waited at the path and allowed us to pass. He would stay at the rear and ensure that there were no stragglers. In the event of an ambush, he would organise the rearguard. We were such a small warband that such plans were necessary. I now saw the wisdom in making the three of us hearth weru. We could protect the hersir while Lodvir and Griotard could organise the rest. As we ascended the path, I began to smell human habitation. Woodsmoke mixed with the smell of urine and human dung and the sounds of cows lowing to be milked confirmed that we were close.

Ahead of us Lars, Leif and Lodvir all stopped. The hersir moved forward and I saw that there was a field before us with a willow hurdle fence. Sheep and goats grazed there. Beyond it, we saw the glow from the farm as the door was opened and then closed. We were now in darkness while, in the west, the last rays of the sun lit the village, silhouetting it against the pink sky. Lodvir and my foster father put their heads together and when they had done Lodvir led us off around the edge of the fence. Lars and Leif would now follow Lodvir. We could all see the shape of the village beyond this farm. It was as we moved silently along the path that I heard the sound of water. It seemed to be rushing. As we turned a corner of the fence, I saw the mill. It was just four hundred or so paces from us and the water was turning the wheel and then rejoining the stream which led to the river. It was good news for if they had a mill then they would have a plentiful supply of grain.

The water also masked any noise we might make, and I saw that Lodvir had sped up. It was as though a candle had been snuffed out as the sun disappeared and plunged us into the complete darkness of a moonless night. I could hear, above the noise of the water which diminished as we drew closer to the village, the sound of people speaking. The villagers' day was almost done, and they would each return to the safety and security of their houses. This would be their last conversation before night. For some, it would be their last conversation ever. I know not who were unluckier, the couple who were leaving the village for an assignation down the path or us. In our case, the girl's scream rent the night and meant we were discovered while the youth, who stood before the girl was skewered. The death of her lover silenced the girl and Lodvir led Lars and Leif into the village.

The girl had just screamed, but it was not as it had been in Wessex. None cried 'Viking!' The scream might have aroused curiosity and even worry but it did not inspire fear nor, it seemed, did it result in men grabbing weapons. The shout of "Vikings!" came when Lodvir ran into the open area, comprising the green and the duck pond.

Sweyn Skull Taker shouted, "Agerhøne!" and he ran with the three of us close by him. I left my shield where it was. As we burst into the open area, I saw two men bleeding out their lives and Lodvir and Lars with bloody spears. The hersir pointed to the church and shouted, "Dreng, take some men and secure the church!"

"Aye, hersir! You four come with me!" Dreng knew that it would only require a handful of men to deal with the few people who might be in the church.

There was a hall ahead of us and it was as big as our longhouse. There would be a thegn who lived there and that was confirmed when the villagers who were in the open area ran for it. The advantage of having Griotard at the rear was that he would send men to deal with any villagers who still hid in their homes. We would have to fight any warriors who felt brave enough to face Danes! Already I could see armed men emerging from the hall and a couple of those who had run to the hall had armed themselves. Lodvir and the brothers were racing to get to the hall before more could join them. They were three brave men for although better armed and armoured than the men they faced, they would be outnumbered until we reached them by five to one. I saw the thegn emerge. He had a high domed helmet with a face mask and nasal. The light from the doorway glinted from the scale armour. Even as Lodvir, Lars and Leif paused to fight five men trying to get to the hall, I saw more mailed men leave the hall. There were at least three of them. We had a fight on our hands.

Sweyn Skull Taker saw the problem and as we neared Lodvir and the other two he shouted, "Shield wall!"

We had practised this, and I swung my shield around and stood to the left of the hersir, locking my shield with Lodvir's and my foster father's. I rested my spear on the locked shields. There was no Griotard yet and Dreng and his church raiders were absent, but we had a solid front rank and I felt shields in my back. Glancing around I saw that it was Ulf and Erik who were behind me. Today would be a good test of their loyalty.

The thegn also shouted out orders and it took me a few moments to realise that I understood them. He was speaking Danish. It was then I

97

knew he was not a thegn, he was a hersir or, perhaps, a jarl. Certainly, he was flanked by hearth weru. The Saxons and Danes formed their own shield wall. Only the middle eight held spears and the rest, whilst they had shields, wielded either axes or swords. It was dark and there were no bowmen although some boys used their slings to hurl stones at us. It was too dark, and we were armoured. The stones were wasted. We did not bother with second rank shields held above our heads. Instead, Erik's shield was pressed firmly in my back.

The hersir began to chant while men were still forming our shield wall. When he pointed forward, we would all be in step.

We are the bird you cannot find
With feathers grey and black behind
Seek us if you can my friend
Our clan will beat you in the end.
Where is the bird? In the snake.
The serpent comes your gold to take.
We are the bird you cannot find
With feathers grey and black behind
Seek us if you can my friend
Our clan will beat you in the end.
Where is the bird? In the snake.
The serpent comes your gold to take.

He pointed at the enemy when we said the first '*snake*'. My spearhead was level with my shield for I wished to thrust. The two leaders would fight each other and so I looked at the warrior to the right of the Norton leader. He had a mail byrnie and a good spear. His helmet was also a full-faced one. The grey flecked beard I saw beneath the mask told me that he was a veteran. I saw the hint of a grin on his face when he realised that I was a young warrior.

The chant helped us to move quickly and the enemy could not move for the walls and doors of the hall were just five paces behind them and villagers were still flooding inside. We had practised thrusting together but that had not been against an enemy who thrust back. It had been against a wall of shields upon which rested spears. The spear came directly for my face and was thrust just a heartbeat before mine. It was a mistake for I had enough time to turn my head slightly. Had the man gone for my leather byrnie he might have injured me. The spear scraped and scratched along the side of my helmet. The warriors of our second rank were still pushing and moving while the line of the men of Norton was static. My spearhead slid diagonally towards the enemy shield but his shield, rather than stopping the strike merely turned it and I hit him in the right shoulder. Saxon Slayer had a slightly tapered blade, and it found a mail link. I pushed and the weight of our wall helped my arm to drive it into the link and find his flesh. I kept pushing as the warrior pulled back his spear for a second thrust. Their line was being forced back and my battle narrowed to the width of my shield and the warrior before me. My shield was still locked with Alf's and his father's but until my enemy was vanquished then I could do little about helping either of them. It was when the tapered head broke not just one link but ripped apart six others that my spear found flesh. It slid between the two bones close to the shoulder. I twisted and felt it scrape across something hard. He began to topple. Even as I pulled back my arm to kill him and claim my mail shirt, Alf's spear drove down and tore into the man's throat. The blood spurted up like a fountain.

My disappointment at the loss of a second mail shirt was brief for the warrior who had been behind the mailed man swung his sword at me. I lifted my shield as I thrust Saxon Slayer, almost blindly towards his chest. My spear hit his shield but with the men behind still pushing it drove him back and I saw that the door was invitingly still open. I pulled back and lowered my thrust. This time when I drove, I did not find wood but the flesh of his leg. When I twisted the head and withdrew it, he screamed. He hopped backwards through the door. I followed and, when I saw him cowering to the side and trying to fashion a bandage around the limb to staunch the bleeding, I ended his life.

What I did next was pure reaction for we had not trained for this. I left Saxon Slayer in the body and drew my Saxon sword. I turned and rammed the sword into the back of the mailed leader of the village of Norton. He had scale armour, but I was able to thrust up between two of the plates. The blow did not kill him, but it made him turn to face the new threat. That was all the opportunity that Sweyn Skull Taker needed. He thrust his spear up under the man's chin and when the spearhead knocked off the helmet and appeared through the skull then we knew that the leader of the village was dead. The battle did not end with his death, but the slaughter did begin. We were fighting our own kind and they knew it was a case of fight or die. They all chose to fight. I was like the cork in a jug. None could get in while I was there, in the doorway, and two warriors turned to fight me.

I stepped back to use the width of the room to swing. They were both restricted by the door frame. I blocked one blow on my shield while the other strike from the axe struck the lintel above the door. My sword hacked through the bare arm and when the axe fell from the hand which could no longer grip, I ripped my sword across his throat. The other sword swung at my head and I just reacted. I flicked up the shield and punched with it. He was not expecting that, and I caught him off balance. He reeled backwards, not towards the door but into the room. I saw that women and children cowered there. I blanked them from my mind as I hacked again at the warrior. He was still off-balance and using his sword to try to regain balance he blocked my sword swing with his shield, but he was forced to step back. When I swung again, this time from on high for the hall had a high ceiling, he used his sword to block my blow. They rang together and it sounded like a church bell but when I raised my sword again, I saw that his weapon had bent. He saw it too. Combat is about confidence and he no longer had any. I brought my sword down and he used his shield. My blow had the power of a year hauling logs and three sea voyages behind it. He dropped to one knee and as his shield's rim touched the ground, I used my shield to punch under his chin. He fell backwards and his arms splayed out. I did not hesitate, and my sword hacked into his neck almost severing his head. Some of the women and children screamed as blood sprayed them.

I looked around for another enemy and, seeing none, retrieved my spear and raced outside to get back to the hersir's side. I had forgotten what my job was. I had defended him but then allowed the battle to dictate my actions. When I reached the abattoir outside the hall, I saw the last of the warriors put to the sword. The hersir and my cousins appeared to be in one piece, but I saw that we had paid a price and at least three of our men lay dead. Sweyn Skull Taker nodded at me as I emerged. "Are any warriors left inside?"

I shook my head, "Not alive and if there are other men in there then they are not warriors and they hide."

"Lars, and Leif, go inside and drive out the women and children. Lodvir, take four men and search the building."

I saw Griotard driving his prisoners before him while Dreng and his men were laden with treasure from the church. "You three did well now search the other buildings and see what can be taken." He must have seen the looks we gave him for he took off his helmet and smiled, "The dead cannot hurt me. Go."

I slung my shield over my back, and we headed to the far end of the village. Griotard and Dreng had already cleared the other end. Sweyn, as the eldest, led and we went to the large building which lay at right angles to the hall. The door was open, and we entered. There was a brand burning just inside the door and I picked it up and lit a second, unlit brand. I handed that to Alf. It looked to be a better house than those ruder ones we had seen when we had first entered the village. It had a wooden floor like the hall although the furniture, so far as I could tell, was homelier. There was a small piece of woven carpet before the fire. The hall had an upstairs while this one did not. We followed Sweyn through a doorway to another room and it was as Sweyn entered that we heard the clash of steel followed by the scream of a girl and then the death cry of a man. With my sword before me, I pushed my way and saw that Sweyn had slain an older man with a well-made tunic. In the corner cowered a girl of, perhaps, thirteen. She held a dagger before her.

"I will kill you before I will let you touch me."

She spoke in Saxon and the other two looked to me for I had better Saxon than they did. The girl held the knife, but it was shaking, and I saw the terror on her face. I sheathed my sword and placed the brand in the sconce. "You two continue searching and I will speak with her. The three of us must terrify her."

Sweyn nodded, "Come Alf."

I took off my helmet and let my coif fall around my shoulders. As I did, I looked around the room. It was a small room and there was just a small table with a single chair. There was a shelf and on it were quills, ink and rolled parchments. I saw writing on some of them. To me, they were squiggles for I could not read. The man must have been a scribe. I picked up his hand and saw that it was soft and stained by ink.

"Do not touch my father, Viking!"

I let the hand drop and turned to face her. "What is your name, child?"

The fact that I spoke Saxon appeared to surprise her, but she recovered quickly, "I am no child! I am a woman!"

I gave a mock bow, "I apologise, my lady!"

"Now you mock me!"

"So long as you hold that knife before you then I can do little else. If I wished I could take it from your hand, but you might be injured while I did that and I do not wish to cause you further harm. I am sorry that your father died. Had he not tried to kill Sweyn then he would live."

Sweyn and Alf returned. They had a chest. Alf said, brightly, "This was buried beneath the soil of the kitchen."

The female shouted, "That does not belong to you! It is the lord's!"

I said, "It looks like the lord of this village kept his treasure here. Have a look beneath the floor of the other room. When I came in, I think I saw a carpet. Look there."

Alf nodded and said, "Will you be safe?"

Sweyn laughed, "He will be safe unless he slips on the puddle she is about to make."

For some reason, I did not like Sweyn mocking the girl and then I realised she would not understand his words. They left and I said, "What did your father do for the Lord of Norton?" I kept my voice even and gentle. It seemed to work, and the blade drooped a little.

"He was the steward and the clerk. He was once a priest."

"Was?"

She nodded, "He fell in love with my mother and left the priesthood."

"And where is your mother now?"

"She is dead and as you have made me an orphan then life holds nothing for me! I will not become a Viking whore! I would rather die!"

I saw the knife raised again. She had increased the fear herself.

I held up my hand, "No one said you would be. What is your name... my lady?"

She smiled a little, "I am not a lady for my parents were only married in the Danish way." I nodded and waited. "My name is Mary, like the name of the church. Mary daughter of Steana."

"Good, well, Mary, you have my word that you will not be used by the men of my clan. You will be taken back to Denmark and you will become a thrall, but you will be well treated. I am able to speak Saxon to you because I was taught the language by Egbert, our thrall." I saw her debating. "Put the dagger down."

"You swear?"

"I will swear on whatever you wish."

And what is your name, Viking?"

"I am Sven Saxon Sword."

She saw the sword, seemingly for the first time, "And that is your sword?" I nodded. "If it is your name then it is important to you." Again I nodded. "Then take it out and swear upon the hilt."

I was happy to do so and I took out the sword held it before me and kissed the hilt. "I swear no harm shall come to Mary, daughter of Steana." It was as I kissed the hilt that I felt a shudder or something like a movement and I thought I heard a voice in my head say, 'amen'. For a moment I did not even see the girl. When I looked at her, she seemed relieved and almost content.

I think that it was the fear of what might happen to her rather than the death of her father which had inspired such fear, and, for some reason, she trusted me. Was that, once again, the power of the sword? Almost absent-mindedly she dropped the knife and said, pointing to the sword, "There is Latin on the blade."

"You can read?"

She snorted, "I am not the barbarian! Of course, I can read!"

After sheathing my sword I scooped up the knife and placed it in my belt. "Now collect your father's papers, I wish to have them. Then we will return and take your father's body. If he was a priest, then he should be buried in the churchyard."

She nodded and looked at the body. Her father had worn black and so the blood was not as obvious but I could see that Sweyn's blow had found the heart. "That is a kind thought. Thank you." She began to collect the parchments and she held them as though they were of value. By the time we had them all Sweyn and Alf had managed to get the smaller box of coins from beneath the floor. They looked up as we passed.

Sweyn said, "What kind of magic have you performed, brother, to tame the wild beast?"

"Just kindness. It does work."

Chapter 11

By the time dawn arrived we had the treasure and the supplies we wanted ready to be taken to the drekar. As I had promised I buried Mary's father, in the graveyard. It amused Alf, I think. The next task was to choose the slaves we would take. Anyone over the age of eighteen was dismissed and as we had killed all of the men there were just a handful of boys left. In all, we had twelve young women and girls along with eight boys. I suspect some had run when we had arrived. Mary had told me, almost threateningly, that the ones who had run would have gone to Stocc-ton which was just a handful of miles away. I told my foster father and he just nodded. He accepted the risk. There were animals and we used those to carry the sacks of grain and treasure. When Griotard and his men had gone to the mill they found it abandoned but full of grain sacks. We began our arduous journey back down the track to the drekar. The tide had come in and although we still had mud to negotiate to get back aboard it was not as bad as it had been. We loaded the sacks and treasure below the deck and then, as noon approached, we loaded the captives. Half of the sheep and two goats were retained as well as one cow for the milk. The other two were butchered and we salted them with the salt we had taken from the village. All this took time and the sentries we had left at the mill came racing down to tell us that a warband was on its way. Mary had not lied. We boarded and pushed off from the muddy shore. Four warriors watched the captives for we wanted none throwing themselves overboard and the rest of us took to the oars and headed back to the main channel.

Rowing steadily, we spied the warriors who, running down the trail to the river, brandished their weapons at us, impotently. I saw as we headed away from the landing place that we had found a natural bay in the riverbed. Now, at high tide, it made passage between Norton and Billingham impossible. It looked like it might be negotiated at low tide, but I could not see the causeway there had to have been. What it meant was we would not be pursued! The captives were relatively quiet and that was a good thing. Thorstein was keen for us to reach the sands where the seals gathered before dark. We had taken food from the village and we could eat while riding at anchor.

It was as we rowed that Alf said to me, "We could have stayed in the village, Sven. Those men who came were no threat. Only two wore mail."

I nodded as we rowed, "But our hersir is a clever man. We would have gained little except for a night ashore in a village. We might have lost men and there may have been more warriors coming from further afield. What care you? You have a mail suit now."

He looked at me in amazement, "But you fought and defeated him."

"And you killed him. The byrnie is yours."

"Thank you, Sven, I will not argue with you."

I think I knew then that I would either have a byrnie made or the one which I won would be as special as my sword. It was then that the name came to me. I just said, 'Oathsword', almost to myself.

Alf said, "What?"

"My sword, it has a name, it is Oathsword. I swore an oath on the hilt and when I kissed the hilt, I felt something. The sword spoke to me."

Sweyn Skull Taker was not rowing but he was looking for a place to land. He must have heard me for he nodded, "That is a good name. King Sweyn coveted the sword and there is more to it than a mere Latin inscription. Is that why you brought the parchments aboard or did you wish to use them to light a fire?"

"The girl I took can read."

"Then you wish to keep her?"

I nodded, "I thought she could be a companion for my mother. She seems bright and despite trying to gut me has a pleasant nature. My mother is lonely, and this seems right."

"She is yours although it seems you have made a poor exchange letting me have one mail shirt and my son another. By my reckoning that is three mail byrnies sent to you."

"But none of them spoke to me, that is the difference. I have Saxon Slayer and Oathsword and when a byrnie finds me then I shall know for my weapons will tell me."

I had done well out of the raid. I had taken two swords and a bent one which could be melted down to make the boss for my shield. I had the dagger which I had taken from the girl. That, too, was a beautiful object with a blue stone at the pommel and another at the cross of the hilt. It was not a weapon of war, but it was a weapon, and it had a beauty about it. I also had the treasure we had found beneath the floor of the hall. While the larger chest would be shared, we had discovered the other chest and it was ours.

When we reached the mouth of the estuary there was enough sun to show us sand dunes to the north of us and, some miles to the north the lights of what we assumed was Herterpol. We anchored a hundred paces from the grass-topped dunes. The cows were milked, and the milk given to the captives. We drank the ale we had taken and ate the food we had found. While we did so the hersir came around to divide us into watches. We, the hearth weru and hersir, were one watch and he had given himself, and us, a hard one.

Thorstein, once the ship was secured, went around to tend to the wounded. Most were minor wounds but he called over the hersir. We three followed for he might need us. The wounded were close to the captives at the mast fish and Thorstein took us to one side so that we would not be overheard, "Sweyn, Einar Siggison has a bad wound. A sword has laid his arm open to the bone. He needs fire."

Thorstein did not make a decision for my foster father but his advice was clear. Lodvir and Griotard had wandered with us. Lodvir said, "The dunes will not have warriors in them and you did say that you wished to hunt the seals."

Sweyn Skull Taker nodded, "But that was before the raid. The men of Norton fought well, and we took more than we expected. We do not need the seals, their oil and their skins."

I had noticed with the hersir and his oldest friends Lodvir and Griotard that they sometimes took opposing views but being a trio they always had a deciding opinion. In this case, it was Griotard who shrugged, "We might as well go ashore and have a fire. The hot food would be welcome, and I need some new boots. The mud did not improve them."

That decided my foster father, "Then in the morning, Thorstein, find a place to land and we will spend one day hunting. No more, mind, for we have little enough room on the drekar as it is."

We returned to Einar. He was the same age as Lars and he had taken a wife who was with child back in our home. It was Thorstein who spoke, "Einar, you have a bad wound. We will land in the morning and use fire to heal it."

"I will not lose my arm!" There was terror in his voice. A one-armed man could do little.

"I hope not." He looked around and said, "We need someone to loosen the bandage every hour or so and make sure he has enough ale to dull the pain."

Sweyn Skull Taker said, "The watch will have to do it."

I saw the girl, Mary, she was sat apart from the other female captives and she was staring at the tableau. "I will ask one of the captives." Until then I had been invisible, but they turned to look at me. "The girl we took in the steward's hall had a father who had been a priest." I shrugged, "She is clever, and this will keep her occupied so that her mind does not turn to mischief."

Thorstein nodded, "That would be best, but can she be trusted?"

I nodded, "I think so."

I walked towards the captives and many of them shrank back. My leather byrnie was covered in blood. It was no wonder that Mary had been terrified of us. The girl was unafraid now. I said, "Mary, we have a warrior who needs a bandage loosening and then fastening each hour. Could you do that?"

"I am cold!"

I saw that she had just a thin shift and was shivering. I unfastened my cloak and wrapped it around her. She nodded and came to Einar.

Thorstein said, "Tell her what I am doing and ask her to repeat it each time the hourglass is turned."

As the healer did so I explained and she nodded, "Is there food? We are all hungry."

I looked up at the hersir, "They are hungry."

Lodvir smiled, "This one is clever. She helps us but at a price. Watch her, Sven Saxon Sword. I will fetch food."

As we headed back to our chest Sweyn Sweynson said, "Lodvir is right, cousin. She is too clever to be trusted and her father was a priest!" Like many of our people, the priests were considered to be the witches of the White Christ.

I sighed as I turned to open my chest and take out my blanket, "She is a captive and that is all. Einar's life may be saved by her presence and so it matters not if we can trust her. I do not believe that she will harm him, look." We turned and they saw what I had glimpsed, she had spread my cloak so that it kept Einar warm as well as herself. "She is a Christian and even though she may hate us she will care for Einar."

I slept fitfully until we were woken. It was not just the cold air of the river and the lack of a cloak; the captive had disturbed me. She had made me use the sword for an oath and had helped to give it a name. Were the Norns using a Christian to weave a web? Had the sword been bewitched? Already our lives were intertwined, and I wondered where the threads would lead.

The morning was dull, and the sun took some time to rise. The hersir roused the crew and we rowed a little way up the coast until we spied an inlet which was close to the mudflats on which the shiny bodies of the seals could be seen. The drekar was turned so that the stern faced the shore and then the ship's boys, stripped to the waist, leapt into the water, and took the ropes that were thrown to the beach. The older boys had wooden mallets and four stakes. The drekar was secure but I knew that once the tide went out a little they might be dragged from the sand. We would have to make them more secure. The wounded men were left to watch the captives and the animals. The rest of us, with just spears, axes and clubs, and, like the boys, without armour and boots, clambered over the side. Thorstein and some of his boys set out to find wood for the fire. Leaving half the men to watch the dunes and the distant settlement the rest of us headed for the seals. The hersir would begin the hunt.

I had never hunted such beasts. I had hunted rodents and squirrels with my sling but some of these beasts were bigger than a warrior. We flanked the hersir. In the water, I have no doubt that these animals were fast and agile but, on the land, they were not. Sweyn Skull Taker chose the largest of the seals. If he had been a land animal, I would have called him the bull.

"Spread out and use your spears to stop him returning to the sea!"

I stood with my back to the gentle waves of a tide which was turning. The beast lurched towards me and he moved faster than I expected. I lunged at him with Saxon Slayer. He came so quickly that the spearhead struck his skin but failed to pierce it! Was the animal wearing mail? Sweyn Skull Taker used a two-handed Danish axe we had taken in Norton and swinging it, hacked through the back of the seal's head. Even though mortally wounded the brave beast turned to snap at his tormentors. His writhing accelerated the loss of blood and he died.

"Let us take him back to the drekar." As we made a bier from our spears the hersir turned and shouted, "Hunt, and hunt quickly. Take the males!" He then used his axe to completely sever the head. It would be less weight for us to bear.

It took all four of us to lift the animal and, despite the cold, we were sweating when we reached the water close to the drekar. Before we took it aboard, we gutted the animal and took out the heart, liver, kidneys and stomach. The rest of the animal would rot more slowly that way. It was easier to move the carcass through the water and lines were thrown to haul the seal aboard. The blood was washed from us by the sea and the hersir said, "Now don your mail and fetch your weapons. We will become the watch."

We climbed aboard and I stripped naked for I was soaked to the skin. I put on fresh clothes and felt much warmer. I put on my byrnie, coif and helmet and strapped on Oathsword. I walked to the mast fish and handed my blanket to Mary. "This will keep you warm and I need my cloak."

She nodded and handed me the cloak, "I hope this blanket does not stink like the cloak!" The girl had an attitude. I could see why the other villagers resented her. She seemed to think she was above all of us!

I smiled, "So long as it kept you warm."

She nodded, "It did, thank you!" Her words and half-smile warmed me.

We would leave our shields on the side of the drekar. Saxon Slayer still lay embedded in the sand. The boys had run out the gangplank and we were able to use it to avoid the deeper water. We passed the fire where a pot bubbled with some of the food we had taken from Norton and some shellfish the boys had collected. I saw that Thorstein was about to use fire to seal the long and ugly red gash. Einar would always be scarred but he might still retain the use of his arm.

"We will be the watch on the dunes. Have your boys fetch us food when it is ready."

"Aye, Sweyn Skull Taker."

Lodvir saw our approach and he led the ten men with him towards the fire, "We saw nothing, hersir, but there is a small settlement just five miles north of us."

"We will watch. I want us to be ready to leave by noon."

We stood on the highest dune. The sandy dunes became grassier to the west and they stretched as far north as the small huddle of huts with the smoke rising from them. Beyond them, we saw the tower of a church but that had to be more than seven miles from us.

"Keep a good watch. Word will have spread that raiders are about and Herterpol may have ships whose captains are foolish enough to take on a drekar."

Alf asked, "But if they are like the warriors in Norton then they will be like us, Danes. They may have a drekar."

His father smiled and shook his head, "These Vikings gave up the sea long ago. I was told a tale about a might Danish king, Guthrum who, five generations ago, brought a mighty army to this land and took it from the Saxons. His army settled here and gave up the sea. The ones we fought are their descendants. They are still fierce warriors, but they are raiders no longer." He nodded to Alf, "The scale mail you took from the warrior you and Sven killed, is ancient. I believe that was handed down from father to son since the time of the Great Danish army." He pointed north, "Now keep a good watch."

An hour later I needed to make water and, as I turned so that I did not pee into the wind, I saw that the seal covered sands were now empty of the animals. The hunt was over. The ones we had not killed had fled back into the sea. I also spied two of the boys hurrying to us with a bowl of food in each hand. By the time it reached us it would no longer be hot but warm food would be welcome on a beach where an icy blast from the east chilled us to the bone.

When he turned for the food my foster father saw the empty sands, "Tell Thorstein to begin to prepare for sea. The hunt is done, and I am guessing that the fire has done its work."

Ketil Svenson nodded, "The smell of the burning flesh almost made Olaf here throw up, but Einar made not a sound!"

"Good!"

They scurried back down the marram grass-covered dune and we ate. The stew was just warm but tasty and mine was finished before I knew it. I was still hungry. I turned and looked north. I saw a movement and even as I looked a head rose and then fell. "The enemy!"

The others turned and the heads appeared again. They wore helmets. Sweyn Skull Taker nodded, "Sweyn sound the horn!"

As the eldest, Sweyn carried the clan's horn. He put it to his lips and sounded three blasts.

Picking up his spear from the sand my foster father said, "Come, we buy the drekar time!"

Thorstein had yet to return with the wounded man and already the men from the north were that much closer. We ran down the dunes discarding the wooden bowls as we ran. They could be replaced! We stopped just twenty paces from the bottom of the dunes and Sweyn Skull Taker had us turn and stand together with our spears ready. Numbers were hard to estimate but I saw at least fifteen. Behind us, I heard Griotard shouting out orders.

As I looked along the dunes, I saw sails, "Foster father, there are ships!"

He glanced and said, "Aye. We work together. Begin to walk backwards. Keep your eyes on them."

We had to have trust and confidence not only in each other but also the rest of the crew. The decks of the drekar would be kept as clear as possible and the men who had bows would be stringing them ready to cover us as we ran back to the drekar. The enemy did not organise a shield wall for they saw only four of us. I heard thundering and saw horsemen galloping down the beach. There were just four of them and they only rode ponies, although some way up the beach they would be a threat to our right flank.

The hersir saw them and took command, "Alf, join your brother on the right." Alf shifted his position leaving me to guard the hersir's left. We kept walking backwards.

The men who ran at us had shields and spear. Most had helmets and at least half had a sword, but none had mail, not even leather. Two had throwing spears in their hands and they hurled them at us. As they threw them from a range of fifteen paces they were doubly wasted. We had time to avoid them and they struck us weakly and secondly in throwing they had to stand. Just five men reached us. My shield easily deflected one blow and allowed me a thrust into the middle of the warrior. I withdrew my spear quickly, twisting as I did so and a nest of red snakes came with it. Two men were attacking my foster father, but his mail meant that their blows did not hurt him. Even so one might get lucky and I was hearth weru. I thrust at the nearest warrior's unprotected left side and drove my spear through his body to prick the other warrior who, distracted, was easily disposed of. The two javelin throwers came closer to hurl their second missiles and they struck our shields. They were not the threat for the four horsemen were almost in range.

"Sven, take these two!" The hersir turned to his right and locked his shield with his sons to face the horsemen.

I ran at the javelin men for they each of them had just one throwing spear left and I did not fear the seaxes in their belts. Neither wore a helmet and so I jabbed Saxon Slayer at the head of the closest one. His javelin struck my byrnie but did not penetrate. It was a well-struck blow, and I would have a bruise, but I was not hurt. As I took the second javelin thrust on my shield my spear found the eye of the first javelin thrower. He screamed and his companion grabbed him and ran away. It would have been an easy pair of kills to run after them and kill them, but I was hearth weru and my hersir was in trouble. I ran back as arrows came from the drekar to discourage the others who were still running from the dunes. I ran at the nearest pony and without hesitating rammed Saxon Slayer into the head of the pony. It died instantly and, as it fell, threw the rider from its back and into the second warrior. When that rider struggled to control his mount then my three kinsmen drew blood.

Lodvir shouted, "Back! We will cover you!"

The biggest threat, the horsemen, were disorganised and while the twenty odd men who were less than forty paces away were a threat, with a rising tide we had the opportunity to escape. Keeping our front to the enemy we hurried backwards until we felt water lapping around our ankles. I slipped my shield around my back and handed the haft of Saxon Slayer to Leif who leaned over the side and then, as he took the strain, walked up the side of the drekar. I felt a thud as an arrow hit the back of my shield. I was lucky. The men cheered as Sweyn Skull Taker slipped his leg over the gunwale. It was as I turned east that I realised the Norns were spinning. We had expected a wind from the west to take us home but at that moment it was from the northeast. As soon as the other three were aboard Thorstein unfurled the sail and we moved away from the shore. Griotard had some of the oars manned and as they began to pull, we drew away from the shore.

Lodvir shouted, "The four ships will catch us. One is an old threttanessa."

Sweyn glanced to the north as did I. The ship looked old and the sail had been hurriedly repaired but she was a warship. The dragon prow did not look like a dragon for the paint had peeled completely. The other ships were the tubby Saxon ships which were better suited to cargo than battle. It was the dragon ship which could hurt us. Until we had our ship under full oars then they could catch us. We either headed into the wind or took a southerly course and headed across the incoming tide. Either way, we would be in trouble.

"Man the oars!"

It was as we all ran to the mastfish that two of the female captives and two of the older boys saw their chance and they hurled themselves overboard.

Lodvir shouted, "Einar, stop the others!" Einar's wound was sealed, and he could still use his right hand. He drew his sword and drove the others closer to the mast fish. Alf and I grabbed our oars and we glanced over our shoulders to get the beat from Leif and Bjorn behind. As the oars bit, we began to move but we were fighting tide and wind. The ancient drekar had the wind and was racing towards us. It was ahead of the Saxon ships which lay to the east and were ready to fall upon us when we were grappled by the drekar. I saw that the captain of the threttanessa was adjusting his course so that he would ram us amidships. We were rowing as hard as we could, but it was as inevitable as night following day that we would be struck.

It was Thorstein the Lucky whose quick thinking saved us, "Larboard oars up." As the left side of the ship raised their oars he must have turned the steering board and with just the steerboard oars rowing we pirouetted on our own length so that we were facing the threttanessa. "Steerboard oars up. Larboard oars, row!"

I had no idea what he was doing for my back was to the enemy now that we had turned. I could see two Saxon ships to the east, but I knew they were not a threat. I heard a crunch as our bows sliced through the oars on the steerboard side of the threttanessa. Then I saw, slightly below us, the lower freeboard of the dragon ship's bow. There were screams from the men who had been sliced and skewered by shattered oars then there was a grinding crunch as our bows hit their steerboard a glancing blow. It was an old ship and perhaps this was a fitting end to an old warrior. As we passed, I saw her begin to break up as our ship sailed over their captain and their crew.

"All oars, row!"

We are the bird you cannot find
With feathers grey and black behind
Seek us if you can my friend
Our clan will beat you in the end.
Where is the bird? In the snake.
The serpent comes your gold to take.
We are the bird you cannot find
With feathers grey and black behind
Seek us if you can my friend
Our clan will beat you in the end.
Where is the bird? In the snake.
The serpent comes your gold to take.

The Saxons in our path had seen what we had done to a warship and they headed towards the men in the water. There would be few of them left. We rowed for an hour and then Thorstein was able to turn and head south-east. That gave us enough wind to take us closer to home. I took off my helmet and coif and unstrapped my sword. Warriors were slapping oars on the deck and shield brothers on the back.

I just looked at Alf and shook my head, "We were lucky there."

Thorstein heard me and said, "No, Sven Saxon Sword, the Norns spin and that was a test." He pointed to the pennant at the masthead, "The wind is changing and soon we will have a fast passage home. It is good to know I still have skills."

Lodvir said, a little louder than he needed to, "As do Sweyn Skull Taker's hearth weru. If Thrond doubted the wisdom of having three young warriors, then today we saw that it was a wise decision. The three of you fought as well as any warriors I have ever seen."

Griotard nodded, "Aye, Sweyn Sweynson, you now have your first song to compose! Lodvir, open the ale barrel. I have a thirst!"

I looked to the mast fish and saw that all the heads of the captives were hanging down for they knew their last chance of freedom had been sunk along with the threttanessa. Mary, however, was looking at me strangely, as Lars and Leif clapped me on the back. What was it she saw?

Chapter 12

We had a swift voyage home and during the voyage, I found Siggi a pair of thralls who might suit him. They were brother and sister. Edmund was the younger and had seen five summers. His sister, Margaret, was seven summers old. I knew that they would suit for their father, whom we had killed, had been the farmer whose field we had passed on the way to the village. I explained to Mary that the new owner would be a kind man and not a warrior. I told the three of them about Siggi and my stories made them smile.

Mary asked, "And am I to be with them?"

I shook my head, "Perhaps I did not make it clear, but you are to be my mother's thrall. She is old but she can speak Saxon well and she is kind."

"You do not wish me for your thrall?"

I shook my head, "I told you in Norton, I will see that no man harms you and that includes me."

She shook her head, "You are a strange Viking."

I nodded, "I know, and I do not even understand myself. I am young and I hope that I am granted time to discover just what I am like." I paused, "I think my mother would like to be able to read. Perhaps you could teach her."

"You have books? A Bible?"

I shook my head, "Just the parchments I fetched from your home."

"She will find those dull for they are just a record my father was making of the history of the land people are calling Englaland."

I shrugged, "Then when we raid other places, I will seek other scribbles on parchment."

She nodded and stroked Margaret's hair as she spoke, "You do not look it, but you are a fierce warrior. How could you kill a pony?"

"Its rider was trying to kill the hersir and I am sworn to guard him with my life." I showed her the scar on my palm. "I took a blood oath."

She looked beyond me and shook her head, "You had better go for the other men find this amusing and I would not be mocked by barbarians."

I turned and saw Alf and Sweyn grinning. I became angry and strode down the drekar, "Have you nothing better to do than to spy on me?"

Alf laughed, "No, not really!"

Sweyn's face became serious, "Enough, Alf, Sven is a shield brother. We do not laugh at a shield brother. Come, the two of you can help me make a song about the battle on the beach."

Composing the song filled the time on the voyage home. As we neared the quay, I saw that everyone had gathered there. Now that we were a smaller clan our return was anticipated even more. My mother, however, was missing. I saw Egbert and Siggi as well as Agnetha but there was no sign of my mother. I hoped nothing had happened to her. I knew that she was old, she was the oldest woman in Agerhøne.

Sweyn was the first ashore followed by the three of us. We dropped our chests on the quay and then helped the rest of the crew to unload. I had spoken to Sweyn Skull Taker about Edmund and Margaret and I waved over Siggi who was waiting. He knew we would find animals and I also knew that he and his father might wish to buy any from which they could breed.

"Here are the two thralls I promised. You will need to pay the hersir what they are worth. Their father was a farmer. Be kind to them."

He gave me a sad smile, "You have seen what I am like about animals. Do you think I could be cruel to two such creatures? You have my word that I shall be more like a foster father than a slave master." Perhaps he had been practising with Egbert, I know not but he said, in Saxon, "I am Siggi and I would like you to help me look after my animals. Let us go." I was not sure he could say more but his gentle voice and smile made them take his hands and head back to his farm. I smiled to myself for I felt that I had done a good thing.

I waved over Egbert, "Where is my mother?"

"She had a cough and I thought she should stay in the longhouse."

I felt relieved and I took him to Mary, "Mary this is Egbert, and he is a thrall too. He will take you to my mother." I handed Egbert the chest of parchments. "These are parchments. Put then close to my sleeping chamber. They are valuable."

After we had emptied the drekar and the animals and slaves were taken care of, then all apart from Sweyn Skull Taker began to clean the drekar. The dead seals were butchered on the quay so that the process of taking the hides and rendering down the seal oil could begin. We would have the stink of seal oil hanging around Agerhøne for days. We had so much to do that it was dark by the time we had done, and we made our weary way back to the longhouse. The smell of the oil drifted from the beach where the young girls and boys stirred and watched the huge pots. In our clan, no one was idle for long.

Apart from the oath, I had not had to use Oathsword, but Saxon Slayer would need to be sharpened and I would have to repair my byrnie and helmet. I then remembered the bent sword I had taken. I had enough work to last a week!

Mother was not in bed, but she was seated at the table before the fire with a beaker of warm honied and buttered mead. She had a woollen cape over her shoulders. From the intricate design upon it, I knew that it was a healing shawl and that Agnetha and the volvas had woven it to put a spell within it. I sat next to her and put my arm around her shoulder. "You should be in bed!"

She kissed my cheek, "You are the best medicine this old body needs. The men are all speaking of your courage, my son. You know I would prefer it if they did not for that would mean you had not put your life at risk."

I spread my left arm, "Not a wound! Not a scratch!"

Shaking her head she said, "Just like your father." She drank some of the mead. "You have brought me a thrall?"

I nodded, "She can read, and I thought you wanted to know how to read."

"When I was young but now... will I have time for I am old?"

"Of course you will. What do you think of her?"

She shook her head, "Her hands are too soft. She has not done any work. What else can she do but read?"

I shrugged, "I know not. She has wit."

A strange twinkle came into her eye, "It is good that you notice such things. I began to fear that women were not for you."

I felt myself flush and I stood, "I did not say that I wished to bed her!"

My mother laughed and looked, at that moment, much healthier, "Of course you did!"

The next event would be the sharing ceremony. The price of Mary would be taken from my share, but I did not mind for we had done well and with the treasure Sweyn, Alf and I had taken, I was becoming rich. I would give mine to my mother for safekeeping. Mary spent each night in our old longhouse with the other thralls. Egbert brought her before I went to the sharing ceremony and I got to speak with her.

She appraised me as she spoke. She always seemed, despite her youth, to not only be in control but also in command. It was disconcerting. "You, it seems, are a man of your word, master. All that you told me has been shown to be true."

My mother was making water and I said, quietly, "My mother is old but I believe that teaching her to read will extend her life. I care not if she can never read but if she tries then she will cling on to life. She lost my father and my brothers. I do not want her to give up on life."

Mary nodded, "I will do so." She smiled, "There is little else I am qualified for. All that I did in Norton was to help my father. That is why the others hated me. They had rough hands and hard lives and I was spoiled." It was the most revealing thing she had told me.

As I headed for the sharing ceremony, I realised why she had not been unhappy to come with us. Her freedom in Norton had been at a price. She had been lonely. She was a slave but lonely no longer.

I spent a week with my mother and Mary just to make certain that they both got on and they did. I had Mary look at all the parchments for I was interested if any mentioned Danes. She read four or five and I was amazed at her ability to decipher what looked to me like the meanderings of a spider which had fallen in ink. The first letter of each page was beautifully drawn, and it was when she picked one out which had a dragon curled around the first word which she said was then that I asked her to read that part.

"*Then the raiding army granted King Alfred hostages and great oaths that they would leave his kingdom and also promised him that their king, Guthrum, would receive baptism; and they fulfilled it. And three weeks later their king, Guthrum, came to him, one of thirty of the most honourable men who were in the raiding army, at Aller – and that is near Athelney – and the king received him at baptism; and his chrism loosing was at Wedmore.*"

She had a good reading voice and I saw my mother smiling as she read them. It was my mother said, "King Guthrum, it was he who led an army which almost conquered the land of King Alfred. In the end, however, the king became a Christian. He lost his power and faded from the lives of his people."

Mary jabbed a finger at the parchment. There were more sections. "This document is about his christening. King Alfred poured the oil, the chrism."

I became intrigued. "If you find any more about this King Guthrum then I would be interested."

Mary nodded and said, "Mistress, if you would learn to read perhaps we should begin with this parchment."

Mother smiled, "It is good of you to take the time with an old lady. Let us do so but if you and my son wish to walk by the shore, for it is a beautiful day, then I am happy to sit here and watch the fire."

I shook my head, "I have much to do and Egbert is waiting at the smithy for me."

I think Mary was disappointed and I know my mother was, but I did have much to do.

When I reached the workshop Egbert was already melting the bent sword. We had stripped away all that was not metal, and there was just a round hole in the shield. Egbert insisted that I carve the piece of wood which we would use to make the impression in the clay. He said it would impart strength to the boss for part of me would be in it. I had spent five evenings working the wood. We knew it had to be bigger than my hand. We could not make it too big for we only had a limited amount of metal. It was late afternoon when we were ready to pour the hot metal into the mould. It did not fill it for we had to put in the carved wood I had used to make the mould. We used the metal tongs to lower the wood into the hot metal. The wood, despite being soaked in water, began to smoke, and burn. Egbert seemed unconcerned. When the metal began to ooze up the sides he nodded and when it spilt a little then he was happy to stop. Egbert was a clever man and he had rigged up a frame to support the cooling metal. I had the task of putting water to the wood whilst avoiding the metal. It was not easy. We watched the iron begin to harden and the wood started to cool.

"We can leave it now Master Sven. Tomorrow begins the hard work of finishing off the metal."

It took three days to file and polish the boss and to make the holes to fix it to the shield. We had taken the cover off and when it came time to fit it, we hammered the nails from the inside so that we could then flatten the points and add to the strength of the shield. We did not cut a hole for the boss, but we wet the leather and stretched it over the glue. That had the effect of making the dragon head even larger and I liked it. The metal boss added to the weight of the shield, but it still felt balanced.

"When it is used then the leather will be cut and the boss exposed but the first time you use it, Master Sven, none will know you have a boss, save you."

I was relieved that my shield was finished for it meant I could spend more time with the parchments. I was fascinated by them. Another of them had spoken of how King Guthrum, before he was converted, captured horses and rode into the heart of Mercia and Northumbria to raid and take the treasure. The lord of Norton might have been descended from such a raider and I remembered the four horsemen on ponies who had seemed happy to attack us. I could ride but I did not see how a man could ride and fight.

I was given barely a week to read the parchments for a rider came from Ribe, we were summoned by the Jarl to serve King Sweyn. We had been ordered to join the fleet off Ribe. King Sweyn had not wasted much time in exerting his power. In theory, even Siggi and the farmers should have been ordered to join us but that was not Sweyn Skull Taker's way.

We held a Thing and when Sweyn addressed the men I knew he was thinking of the meeting with the king. He would not lose men just for Forkbeard's ambition, "I will take just those who raided Norton. We were a good warband and the raid helped to temper the weapon that is our clan!"

I saw the relief on Siggi's face as he realised he would not have to sail. We had lost men in our raid, but they would not be replaced at the oars.

Dreng asked, "Is this war with Norway?"

Sweyn Skull Taker shrugged, "The messenger said to meet Jarl Harald Longstride at Ribe seven days from now."

"Then we know not how long we need to be away. What of our home? Who will protect it while we war for Forkbeard? We know, hersir, that when you lead a raid, we can count the time we are away in days not weeks. What if he wishes us to winter somewhere and raid?"

"You ask the impossible Dreng, son of Aed. You expect me to read the mind of a man I barely know."

I had yet to speak at a Thing, but I felt obliged to speak for the hersir, "I was at Heiða-býr and I saw King Forkbeard. He does not think that the men of this clan have done enough for him. No matter how far we travel or how long we are away we will have to obey him, or the consequences do not bear thinking about. We are a small clan and a tiny part of King Forkbeard's army. He could, if he chose, squash us like an insect."

Lodvir smiled, "That would leave us but one choice and do what the Norwegians did when King Harold Finehair decided to impose his will. We could sail to the land of ice and fire where there is no king." He shook his head, "For my part, I would rather serve this king no matter how long it takes. I like our home and if the sacrifice to live here is a voyage of months and a war for a man I do not like then so be it. Dreng, we will be fighting as a clan and we will fight together. I am content to stand in a shield wall with all of you for there are no longer any bad apples."

It was wise Lodvir who convinced the clan.

The hersir turned to Thorstein, "'*Sea Serpent*', she is ready for sea? There was no damage after we sank the drekar?"

"It is repaired, and I will strengthen the prow before we sail. I have sailed with a fleet and know that not all those who steer the dragon ships are as skilled as I am, nor as lucky. There may be collisions!"

119

That brought a smile and we left to prepare. We had killed enough seals so that all of us could have a new cape and boots. I was not given any seal skin for I had both already. All that I gained from the seal hunt was the seal oil given to the hersir. I did not mind for although my boots and cape were old, they were serviceable and there would be other hunts. Egbert and I added more varnish and tar to my shield and oiled my cloak. Siggi gave me a sheepskin and we used that to line the cloak. If King Sweyn chose to fight the Norwegians, then I would need it. I had my beaver fur hat and that was packed in my chest.

My mother appeared more philosophical about this voyage. Each day was filled with work and preparations but, in the evening, after we had eaten, I sat with her and Mary. While the rest of our thralls were in our old longhouse Mary would stay with my mother. The two had grown close in the short time we had been back. My mother had only borne sons. For the clan that was a good thing, but my mother had pined for a daughter. I think Mary filled that void. Mary's mother had died some years ago and she, too, took comfort from the relationship. Both had an opportunity to mother me and share the worry. My mother had never been to sea, but Mary had seen what it was like on the tiny drekar. It did not increase my mother's worry but gave her other things to dwell upon. I did not mind as the two of them fussed each night and came up with more supplies for my chest.

By the time it came to load my chest on the drekar, I could barely carry it. We loaded the drekar in the evening for Thorstein wanted to make the short journey to Ribe early and snatch a good anchorage while we waited for the orders. When I returned to the hall, I took out the silver cross I had taken from the Saxon with the dragon sword and I handed it to Mary, "Here is a gift for you." I suddenly felt embarrassed. "It is of no use to me and you might well find it a comfort."

She smiled, "Thank, you, master." As she took it our fingers touched. I wished that I had more to give to her.

The hersir held a family feast. Until we returned Agnetha would rule the clan and the feast was a symbolic handing over of power. Mary acted as a servant for my mother and fetched her food. She had managed to make my mother eat more since her arrival and given her an interest in life. Mary did not believe in the three sisters, but I knew they had been spinning. She fetched my mother's food and mine. I did not ask her to do so. My foster father had other thralls to do that, but she brought me the choicest pieces of meat and fish.

Sweyn Skull Taker was in an expansive mood and as he was flanked by his wife and his three sons his words were intended for our ears. "It seems our cosy world is about to be shaken, my love."

Agnetha smiled and patted his hand, "Fear not, husband, for King Forkbeard cannot shake the roots of this family and this clan by his ambition. My sisters and I have spun and woven a spell. You and the men of Agerhøne will be protected. The White Christ of Sweyn Forkbeard will not save him."

Her son Sweyn said, "You have seen him die?"

Shaking her head she said, "No, but any man who abandons his father cannot expect help from the spirits. He may have taken the cross, but he was born to the old ways and the Norns spin. I care not for Denmark and the ambitions of its king. We protect our own."

My foster father drank from his horn of mead, "And we do the same when we go to war. Our clan fights as one and we stay together. It is unlike a single arrow that can be broken, a bundle of arrows is hard to break. We will be that bundle of arrows." He smiled at us. "You three have exceeded even my expectations. The choice of three was a wise one and it is good that you fight as one. Even Lodvir and Griotard the Grim praise you."

Alf shook his head, "That I doubt, father, for they are ever critical of all that we do."

Agnetha smiled, "The two are a pair of old men who are set in their ways. It is in their nature to be critical of all but you three are held in higher esteem by them than any other warriors."

The hersir nodded, "Your mother is right, Alf. They are happy to let you three watch my back. At Norton, Griotard did not even see our first battle and when we watched on the dunes the two of them did not race to my side as they would have once. They organised the drekar knowing that my three hearth weru would be there for me."

It was at that moment I knew I had become a warrior. When I had killed my first Saxon in that foetid ditch I had thought I was lucky, but now that I knew Lodvir and Griotard approved of me, then I knew I was not only a man but a warrior who was respected!

We did not stay up late. Sweyn had a bride who was keen to share his bed for one last night and so I made my way to my bed. As I pulled back my sleeping blanket, I saw something on the sleeping platform. It was a woven cross. As I picked it up, I smelled the scent of Mary. She had left it there for me. That meant she had to have made it. Agnetha had taught her how to use the bone hook to make fine pieces of woven wool. I had seen her with my mother as she practised. She had made it for me. I knew that it was a cross and a sign of her faith but that mattered not. I picked it up and placed it in the leather pouch I wore on my belt. In it were a whetstone and a flint as well as the spell Agnetha had given to me the first time I sailed to war. I put the cross there with the other treasures. Perhaps Mary had put a spell of the White Christ in the cross. It could not hurt and, as I went to sleep, I had a warm feeling.

Chapter 13

It was still dark when I was awakened. I slipped out of the longhouse with the other hearth weru and we walked through the chill air to the drekar. I am not sure how much sleep Thorstein had enjoyed but he and his ship's boys were already there. The last voyage had been when they had learned their duties and they each had the bruises and scars to prove it. I noticed as we walked up the gangplank, that they appeared more confident this time. We were the first aboard and Thorstein smiled as he pointed to the pennant, "We shall have the wind for Ribe! The gods are kind!"

The three of us were the first to hang our shields from the side. In preparation for this voyage, every warrior had refreshed their shield but mine was the only one which had been improved by a boss. I fixed Saxon Slayer to the gunwale and folded my cloak to make a seat. I had seen Lodvir do it on the first voyage and now I understood why. Long hours at the oars needed a degree of comfort. I unstrapped Oathsword and used cords to fasten the baldric and scabbard to my sea chest. I was ready for sea and the three of us waited by the gangplank for the hersir. The first hint of light was in the east when he led the warriors aboard. His mail byrnie and helmet were in his chest, but he had his shield, sword, and spear with him. I took the shield and fastened it to the gunwale while Alf fixed his spear to the side and Sweyn attached his sword to his sea chest. Sweyn Skull Taker stood with Thorstein and they looked to the north.

The rest of the clan boarded. Most had left warm beds they shared with their wives. Not all came to see them off. Some women thought it brought bad luck. I knew my mother would not be there for she still had the remnants of the cough which had laid her low. That meant Mary would not be there and when Bergljót came to wave to Sweyn I felt jealous. It was foolish, I knew, for Mary was a thrall and a Christian. The woven cross was an attempt to convert me but even so…

There is little time on a drekar for self-pity and as the gangplank was taken aboard and the sail loosed Alf and I took our place at the side of Sweyn Skull Taker. We left silently. The women on the quay waved. I saw Agnetha fingering the spell she had woven and that gave me comfort. We had the wind and so needed no oars. It was not a long voyage to Ribe. The journey by road might take half a morning with a slow cart but with the wind with us, we reached the port within two hours of leaving Agerhøne. We could have done it quicker but

Thorstein had fitted new sheets and stays. He had them adjusted as we headed north.

We saw the masts of the assembled fleet long before we reefed our sail. There were already fifteen ships in the harbour. Jarl Harald's drekar, *'Stormbird'*, was larger than we were but the ship next to it dwarfed it. There were twenty oars a side and we learned, after we had tied up, that it was Sweyn Forkbeard's, *'Golgotha'*. We were told it was the name of a holy place associated with the White Christ. Thorstein did not like it for the ship still had a dragon prow and he was sure the two religions could not sit side by side.

We landed at the quay so that the hersir could visit with the jarl and the king. We donned our byrnies and strapped on our swords. We donned our helmets and walked behind Sweyn Skull Taker as he headed for the mead hall. Thorstein took the drekar to anchor safely. Jarl Harald had a feasting hall which was almost as impressive as the king's. The hersir and jarls who had arrived were there already and as soon as we walked in, I felt like a pauper at the feast. Sweyn Skull Taker's mail was as impressive as any and both Sweyn and Alf had mail, but I was the only one in the room with a leather byrnie. I found myself sheltering behind Sweyn and Alf. Karl Three Fingers greeted us and took the hersir to sit at the table. We were directed to the ale barrel where the other hearthweru waited. A thrall filled our horns and I tasted it. Not as good as that we enjoyed at home, it was nonetheless palatable. Looking around I saw that we were not the only young hearth weru but while others had just one who was young, we were the only ones where all the hearth weru were as we. I think we were all intimidated and we pressed ourselves into the wall as more leaders arrived. By noon it was clear that all were present for Karl Three Fingers banged a spear on the wooden floor and King Sweyn Forkbeard stood.

"Thank you for coming." There had been little choice! "This is not the entire Danish fleet. We leave as many ships as possible in the Østersøen." That was the huge sea which faced Sweden and Pomerania. "We go to raid the lands to the west of Englaland. Some of my captains sailed and took Man last year but we have Sweyn Skull Taker to thank for this raid. He found the weak underbelly of Wessex. We intend to exploit that. We will sail around the jagged headland to raid the abbeys and farms of land to the south of the river the Saxons call Sabrina. Mercia and Wessex have their defences and their burghs facing the east. We will show them that we can attack from the west too! Do not expect to see your wives and sweethearts any time soon for I intend to winter there!"

I knew I would not be the only one from our settlement whose heart sank at those words. We owed the king nothing and his share of the treasure we might take would dwarf ours. No one showed open displeasure however and all the men at the king's table dutifully banged it.

The king allowed the noise to subside and then said, "One day the land of Englaland will be ruled by a Dane!"

That caused an even greater outburst of acclamation and I saw the scale of the King of Denmark's ambition. He would gain a kingdom, but it would be bought by the blood of his warriors. I counted the leaders and worked out that we had more than thirty drekar. Some would only be threttanessa but there would be others almost as large as *'Golgotha'*. We would have twelve hundred men. That was an army. From the parchments Mary had read I knew that the army the Northumbrians called, *hæþen here*, the Great Heathen Army numbered two and a half thousand. We would be a formidable force.

The king sat as his steward, and obvious military adviser, Karl Three Fingers stood. He gave the detailed instructions related to the formation they would use, the signals they would need and how they would sail at night. That impressed me for I had worked out that it was one thing to try to sail almost a thousand miles but it was another to arrive safely. When all was done then thralls brought in food and ale. I also saw that the king's son, Cnut, was fetched and seated at his father's right hand. I wondered if he would voyage with us. Another two tables were brought for the hearth weru. We sat at one end where we would not have to speak to others. As it turned out we were ignored and that suited us. When we spoke it was almost a whisper. Who knew what spies there were? It was known that King Sweyn was a suspicious man.

"We know some of the waters, anyway."

I nodded, Alf was just filling the silence, "We could sail across the empty sea with Thorstein and I would feel safe. What is in my mind is that if these abbeys are richer than the small one we burned, will they not be protected?"

Sweyn nodded, "And if we are there for the winter then the Saxons will have time to muster a huge army and bring us to battle."

The hearth weru who was next to me must have heard us for he said, "Fear not about the men of Wessex. Our hersir, Snorri Sturluson sailed there last year as a merchant and he discovered that the abbeys have little protection, and they are filled with great treasure. Their army faces the land of the Danelaw." He smiled, "As for their armies? Their King Aethelred is no Alfred. He has fleets of ships which do nothing, and he has to wait to discover where we will land. If they do come," he rubbed his hands together, "then they wear mail byrnies, use fine swords, and could not fight my aged mother. If they fight us, we will win and even you, the warrior with the dragon scabbard, will own a mail shirt!"

I know he meant nothing by it, but I felt embarrassed and gave him a weak smile.

Sweyn Skull Taker could not wait to leave the gathering. I could see, from our table, that those who sought to ingratiate themselves with King Sweyn sat the closest to him. The hersir, like us, was at the end of the table. It was a though we were on the periphery of this royal court. Sweyn could not leave first for that would have been deemed to be an insult but when one hersir was forced to leave because he was unwell our hersir and two others who had small clans managed to excuse themselves. We hurried after him and the four of us made our way to the quay. The Jarl of Ribe had thoughtfully arranged for ferries to take us to our ships. Until we were back aboard ours then I knew the hersir would say nothing.

The ferryman was an affable man and he chattered away like a magpie. Although he said nothing, on the crossing he let certain information drip from his lips. I do not think it was intentional. There are some men who gossip like women when they are at the river beating clothes; he was such a one. He let drop that Eirik Hákonarson, Jarl of Lade, was also due to join us on the raid and his would be the last ship to arrive. I now saw a conspiracy to gain not only Englaland for Forkbeard but also Norway. We also learned that Jarl Harald of Ribe was a popular leader and that made me happier. We owed him allegiance and if he needed our help then I would gladly fight for him.

We slipped the ferryman coins for it did no harm to have friends. Once aboard Sweyn said to his father, "Did you hear the news about the Jarl of Lade?"

His father nodded, "Aye, but we had already heard of the connection when we visited the King. Still, another drekar cannot hurt."

As we made our way to the steering board where Thorstein, Lodvir and Griotard awaited us, Alf asked, "Will there be enough treasure for so many ships and warriors?"

My foster father laughed, "Except for Miklagård it is the richest country in the world. There will be enough, and the king is quite right, the warriors there are not what they used to be. I do not mind the raiding, but I wish we were not staying so long. There is no need."

He did not need us and so we went to put away our weapons and helmets. He told the others what would be happening. I took the opportunity to arrange my chest. The treasures my mother had given me such as the skin of mead, honeyed cakes and pickled herrings would have to be husbanded now for longer. They would be a reminder of home and my mother as well as a treat. I put my boots in the chest as bare feet gave a better grip on a wet deck. I had eaten a hot meal, but the crew would be on cold fare. I wondered when we would have our next hot meal. A thousand milles with little progress in the night might mean a journey of eight or ten days depending upon the winds and if the Saxons had a fleet watching for raiders then we would either have to battle them or avoid them.

The *'Ice Wyrme'* was a big drekar with eighteen oars a side and when she disgorged her warriors at the quay where a berth had been reserved for her, I saw that most of the oars were double crewed. The Norse had come. They arrived just after dusk and that told me that they knew the port well and that the Jarl was being as discreet as he could. King Olaf and King Sweyn were sworn enemies. Sigrid the Haughty was the wife of King Sweyn and she had been due to marry King Olaf before she had married King Sweyn. The reasons why the marriage never took place were the matter of gossip but whatever the reason Sigrid the Haughty hated King Olaf and that enmity was reciprocated. King Sweyn not only had ambition as a spur he also had his wife's hatred too to fuel the feud.

I was close enough to the steering board to hear the conversation between the four men who led us. "Will you go ashore again, Sweyn?"

"No, Thorstein, for most of those who will be in the mead hall are those who seek to ingratiate themselves with the King. I have no wish to do so. We know where we sail, and we know the orders. You know the waters around the Sabrina channel?"

I saw Thorstein shake his head, "I am not sure any of our ships know them. The people on the north bank are the Walhaz and they are a poor people. The Vikings on Man and Dyflin have taken all that is worth taking."

Lodvir drank some more ale. The Jarl of Ribe had sent us a barrel which we would finish before we sailed. "The king has been advised well. The richest abbeys of Wessex are in the west. The farms there have abundant animals and produce wagonloads of grain. If they have a fleet, then it will guard the land around Lundenburgh."

Sweyn Skull Taker asked, "Then you are happy to raid?"

I saw Lodvir sigh, "I was not at the meeting with the King but from what you have said then we have little choice. We either bend the knee or he brings his wrath down upon us. We are a small clan with one drekar…"

127

No eyes turned towards me, but I knew that their thoughts did. My father had brought about this situation. When we had three drekar then we had enough men, along with allies, to fend off anything but the full might of the King and his army. Now we could be wiped from the face of the earth with a flick of his imperious hand.

Thorstein ended the silence, "Aye, well, it is good that we hunted the seal for we shall need seal oil to light the pot at the stern. We have three such pots. As for the rest, the ropes were renewed, and we have a spare sail. We are not the biggest ship in the fleet nor are we the smallest and the warriors you lead, hersir, have proved themselves." Thorstein was always the voice of reason and calm.

We left the harbour after dawn for the king wished no collisions. It took two hours for the fleet to assemble, for I watched the hourglass turn, to leave the harbour and take our positions. The king, the Jarl of Lade and the Jarl of Ribe were at the fore and then ships took position behind them. Thorstein's skill enabled us to find the extreme left of the second line of ships. Being close to him I heard the conversation between him and my foster father.

"I would rather have sea room to larboard, Sweyn, for after we leave Ribe that will be open ocean. The ones on the steerboard side of the fleet will have the coast of Northumbria, Essex, Wessex, Om Walum and Mercia to contend with. I do not know the competence of the other captains but from the sloppy way some of them left their anchorage I fear that they know not larboard from steerboard."

We were next to a threttanessa, *'Fire Dragon'*, which came from a village to the north of us. We kept her company for most of the voyage, but we never once spoke to them. I had not sailed in such a fleet before and I wondered at that. We were not all of one mind and one heart. When King Guthrum had sailed to the land of the East Angles to take the land all his captains and warriors had volunteered to sail with him. We had been ordered. There lay the difference.

For the first five days, as we sailed south to head west, we saw ships, but they were on the horizon and fled when they saw our mighty fleet. Then we headed into deeper waters and an open sea. We rowed more than when we had raided and so I was able to see the skills, or lack of them, amongst the ships who followed us. At night, when we stopped rowing and reefed our sails to keep way, we had the whole fleet behind us. Each morning we saw fewer ships and it took time for the stragglers and poorer sailors to rejoin us. We were lucky that the weather was benign. It became clear that King Sweyn was taking us well to the south and east of any Saxon fleet which might be waiting for us. He wished us to disappear. Frankia and the land of Al-Andalus were to the south and east. The ships who saw our masts might tell Aethelred and his Eorledmen that we were heading there. It was a clever move for it meant we could pick up the south-westerlies and while they made sailing a little more hazardous it also added to the speed.

As I drank some ale and spoke to Sweyn Skull Taker he gave me his views, "Karl Three Fingers is a good warrior and has a wise old head on his shoulders. He may no longer be able to be at the fore of a battle, but his mind is still sharp. It is he who advises King Sweyn. A good leader needs such men around him."

I nodded, "And that is why you have Lodvir the Long and Griotard the Grim."

He laughed, the two men were taking advantage of a good wind and were sleeping, "Aye, no one keeps Griotard the Grim for his pleasant company, but he knows battles and how to lead men. I hope my son is as wise when he leads the clan."

It was as we passed the islands called Syllingar which were the home, it was said, of witches and the rocky edge of the island called An Lysardh by the locals, that we lost two ships. The seas had boiled and bubbled, and the winds had blown hard as we had turned before dark to take the passage to the Sabrina. We had reefed our sails but Sweyn had kept half the crew on watch during the night to help Thorstein and his boys keep way upon the ship. His wisdom in choosing our position was justified for when we woke it was to an empty sea. We knew that the fleet had to be to steerboard of us for that had been where we had seen the lights. We spied the sails of the ships and headed for them but then we found the wreckage. It could have been from some storm weeks earlier but when we grappled an oar and saw runes carved upon it then we knew it was from our fleet. Forkbeard waited until almost noon for the two ships which failed to rejoin us and then took us, with a much stronger wind behind us, northeast towards the coast of western Wessex.

Part of the instructions we had received in Ribe had been the orders for our approach to Wessex and our landing. Once we had turned then we would form a long column four drekar wide with the three leaders forming the arrow. When King Sweyn turned to head towards the land then the eight drekar which followed him, whichever ships they might be, would continue sailing north and east and turn when they had sea room. We would all land at the same time. When we saw the land, for the first time since leaving Ribe, we knew that soon we would be landing, and the raid would begin. As I looked up at the skies and we pulled on the oars I felt the first hint of early autumn in the air. I assumed that it had been planned thus but I was impressed for it meant we would be landing when the men of Wessex would be working in the fields, harvesting crops and beginning the autumn cull. They would not be concentrated in towns and villages. As Alf and I drew back on the oar I reflected on the problem the Saxons would have. The island the Romans had called Britannia had a long coast. Raiders like us could land anywhere. This would not be like the raid on the Fal. Even if we were seen, there were so many of us that we could not be opposed until the hundreds had been summoned. I wondered what plans Karl Three Fingers and King Sweyn had made.

Chapter 14

With so many ships and a coast none of us knew, we had to land in daylight. We were in the group which would sail north of the king's ship and land there. We headed east as dawn broke and the coast drew closer. I saw that to the northeast of us was a bay and I saw houses of a small port. The orders which had been given in Ribe were to secure the land for a mile or so inland and give ourselves a base. We had two days to do so and then the king would send his scouts out to find suitable sites to raid. As the wind was with us Thorstein allowed the sail to take us in and, unlike the four drekar closest to us we had already put our oars on the mastfish when we were still four hundred paces from the beach. Whoever had navigated us had done a good job for there appeared to be no jagged teeth to rip out our keels. By the time the sail was being reefed we were all armed and ready to leap ashore. The other drekar were still stacking their oars as, having secured his ship to the land, Sweyn Skull Taker jumped into the surf. I had not bothered with my cloak and my shield was on my back. He began to run up the beach towards the distant settlement which looked to be a fishing village. The three of us easily kept up with him and Lodvir, Lars and Leif followed us. The other drekar captains would have seen the fishing ships and as we passed *'Njörðr'*, her hersir led his men to join us. Sweyn, Lodvir and Griotard might have known the identity of the Danes who followed us, but I did not. It mattered not. We knew what the Saxons looked like and they were the prey.

The settlement was just a mile from where we landed, and I heard the church bell tolling as we ran. The sand was firm, and the running was easy. I wondered at the flight of the people. Where were they running? It suggested that they did not have a wall around the village. There would be ships there and, possibly, warehouses or fish sheds. We had to leave the sand and head up the grassy slopes to the houses and there Sweyn halted and raised his spear. I saw that the settlement was little more than a small fishing village. The boats were drawn up on the beach and I saw whence the villagers had fled. There, less than half a mile away, was a castle. It was wooden and it was Saxon, but it was a place that they could defend. It had ramparts, riches and a wooden palisade; there was, it appeared, one gate only. It had been hidden from view by the low ridge.

Sweyn Skull Taker turned to Folki Drengson, "Find the king or the jarl and tell them we have found a Saxon stronghold."

131

"Aye, hersir!"

He then turned and shouted, "Let us see what the village holds!" We hurtled down the slope to the now deserted village. The treasure we found was of the edible kind. The fishing boats had been out the previous day and the fish they had caught was salted and drying. There was enough there to feed the crews of ten drekar. We were warriors but the ships' boys would be sent to collect the sea's harvest. We followed the hersir as he went into the largest hut. We threw the table outside and examined the soil floor. It had not been recently disturbed and Sweyn nodded to Alf who used his sword to slide it beneath the soil. We heard a noise as the metal struck wood and Sweyn Sweynson and I went outside to fetch spades. We began to dig and found a small chest of coins. They were mainly silver and copper. It was a start. It did not take long to find all that the handful of mean cottages had to offer. Alf was given the chest to carry.

As we returned to the ridge, I saw that a river bent around the back of the castle. It explained its position for it had water to defend it on three sides. The gate formed the fourth. Shouting, "Agerhøne!" Sweyn Skull Taker led us towards the castle. The other drekar crews were also heading in that direction. We could see our ships, but the ridge hid the others from us. What had King Sweyn discovered? Three more drekar crews were heading towards the castle. Had they been sent by the king? When stones were thrown at us from the walls, we halted while the hersir assessed the situation, "Lodvir, take ten men and cut off the road!"

"Aye, Sweyn Skull Taker." It was clear now that the castle had been built on a narrow neck of land between the sea and the river. The neck of land looked to me to be less than a mile and a half wide. There was a single ditch, and the palisades were just eight feet or so high. Two towers flanked the gates and there were small wooden towers at regular intervals. None of the towers had a roof. There had been a bridge over the ditch but that was now drawn up before the gate.

The hersir of 'Njörðr' joined us, "I am Beorn Bear Killer. What do we do?" It was interesting that the young warrior who led the crew of a threttanessa deferred to Sweyn Skull Taker. His mail looked to be of similar quality and perhaps it was that he had little experience in these matters.

"I have sent men to cut them off. We use our bowmen to keep down the heads of the defenders and advance using our shields. When we have crossed the ditch, we use our shields to boost men up to the walls." He waved his spear, "So far as I can tell, there are fewer men on the walls than in our crews and the two others which are joining us. If we take the castle, then the king has a base."

Beorn Bear Killer nodded and grinned, "Aye, and a roof over his head not to mention a kitchen and food!"

It did not take long to organise the archers and the handful of slingers who had followed us from the drekar. As their arrows and stones landed on the fighting platform so the heads disappeared from the ramparts. Sweyn Skull Taker pointed his spear forward and almost a hundred men ran forward with our shields held before us. Even as arrows thudded into our shields, I heard cries from ahead as the brave Saxon bowmen who had stood to loose were, themselves, cut down by our archers. We did not race blindly across the ditch.

"Sven, Sweyn, descend into the ditch and see if there are traps."

The ditch looked to have rainwater in the bottom and was overgrown with grass and weeds but that did not mean there were no ancient spikes hidden there. I kept my shield above my head as I used Saxon Slayer almost as a walking stick to sink into the soft earth seeking wooden spikes. There appeared to be none. Still holding the shield above my head I turned and shouted. "This part is clear!" Just then a Saxon must have dropped a rock on to my shield. All that I knew was that it felt as though someone had smashed a sword into it, but all the work Egbert and I had done paid off for it hit the boss. Of course, after the shock, I was angry that my new shield had been damaged but it had done its work and when there was a cry and a Saxon fell at my feet with an arrow in his chest, I did not feel so bad.

"Clear!"

I heard Sweyn Sweynson emulate me and shout, "Clear here, hersir!"

Turning to the other warriors our leader called, "Into the ditch and follow my hearth weru to the walls!"

Using the long tussocky grass I hauled myself up the bank. It was hard doing so one handed but the year of running to the wood to carry back logs helped me, and I stood with my back to the wooden wall holding my shield above me. The chest left at the top of the ditch, Alf followed me, and I held my spear for him to use to pull himself up. Sweyn did the same for his father. Griotard, Dreng and the others followed. Our bowmen still sent arrows at the wall above us, but stones continued to be dropped.

Sweyn Skull Taker turned to Bergil the Brawny, Sigismund, Eidel Eysteinsson, and Snorri. "Make two platforms for Sven Saxon Sword and my son Sweyn." He looked at us and nodded, "This is your time! May the Allfather be with you!"

I nodded and stepped back. My shield was before me and I angled it to protect my head, but I could still see. I ran and stepped on to the shield which Bergil and Sigismund lifted. It was good that I was ready and had Saxon Slayer thrust before me for a Saxon swung his sword at me as I rose. I blocked the strike with my shield as my spearhead found something soft and the man cried out. I jumped over the top of the rampart and landed on the fighting platform. Sweyn would land to my left and I had wounded the Saxon who had been there. I whipped around to my right and was just in time to see a pair of Saxons run at me with spears held before them. The platform was too narrow for two men abreast and one was slightly behind the other. I had never fought in such a situation, but I knew that my shield protected my left and if the first Saxon thrust with his spear then I should be able to deflect it. I punched hard with Saxon Slayer. The first Saxon's shield was not as large as mine and did not have layers of wood. It was planks nailed together. The spear split the shield and stuck. I dropped it and drew Oathsword. The Saxon's spear slid along my shield and did no harm. I had no one behind me and as I swung my sword over my head I stepped, as Lodvir had shown me, on to my right leg. The movement made the Saxon flinch and that cost him his life. Oathsword slid down the side of his helmet to first break flesh and then bone before finally finding something vital so that blood gushed. The step forward had also confused the second Saxon who had the falling body of his comrade to negotiate. His shield was slow in coming up and my blade hacked through his upper arm close to his shoulder. He tumbled from the fighting platform.

I heard Sweyn Skull Taker's voice behind me, "Take the gate! I am behind you!"

I ran down the fighting platform. I felt like I was immortal but a little voice inside me told me the reason was that the men I had fought had no armour and were not real warriors. They were fishermen holding weapons. I was hearth weru! Two young men, each armed with a short sword and small shield ran from the wooden tower to try to stop me. With my foster father, Sweyn and Alf behind me I was not afraid, but they must have been for they made the fatal mistake of slowing. I did not. My shield was bigger than theirs and I was a bigger warrior. I held Oathsword before me and ran into them. They flailed their short swords, and one struck my shield while the other scraped and scratched along my helmet but neither hurt me. My sword sliced deeply in the left arm of the one nearest to the palisade whilst my shield threw the other screaming to the ground below. I almost lost my footing so suddenly were they moved and then I saw the ladder which led to the gate.

The Dragon Sword

We had taken our section of the wall and we had, to all intents and purposes, taken the castle but so long as the gates remained closed then the defenders had the chance to hurt us. I reached the ladder before the two Saxons with good helmets, large shields and spears stepped from the tower. Leaving my foster father to fight them I descended the ladder. It was then I was vulnerable, and I knew I was lucky when it was just a stone from a sling which thudded into my back. I knew not who was behind me, I guessed Alf, but it made little difference. I had to clear the gate and then open it. Two fishermen with long axes stood to bar my way. Both were older than even the hersir.

"Do not bar my way or I will kill you both!" I saw their eyes widen when I spoke Saxon but they both rushed at me swinging their axes. Years of hauling nets filled with fish from the sea had given them muscles and I knew that if they hit my helmet then I was a dead man. Sadly for the two they both went for my head and holding my shield above me I ran towards them and slashed with Oathsword. I closed the gap so quickly that the hafts of their axes struck the rim of my shield. Oathsword sliced into the side of one, who fell and then ripped up into the belly of the second. They both fell to the ground. They were not yet dead, but they soon would be.

Alf appeared next to me and he drove his spearhead into the ground, "Save some Saxons for me eh, brother?"

I sheathed my sword and we both lifted the bar on the gate. As it opened, I saw the ropes which secured the drawbridge and we both lowered together. When it began to descend, I saw Lodvir and his men waiting for us. He was grinning, "Well met, Saxon Sword! Now let me wet my blade!" We stepped aside as they and the others who had been trying to ascend the walls rushed in. I did not have to unsheathe my sword again for we had won, and the castle was ours.

The men we found were all put to the sword. They had defied us and had to be punished. If it had been us who had been in such a position then we, too, would have fought to the death. The difference would have been that we would have taken more of the enemy with us. It was dusk before order was restored, the bodies burned, and the captives secured. It coincided with the arrival of King Sweyn and the Jarl of Lade, they were riding captured horses.

He waved his sword around at the castle, "You have done well! Now it is time for you to draw your drekar above the high-water mark. Take what food you wish and any women you need. We have made a good start. I will send your orders for the morrow!"

With that, we were ejected from the castle. I found Saxon Slayer still embedded in the planks of the shield and retrieved it. We took the food we had found and the chest of coins. Beorn Bear Killer and his men trooped back with us to the beach. Despite being the first over the wall we had not suffered any losses. As none of us had bothered to bring any of the poor arms we had found perhaps the ease of victory was down to the opposition.

The two hersirs walked together and their hearth weru guarded their backs. Sweyn Skull Taker said, "You know King Sweyn well then or are you a galdramenn that knew he would take the castle from us?"

"I have raided with him before. He has a good sense of self-preservation! Your men fought well. Have you raided much?"

I saw our hersir nod, "But normally, alone. This is the largest raid I have been on."

"And me but the next ones will be larger. This is to get the gold to pay for newer, larger drekar!" The young warrior was a mine of information.

More than half of the drekar were already drawn up on the beach. Fires were burning to prepare food. Thorstein, the ship's boys and the other crew would stay with the drekar. Knowing Thorstein he would not waste having the ship out of the water and he would clear the weed from the keel. We had enough food for us and the crews of the drekar who had fought with us. However, I knew that each day we would have to forage for food as well as seek treasure.

The boys had collected shellfish and with some salted meat in the water, we would have a tasty stew anyway. When the salted fish we had found were added then it would be a feast! We had also taken barrels of ale from the houses as well as fermented apple juice which we found in many of the homes.

Thorstein was still aboard the drekar and he shouted, "Do we need to pull her ashore?" I noticed that the mast had already been stepped. That made sense for dragging a drekar with the mast in place risked damage.

"Aye, we are here for some time. We have many dried fish. When we raid tomorrow, I will try to get some meat."

Two of the ship's boys were aboard and they threw out two heavy hawsers. Lodvir shouted, "Fetch the cords of wood to make a wooden road."

Karl Three Fingers had planned well, and the logs had been brought from Heiða-býr. Placed on the sand they made pulling the drekar easier while causing little damage to the keel. It was dark by the time the drekar was propped up above the high-water mark. Thorstein had made us pull it stern first. It took more work but meant we could launch the drekar quicker if we had to. The chest was placed aboard the drekar and we took all that we would need ashore. We ate and spoke of the battle. My name, as well as the other hearth weru, was praised and Sweyn gave us his first attempt at a saga. It was the story of the raid on Frankia.

When the clan of Agerhøne sailed the Somme
When the warriors fierce were to Frankia come
When Sea Serpent bared her bloody teeth
Her crew were filled with blood-filled belief
The Sword of the Saxons is strong and true
With a dragon sheath bright and new
The Sword of the Saxons is strong and true
With a dragon sheath bright and new
Skull Taker went to find monk's gold
Hidden in a church, made of stone and old
The Franks could not face his bloody blade
All who came near were quickly slayed
The Sword of the Saxons is strong and true
With a dragon sheath bright and new
The Sword of the Saxons is strong and true
With a dragon sheath bright and new
Sven Saxon Sword fought like a bear
Three men were killed in the farmhouse there
Then a jagged spear broke his skin
Baring the bones and all within
The Sword of the Saxons is strong and true
With a dragon sheath bright and new
The Sword of the Saxons is strong and true
With a dragon sheath bright and new
As the ship sailed home a trap was laid
But Agerhøne clan were not afraid,
They rowed and worked as a single man
Determined to thwart the Frankish plan
The Sword of the Saxons is strong and true
With a dragon sheath bright and new
The Sword of the Saxons is strong and true
With a dragon sheath bright and new
The Njörðr played a cruel joke
The tide was turned, and their hearts were broke
Then as Frankish ships loomed at their side
A hero rose the battle to decide
The Sword of the Saxons is strong and true
With a dragon sheath bright and new

The Sword of the Saxons is strong and true
With a dragon sheath bright and new
Sorely hurt with sword in hand
Sven Saxon Sword saved the band
He hacked and slashed at Frankish skin
Fuelled by the power which lay within
The Sword of the Saxons is strong and true
With a dragon sheath bright and new
The Sword of the Saxons is strong and true
With a dragon sheath bright and new
When Thorstein rammed the enemy boat
And Sea Serpent remained afloat,
Njörðr smiled and the clan had won
Saved by Sven, brave Bersi's son
The Sword of the Saxons is strong and true
With a dragon sheath bright and new
The Sword of the Saxons is strong and true
With a dragon sheath bright and new

When he had finished Sweyn looked around the fire nervously. There was silence then Lodvir said, "I need it again, Sweyn. You tell a good tale, but you raced on a little too quickly. A good song is like a fine mead, it must be savoured."

Sweyn was happy to do so and the second time was better for he paused at appropriate moments and his extra confidence gave the tale life. When he had finished the warriors cheered and applauded him. Later, as we huddled under our cloaks he said, "I had to put in our father, Sven. He is hersir but I thought to put Bersi in too. That is how men will now remember him, a brave warrior, and your father! Even Thrond cannot change that now."

As I curled up to sleep, I reflected that I had not thought about my actions on the river in Frankia but now that the song was sung and would be passed on through the clan then my father's name would no longer be blackened. *Wyrd!*

Chapter 15

The next morning a messenger arrived with King Forkbeard's command. He wanted every drekar crew to travel as far as they could and take as many supplies as we could. Sweyn Skull Taker was less than happy about the order. He summoned Lodvir and Griotard and we heard the debate as we donned our helmets.

"There is no order to this, Lodvir! I do not see the hand of Karl Three Fingers in this."

Lodvir had donned his mail already and he nodded, "This reeks of Forkbeard. It might be that there is no opposition, and we bring back a great quantity of supplies but if any of the bands find opposition and perishes then that does not harm the king and he will know where he must concentrate his thrust. We are being used as scouts."

Griotard nodded, "I would bet a suit of mail that neither King Sweyn nor his Norse Jarl will venture forth from the castle." He shrugged, "It matters not, Sweyn Skull Taker. We can defeat any but the largest army. Even if a Saxon hundred is summoned we are well prepared, and the training will pay off."

We formed up and headed south-west towards the distant spirals of smoke which suggested farms. We saw the other crews, some of whom shared the roads with us while others headed across farmland. As we came upon more roads and warbands peeled off then the numbers dwindled. Some of the warbands had found farms already and we came upon captives and animals being driven back towards the beach. We saw a river to the west and that guided us. We followed the road which ran parallel to it.

It was almost noon before we outran the other warbands. Griotard and Lodvir had driven us on and we came upon a village which looked as though they had not heard of a warband on the loose. We saw animals in the fields which were close to the houses and Sweyn Skull Taker took the decision to surround it and take it. The twenty odd houses suggested that there might be as many as thirty or forty men but that was a number we could manage. Lodvir led ten men in a long loop to the south-east while Griotard led the same number to the river which lay to the south-west. The remainder we kept with us. We had but a handful of warriors with mail, Sweyn and my two cousins, but we had numbers and we spread out in a long line with the four of us at the centre. Bergil the Brawny was at the western end of the line and

Sigismund at the east. We turned our shields to the fore and with spears poking over the top we advanced.

Lodvir and Griotard had run their men and the hersir kept us at a steady pace. We were seen just two hundred paces from the first house. A farmer was striding across the fields to see to his animals, the sheep which lay before us, and, as the flock panicked, so the man shouted, "Vikings!"

We continued our steady pace for so long as the attention of the villagers was on us then Griotard and Lodvir could close the trap. The farmer we had frightened disappeared into his home and, as we neared it, we saw that he had armed himself and was leading his family south. It was then that Sweyn Skull Taker shouted, "Agerhøne! Charge!" We ran. The four of us kept together and as we ran around the side of the farm, we saw that the Saxon men were forming a shield wall. There looked to be twenty already with more joining. "Wedge!" There were just six of us who were close together, but we slipped into the wedge formation easily for we had practised this many times. The four hearth weru were a diamond at the fore and as others heard the shout so they joined in. We went from a walk to a steady run while the Saxons were still trying to form up. I was on the left and I pulled back Saxon Slayer when we were just fifteen paces from the line.

The Saxons had a variety of weapons but the ones which we would face were spears for the hersir had chosen the strongest part of their line. Our shields were larger and better made. It was Sweyn Skull Taker who would have to bear the brunt of their attack but with the best mail and helmet, he was well suited to the task. He punched a heartbeat before Sweyn and me. The Saxons made the mistake of aiming their spears at Skull Taker and that allowed me to spear the young man to the right of the leader who was skewered by Sweyn Skull Taker. Saxon Slayer struck the warrior in the chest and cracked through his tunic and breastbone. Enough men had joined us to put their shields in our backs and as the man fell from my spearhead, I punched the boss of my shield into the face of the Saxon in the second rank whose spear pointed to the heavens. As he fell Alf stamped hard upon his face and I heard his skull crack.

The men had been trying to buy their families time and with their best warriors dead the ones at the rear tried to flee. The wail from ahead told them that their attempt had been futile as Lodvir and Griotard appeared in a long line like a human fence and the women and children fled back to the centre of the village. The men who still remained were being slaughtered and I saw that Sweyn Skull Taker had been wounded.

I shouted, in Saxon, "Throw down your weapons and live! If you do not, then you will be slaughtered."

My foster father, although wounded, understood enough of my Saxon to shout to our men, "If they throw down their weapons then let them live."

Only two men were foolish enough to fail to obey my command and they were quickly butchered. My cousin, Sweyn, saw that his father was hurt, and he took command, "Lodvir, secure the village. Dreng find a wagon or cart for the hersir. He is hurt!"

I saw that a spear from the dying Saxon we had first killed had sliced into my foster father's leg above the knee. I stuck Saxon Slayer in the ground and using my seax cut a long piece of cloth from the tunic of a dead Saxon. I tied it above the wound as Dreng and Folki fetched a cart. Alf and I lifted the hersir on to the cart.

"I do not need this!"

Lodvir looked at the wound, "Aye, you do, hersir, for you cannot walk and we have twelve miles to travel back to the beach. We will see to the rest. Sweyn, you, Sven and Alf fasten a horse to the cart and be ready to move. We will gather the supplies and burn the village." He shook his head, "The Norns are spinning, Sweyn Skull Taker, for the only man with a serious wound is you!"

I saw that the loss of blood had made my foster father weak, for he lay back and said, "Aye, and for that I am grateful. Better me than my sons, eh?"

We learned from the captives that the village was called Haldeword and we had slain the thegn. That he was not a great warrior was clear when we found his hall. He had no mail byrnie but there was treasure. When Sweyn Skull Taker passed out due to the loss of blood Lodvir took over. "Take the thegn's family as hostages. Sven, tell them that if any man from this village takes up arms against us then the captives die!"

It was not as terrible a punishment as others might have inflicted but Lodvir was being wise. If we were here for the winter, then the last thing we would need would be the populace rising against us. Enough of them would do so, we knew that but if we could lessen it then that could only be for the good. I told them and I saw the four of them resign themselves to their fate. Griotard slaughtered the flock of sheep and their carcasses were piled on a wagon. There were three horses and we hitched them to the wagon and the cart. We took all their grain as well as the treasure and the weapons. The weapons were poor ones but if the villagers had none then they would not be able to resist or to fight.

It was well after dark when we reached the beach. We loosened the bandage on the hersir's leg every couple of miles and kept him dosed with the ale we had taken. The three of us walked with the cart and it was Lodvir who led the warband with Griotard as the rearguard. Thorstein was alerted to the hersir's wound by Folki Drengson who ran all the way back so that by the time we reached the beach then there was a lighted camp and fires ready for us. We stood with Thorstein as he examined the wound. My foster father was awake, and I saw the fear on his face. A lame warrior was no warrior at all. Thorstein prodded and poked. Sweyn Skull Taker bore it all stoically. When Thorstein stood and nodded we all smiled, "The wound was a clean one and did not touch the bone. I will use fire to seal it but, hersir, it will take many days before you can put weight upon it."

He gave a weak smile, "Then Lodvir will lead the band and I will watch the ship with you, Thorstein."

For the next week, we mopped up all the places which had been missed. We gathered flocks and herds which we did not slaughter but kept as winter food. We even had bread ovens built on the beach so that we could have fresh bread. King Forkbeard had raided north of the river and at the end of the week decided that we would take the whole warband and head to the nearest town, Ocmundtune. The king had discovered another large town, Beardestapol, to the north but, for his own reasons, he decided to head south-west. He and the other two jarls as well as their hearth weru all rode horses, but we marched. The weather had turned over the last week and become more autumnal. The rain made the ancient stone roads slick and slippery. Lodvir led us through the fields which, whilst muddy in places had been cleared of crops and we made better progress. A Viking army, even when afoot moves far quicker than one might imagine, and we reached the town of Ocmundtune before noon. You cannot hide an army of a thousand men or more and we had been seen. The animals in the field had been abandoned and the Saxons had taken refuge in the burgh. The burghs were like their castles. There was a ditch around the town and atop the spoil from the ditch, they had embedded wooden palisades. The difference was that there were four gates as opposed to just one. That gave us four points of attack. It was not King Sweyn who told us that but Lodvir who knew such things. We surrounded the ditch in no particular order except that the king and the Norse jarl took the main gate and the Jarl of Ribe the one on the opposite side. That marked where we would attack.

Harald Longstride quickly organised slingers and archers. He also had men hew some trees and saplings. Instead of risking stakes in the ditch, we would make a bridge. My foster father had offered me his mail byrnie, but I had declined the offer. The reason was that I feared I might damage it but, as we stood behind our shields, having been designated as the clan which would protect the tree carriers, I rued my decision for whilst my shield was large enough and well made, it could not cover my legs and I had seen how close Sweyn Skull Taker had come to lameness! We locked our shields and advanced. Now, instead of flanking my foster father, Alf and I were next to my cousin Sweyn. On my left were Lars and Leif. I was the only one who had no mail and I felt almost naked.

The arrows from the walls flew first. The ones that reached us had been loosed from too great a range and they bounced harmlessly off helmets and shields. As we drew nearer to the ditch, so the arrows pinged off helmets and thudded into shields. Then the stones began to pelt us. It sounded like a hailstorm on a drekar's deck. I was lucky but the cries from further down the line told me that others were not. I now had a thicker helmet liner, and I felt that I was protected. When we reached the edge of the ditch we had to endure ever more of the stones and arrows as the logs were pushed from behind us across the gap. It took three men to do so for this was a wider ditch than the one at the castle. One of Jarl Harald's men pitched forward into the ditch as a moment of carelessness allowed an arrow to find a piece of bare flesh. When the last tree was in position, we had to shuffle them together so that they made a bridge. With men sitting on the ends to prevent them from moving Jarl Harald shouted, "Across!"

I knew the dangers of running over the crude bridge. I had fallen more than once when I had been felling trees. I ran, not on one trunk but two different ones. As arrows were hurtling towards us as we did so it was one of the hardest things I had ever done. Once my feet touched the top of the rampart, I threw myself against the wooden wall and placed my shield over my head! It was not a moment too soon for a huge rock was dropped on to the shield. I had learned from the attack on the castle and the shield was angled so that it rolled down the face of the shield and into the ditch.

The more men who ran across the bridge made it safer for those of us who were already there as the defenders had easier targets. We had to wait until there were enough of us to use shields to climb up. The Jarl had our archers and slingers keeping down the enemy heads but warriors rushing across the crude bridge were still being struck. Sweyn and Alf joined me as did Leif and Lars.

Sweyn said, "Sven, you have no mail yet. Hold the shield with Alf and let we three climb. We will help you to ascend!"

Neither Alf nor I liked it, but it made sense and, slinging my shield over my back we held Alf's. We had done this at the castle and Alf and I knew what we had to do. As Sweyn stepped on to the shield we hoisted him up. He jabbed his spear at the face which appeared and then leapt across the top of the wall. When we felt him jump, we lowered the shield and Lars stepped on to it. He was heavier but we had Sweyn on the top to give him some protection as he joined my cousin. We lowered it for Leif and heard the sounds of battle above as the two men with a foothold fought to enlarge the section of wall we held. Lars was boosted next and once he had jumped Alf slung his shield and we waited for help. A rope snaked over and, as I wore no mail and was lighter, I grabbed it and began to walk up the wall. I had had to leave my spear as I needed both hands to climb. A dart was thrown from the side and it hit my leather byrnie at the shoulder. The tip actually pricked me but did no harm save to make me climb even faster. Once on the top I simply rolled over the wooden palisade. The axe which hacked at me hit the boss of my shield and as I stood, I whipped out Oathsword. The Saxon raised his axe for a second strike, but I slashed my sword sideways and connected with his side. I sawed it backwards and drew blood. He was brave and tried to raise the sword again but this time I swung it at his face and not only bit into his flesh but knocked him from the fighting platform. Unslinging my shield I moved down the walkway so that Alf could have an easier time.

Sweyn, Lars and Leif were working their way down to the gatehouse and I held Oathsword before me so that Alf could gain a foothold behind me without the danger of a Saxon spear. He stood to my left, "Ready Sven." It was not before time for we had been seen and some of the townsfolk ran at us with spears and swords. They saw just five warriors atop the wall and meant to sweep us away. Alf and I did not hesitate but ran at the Saxons with our shields held before us. My red shield with the dragon was no longer pristine. It was cut and bloodied but it was still whole and when our two shields struck the Saxons, whose spears ineffectually hit either our helmets or shields, then the warriors were hurt. The boss on my shield crunched into a young warrior's nose for his helmet was an open one. I punched with the hilt of Oathsword as we were too close to allow a full swing. The edge of my blade sliced into his cheek and he reeled. Alf's opponent had the luxury of the open side of the fighting platform and he was swinging his sword in a wide arc. The falling Saxon I had hurt hit him and the two of them tumbled over the side. I brought my sword from on high and hit the next surprised warrior on the shoulder. One moment he had been protected by two of his fellows and a heartbeat later a Viking was slicing down his sword. The sword hacked into flesh and broke bones. I swung the edge of my shield up into his face and stepped forward.

Behind us, I heard a cheer, not only had others climbed up the rope but Sweyn and the others had opened the gate. Men were pouring through the opening. The last two warriors knew that they were doomed, and they turned and ran. They showed us the ladder down and we hurried after them. This was a walled town and we had breached their defences. The town was lost. Alf and I ignored the fleeing Saxons and ran to join Sweyn, Lars and Leif. We fought better as a clan. Sweyn nodded to us and Alf and I stood to the side of Leif and Lars. Raising his sword Sweyn led us down the centre of the town. Other warriors were racing recklessly towards the houses and I saw one warrior, not from our clan, struck in the head by an axe as he kicked open a door. The house was a small mean one and Sweyn knew there would be little treasure there. We hurried on. Few Saxons would face five men and we were unhindered as we hurried towards the centre of Ocmundtune. The larger and better houses would be there.

We began to catch warriors with helmets and weapons. Two turned to slow us down but our swords ended their resistance quickly. Thus far we had not seen any warrior who wore mail. It was Alf who spied the men guarding the door of the large house to our left. There were three of them. I guessed that they were taking either nobles or treasure to safety. To the Saxons that meant the church. King Sweyn was a Christian and there was a chance that he might spare those who hid there. We were five pagans, and we were not bound by such restrictions. The warriors were house warriors, housecarls, their arms and tunics told me that, and that told me their paymaster was important and rich. They were hired swords and would be better than the warriors who had stood on the walls. Sweyn had taken over his father's mantle and he bravely stepped up to them, raising his sword as he did so. For the first time in a long time, it was not Alf and me who flanked him. Lars and Leif were good, but we had fought as one for so long that we knew each other's moves. As Sweyn punched his shield at the central warrior and brought his sword down towards the Saxon's helmet the warrior to his right jabbed his sword at my cousin. I know not if it was a lucky strike or the Norns were spinning but the blade found Sweyn's eye. I heard the cry from my cousin. Lars was slow to react, but I was not, and I lunged with Oathsword. The sword found the Saxon's neck and the man who had maimed my cousin died quickly. The wound angered us all and the three lay dead.

I shouted, "Alf, see to your brother!"

145

"I am well!"

Lars shouted, "You have lost an eye. Sweyn, stay with your brother. The three of us will clear the hall!"

"Go, I will watch him!" Alf was already tearing the tunic of a dead Saxon housecarl.

It was not the lust for treasure which made us race inside but the thought that there might be more warriors. We also sought vengeance. If you hurt one of us, then you paid and that payment would be both terrible and final. The rolls of cloth in the storeroom to our left told me that this was the home of a merchant. The cloth was valuable, but we needed to clear the house first. It did not have an upper storey, but it was large. We moved silently. The battle at the door would not have been heard above the cacophony from the street. Ahead I could hear noises and knew that the merchant was retrieving his gold. That would save us a task. The room was at the back and looked to be where they prepared the food. Two men were digging a hole and a woman and the merchant watched.

We entered silently and it was the woman who screamed and picked up the meat cleaver. Lars just reacted as any warrior would do and he slashed with his sword to tear open the woman. The merchant roared and the men who were digging reached for their weapons. I whipped Oathsword in an arc and ripped across the merchant's chest. Lars and Leif wasted no time in ending the lives of the two diggers. As the merchant lay bleeding on the floor, his lifeblood slipping away, he saw the writing on Oathsword and said, "Alfred's Gift, how...?"

He said no more. I think I was the only one who either heard or understood the dying merchant's words for they were in Saxon.

Lars looked at the woman. He was not a cruel man and I knew that he had not deliberately killed her, "Why did she attack me? She might have lived!"

His brother put his arm around him, "It is the Norns, brother. Put it from your mind." He pointed to the large chest, "And here we have weregeld for Sweyn's eye!"

I nodded, although still distracted by the merchant's words Lodvir had taught me well enough to know that we had to see to Sweyn and to guard our treasure. The warband had Vikings we did not know and certainly did not trust. "Let us secure the house. One of us should find Lodvir." I pointed at the food and the barrels of ale. "This looks to be a good place to hold up."

Lars sheathed his sword, "I will go."

Leif lit the brands so that we would have light. The table had been moved from where it guarded the treasure hole and lay against one wall.

Leif began to clear it and I went for Alf and Sweyn. Alf was helping his brother down the passage to the kitchen. He shook his head. I nodded, "Come cousin. We have treasure and we have the means to tend to your eye."

He had his hand over the missing orb, and he nodded, "I thought I would be Sweyn the Skald, but it seems to me I will be Sweyn One Eye!" We said nothing for what could we say? "What will my wife think?"

Alf said, "Bergljót will see a warrior and you can wear a patch."

I was able to stand back and reflect on this turn of events, "It is the Norns cousin, they weave, and they plot. Your father was hurt but not killed and you have lost an eye. Do you not think my father would prefer to be alive and one-eyed than butchered by Saxons?"

"Aye, you are right and there will be a song in this."

We took his cloak from him when we reached the table and laid him with his head upon it. Leif was the eldest and whilst not a healer like Thorstein he had tended his brother when his cheek had been laid open. "Sweyn, I must look at the eye."

Sweyn took away the bloody cloth. The blade had ripped open his cheek and the eye was gone. There was a bloody mess where his eye had once been. Lars said, "This needs fire!"

Sweyn nodded, "Give me ale first."

He was given a large swig from the ale skin and then Alf and I held his arms as Lars took one of the fiery brands. He said, quietly, "May the Allfather be with you." He placed the brand on the eye and there was a smell of burning flesh and hair. Sweyn gritted his teeth and his back arched but no sound came from him. When his body became limp then I knew he had passed out. While he was unconscious, we applied honey and made a bandage.

While he slept, we searched the kitchen and found fresh bread. Leif put a pot of water to boil while Alf watched his brother. I knew that the wounds to his father and his brother were having an effect on Alf. He was the only one of us now not to have suffered a serious wound. The next time we fought he would have them in his head.

I went around the rest of the house and found another bag of coins and also more bolts of fine cloth. It was a different treasure. I dropped the purse into the chest we had dug up and then began to pile the cloth in the room the family used for eating.

I saw Alf staring at his brother. Sweyn was asleep and he needed none to watch him. Alf needed occupation, "You had better close the lid on the chest in case we have to leave quickly." We would not but I needed him to be busy. He nodded and left Sweyn. Agnetha had always said that sleep was the best medicine and Sweyn did not appear to be in mortal danger. I heard the door open and drew my sword. It was Lodvir.

He nodded, "He lives eh?"

"Aye, Lodvir the Long and we have treasure for the clan. The cloth is valuable. We can tell the king that was what we found."

Lodvir grinned, "It is as though you have read my mind, Sven Saxon Sword."

I was tempted to tell him the merchant's dying words, but something told me that this was a puzzle for me to untangle. Griotard and the remainder of the clan entered. "The rest of the warband is busy wrecking this burgh. You five have done well and this is as good a haul and a place to rest as we could have hoped." He nodded to Bergil and Sigismund. They held more chests. "I think the king will stay here for some days and the ones who did not find the riches we did will raid further afield."

I sliced some hunks of ham from the bone and then dropped the bone into the boiling water, "Lodvir, why did the king attack this burgh and not Beardestapol?"

"Karl Three Fingers, I think. The king wants Athelstan to send men to fight us. This is closer to his abbey at Tavistock which is less than ten miles from here and the taking of this burgh may spur him to attack us now before he has a full army. We are far enough from Wintan-ceastre and Lundenburgh for it to take an army a long time to muster and reach us. He is poking a stick at the dog in the hope that it attacks us." He smiled, "And now let us eat and enjoy good ale, eh?"

Sweyn awoke in the middle of the night. Alf and I were close by him as he first moaned and then sat bolt upright. One brand burned in the kitchen and gave us enough light to see him. He winced, "It was not a dream then?"

Alf shook his head, "No, brother. You are now Sweyn One Eye. You have slept for some hours. Are you hungry?"

He shook his head, "No, but I have a thirst on me." I poured ale into his horn. "Did we lose any men?"

"No, cousin and yours was the most serious wound. We were lucky. Lodvir told the king about the cloth. Tomorrow we are to return to the ships with the cloth and the wounded. We stand high in the king's opinion."

"And all it cost me was my eye."

Lodvir had entered the room silently, "And you can still be a great warrior and a skald. I heard of a warrior who followed the Dragonheart in the Land of the Wolf. Haaken One Eye was an Ulfheonar and a

148

skald. He lived and fought for more than sixty summers. He did not let the loss of an eye stop him."

Alf asked, "The Land of the Wolf?"

"It lies many leagues to the north; a land of mountains and water, it is protected by a witch. Dragonheart was also called Danish Bane."

I nodded, "I have heard of Danish Bane, but I thought it was a weapon."

"It was the Dragonheart, but he had a weapon too; it was a sword touched by the gods. It has long been lost but was said to be the most powerful sword in this world."

I said, quietly, "More powerful than a Dragon Sword?"

"Aye, Sven. Yours is a good sword but it is not magical. One day yours shall tell us its whole story."

Sweyn smiled and I saw that it hurt him to do so, "And I shall tell the tale, Sven."

"You will have time Sweyn, for like your father, there will be no further raiding this season. You will have to learn to fight with just one eye. It will take time but next season you shall be as good as you are now; probably better for with such a wound comes wisdom, does it not Sven Saxon Sword?"

I smiled, "Aye, Lodvir!"

Chapter 16

It suited us to be heading back as the warriors in Ocmundtune had drunk too much and there were fights which sometimes ended in death. Even as we were leaving King Sweyn Forkbeard had two warriors executed for murder. We were better off on the road. This way we could secure our treasure in the drekar. The bolts of cloth were in a wagon along with the wounded from other warbands who were unable to walk. We had plenty of ale and food. That was not the king's doing. We had emptied the house. There had been a thrall hall attached as well as a granary and that was taken before any other knew it was there. Lodvir felt no obligation to a king who let others be the first across the ditches and over the walls. We had taken the risks and we deserved the rewards. We spent some days travelling through a land we had completely emptied. It was a dead land and with the leaves now falling from the trees, looked even more skeletal. It was as though we were picking over the bones of Wessex.

Sweyn Skull Taker was now walking but it was with the aid of a staff. Sweyn One Eye was in the wagon and when his father saw the bandage across his head he clutched at his hammer of Thor. Thorstein insisted upon examining the wound which was still red and angry from the burning. We unpacked the treasure and the food while he did so. The ship's boys were happy to have something to do rather than finding shellfish and kindling. While Thorstein looked at the wound Lodvir told the hersir of the taking of the town.

"Your hearth weru were the first warriors over the wall and it was your son, Sweyn, who led the five of them to break into the hall. They are all great warriors."

The hersir nodded, "I knew that already and did not need this monument to Forkbeard's ambition to tell me so."

Griotard had joined us, "I spoke with Karl before we left. He said that the king wishes a battle before we go home. He wants Athelstan to fear us." He paused, "There are plans for another raid next year, but Karl was close-mouthed about where."

Thorstein seemed satisfied, "Sweyn One Eye will heal well. Leif did well and all that Sweyn needs is a patch."

It was almost as though the hersir had not heard him, "So the king wishes more men to die to gain him a kingdom!"

Lodvir said, "Be wary, Sweyn, there are others who can hear you. The king is already suspicious of us."

"And what more can he do to us? My clan has taken two strongholds for him. We may be a small clan, but we are a skilled one."

"But, my friend, we will have to obey the king. We both know that!"

I saw my foster father's shoulders sink in resignation, "Aye, I know. Come we shall eat well, and my son and I can recover together."

The army did not return for over a week and when they did, I saw that more men had died whilst they had raided the land around Ocmundtune. The Saxons were fighting back. The weather had definitely turned and the warband which marched to the beach and Forkbeard's castle home was so muddy that there appeared to be little difference between those that wore mail and those that did not. That his ambition was not satiated became clear when, a week later, he sent scouts to Beardestapol. They discovered that it had been abandoned. Lodvir was critical of the king for he said he should have kept a better watch so that we could have attacked them when they fled. All we found were empty homes and no food. Forkbeard was angry and he had the place burned. When men began to complain he had two more executed but there was a mutinous mood amongst some crews. Ours was wise enough to remain silent.

Scouts ended the mutiny when they reported a large Saxon army heading from the burned town of Ocmundtune. It was led by Eorledman Ordwulf, King Athelstan's uncle and there were many mailed men with it. The scouts had not done their job properly and we had no idea of actual numbers. The hersir took matters into his own hands. We refloated *'Sea Serpent'* and crewed her with our wounded warriors aboard. We dared not leave but if things went badly for us then we would not have to rush to float the boat. King Forkbeard would have his battle, and our army was organised to face the Saxon fyrd. We had less than eight hundred warriors and when the Saxons made a shield wall, we saw that they had more than twelve hundred men to face us. The king did not flee but had slingers before us and archers behind us. We waited for the Saxons to advance.

We were not on the flanks nor in the middle. We had our small crew next to Beorn Bear Killer's clan and that pleased me. Lodvir stood in the centre. Leif and I flanked him. I took it as an honour. Saxon Slayer had been well sharpened, and I knew, as I grasped the spear, that it was eager to drink Saxon blood. I still felt almost naked for I was just wearing my leather byrnie. I know that had I asked Sweyn One Eye would have loaned me his but something stopped me. We began to bang our shields as the Saxons approached. If this had just been our clan we would have sung one of our songs but King Sweyn Forkbeard did not appear to want pagan chants. This time, at least, he was in the front rank along with Karl Three Fingers and the Jarl of Ribe. The Jarl of Lade had sailed back to Norway after the raid on Ocmundtune. The Saxons had priests before them, and they had relics held high. The king forbade us to kill their priests. It angered Lodvir and Beorn Bear Killer, for these carriers of relics were like witches and they gave their warriors heart. I touched the woollen cross Mary had given to me, not because it was Christian but because it was a memory of comfort and home. The fact that it was a cross could not hurt.

The Saxons had many with them who were not warriors. They were on the flanks. The ones in the centre were warriors and they came directly for the king. They had not practised breaking a shield wall and so they just advanced steadily. They had no chant to help them run and so they came at us with a fast walk. Their spears had small heads; some were hunting spears. Saxon Slayer's broad head had a tapered point which could tear through mail and then rip into flesh. As we closed it became clear whom we would fight. I knew which Saxon I would face. He had a hunting spear, leather byrnie and a shield which was simply some boards nailed together. We both thrust at the same time. My weapon found the tiny gap between two planks which made his crude shield whilst his hit my boss and bent the poorly made head. My spearhead went through the boards and across his arm. As I jerked it back the shield was rent asunder and before he could react, I had thrust again, and Saxon Slayer tasted more Saxon blood. I found his stomach and saw the terror in his eyes as my spear twisted to wrap guts around the head so that when I pulled it out it was as though he had eaten a bowl of bloody eels. He sank to the ground.

The two lines were now intertwined. Some Saxons had done as I had done, killed Danes, and some of our men had also slain Saxons. I stepped forward to stab at the next man and Folki, behind me, thrust his spear at the man fighting Dreng next to me. I rammed Saxon Slayer down towards the Saxon's leg. He was not expecting that blow, and my spear scraped along his thigh bone. His spear hit my helmet. It was a good blow, but I had renewed the leather straps and it held. I punched my shield into the man's face and when I could not lower my spear to gut him, I continued to punch him in the face with my shield and the haft of my spear. As he started to slip, I smashed the haft of my spear into his already broken nose. It drove through his skull as though it was parchment. Folki, Dreng and I, along with Lodvir had managed to create a hole in the Saxon line. We locked shields and after driving Saxon Slayer into the body of the man I had just killed I drew Oathsword.

The Dragon Sword

The Saxons threw themselves at our shields, but we had larger shields and better helmets. Their best warriors were at the fore and we had destroyed those near to us. The biggest danger we faced was blunting our weapons. I know not exactly how many Saxons I slew for I had no time to count and I slashed, stabbed and sliced at any face, arm, neck and leg that I could. I was not even aware of time but suddenly there were no Saxons before us for they had started to fall back.

Bjorn Blond Hair shouted, "We have won!"

Lodvir spat out a tooth, "You fool! Look down our line. It is coming on to night and no man fights in the dark unless he has to. The battle is ended for the day!"

I looked down the line and saw a mound of bodies, Saxon and Dane, intertwined in death. Alf lived as did the warriors with whom I had fought before but my former tormentors Erik and Ulf both lay dead. *Wyrd.*

"Fall back to the beach!"

We walked backwards and I retrieved not only my spear from the dead Saxon but also the three best swords from the dead. None of them had a better helmet and I could not see purses. I had fought in my first real battle and I was just happy to be whole! We reached the beach and I saw that other drekar had also been launched. When *'Golgotha'* was made ready then I knew we were leaving. I was pleased to be heading back to Denmark. We had not had to spend the winter in this land and we would be returning home richer. The king had much to collect from the castle and it was one of his hearth weru, Gandálfr Oakshield, who came to speak to us.

"The king has lured the Saxons here so that we can sail around to the Tamar and raid the abbey at Tavistock. Ordwulf himself built it and it is said to be the richest in Wessex. When we leave you are to follow Jarl Harald's drekar!"

There was no discussion nor opportunity for us to object. As we boarded the drekar I heard Sweyn Skull Taker say, "And by having us follow the Jarl we cannot become lost eh, Lodvir?"

"Perhaps it is a compliment. We lost fewer men than other warbands and he now knows of the courage of our clan. I do not mind raiding a church. It is on the way home and they are always filled with riches."

Griotard sniffed, "Our King, it seems has a practical attitude towards his new God!"

After placing my swords in my chest I sat upon it and Sweyn One Eye sat on his, "Cousin Sven, you are a clever warrior. What makes the king so certain that this Ordwulf will not rush back to his abbey?"

I pointed to the sky which was already darker, "They will be in their camp and planning how to defeat us. It will only be dawn when they realise we are gone and by then our ships will have disappeared. Where will they search? We could go north or south or simply cross the river. The Saxons were all afoot and they will take some days to search. We have time."

Alf had been listening, "You are cleverer than I am Sven. Perhaps the gods gave you the mind to make up for taking your father and brothers."

"Then I would be happier to be Bergil the Brawny and have my family alive. It was not an exchange I would have made."

Sven One Eye said, "That is my brother-in-law you are speaking about!"

I laughed, "And he has the heart of a wolf but, I fear, the mind of an ox!"

Sweyn thought about it and then laughed, "Aye, you are right." He looked at my byrnie, "And still no mail shirt."

Lodvir had just boarded and sat on his chest, "He does well enough without it. Perhaps the lack of metal on his body means he has to be cleverer when he fights. You will not need it against the monks!"

As soon as *'Golgotha'* was ready her sail was lowered and the oars manned. Thorstein shook his head as he ordered our sails also lowered. He then pointed, "See he does not wait for the others. Some drekar are still on the beach!"

We took our oars and, as Jarl Harald's *'Stormbird'* passed us, we began to row. I thought then that if the Saxons had followed us then they could have caught many crews on the beach. However, they stayed in their camp and the gods smiled on us. By the time dawn came, I saw that, as we took the first row of the morning, there were just eighteen drekar with us. Had some deserted or merely become lost? I suspected the former as we had all done well out of the raid. If King Forkbeard asked questions, then they would simply say that they had lost sight of the ships ahead. We had no choice for we followed our jarl. It was as he neared the southwestern coast of Wessex and turned east that we realised we had lost another ship. There were now just seventeen of us. It was as though we had a serious wound, and our fleet was haemorrhaging. I wondered if there would be retribution when we returned to Denmark.

Two days later we rowed up the coast towards the River Tamar. We were helped by the fact that there was an autumn mist on the water and with no sails to mark us we were as invisible as we could be. This time we had a local to guide us. When King Sweyn had taken over the castle

he had gathered prisoners he thought might be useful and we had the
thegn's family as hostages, still. I do not know how he discovered the
one who had treacherous tendencies, but he did. Not all Saxons
supported their king and for whatever reason, the Saxon who was
simply called the guest of King Sweyn was at the prow of *'Golgotha'*
and guided us up the river.

Unlike our previous forays, this one felt easier. We were the third
ship in the column and all that we had to do was to follow *'Stormbird'*.
With Olaf, the ship's boy at the prow all that Thorstein had to do was
obey his directions and Olaf's job was made easier in that he could see
the shadow of the leading drekar and could anticipate changes in
direction. We twisted and turned through the fjord-like river valley. We
were followed closely by Beorn Bear Killer's threttanessa. That gave
me comfort for he was a man I liked, and I knew that Sweyn Skull
Taker trusted him. The hersir could not fight in a shield wall but he
could row, as could his one-eyed son and our ship powered through the
water. If anything Thorstein was hard pushed to keep us from ramming
the stern of the jarl's ship. His men had suffered in the fighting against
Ordwulf and the fyrd. Their ship, like the king's, had fewer men
available to row.

It was almost dawn when Olaf gave us the signal to turn to larboard.
Thorstein knew that we were ready to land for the river was narrowing
and we would not be able to go further upstream. The larboard oars
were raised and after we had turned and the steerboard oars were raised
we slid on to a grassy bank. The ship's boys had learned skills on the
voyage and they had us secured to the trees which lined the banks faster
than the other drekar. I grabbed my shield and slung it from my back.
With my helmet on my head and Saxon Slayer in my hand, I was ashore
before even Alf. He clasped arms with his father and brother. There was
a reason for this. The hersir and his brother would not be coming with
us. Lodvir would lead the clan. Alf had been largely silent as we had
headed to the Tamar and I knew the reason. He feared a wound. He was
not a fearful warrior but three of us had suffered life-threatening
injuries. The fact that we had all survived meant nothing for if he was
wounded then his might be the wound which would end his life. He was
bidding farewell to his father and brother.

As the sun rose in the east so Karl Three Fingers circled his spear,
and we made our way to join him. The traitorous Saxon was with him.
He wore a byrnie and carried a sword, but he was a Saxon. He was
guarded by two of the king's hearth weru. It was those three who, along
with half a dozen lighter armoured scouts, loped off along the path. In
the distance, I had the whiff of woodsmoke mixed with incense in my

nostrils and could hear the tolling of the bell calling the monks to prayers. Lodvir had said that there could be a thousand monks in the Abbey. I did not believe that but, as we hurried to the church which took shape and form as the sun rose, I began to believe that it might be the biggest church I had ever seen. To me, it appeared to be a small town. There were many smaller buildings gathered around the monumental church. The hurdled fields contained sheep, pigs, goats, and cows. There were fields planted with winter crops. I spied granaries, barns, and cow byres. However, it was mainly a place of worship and the priests who lived there either looked up to God or down to the floor. They kept no watch. It could have been that even though they knew Danes were on the loose, the fact that King Sweyn was a Christian made them believe they were untouchable. They were about to be proved wrong.

I had learned just how good a general was Karl Three Fingers. He planned meticulously and our crew, along with Beorn Bear Killer's had been given the task of leaving the main band to run around the far side of the abbey and prevent them summoning help. Half a mile after we had joined the river path the two warbands left the main track to run across fields. We were able to move faster than the rest of King Sweyn's diminished army. Lodvir led for he appeared to have a nose which could sniff out danger. I ran just behind him. I had not been assigned that place, but it just felt comfortable to be behind him. I also took comfort from the fact that he seemed to trust me.

The Saxon shepherd who crossed our path was just unlucky. He must have stopped on his way to his flock to empty his bowels and, as he stood, he spied Lodvir who was just ten paces from him. The man may have been slow-witted for even as he thought to form the word, 'Vikings', Lodvir had taken four more strides and skewered him with his spear. It was a warning and Lodvir ran even harder. We saw, in the distance, the road which led from the abbey to the nearest village, Lydford. We had spied the village before but from the north for it lay to the south of Ocmundtune. Even now Eorledman Ordwulf might be marching back to his town. It was as we neared the road that I realised just what advantage raiders like we had. The Saxons knew not where we would strike and our ships gave us such mobility that we could move faster on the seas and rivers than they could march. Even if word reached the Saxon general then the odds were that we would be on our way back to Denmark before they could get close.

We had barely reached it when we heard a bell tolling. It was an urgent bell, a warning. The king had struck and we saw the effect immediately. Two horsemen suddenly galloped from the wooden barn which lay just fifty paces from the nearest stone building. We had approached the church from the north-west and, perhaps, they had not seen us for they appeared to look over their shoulders. Whatever the reason by the time they turned and spied us it was too late and our spears killed the messengers. Leaving four men with the horses Lodvir and Deorn Dear Killer led the rest of us towards the church. We had done what we had been asked and we could now raid and plunder like the rest. Alf and I ran together, watching Lodvir's back. There were smaller buildings around the large church and Lodvir ran into one of them while Beorn Bear Killer took his crew to the slightly larger one next door. We all followed Lodvir. The priests who were within were gathering parchments and books. As soon as they saw us, they dropped them and ran.

Lodvir turned to me, "Sven, you and Alf see what treasure there is to be had in here. Take whatever you find back to the drekar."

The rest of our shipmates followed Lodvir and I laid down Saxon Slayer. "Alf, see if you can find gold. I will put some of these parchments in this chest."

"Parchments? We were told to find treasure."

I nodded, "This is a treasure, of a sort. Mary can read and I wish to know more about dragon swords. The Saxons and the Christians do what we do not. They write things down. Do not worry, I will carry the chest and you may carry any gold that you find."

There were not many parchments. It appeared that the building was one they used for the monks who wrote the parchments while the finished documents were stored elsewhere. There were frames for the parchments, quills, and ink. I left the ones they had just started. Alf found some candlesticks and candles. He put them in the chest with the parchments. There was also, amongst the inks, some gold and some silver leaf. When we found the treasure of the leaf Alf shook his head. Why waste gold leaf on parchment which is only good for kindling?"

I said nothing for I knew that it was treasure and that the squiggles on the parchment were like a treasure map. When we had filled the chest and nothing remained, we hefted the chest on to my back and we were about to leave when Alf spied a small door behind a curtain. The screams and shouts had faded, and we knew that we were alone. We took the curtain and placed it in the chest. Alf opened the door and peered in.

"It is a room but a small one and I can see little." He took off his shield and laid down his spear. He was able to crawl into the space. It was not a large chamber for his legs were in the larger room when his echoey voice said, "I can feel the far wall. There are spiders' webs."

There was silence and then I heard something being dragged. "There is a chest. Pull my legs, Sven, for it is heavy."

I put down my parchment chest and pulled. He emerged with a chest and, when we opened it, we found it was filled with silver and gold coins. We had our treasure. Taking Lodvir at his word we headed back to the drekar directly. To be truthful the sight of slaughtered priests was not my idea of war. As my foster father had shown you could raid the priests of the White Christ without massacring them. When we clambered aboard the drekar Sweyn Skull Taker cocked an eye at the larger chest which contained just parchments, some candles, and some candlesticks. I gestured to Alf, "Alf here, has a great treasure. Let us say this is for me."

Sweyn One Eye shook his head, "You still believe that you will find out who owned the sword from parchments? The blade is too old for men to have written down its history."

I took a deep breath, "The merchant I slew in Ocmundtune recognised it. He called it *'Alfred's Gift'*. I believe that is King Alfred and that men would write down to whom it was given. I need to know why a Saxon had a dragon sword made."

My foster father nodded, "Just so long as the quest does not consume you. Your father sought a treasure too. I did not know what it was, but I know that it killed him and two drekar crews. I would not like you to waste your life."

I said nothing but I believed that my father had not wasted his life. I did not wish him and my brothers, dead, not to mention the other crews but men had died in this raid and for what? A King's ambition. Perhaps a quest for the story of a sword was no worse.

It was late afternoon when Lodvir and the rest of the crew returned. They had slaughtered some animals and they were cooked for the voyage home while the treasure they had taken was stored below the decks. He spat over the side and then turned to speak to the hersir, "Forkbeard ensured that he took the choicest of the treasure. He has a chest which took four men to carry. Jarl Harald also took a large chest." He nodded towards the modest one he had taken. "This will have to do."

Sweyn Skull Taker said, "Sven and Alf found one of a similar size. With what we have taken already we are rich, and we can build a second drekar."

"A second?"

My foster father smiled, "Aye, Lodvir the Long, for now that I have hearth weru you can captain your own ship. When next we raid alone, we will have twice the strength we do now. We have boys who have become men."

We camped at the river for it took some time for the other drekar to be loaded and left at dawn. The seventeen drekar were laden and the king did not wish us to be attacked by Saxons. We sailed away from the land to avoid the fleet we knew guarded the river close to Wintan-Caestre. However, on the third day, we spied wreckage and a body. When it was hauled aboard, we recognised it as one of the drekar which had not followed us to the Tamar. The Saxons were still dangerous and the king's decision to sail together was a wise one.

We did not have to row as the wind was with us, and once we spied the cord road most of the ships left us to sail directly to Heiða-býr. Only those who lived by Ribe, four of us, continued north. I had never been away from Agerhøne for such a long time before and I felt unbounded joy when I saw our home. I now understood my father's face when he had returned from the sea. It was good to go a-Viking but even better to return home.

Chapter 17

We had lost men and as Ulf and Erik had been almost the last of their family in Agerhøne I wondered if their mothers and sisters would stay. As we tied up and the women of the clan scanned the drekar for their loved ones I saw their family bury their faces in their shawls. Agnetha also saw her scarred son and limping husband as they stepped from **'Sea Serpent'**, but the smile never left her face. She was a strong woman and whilst she might be grieving inside, she would keep any tears for the longhouse. Neither my mother nor Mary were there but Egbert was. He was smiling and I knew that my mother would be well. I stayed with the other warriors to unload the treasure and the supplies while my cousin and foster father left for the longhouse with the other warriors who had wounds. I knew that Alf and I had been lucky. We were amongst the handful of men who had not been wounded. Even some of the ship's boys had been hurt. I had four of them help Alf and me to carry the chests to the longhouse. The most important to me was the least important to anyone else and so I carried it.

Mother was seated in a chair by the fire. With autumnal air, she was suffering from the cold. She had a shawl around her shoulders and Mary held a platter of food before her. They both looked up as I entered. I smiled and said, "How are you mother?"

"Alive and pleased that you are whole. What happened to your cousin, Sweyn?"

Father had never told my mother all that went on during a raid and I maintained the tradition, "He was unlucky, and a spear took his eye. Thorstein says that he will make a full recovery and his father's wound is almost healed. All is well."

"Yet Erik and Ulf sleep beyond this land."

I nodded, "That is in the nature of war."

She pointed with her wooden spoon at the chest in my arms, "And is that treasure?"

"Of a sort. It is parchments and writing. Mary can use it to teach you to read."

My mother shook her head, "I have given up on that. I cannot make out the squiggles and my eyes grow cloudy. She reads them to me, and they are interesting for they talk of a different people to us. I like to hear them with Egbert for he, like Mary, is a Saxon and their ways seem strange."

Mary must have worked hard for she seemed to understand my mother's words and rolled her eyes. She had yet to learn how to behave as a thrall! I put the chest close to my sea chest and sleeping mattress. I then took off the tunic I had worn at sea. We had all taken advantage of one pleasant afternoon at sea and poured buckets of icy seawater over each other. When we had another such day I would walk to the river and cleanse the salt from me. I changed to my better tunic and began to comb my hair. I had not managed to do so as often as I should whilst on the raid and it took some time to untangle the mess. I heard my name shouted and turned to see Alf with a horn of ale for me.

"Come, oar brother, all wish to hear of our exploits, and I know you have a better memory than I do."

I really wanted to sit with my mother and Mary, but Alf and I were the only ones in the longhouse who had witnessed all the events, battles and fights. I gave an apologetic shrug to Mary and my mother and went to the table where the others were gathered. I was no skald, but I had a good voice and when I spoke, I made sure that my voice could be heard by my mother. I know that a skald would have made the story more exciting but that would have made my mother even more worried the next time we went to sea. I kept it simple and as bloodless as possible. When I had finished, and Alf had nodded then the others banged the table in approval.

"A good tale, foster son!"

Sweyn One Eye nodded, "I will give you lessons, Sven Saxon Blade so that you may entertain us!"

Shaking my head I said, "No cuz, I will not take that from you. You will heal and be able to do justice to the story of the clan!"

The hersir then spoke his thoughts about his hopes and fears for the future, "We will go to Ribe and commission the new drekar for Lodvir. I spoke with him and Thorstein on the way home. It will not be ready for a year but better that we start it now so that the hard work can be done before next spring."

Agnetha had not left the table since we had returned and that was a sign that she was concerned about her husband and son, "And now that you have fulfilled your obligations to the king, he will leave you alone? From what Sven said," she smiled, "and tried not to say, the clan did more than most to help achieve King Forkbeard's ends."

My foster father emptied his horn and shook his head, "I think it has merely whetted his appetite. Before we left the Tamar, Karl Three Fingers spoke of plans the king had to raid Lundenburgh. He wishes to emulate King Guthrum, who took it from the men of Mercia. It may be that we have to raid again before the second drekar is built." He saw that his words had disappointed his wife and smiled, "We have little choice for the alternative is to find a new home and I do not relish sailing to the Land of Ice and Fire where they have no kings!"

What remained unsaid was the third way; to try to wrest the crown from Forkbeard. It was not even a possibility, but men had spoken of Sweyn Skull Taker's skill as a leader.

It was late when the feasting and the drinking ended and Mary had put my mother to bed by the time we had finished. I walked Mary back to the old longhouse which was now our thrall hall. Egbert could have done so but I wanted to talk to the Saxon woman.

"Thank you for caring for my mother."

She turned and stared at me, "I am a slave and I do what I am ordered." I heard the venom in her voice.

"Your people have slaves. When we raided Ocmundtune we saw the slave halls and I saw slaves who had been burned. You are not ill-treated."

"No, but I am not free. Where could I go if I were free?" She swept a hand around the houses that made up Agerhøne.

What she said made perfect sense, but I was afraid to free her in case I did lose her. I chose to ignore her request. "We brought back some fine bolts of cloth. You could have a tunic made."

"I do not sew!"

I sighed, "We have thralls who do. Why must you make it so difficult? I am trying to be kind to you."

We had reached the door of the old longhouse and stepping in she gave a thin smile, "Then you have failed!" She did not slam the door, but I had seen slaves beaten for less.

I turned and headed back to the longhouse. I would try again the next day.

Egbert roused Mary before dawn and she was already attending to my mother, helping her to her toilet, by the time I woke. The house slaves had food prepared and I joined Alf. Sweyn and his father were enjoying the company of their wives. Alf was in a good mood, "What will you do to today, Sven? I thought we could go hunting!"

It was almost time for the cull of the deer and wild pigs but not quite. I shook my head, "The start of the next month will be sufficient and, besides, we will be needed to go to Ribe with your father and negotiate for the new drekar. I will repair my shield. Perhaps, you should make yours stronger too."

"I am content, and I would not wish to bring it bad luck by changing it."

I did not like lying to Alf, but I was anxious to have Mary start to read the parchments. I had all winter to repair the shield and, in truth, the damage was superficial. I needed a new skin over the shield, and I would have to repaint it. Alf took himself off to practise with the other young warriors. It would have done me no harm, but the writings seemed to draw me.

When Mary had finished feeding and helping my mother to wash, I brought out the top few parchments. Mary sighed but when she saw my look of disappointment then she smiled, "Very well. Let us begin with this one. She read through four parchments before the noon meal. They were interesting enough and they were about King Alfred and his children. As an insight into the mind of the king who had been given the title, 'the Great', they were invaluable. None of them, however, mentioned a sword, dragon or otherwise. The Saxon king seemed obsessed, during his reign, with making everyone a Christian. I saw that some men appeared to use him by pretending to do things for Christian reasons. Perhaps it was Mary's reading of them, but I became suspicious of some of the men who advised the king. After the meal, we read a few more but when my mother fell asleep, Mary said she had endured enough reading and her eyes hurt. She asked if she could walk by the beach. I agreed but my reasons were selfish. I wanted to spend more time in her company. Despite her haughty manner, I found myself increasingly attracted to her. She was growing and was no longer the young woman I had called a child. I even contemplated acceding to her request to be freed but I did not for I knew that even if she was free then she would have nothing to do with me. It was better that she was my property.

I enjoyed the afternoon with her. We walked for many miles and she saw parts of our land she had never seen before. As a thrall, she was limited in the places she could visit. I knew it as well as any. When I had been the one looking after my mother, I had spent many hours wandering the land and getting to know it. She smiled more on that late afternoon in Gormánuður and I was reluctant to have it end. I knew it would for Mary said that my mother would need her, and we went back.

Looking back I think that my mother pretended to be asleep so that we could be together. Certainly, for the next three days, it became earlier each day when she fell asleep, but I enjoyed the time with Mary. Of course, Alf commented on it and began to tease me but, surprisingly, it was Sweyn One Eye who told his little brother to grow up. Was there a conspiracy to throw Mary and I together? I did not mind but I knew that Mary would not entertain thoughts of me as a suitor. After three days we had still to find any reference to a sword and the reading had to stop for the hersir, his hearth weru and Lodvir would be going to Ribe to negotiate for a new ship. I had one of the other thralls use some of the fine cloth we had taken from the merchant to make tunics for my mother and Mary.

We did not have to travel armoured for this was our land. We rode four ponies and just took our swords, cloaks and our warm hats for the weather was becoming colder day by day. Sweyn One Eye had good news for Bergljót was with child and he intended to buy his wife a present from Ribe. We not only had clan coins to spend we each had a bulging purse and Alf was desperate to spend his. Ribe's market was much smaller than Heiða-býr's but enough merchants and ships used the port to ensure that there was a wider range of goods available than in Agerhøne. Before Sweyn Skull Taker would allow us to visit the market we had to visit the shipwright, Bolli Strakemaker. He was the best shipwright in Ribe but that was because he was the only one who built drekar. The other two made knarrs and fishing boats. If we could not agree on a price, then we would have to go further afield and none of us wished that. Ribe meant that we could easily travel to see the progress on the ship.

That was the day I discovered my fame. Bolli knew the hersir and as my father had paid for his own drekar, built by Bolli then my family was known to him but what surprised me was that I was the one he first spoke to after the hersir had said that he wished a drekar to be built for us.

"I hear, Sven Bersisson, that you now have a new name. Men who returned from Wessex speak of Sven Saxon Sword. I am intrigued. Before I took to shipbuilding, I sailed the seas and I admire a fine sword. Could I see it?"

"Of course." I took it from the scabbard and held the hilt for him to hold it.

He balanced the weapon. All those who had touched it commented on the balance. Some swords looked good but when you held them then they felt unbalanced. He then began to examine it. I doubted that he could read the writing, but he ran his fingers over it. I watched him trace the line to the hilt and then the pommel. He handed it back to me and nodded, "It is a dragon sword. Some of those who told me the tale doubt it, but I know it is one."

I was intrigued for this was a man who had not been to war or to sea for ten years, "How do you know?"

He must have heard the scepticism in my voice for he smiled, "I know I have not been to sea lately but I have seen and held a dragon sword."

Even Lodvir and Sweyn Skull Taker were taken aback by the statement.

"King Olaf Tryggvasson of Norway has one and I have seen it. He bought a ship from me five years since. It does not have the same writing as yours and his has a dragon on the hilt, but it has the same balance and the pommel decoration is the same." I looked at the sword again. He continued, "If you want my opinion then the sword lost its dragon when it was taken by the Saxons. They are Christian." He shook his head, "If King Sweyn has his way then so shall we. Take care of this Sven Saxon Sword for it will care for you." He paused and frowned, "Why were you not named Sven Dragon Sword?"

Lodvir answered, "We saw the Saxon sword and it was only later that we determined the truth. Perhaps this is better. If men think he has a dragon sword then his life may be in danger. He is a good warrior but still needs more experience."

That satisfied the shipwright who nodded and said, "So Sweyn Skull Taker, what size ship do you wish?"

"A threttanessa. We are a small clan, and it will only be when my first grandson is ready to go to sea that we shall need anything larger!"

"That is wise and there is less to go wrong with such a ship. It will take half a year. Come back at Gói and we can discuss the dragon."

Sweyn One Eye said, "You have not given a price!"

Bolli smiled, "I will take a hundred pieces of silver now and by the time you return at Gói I can tell you the final price. You will not be robbed, Sweyn One Eye, and that is why your father does not ask the question. This arm clasp seals the bond." He held his arm out and my foster father did the same. We would have a new ship in less than a year!

We then went to the hall of the Jarl. Our presence in his walled town would have been noted and he may have been insulted had we left without visiting. Jarl Harald, as I had learned in Wessex, was a real warrior and one of us. He had endured the hardships of the campaign even when the Jarl of Lade had joined the king in the relative comfort of the castle. He was also a thoughtful leader and asked after the health of his two warriors who had been wounded. When we told him the purpose of our visit to his town he was pleased. He rarely did so but he was entitled to summon us to sail to war with him. Having another drekar would be useful.

It was after he had toasted us that his face became serious, "Two of your men sought me out before the raid. They said they had left your service and wished to sail with me." He shook his head, "One had a face which told me he would cause mischief amongst a crew and, to be honest, I knew that you needed every warrior you had. I wondered at his reason for leaving. I fed him but sent him on his way."

We looked at each other. We knew who it was. My foster father said, "Thrond and his young brother Karl left us for they had a blood feud with the family of my sister. Where did he go?"

The jarl shook his head, "I know not save that it was north and not south. I had thought he would find a berth with another drekar and that we might have seen him in Wessex. We did not."

I could not help wondering what might have happened had Thrond sailed to war with us. Such was his enmity that there would have been blood.

I was suddenly aware that the others were all looking at me. My foster father smiled, "I am sorry for my foster son, Jarl, he is a dreamer. The Jarl asked about your sword, Sven."

I drew the sword, "I am sorry, my lord, my mind was elsewhere. Here is the sword."

He examined it, almost reverentially, "There are few of these left in this world. The warriors who wielded them normally died with them in their hands. Now many would frown upon them for they are pagan."

The Jarl had been a practical and pragmatic man and as his wife was a Christian so he, ostensibly, worshipped the White Christ. His words told me that, at heart, he was still one of us.

He handed the sword back. "The Saxons made good swords and also made pretty knick knacks." He waved his hand and one of his hearth weru went to a chest and returned with a small metal object. He handed it to the Jarl who placed it on the flat of his hand. It looked to be a scaled creature, but it had no teeth and no wings. Where its mouth would have been was a hole. I saw around its body writing such as was on my sword but the lettering was different.

"What is it Jarl?"

He shook his head, "It was a gift from King Alfred of Wessex to someone, I know not who. My father took it in a raid on Lundenburgh. He also brought back a monk who translated the writing for him. It says, '*Alfred had me made*'. I learned when I was young, for I was curious, that the Saxon King had such pretty things made to give to those who joined him. Wessex was a rich and powerful kingdom once. Perhaps this was something to point with or might have had a quill for someone to write." He shrugged, "I know not but it shows what the Saxons are capable of that they can work so hard on something which is not used for war. I wonder why they make dragon swords no longer."

One of his hearth weru, Galmr the Grey ventured, "Jarl Harald, I lived in Jorvik when I was young and there, I heard a tale that the

166

The Dragon Sword

swords were commissioned by Danes and Norse chiefs who wished a mighty weapon. Before they began to follow the White Christ, the Saxons followed the old ways, and they were happy to make such pagan weapons. They still make good swords, but they do not make them dragon swords." The grey-haired warrior lowered his voice, "It was said that a good dragon sword was tempered in blood."

We all nodded, and Jarl Harald said, "Thank you, Galmr. You have a powerful sword, young warrior, but I think it was intended for you. I saw you in Wessex and you fight well. Does the sword help you?"

I nodded, "When I hold it in my hand then I feel that I am unbeatable. Saxon Slayer, my spear, is a good weapon but the wounds I suffered came when I held the spear. When I use the dragon sword that does not happen."

"Then guard it well. Beware those who would steal it from you. While you are close to Ribe that will not happen for my law here protects all and I would punish, severely, any transgressor."

After we had visited the market, we headed back to Agerhøne. I had much to occupy my mind. I had thought the sword might have come from Alfred. The merchant's words had suggested that but from what the jarl had said and the pretty object I had seen, if that had been the case then it would have said *Alfred* and not *Melchior*. The others did not notice my preoccupation and they had much to occupy them; the new drekar, the news about Thrond and the purchases that they had made. I had found a small silver cross which I had bought as a gift for Mary. It was prettier than the one I had given her. This one had four small blue stones set into it and the filigree work was intricate. I thought it might make her smile. It was after dark when we reached home, and Mary was in the thrall hall. Agnetha had kept food for us and it was almost a celebratory feast as gifts were given. I retired early for I was still lost in my thoughts. I was no nearer to finding out the owner of the sword and, for some reason, that was important. Galmr the Grey's words had been the most interesting for I now understood why dragon swords had been made by Saxons. From what he had said they were normally made as a gift and whoever the first owner had been, he had been an important man.

I was up early the next day and after Mary had seen to my mother, I took her outside and gave her the cross. I was not given the reaction I expected. She nodded, "And is this payment for services you expect me to deliver?"

I felt as though she had slapped my face and I reddened, "The first time I saw you I told you that you were safe and would remain a maiden

167

as long as you wished!" I felt my voice rising, "Has anyone tried to touch or harm you?"

I saw the effect of my raised voice for she recoiled a little, "No, Sven, and this is a kind gift, but I am still a thrall."

"And an ungrateful thrall you shall remain!"

I stormed off to practise with Alf. Relations were strained for some days and I spent time with the other warriors. I spoke only to give commands when I saw Mary and I did not look at the parchments. My mother noticed and, one night, as I said goodnight to her, she said, "You have upset Mary!"

"She is a thrall mother! Why should I care if she is upset or not?"

My mother's eyes flashed a little and she nodded, "I thought I had brought you up to be kind, but it seems you are not. You took the girl from her home and brought her here across the sea. She is younger than you. What would you have done had you been made a slave?"

I said nothing.

"I can see that there is more to this than meets the eye. Do not be so stiff-necked, my son. We do not have long on this earth and you like Mary. Do you enjoy this distance?" She waited for an answer and I shook my head. "Then heal the breach for I am old, and I do not like this discord around me. You brought Mary to help me and she does or at least did until you fell out with her. If you cannot live with her then sell her or give her to another!"

That night I could not sleep. My mother was right, I was stiff-necked. What had I expected when I gave her the cross? I could see how it looked, an exchange of the cross for her maidenhead. The thought of selling her was something which I could not countenance. I determined to heal the breach the next day. The Norns were spinning and my foster father announced at daybreak that as the omens for the day were good, we would hunt and cull the wild herds which lived in the forests nearby. That I had to go was clear. Not only was I hearth weru I also knew the woods well from my time hewing logs. Mary entered the hall and gave me a weak smile. In return, I gave her a wave but then I donned my leather byrnie and took my boar spear and javelins. Any words we exchanged would have to wait!

Many of the men in the village had their own farms and families and would not be on the hunt. The hunters would be my foster father, his hearth weru, Lodvir and Griotard. Sweyn One Eye would be there to guard our backs. His one eye would be a hindrance in a hunt. He was still learning to use just one orb. Similarly, Sweyn Skull Taker's leg would also mean he had to use his bow. The six thralls we took with us would carry the fruits of the hunt but there would be just four of us who

actually hunted. I had never learned to use a bow well but the others
could and so I would be the one who found and followed the trail.

It had been some time since I had been in the woods, but I
remembered every trail and within an hour I had found the deer spoor. I
may not have known how to use a bow well, but my father and uncle
had taken me hunting since I was five summers old and I knew how to
use the wind, water and cover to my best advantage. The wind in my
face told me that the deer would not smell us and the track which led
down to the water had enough autumnal undergrowth to hide us. It was
an old stag we found. I could see that his body was recently scarred
from the rut. Had he been successful then he would have been with the
hinds. I raised my hand and then circled it. The others spread out.
Sweyn One Eye stood close to me. We moved silently as one and when
the hersir loosed, so did the others. The four arrows all found flesh, but
the stag had a heart and he raced down the beck. He made just ten paces
before he fell to the ground.

The carcass was hauled from the ground and he was quickly gutted.
Had this been anyone's first hunt then the heart, still warm, would have
been given to them to eat. As it was not then the heart, kidneys and liver
would be taken from the dead animal and the hunters would enjoy them
cooked with blackberries and mead. Two of the thralls placed the stag
on a sapling and carried it and the offal back to the longhouse.

None of us spoke for noises such as a stag racing through the woods
would not overly alarm animals, human voices would, and we were like
warriors on a raid. We used hand signals. This was how we trained for
war. Hunting wild animals honed senses and reactions. We found
another trail a short while later and this time it was not a solitary deer, it
was the herd. We would be hunting the older hinds. The herd had left
the water and were grazing in an open area. I held my javelin ready to
hurl but I did not expect to do so. A stag was harder to kill than a hind
and when the four archers saw the two targets, divided the archers into
two. The hinds might run further but they would succumb. It was that
day I saw the skill of Lodvir. The four arrows flew and Lodvir's killed
one hind instantly. The second was hit by two arrows but neither was a
mortal wound and it raced off. Lodvir nocked and loosed a second
arrow so quickly that the hind managed a bare five paces before it fell.
The two carcasses were sent back, and we sat down to eat and drink for
it had gone noon. We would wait for the thralls to return. Still, no one
spoke and that, too, was the best training for war.

When the thralls returned, we set off looking for more spoor. We
had not culled all the old stags and hinds, but we had done enough to
make the herd healthier. With the sea so close we always had a supply

of food but if the winds and the seas kept our fishing boats on the beach then we would hunt deer. It helped to keep a healthy herd. Although I was at the fore it was Griotard who spotted the tracks of the wild pigs. They were to the side of the track. He tapped me on the shoulder and I stopped. There appeared to be a number of animals and as it was still early afternoon, worth investigation. The herd was such a large one that they had spread out. I had often seen the herd when I had been hewing trees. I was not a fool and I had moved away from them when I saw them. A wild pig with tusks could tear out a warrior's guts in a heartbeat. The herd was heading into the part of the wood which was covered in blackberry bushes. Most of the fruit had either been picked or eaten but there were still enough, along with crab apples, to make a meal for the herd. It was almost impossible for us to follow them into the spiky bushes, but their thick hides could brush off the thorns. We were forced apart. It was as we spread out a little that the herd was spooked. They raced out from the undergrowth. The Norns had been spinning. I was isolated when the old, scarred boar ran towards me. As I readied my boar spear, I had time to notice that one tusk was broken in the middle and there were jagged shards which made it an even deadlier weapon than a whole one.

The squeals from my right and left told me that the others were dealing with pigs which were trying to escape the hunters, but I would have to fight the old boar alone. I had never done so but I knew what I ought to do. The boar spear had a bar which prevented the spearhead from penetrating too deeply. I had been told of boars which were still able to kill with four ordinary spears in them. I knew to aim for the head and, preferably, the mouth. Talking in the longhouse that would seem easy but with the beast which seemed the size of a huge fat pony, I thought it an impossible task. I lunged as it came at me, but it had not lived so long without becoming cunning. It had been hunted before and it turned its head. The twist meant that its teeth and tusks could not strike me, but it also meant my boar spear hit its shoulder. I was knocked to the ground and the boar spear torn from my grasp. I was only saved by two things. The boar tried to shake the spear free and I was young enough and fit enough to rise to my feet. I drew Oathsword as the boar shook the spear from its shoulder and turned to charge me and finish me off. I only had one chance and I took it. I swung my sword from left to right as it leapt at me. Its tusk was just an arm's length from me as Oathsword struck the side of the boar's skull. It had thick skin, but the dragon sword was sharp and well made. The strength of my arms knocked the animal to the side and took its deadly tusks from me. My action also cracked open the animal's skull for it hit the side and drove into its brain. It fell in a heap at my side.

I was panting. It was not just exertion it was fear. I had fought in battles, but this was as close to death as I had come. Any hesitation on my part would have resulted in a softer blow and the boar would have lived. Oathsword and my strength had saved me. It was a lesson learned!

I saw the others, on the other side of the brambles. They stared at me. I raised my sword, "Oathsword has saved me! The boar is dead!"

Chapter 18

The others had killed a sow and a young boar, but they were forgotten as they looked at my kill. Sweyn Skull Taker took the sword from my hand, "To kill a boar with a sword," he shook his head, "it is unheard of!"

Griotard gave a rare grin, "Aye, and lucky! Remind me to stand next to you in the shield wall!"

We laughed. For my part, it was relief to be alive. I had just reacted and not thought about the possibility of death but looking at the animal, which took four thralls to carry, I knew just how near I had come. All the way back to Agerhøne I was silent. I had been close to death in battle but somehow, fighting alongside shield brothers made me believe that I would live. Fighting alone was another matter. When we reached the village the fishing boats had returned and landed their catch but when they saw the boar, sow, and young boar they raced over to hurl questions at us. Sweyn One Eye showed he was a true skald. He had not had much to do in the hunt save to watch and now he gave a blow-by-blow account. By the time we had gutted and skinned the animals, word had reached the hall so that when I entered, I was cheered by all except for Mary and my mother who held each other fearfully. I had washed my face and hands outside but now I went to my chest to change into clean clothes that did not reek of boar's blood.

I gave a wan smile to mother and Mary as I passed them, "I am well. Sweyn's tale grew larger in the telling."

I could see that I had not convinced them. Even when I was dressed, I could not speak with them alone for all wanted to hear the tale of how I slew a boar with one strike of a sword. I tried to tell them that I had speared it already, but they chose to ignore that side of it and focus on the one blow. It was the evening, after we had eaten when I was able to speak to Mother and Mary. Mary had not left for the thrall hall, Egbert waited outside for her. Mother was still seated by the fire and it was clear she would not go to bed until she had spoken with me.

I had not even had the opportunity to give my version of events before she tore into me! "Today, my son, was a warning."

"I went hunting was all."

"And kept no one at your side! I never hunted but your father taught you to always have someone by your side." She was right and I had no answer. If I had said the bramble bushes prevented me, it would seem like a poor excuse. I said nothing. "Mary here fretted about you for the last time you spoke it was harshly. Had you died today then that would have lived with her. I wish you to make it up to her!"

I whipped my head around, "How?"

"You were wrong to speak harshly to her, apologise!"

Had another asked me then I would not have acceded to their request, but she was my mother. However, it was the wrong thing to do for there were others who overheard. They said nothing but I knew that they had heard. "I am sorry for speaking harshly to you. I was wrong." The words did not sound sincere and I knew it.

She gave a half-smile, "I was worried about you. There are many things about you which annoy me, but you have good qualities too."

That was the moment when one of us should have taken the other's hands and it may have turned out differently had we done so but, instead, she turned to my mother and said, "Come, it is past the time for you to sleep and I need to be fed too." She helped my mother to her sleeping mattress and the moment was gone. I was not allowed to think further on the matter for Alf and Sweyn came over, they had drunk more mead than was good for them and they wished me to hear Sweyn's song about the hunt. I went with them. Sweyn sang good songs but not when he was drunk. The one he and Alf attempted to sing was forgettable and when they retired to bed Mary had gone and I dwelt on what I should have said.

The next day we were working from the moment we rose until darkness fell. The animals we had slaughtered would, if we were careful, provide food for us for some time. Many of the bones and antlers could be used not to mention the tusks. I did not get to speak to Mary until the following day and too long had passed since the forced apology. We were uncomfortable and even when she read from the parchments there was a dullness in her voice and little interest.

Then in Mörsugur, a week before the Solstice and when the days seemed to last a heartbeat, a messenger arrived from King Sweyn. He sent a gift for the hersir, it was a brooch with silver work upon it. It was a fine gift except that it was in the shape of a cross. My foster father smiled and accepted it graciously, but we all knew he would never wear it. The messenger also brought a command. We were to meet at Ribe at the spring solstice during Einmánuður. We were raiding again. The messenger was close-mouthed about the destination but when we sat and drank during the long nights we speculated, and the consensus was that we would raid Wessex. We had not lost when we had fought the Saxons but neither had we won, and King Sweyn wished to emulate King Guthrum and defeat them so heavily that the money they paid us not to raid would make his whole army rich men.

It was Þorri before we began to read the parchments again. Things were still not right between us, but my mother had taken a turn for the worse not long after the solstice. Agnetha had spun and woven a spell. Special concoctions had been given and she had recovered. The Christian Mary was kept from my mother's side during the illness for a Christian could only bring bad luck. I think the time she spent apart from us made her warm a little to me for when she returned, she smiled and asked to look at the parchments. I had long given up on finding anything in them but the thought of sitting close to her while she read made me eager and we sat and she read.

Both of us jumped when she read the words, *'King Alfred's Gift'*. *"And so was made, King Alfred's Gift."*

My mother had been sat with her eyes closed but she opened them when the silence erupted with the words. "What is amiss?"

I shook my head, "We have found words which give me hope."

"The squiggles on the parchment?" I nodded and she picked up the woven spell Agnetha had made for her and kissed it.

"Read on."

"And the King of Wessex was so pleased that the God had triumphed and brought a lamb to the fold that he ordered his finest weaponsmith, named Melchior, after the Magi, to make a sword which he would give to him."

"Who is the *'him'*?"

She scanned up and down the parchment and shook her head. "It does not say. Perhaps it was obvious at the time." We spent hours going through every document looking for the name of the lamb. I knew enough to know it was not an actual lamb. It had to be either a pagan or a Christian who had betrayed Alfred. While we did not find the answer, we did find each other again for as we searched the parchments our fingers touched and when we looked at each other we both smiled. No words were spoken but the Oathsword had, once again, bound us.

It took another two weeks to read through every parchment, but the one reference was the only one we found. Then we had to travel to Ribe to see the progress on the drekar. It was as though Mary and I had been, along with my mother, isolated from the rest of the clan. Things had happened but they had passed us by. Bergljót was now clearly pregnant. Other warriors had become fathers and some, like Lars and Leif, also had wives with child. The long nights of winter did that. Lodvir had also managed to father a child but, in his case, it was a captive we had brought back from Frankia. He would raise the child, but the thrall remained just that, a slave.

The talk, on the road to Ribe, was all about the raid. None of the others now thought it would be to Wessex. King Forkbeard would want rich plunder and that meant the south and the east. Cent and Essex had abbeys and monasteries as well as rich merchants. The cloth merchant we had found had shown the king that there was treasure other than gold to be had. This time we went to speak with the Jarl first. Like us, he had not been told of our destination, but he agreed with our prediction. He did have a warning for us, "King Olaf causes mischief. He and Sigrid the Haughty hate each other and King Olaf has now instructed his ships to raid Danish ones. Even his merchant ships are encouraged to create trouble. One knarr crew wrecked a fishing ship and fled before we could react. I have now banned all Norse ships from entering the harbour."

My foster father asked, "How can you do that? It is hard to tell a Norse drekar from a Dane and as for knarr there is no difference."

The Jarl nodded, "Unless we recognise any ship, we assume it to be an enemy. I fear trade has suffered. You need to keep a sharp eye out at Agerhøne. You have fewer warriors than many other places."

I knew not about the others, but I wished to race back to protect Mary and my mother.

We went to the shipyard and the keel had strakes covering the lower part. The worked wood smelled fresh for no pine tar had been used. We saw the masts and the other elements which would be used to finish her. The hersir and Lodvir were happy, the price agreed, and the silver was paid. Bolli then asked what the ship would be named.

Once again, I had been so engrossed in my search that I had missed the discussion. Although it would be Lodvir's ship it was my foster father who was paying for it. He said, "'*Hyrrokkin*'." It was an interesting choice of name for she was a female Jotunn who was responsible for launching the largest ship at Baldr's funeral. It had been a feat which the gods could not emulate.

Bolli did not seem put out at the unusual choice, "Then you wish the dragon to be female?"

"Aye, for our drekar are females anyway."

"I could give the dragon features of your wife if you wished."

We had not thought of that but it seemed a good idea and we left, to head south in a buoyed frame of mind. We spoke of the threat from Norway as we headed home. "Perhaps King Sweyn should make war on the Norse!"

Lodvir shook his head, "The Norse are pirates. We make homes and King Sweyn, for all that I do not like him, makes war on a place we can farm. The Norse have nothing worth taking! No one attacks them for their fjords are like fortresses. The only place to catch them is either where they raid or at sea and they are too wily to be caught at sea."

Perhaps it was those words which made Sweyn One Eye look to the west. He only had one eye, but we had noticed that since he had lost one his other seemed to see more! *Wyrd*! "There are two masts out to sea!" We all looked, and against the setting sun, we could see the two masts. They were drekar.

Griotard laughed, "If there were two masts to landward then I would worry but sea?"

Sweyn Skull Taker reined in, "Before you mock my son, Griotard the Grim, think on this, we saw no ships ready to leave Ribe and these ships are sailing south. Had Jarl Harald not spoken of Norse raiders then I would not be worried as it is… let us ride!"

Griotard was the only one with no one in Agerhøne to whom he was attached. The rest of us did and we whipped our ponies and flogged them all the way to our home. We arrived to a peaceful place but the hersir began shouting as soon as we were close to our home, "Alarm! Alarm! Arm yourselves."

The men who lived on the outskirts of the settlement emerged as Lodvir shouted, "Arm yourselves and get your families to the longhouse." He turned to me, "Sven, he is your friend, fetch Siggi and his family."

I nodded, for as much as I wanted to be with Mary and my mother, Siggi was my friend and an isolated farm would be easy to take! I headed up the track to the farm. My pony was already lathered when I reined in and Siggi and his father emerged.

"Arm yourselves and get your families to the longhouse! We think that there may be two Norse drekar hunting!"

Siggi's father said, "But you do not know?"

Siggi put his arm around his father's shoulders, "Let us trust Sven Saxon Sword eh? At worst we lose a night's sleep. At best we save our lives." He turned back to me and shouted, "Go, we will follow!"

By the time I reached our home, everyone was armed and armoured. Night had fallen and it was hard to see further than half a mile out to sea. My foster father had cast the bones but Siggi was right. If this was not a raid, we would lose a night of sleep and the hersir might look a little foolish. I hurried into the longhouse and donned my byrnie. I grabbed my shield and Saxon Slayer. Already the hall was filling with the women and children. Agnetha would take charge.

"Hurry Sven!" Alf's voice came from the door. My mother grasped my hand as I passed, "Take care, my only son."

"I will."

To my great surprise, Mary did not take my hand but threw her arms around me and kissed me full on the lips. It was fortunate I had not donned my helmet! "Come back whole!"

I could not form the words and I just nodded.

Once outside the warriors were gathered. This was the whole clan and not just those who raided. Many just had a simple helmet, shield and a spear. Sweyn Skull Taker pointed to the drekar, "The hearth weru and those with mail will board the drekar. Dreng, you take charge of the rest and make a shield wall outside the longhouse."

Siggi, his father, family and slaves had just arrived and Siggi's father shouted, "And if they do not come?"

"Then choose another hersir!"

His words were greeted by cries from our men and it was clear they were all happy with our hersir. Since Thrond and his brother had fled there had never been a word spoken against the hersir and now it came from one who lived outside the clan.

Dreng shouted, "We will defend your families Sweyn Skull Taker! Form a shield wall."

Thorstein had armed himself and he led six of his older ship's boys, "I want only warriors, Thorstein!"

The old man shook his head, "The Norse will try to take my ship. My boys and I will defend it!"

We clambered aboard. Without the chests and with the mast and oars stacked on the mastfish and beneath a piece of old sail the ship looked different. The steering board was ashore and there was no prow at the bow.

"We hide beneath the gunwale. If there are raiders..."

Lodvir growled, "There are raiders out there, hersir, I can smell them!

"If there are raiders then they will leave guards on their ship and then get to the longhouse as soon as they can. We wait until they have passed then we attack them in the rear."

"That is the plan?"

"If you know of a better one, Griotard the Grim, then now is the time for it."

Lodvir knew Griotard better than anyone, "Griotard, it will work. Dreng and the others will hold them, and we will have the warriors without mail who are at the back. There are eleven of us and ten of us wear mail. You can kill two men without armour in a couple of strokes, can you not?"

Griotard snorted, "I could kill six!"

"Then stop complaining!"

177

Gandálfr's son, Galmr, was the one who saw the two drekar. He hissed, "Hersir, there are two drekar, threttanessa heading for the quay."

"Then let us be ready."

I never liked waiting and as we crouched beneath the gunwale, I found myself hearing sounds which were not there and imagining all sorts of ends to this. It was almost a relief to hear the first drekar bump alongside the quay and then the thump of feet as men clambered on to the wood. They were not as disciplined as we were for they spoke and we could hear every word. The shock was that one of the voices I heard was Thrond's!

"The two longhouses we must take are in the centre of the village. They will be the ones with mailed warriors and the only ones who are a threat."

"Then you and Karl lead us there!" His brother had betrayed us too. That we all heard guaranteed we would have vengeance. Now the raid made even more sense. Not only was it a vengeance raid, Thrond and Karl knew about the sword!

We heard them pass along the quay. Even had we not seen them along the coast we would have heard them. They were counting on sleepy men who had drunk too much facing them. The numbers who passed us seemed too many for just two ships, but I calmed myself. This was my imagination at work. Sweyn Skull Taker waited until there were just a few footsteps and then he stood and slid over the side. We all followed him. I pulled around my shield as Lodvir and Griotard slammed their spears into the middle of the last two tardy raiders. They had turned to see who was behind them. Ahead I heard shouts as the Norse raiders saw our shield wall and knew that they were expected. Knowing that our men were under attack spurred us and even though his wound had not completely healed, Sweyn Skull Taker led us from the front. He was flanked by his sons and I was behind him.

Once we left the quay there was no need for a narrow front and we spread out. I was between Sweyn One Eye and Lodvir. I felt safe! As the Norse made the third line to their shield wall we attacked in the centre. I pulled back Saxon Slayer and rammed it into the tunic of a Norse warrior. I think I punched so hard that it went through him and speared the one before him. I pulled back the spear and thrust it at the man I had wounded and who had turned to face the new threat. The spear gutted him, and he fell from the bloody head. The warrior whose back was to me wore mail. In two thrusts we were near to their best warriors. The Norse tried to turn, and I stuck my spear into his side. His turning made the blow less effective, but he was hurt. He used his spear to punch at four of us and then I saw Dreng's axe hack into the side of his neck.

While the Norse flanks were largely intact their centre had been broken. I saw Agnetha and the women wielding swords and spears as they joined the shield wall. Sweyn Skull Taker was an angry man, but it was a cold anger and when he faced the Norse leader, he set about killing him quickly and efficiently. We three hearth weru knew our task. Whilst others could kill whom they chose, we had to protect our father from harm. The Norse's hearth weru were doing the same as we but they also had men and women behind them; the whole of our village was fighting them. Folki Drengson was the same age as me but he wielded the axe well and he split the helmet and skull of the warrior fighting Sweyn One Eye. I lunged at another hearth weru with my spear and it tore a hole in the side of his mail. It was at that point that Sweyn Skull Taker lived up to his name and in one mighty sweep hacked through the coif and neck of the Norse leader. His hearth weru were either dead or wounded and when they ran it became a rout. More Norse died when they fell back than in their attack. With our womenfolk, we outnumbered them and ran after them.

None was given quarter. I saw four women beat a wounded warrior to death with clubs and cleavers. The quay was slippery with blood. I saw the sail of the nearest ship billow as the handful of men who had reached it set sail without waiting for the others. The rest ran to the second threttanessa. I had followed Sweyn Skull Taker but now he tired, and he waved me forward, "You have done your duty! Go!"

I ran as hard and as fast as I had when I had been training. I dropped my shield and my spear for they were slowing me down and when I saw a gap appear between the quay and the ship I just leapt. Had I held a weapon I would not have made it, but the gods smiled on me and my hands found the gunwale. I saw a sword raised to end my life but an arrow flew from *'Sea Serpent'* and the man fell dead. That spurred me and I pulled myself on to the stern of the drekar. I think I would have died had the crew not been busy grabbing oars and pulling on the stays. As it was, I drew Oathsword and turned to hack into the man at the helm. He wore no mail and my blade ripped through his stomach which poured its contents to the deck. The ship's boy who was near to him raised a hatchet and my sword sliced into the side of his head. I turned as the crew saw me and a couple advanced towards me. I raised my sword and hacked through the steering board withy. The ship could now not be sailed and then I turned.

I saw Karl and another warrior who wore no mail. I drew my seax for I had two weapons to face. "You traitor! Your family live in Agerhøne!"

Karl now had a long scar running down his face, "And my brother would have been hersir had we succeeded. At least you shall die!"

I was aware that the drekar was heading for the rocks which lay to the north of the port. We would strike and the drekar would die.

The two warriors separated to give me a harder task. I suppose I could have turned, run for the stern, and hurled myself over but Karl had betrayed us and he deserved to die. I brought my sword over to strike at his head. His sword was shorter and although he blocked the blow the edge of Oathsword drew blood from his shoulder. The other warrior took his chance and lunged with his sword. It was pure reaction made my hand flick out and the seax deflected the sword enough to miss. I could hear shouts from *'Serpent'* as my clan shouted for me to jump overboard. Karl reacted too slowly and his attempt to skewer me was clumsy and predictable. The seax which had thwarted one blow now locked against the hilt of his sword. I was dimly aware of the rest of the crew attempting to use the oars to steer the drekar away from the rocks, but they were doomed to failure. The other Norse warrior saw his chance and he tried to ram his sword into my side. I brought Oathsword around in an arc and as his sword struck my byrnie so Oathsword struck him between his neck and his shoulder. He screamed and dropped his sword before plunging over the gunwale. I did not see Karl's next strike, but I must have sensed it for I stepped back on my right leg and his sword struck the gunwale. The tip had hit wood and as he tried to pull it out, I stepped in close and said, as I ripped the seax across his throat, "So die all traitors and when I find Thrond he will suffer it too!"

As he slipped to the deck, I heard the first of the oars shatter on the rocks. I sheathed my sword and leapt into the icy darkness of the sea. I wore no mail, but my helmet tried to pull me down. I tore it from my head and then kicked hard. The sea above me was as black as night and even though I kicked with all my might it seemed impossible that I would break to the surface. I wondered if I should shed Oathsword too, but I gave one more kick and my head popped above the waves. I heard a cheer and knew that the clan had seen me. Coughing up seawater I sculled my hands to turn. The Norse drekar had been driven up onto the rocks and now holed, she was slowly sinking back into the sea to die!

I was dragged from the water more dead than alive. The fighting and the descent to the seabed had taken its toll. My foster father looked at me anxiously as Sweyn and Alf helped me close to him. I gave him a sad smile, "I appear to have lost my helmet!"

That made him smile and the band laugh. They began to cheer my name.

"There are plenty to choose from! You shall have your pick."

I nodded, "I killed Karl, but I did not see his brother, Thrond."

I saw a frown on Sweyn Skull Taker's face, "We hoped he was on the drekar which sank. We have not yet found his body and I fear that the snake has escaped us." Just then there was a wail from the longhouse. "Lars, go and see what that is. If any has caused mischief, then I will give the blood eagle to the prisoners and not the warrior's death I promised them." I saw the eight prisoners who were guarded by Griotard and ten of our biggest warriors.

I looked at Alf, "Did we lose many?"

He shook his head, "Our line held and with the women and girls using spears the Norse were kept at bay and our attack broke their hearts."

Sweyn One Eye said, "Had they been better led they might have succeeded. Their leader was brave but had no sense and when he died his men broke. We were lucky."

Lodvir smiled and put his hand on my shoulder, "A man makes his own luck!"

Just then Lars came back. He looked sad, "It was Thrond and Karl's mother, she took her own life."

I saw the anger on my foster father's face. He drew his sword and strode over to the prisoners. He pricked the neck of the first of the Vikings. "I am an angry man. You have tried to hurt women and children and for that, you will die! The manner of your death is in your hands. Tell me all about the planning and execution of this raid and you will die a warrior's death with a sword in your hand. If you do not, then you will be given the blood eagle."

The warrior with the torn mail byrnie and the deep cut on his right arm, I could see the bone, spoke. He was defiant, "I am Faramir the Fierce, for me I would be happy to have the blood eagle for all that we have taken here this day is shame. We were beaten by women and boys." He was looking at me as he spoke but then his eyes dropped to the dripping scabbard and he gave a wry laugh, "And all this way to steal a sword "

I looked at the blade and began to wonder if it was a gift or a curse. My foster father said, "You came for the blade?"

"Aye, Aethelstan's sword, given to him by King Alfred himself. The king they called the Great gave it to his grandson when he was but five." The man looked at the scabbard and asked, "If you will show me the blade then I will tell you all. The blood eagle does not frighten me, but I would die happier if I could see the sword." Sweyn nodded and I unsheathed it. The warrior's eyes widened when he saw the blade with the writing, and he smiled. "Men will seek it, boy, for it was wielded by a better king than rules Wessex now. We sailed with Ulf of Tromso, the king's cousin. When Thrond the Dane came to us with his brother and this tale of a sword in a pigsty in Denmark Ulf thought to take it. If he had the sword then he could use it to conquer the Saxons. Thrond the Dane told us it would be easy for you had no defences." He snorted, "He was wrong!" He looked up at Sweyn, "Now before I bleed to death put a blade in my hand and send me to Valhalla!"

I admired the man for he died with courage. I was not sure about the others, but his fierceness forced them to obey. Each one of them was given a sword and then they were all slain at the same moment by a sword thrust into the neck. It was over.

Chapter 19

It was daylight by the time we had burned the bodies and taken the mail and the weapons from the dead. We saw the tide take out to sea the bodies of Karl and the others. They would feed the fishes. Our own dead were buried and then we ate. It was as we were eating that my cousins commented on the news we had heard. "Well Sven, at least you know the owner of the sword. It is even more valuable than we thought."

I shook my head, "They were wrong. This is not the sword of Aethelstan."

Lodvir, Griotard and my foster father were all close by and they stopped eating. The hersir said, "You must be wrong, Sven. The story makes sense."

I nodded and swallowed the food I had just chewed, "It would make sense but for a number of things. Would a Christian king give his grandson a dragon sword? The dragon was partly chopped off so that it could be used by a Christian Saxon, but a Christian king would make it have Christian symbols and there is something else." I paused as Mary fetched more ale and poured it in my horn. Our eyes met and I smiled. She smiled back. "We two have been reading the parchments I brought back from Wessex. They speak of a gift, a sword given to a pagan by King Alfred. This is that blade for the parchments speak of Melchior who was one of Alfred's weaponsmiths. I know not which pagan, but it has to be a Norse or Dane and from the time of the Great Army which took half of the land of the Saxons."

Lodvir said, quietly, "What you say sounds true but Thrond, who now calls himself the Dane, has begun a poison which will spread. Now every man will believe that this is the sword of Acthelstan, the first Saxon King who ruled their land. They will all believe what they want to believe. More men will come."

Mary still stood close by and I looked up and saw the horror on her face. She had been a quick learner and could now speak our language fluently. She understood Lodvir's words and their implication. I could not stay and endanger them all.

"Then I will leave Agerhøne and become a sword for hire. I will not draw danger to my family and my home. My father caused enough grief here and I will not compound it."

Sweyn Skull Taker said, "That is not your decision to make. The blade was sent to you while we were on the vengeance trail. It was sent to the clan and not to you. When first we took it someone called it weregeld and it may well be. You do not spurn weregeld for you risk punishment. We will be more vigilant. Faramir the Fierce said we were without defences and he was right. Any could walk in here and raid while we are at sea. Beginning tomorrow we build a ditch such as they have around Heiða-býr. It will not be as high, nor will the ditch be as deep, but we will make a channel to the sea so that it is a watery defence. We will use the five largest longhouses to be the centre and put a wall with a fighting platform around them. We shall build a watchtower and our young men who do not sail will keep watch." He nodded towards the newly made graves. "I would rather dig a ditch and walls than graves!"

When the whole clan approved of the idea, I felt a little better, but I saw the fear on Mary's face. We had grown closer again but would the knowledge that my sword made me a marked man change her opinion of me? I did not get a chance to talk to either Mary or my mother as the day was spent repairing the damage from the raid. My eye was constantly drawn to the wrecked drekar as the sea gradually took more and more of it. I knew that it would leave part of it, a skeleton, as a reminder of the day we almost lost our home. We would not move it as it would act as a warning to others that the clan of Agerhøne were not easy prey. I headed back to the longhouse as dusk fell. No one objected to me leaving early as I had been responsible for the destruction of the drekar and I was lauded as a hero. I did not feel like one for I had brought death and destruction to my home. Had I not drawn attention to the sword with the dragon scabbard then perhaps none would have sought the sword. The women were preparing food and the longhouse had just Mary and my mother within. My mother looked grey and ill.

I hurried to her side, "What is amiss, mother? Mary, why did you not seek me?"

"Do not fuss, my son. I am overtired is all!"

I looked at Mary who shrugged, "She was up all night and may be right, but she worries about you. As do I."

"Perhaps I should leave Agerhøne and take away the worry."

Mary turned and snapped, "And that would have the opposite effect! Just stop playing the hero. You had no need to leap aboard the pirate ship!"

I sighed, "And if I had not then twice the number of our enemies would have been free to return. I am tired. Forgive me for being who I am but we cannot change what is in our hearts." I looked at my mother, "You once told me that you knew my father's faults and yet you still loved him. Do the same for me."

"But you are my last."

For that, I had no answer. I changed from my bloody clothes and then joined the others for the food. Mother was asleep and Mary had gone when I had finished. I could see no solution to this dilemma. The Norns had spun and their web was as complicated as any. I had not the wit to try to untangle it. My course was set, and I would have to follow it.

When we should have been preparing for Forkbeard's raid, we were improving our defences but, in many ways, that was preparation. The clan worked as one and the physical labour was as good for us as training with a spear and shield. I was also rewarded with the mail shirt of Ulf of Tromso and his helmet. Both were well made but in need of repair. When I was not toiling at the ditch and rampart I was working in the smithy.

When the time came to obey King Sweyn's command we had only built the gate and embedded a few of the hewn trees in the rampart but we had a ditch and more security than we had before. The women had shown that they could defend Agerhøne and we now had many more weapons with which to do so. Agnetha was determined to defend our settlement. My mother had recovered a little, but each bout of illness weakened her and I feared she would not see another solstice. Our goodbye was poignant for neither knew if we would see the other again. Mary, too, wept as I carried my chest aboard. We had shared one kiss. I wanted more. I think the others recognised my distress for even Alf kept apart. They were men and uncomfortable with such things. I placed my chest and secured it to the ship and hung my shield from the side. Saxon Slayer was placed in the rack and I rolled my cloak for a seat. The preparations were now almost second nature and I could do them without thought. That was not a good thing for it meant my head was a void and became filled with fears and doubts. That was not a good way to start a raid.

We sailed up the coast as we had done the first time but we now knew what to expect. The fleet was far larger this time. Many more ships had arrived. I recognised Beorn Bear Killer, but many others were new to me. When we went ashore to be given our orders, I heard strange accents and deduced that these were from the Østersøen. I was now wearing my new mail byrnie and had a better helmet on my head. It had taken some time to get used to wearing the mail but it was lighter than I had expected. I had grown considerably over the winter and my beard was no longer thin. Whereas before I had seen men look at me askance, now they viewed me more respectfully. Perhaps the story of my sword and the battles in which I had fought also helped. Sweyn's eye patch also marked us as battle-hardened warriors. Now it was Alf who stood out for he still looked both younger and smaller than I did. Lodvir came ashore with us so that he could visit with Bolli. He left us when we entered the hall.

There was a different doorman, but he knew us for he took us directly to Jarl Harald who was with his hearth weru. When he saw us approach, he dismissed them, "It is good to see you, old friend. I was sorry to hear of the raid but pleased that you dealt with it so well."

My foster father nodded, "And thank you. But for your warning, things might have turned out differently."

"To be truthful I heard that the brothers who fled your clan planned mischief. There was a rumour that they had gone to Norway, but I had no proof. I am just pleased events turned out as they did. I wanted to speak with you alone for the king is pleased with the men of Agerhøne." He nodded towards the King's adviser.

Karl Three Fingers was close by and he came closer, "King Sweyn seeks to reward you. He has spoken to Bolli and the drekar you have ordered will be paid for by him."

That sounded like good news, but I saw suspicion on my foster father's face, "And what does he want in return?"

Jarl Harald had the good grace to smile, "Your support. It is no secret that he seeks Norway and after our last raid he seeks the crown of Englaland."

"But that is a poisoned chalice. Even the men of Wessex and Mercia cannot hang on to it. As we proved it is simple enough to raid anywhere on that island and take whatever they have!"

"I did not say it would be easy but you, your sons and your men have shown that you are men of your word and good warriors." He saw the continued doubt and added, "He asks for nothing more than you offer him already. The difference is that you will be rewarded more!"

"Then under those terms, I accept."

By the time evening came the feasting hall was packed and the hersir and jarls had to sit cheek by jowl while the hearth weru were herded against the walls. We discovered that our speculations had been accurate. We were to raid Cent and Hrofescester in particular. The town had been granted permission by Aethelred to produce coins. There was a mint there as well as a cathedral and we could guarantee much gold and silver. It was almost as though they were gathering the coins for us to harvest! It was also a rich farming area. The lords there were close to Lundenburgh and they had many fine objects in their homes. No one gainsaid the suggestion and even Sweyn Skull Taker saw the wisdom. We would sail up the river they called the Medway for there was a bridge at Hrofescester. Once more Karl Three Fingers had been meticulous in his planning and we saw his handiwork all over the details. Satisfied that we had our instructions we left.

Lodvir was waiting for us. He looked pleased and I guessed he had discovered who would be paying for the drekar. "As the king is paying, I added a few extras to the drekar, hersir. The bow will be strengthened and there will be an extra oar hole on each side."

"If he finds out…"

"Bolli does not like the king. He will say nothing. The drekar will want for nothing." He hesitated, "There is something else."

We stopped for this was not like Lodvir. "Aye?"

Lodvir took a breath and sighed. "This is not like me, Sweyn Skulltaker, but I met four warriors who sought a berth. They had been helping Bolli build the drekar. Bolli spoke up for them and I offered them a berth. We will need more men when the second drekar is built." He added hurriedly, "I will be responsible for them!"

Sweyn nodded and then smiled, "And they might become your hearth weru."

Lodvir's mouth dropped open, "How…?"

"There is little surprise. Since my sons became my hearth weru you have felt you needed your place. It is one reason I offered you the drekar. By choosing four men who are not from Agerhøne you are making men who will be loyal to you before me and that is right and proper. We are shield brothers, Lodvir, and we know each other. If I cannot trust you then I should hang my shield from the longhouse door!"

The four warriors were waiting by the quay. Once more our garrulous ferryman was awaiting us. He would not take the four of them for he had no orders to do so. The four were young. At a first glance, they were of an age with Alf and me and I understood why Lodvir had chosen them. None had mail, their helmets were poor, but each had a spear, shield, and short sword. They were clay and I knew that he would mould them as he had moulded me. In my case, it was a favour to my father. Now it was for himself.

When we reached them Lodvir gestured to Sweyn Skull Taker, "You have sworn an oath to me when you asked me to take you, but Sweyn Skull Taker is the leader of our clan and I would have you swear to fight for him and obey all of his orders."

There was a lighted brand by the ferry ladder, and I saw that the four of them were gaunt. They had not eaten well. However, they were all eager and all offered their swords to my foster father who touched each hilt and said, "Welcome to the clan of Agerhøne. These are my hearth weru!"

As each of them spoke his name they bowed, "I am Aksel Moltisson."

"Bodulf Therkilson."

"I am Diuri Therstenson and Aksel is my cousin."

"Enwald Ubbisson."

"Welcome." He shouted down to the ferryman, "Can you take another four or will it need two trips?"

As I expected he opted for the latter as he would expect two tips. Lodvir frowned for he knew the game. "Take Aksel with you and I will come with the other three."

As we boarded the ferry and the ferryman smiled, I knew that he was in for a shock. The ferry could have taken us all in one trip and not only would there be no tip the ferryman would have to endure the sharp end of Lodvir's tongue.

I sat next to Aksel and asked, as we pushed off, "Where is your home?"

"Roskilde."

I knew that to be an island and that Harald Bluetooth, the father of King Sweyn had made the town it's home. Perhaps that explained why they had not obtained a berth on any of the other ships from that side of Denmark. King Sweyn had banished his father. I did not pursue it. If Aksel chose to offer an explanation that was one thing, but it did not do to delve too deeply into a man's past.

When we clambered aboard, I helped to haul his chest. It was very light. He did not have much. The stranger made everyone look, "Get back to what you are doing, idlers!" It was Aksel's first introduction to Griotard and I saw the effect immediately.

The hersir said, "Sven, take him to the prow. He and the others can occupy the oars you and Siggi had when you first sailed. Perhaps they will enjoy your luck."

As we walked down the drekar he said, "Luck?"

"I took a dragon sword!"

There was little point in hiding its existence from him. The rest of the crew would tell him and, indeed, the song we sang when we went to war would reveal its presence. He saw the scabbard and said, "Then you are truly lucky…"

"Sven Saxon Sword. I am Sweyn Skull Taker's hearth weru and his foster son."

Aksel was an affable young man and he grinned, "Then you are a man to be close to for the gods smile on you." That told me he was a pagan and perhaps offered another explanation of why he had not been given a berth on another ship.

I shrugged, "If the gods know you then the Norns do too! I would prefer to be anonymous, but a man does not choose his own fate."

He clutched at his Hammer of Thor and nodded.

"This is a good ship and a happy one. Griotard barks and he does not suffer fools gladly, but you are Lodvir's men and he is well thought of."

I sat with him and chatted until Lodvir and the others arrived. Lodvir was grinning. He gestured towards the ferry which headed back to the quay, "I have not made a friend there. Where do you want my men, Sweyn?"

"At the prow. Aksel is there already."

It was cold fare, but the food was good and I joined the rest of the crew to devour freshly cooked bread with cold fish, ham and cheese. All were curious about the new men but, at the same time, pleased to have our numbers bolstered. It meant we could row for longer if we needed to and have more men in our shield wall. Sweyn had given them the bare bones of the story of the new men. That would be all that they would hear unless the four Roskilde men chose to open up. I knew that Lodvir would tell us the reason why he had taken them on. It was late in the evening when he eventually sat with us, Griotard and Thorstein. He spoke quietly to us, not wishing to be overheard.

"Theirs is a typical tale, hersir. The father of Diuri and Aksel's uncle was Harald Bluetooth's hearth weru; he died when the king was in exile. The other two had fathers who also followed Bluetooth. Because of that, they were shunned. The fact they refused to become Christians also turned captains against them. Most of the ships which come from Østersøen are Christian."

Sweyn Skull Taker nodded, "What you three do not know is that we are held in special regard by the king. He views us as reliable. That may be why he has not tried to have us converted."

"It would do him little good!"

The hersir sighed, "I know, Griotard. Let us make coin while we can. This raid could make us more than even the last two. We raid the town where they mint the coins for the southern part of Englaland." He could see that Griotard was not convinced. "And he has paid for '*Hyrrokkin*'! And before you ask there is no obligation tied to the ship save the normal fealty we owe our king."

Griotard spat over the side, "I still do not trust him, but I cannot see how he could betray us."

The voyage was a short one, just over four hundred and thirty miles. With a good crew rowing, it could be completed in two or three days, but we had fifty ships and I think that King Sweyn was aware of the problems we had last time. He wanted us to stay together. This time the Jarl of Ribe was his most senior jarl and we sailed to steerboard of *'Stormbird'*. It was a place of honour. This time we risked the Saxon fleet which Aethelred kept at sea whenever he could. The extra rowers and our clean hull meant that we had to row less often than other crews for we were a faster ship. It was an easy voyage. The new crew from Agerhøne, ship's boys who had been promoted, did not suffer as much as Alf or Siggi had. None said that this boded well. It did not do to antagonise either the gods or the Norns. We were spied, on the third morning. We were highlighted against the rising sun but by the time we spotted the ship, in the darkness to the west, she had disappeared.

Thorstein was philosophical about it, "They know not where we land. There is the whole of the southern coast that they must guard. In fact, this may help us. By looking everywhere they cannot defend in depth. When we sail down the Tamese they will assume we go to Lundenburgh. That will draw their defences."

Griotard nodded, "And before the Tamese is Cantwareburh. That is a rich church and the most important one in the land."

Lodvir shook his head, "And only a fool would try to take it for there is a Roman wall around the town. We would have to besiege it and that rarely ends well. The moneyers and the mint will suffice!"

The mouth of the Tamese was wide enough for twenty ships abreast and we used every uncia of it. We saw beacons lit to the north and south which told us they knew that wolves were about and were warning their sheepfolds. I was now at the oar and we were pulling against the current. I had time to think about the words of Lodvir and Thorstein. If I was a Saxon lord, I would think we were going for Cantwareburh or Lundenburgh. I would send to my neighbours for help. I would raise the fyrd, not just close to the river but up to sixty miles away. Danish armies had been known to take horses and forage for up to fifty miles. Every river which fed the Tamese would be alerted too. How could they meet us with a force as big as ours? The answer was simple. They could not. This time we had fifteen hundred warriors. In addition, we had well-armed ships' boys who were more than capable of repelling any attack on our ships. However, I was not certain if King Sweyn relished another battle after we were so roughly handled by Ordwulf.

We passed through the channel between the Isle of the Sheep and the Isle of Greon. The land on either side was marshy. If we struck, we would not have a hole gouged in our keel, but it would take effort to extract us. It was late afternoon when we saw the spire of the cathedral and could hear its bell tolling, they knew we were coming. There was little that we could do to reach the town quickly for the river twisted and turned. This time the orders were to allow the king and the jarl to land first and for the rest of us to land on either side of them. Our position meant that we were able to pass the king's ship and the Jarl's as they turned to the riverbank. It enabled us to land almost as soon as they did. We had donned our mail and helmets when we were off Gippeswic.

As the boys leapt ashore to tie us to the quay, I grabbed my shield and slung it around my back. I left Saxon Slayer on the drekar for the narrow streets of Hrofescester were no place for an eight-foot-long spear. Alf and I landed ashore together, and we drew our swords. Sweyn and his father were just behind us. When Lodvir and his new men joined us followed by Griotard and the mailed men of the ship, then we were ready to advance. The town had a gate from the port to the town and it was barred, but Jarl Harald's men had found a good length of timber and were using it as a ram. We protected the hersir with our shields. I did so with more confidence for I now had a mail shirt. Whilst not new it afforded me more chance of surviving. My mother and her thralls had made me a padded undershirt so that I was comfortable, and the weight was spread about my shoulders. I was not sure how I would fare fighting in high summer, but the chilly waters of the Medway meant I had no such problem. More drekar were disgorging their warriors on to the quay while others had tied up on the river side of our drekars and were using them like a longphort, walking across the decks of the ships attached to the land. It also prevented any boats who were upstream of us from escaping to the Tamese.

Jarl Harald had lost men in the assault but not enough to deter us and when the gate gave with a creak and then a crash, we followed his men and then the king's into the city. The orders were quite simple. Secure the gates and make sure that none left with treasure. The town was a Roman one and laid out with straight roads. There would be another three gates and Sweyn Skull Taker led us to the one on the far side of Hrofescester. The jarl and the king were heading for the mint and the cathedral, respectively. We shared the same route for two hundred paces. More than two hundred Danish warriors racing through narrow streets had a dramatic effect. The ordinary people fled, and the warriors designated to guard the important buildings were hurrying to their duties. My sword was not needed until we neared the far gate.

A press of people were trying to get out. I knew that some of our warriors had been ordered to destroy the bridge over the river and I guessed that there would be even more trying to cross the river before that escape route was barred. The Saxons, who were at the gate, saw us as we ran up and formed a shield wall of twenty men to enable as many people as possible to escape. As we ran Sweyn Skull Taker shouted, "Wedge! This time Lodvir would not be in the wedge. He would be with the lightly armed men protecting our flanks. We had taken mail from the Norse raiders and it was a heavy block of warriors which struck the shield wall. We were hampered by having no spears but as the Saxons were not wearing mail and had smaller shields it was a risk worth taking. I had Lars and Leif behind me, and they were big men. Holding Oathsword before me I was propelled into the wall of spears. They were just two deep, but three spears still came for me. My new helmet had a better fit than my old one, but my eyes were still vulnerable. One spear hit my shield and one, my shoulder. The third was coming for my eye and I envisaged a life like Sweyn's. I made the slightest of turns with my head and the spear struck not my eye but the nasal. It glanced off and struck the side of my helmet. By then Oathsword had driven into the shoulder of one warrior while Leif's sword had stabbed a second in the thigh. Sweyn Skull Taker's sword had skewered the captain of the guard and the three of us at the fore had bowled over the warrior in the second rank. When he fell, we almost tumbled to the ground but the three of us retained our footing and Sweyn Skull Taker shouted, "Break!"

I turned to my left and was quicker than the Saxon who had Lodvir and his four men before them. I rammed Oathsword into his unprotected side and twisted. He slipped to the ground.

Lodvir shouted, "To the gate!" He led his men to secure the gate and to trap any more of the men of the town who wished to flee. The Saxons who had tried to defend the gate now lay dead, wounded or, in the case of four of them, fled. The gates were in our hands now and for the ones who remained, there was no escape. The best that they could hope was to ascend the walls and climb over.

Sweyn Skull Taker pointed to four of the younger warriors. Folki Drengson was amongst them, "Guard this gate. We will ensure that you get the treasure which is due to you."

They looked disappointed but that was not because they thought they would be cheated, they wanted action. Griotard pointed at a church which lay down a short street. "Sweyn?"

"Aye, that will do. Leif and Lars take some men and ensure that none escape with the treasure."

192

They hurtled off and we advanced on the church. Once we opened the doors, we saw a dozen women and children and a priest guarding them with a sword. My foster father looked at me, "Sven!"

"If you wish to live then leave. You will not be harmed by us!"

The priest shouted, "And the church?"

I smiled, "Is a different matter. You can make more candlesticks and write more books, but you cannot easily remake a life. I say to all of you, run while you can."

Some would end their lives as captives, but some might be lucky. All that we were doing was giving those who wished the chance to escape. Suddenly a woman and her three children passed us and that was like the start of an avalanche. Soon there was just the priest left and I advanced towards him. He raised his sword and Lodvir shouted, "Kill him!"

I knew at that moment that I could not for Mary would not have liked it. As the priest's hand came down to smite me on the head, I raised my left hand and held his sword hand. He was a weak man. I punched him hard in the face with Oathsword's hilt and he fell in a heap on the ground. I picked up the priest's sword. It was a good one. I saw that it had lain above a tomb on a wooden stand. It was better than my spare and even though it had no scabbard I slipped it into my belt.

Lodvir stormed past me as he led his men to search the place the Saxons called the vestry, "You are a fool, Sven! That girl has cursed you. Next time kill him!"

I smiled and sheathed Oathsword, "There was no need. My mother could have felled him!"

There were valuable goods in the church: candlesticks, paraphernalia of their services, fine clothes, incense, holy books, and richly decorated vestments. There were also relics in boxes. We threw the relics to the floor for the boxes were decorated and of more value.

Alf said, enviously, "The sword you took was the greatest prize. We should call you lucky!"

I laughed, "Do not worry cousin, you will find a name soon enough!"

Griotard overheard and chuckled, "A name chooses you, Alf No Name, not the other way around! Perhaps we should call you that, eh?"

It had all gone so easily that Griotard could joke and that was unusual. By nightfall, we had the town, and the bridge was burned. If help was to come from Lundenburgh then they would have a long route. We found food and we found ale. We took up residence in the church. The priest had awoken and fled while we had searched the building. The gates were still guarded and so the odds were that he would end up a prisoner. We first sent food and later took the treasure to the drekar. We were, indeed, a longphort and our deck was already dirty and bloody from other ships' crews which passed over ours to take the treasure back to their own ships.

Thorstein grumbled to the hersir when he secured our treasure and that was unusual. Sweyn Skull Taker pointed to the quayside, "Take the timbers there that have been unloaded from some other ship and make a proper bridge. We can always take the timber home with us."

Thorstein brightened up. He would be able to keep his deck clean and we would have a profit. We passed Karl Three Fingers who was hanging three Danes. We stopped and said nothing. Karl shrugged, "There is a convent and these three thought to rape the nuns. A warning to your men. You can steal from them but try not to kill or hurt their priests and nuns!"

I looked at Lodvir with a superior look. He shook his head and grinned, "Lucky!"

For six days we raided along the Medway and the southern bank of the Tamese. We took many sheep from the Isle of Sheep. We slaughtered and salted them. We took the treasure from the smaller churches and we had taken so many coins from the mint that the king was forced to distribute half of it amongst his drekars to prevent his ship from sinking on the way home. Then, a week after we had landed, scouts who had been raiding to the south-west galloped in on the ponies they had been using.

We happened to be close to the king and heard the report, "There is a Saxon army, my lord, and they are heading from the south and west."

Jarl Harald said, "We have a battle then! Unless we sail away!"

The king then showed that he was no fool, "If an army comes then I do not doubt that their fleet will soon follow. We will fight this army but have the ships made ready for sea. This time we will take the treasure home and I will keep my army intact. There will be no desertions."

The hangings had served a dual purpose!

Chapter 20

A few men had been wounded and they were left to guard the captives. If things went badly for us then the king would simply use the Saxons as hostages. We took the last of our booty to the drekar and picked up our spears. A battlefield would need a shield wall and spears. We marched quickly with the Medway to our right. That way we had a secure flank. The road passed through a huge forest and King Sweyn wisely kept as many scouts out as he could manage to mount on Saxon ponies and horses. The last thing we needed was to find ourselves ambushed. It was fortunate that the king had done so as they found the Saxons waiting for us less than half a mile from the edge of the trees. Our army halted and we shuffled into our positions. We would have a battle. We were not close to the king, but we saw from the banners that the army was led by Ordwulf once more and I do not doubt that he sought revenge for what we had done to his abbey. We knew that we were in for a bloody fight; this eorledman knew his business. The last time we had fought neither side had won. It had been indecisive. What would happen this time? We formed a shield wall three hundred paces from the trees.

Lodvir said for the benefit of his new men who were in the second rank for they were not mailed, "The king is cunning. We have enough space to fall back and to use the trees to evade capture." No army liked to be trapped and the forest was not dense enough to be an obstacle.

The men who faced us were from Wessex and Cent. More were from Cent but as Eorledman Ordwulf led the men of Wessex and was the most senior he looked to be in command. As usual, they had priests and relics with them, as well as holy banners. Less than four hundred of their warriors appeared to be mailed and the majority of those who faced us was the fyrd. These were farmers, burgesses and yeoman who would train once a week, supply their own weapons and fight amongst friends. The greatest weapon they possessed was that they were fighting for their homes. What they lacked in skill they would make up for in courage. The best warriors, the housecarls and thegns, were mailed and it was they who protected the relics and the Eorledman. Their priests began singing and, as we knew that would take time, we ate, drank, and made water. We did not need singing to bolster our courage. We were Danes and were facing the same Saxons we had beaten in the past. The singing stopped and Eorledman Ordwulf stepped before the Saxon army. A priest came with a box. I knew it contained some relic, but it

195

looked to be a long, narrow one. My guess was the leg bone of some long-dead saint. The Saxon had a powerful voice. I heard him shout, for the benefit of his army for he was speaking Saxon, "Lord, bring us your help to smite the pagans." The priest took out a sword and handed it to the Eorledman who faced us and shouted, "Here is the sword of Aethelstan and with it, we shall send these barbarians back to the sea from whence they came!"

The Saxons began to chant, "Aethelstan!" over and over. I knew that the eyes of the hersir, Lodvir and the hearth weru were on me. I had been right! The Norse had come for the wrong sword.

However, the sword had a profound effect on the Saxons. It seemed to inspire them, and I knew that their King Aethelstan had to have been a great king. With the old Eorledman at their fore and the Christian banners above them, the whole mass of men hurtled towards us. There were few Saxon archers but their slingers, the youths, and boys scurried forward to pelt us with stones. We had archers and the boys fell. Some of their stones struck us but a Danish shield is always bigger and better made than a Saxon one. Perhaps that was why Egbert had taken such care in the making of mine. He had seen the deficiencies in those of his own people. Some of the arrows also found flesh amongst the Saxon clergy. Some relics fell and were picked up by men who would have been better wielding a weapon.

"Lock shields!"

With Saxon Slayer poking over the top of my shield we awaited the Saxons. This was a proper shield wall and spears from behind me rested on our shields as well as my shoulder. I saw that the Sword of Aethelstan was not in the fore. Eorledman Ordwulf might be a brave man and a good warrior but he was no longer a young man and holding a sword aloft while you run is no easy thing. The first men who hit the shield wall were fanatical young men who were inspired by the Christian relics. They wore no mail and relied on, I think, not military skill but divine help. They discovered that an eight-foot length of ash with a metal head cares not for any god, pagan, or Christian. They slammed into shields and spearheads and fell before us. Behind them came Eorledman Ordwulf's housecarls. Dressed in mail with a shield and spear the equal of ours these were true opposition. They had also managed to form ranks. Perhaps that was one reason why they took time to reach us. I saw the Sword of Aethelstan still raised in the air, but it was three ranks back. The housecarls and thegns would defend both the sword and Eorledman with their lives.

The line did not hit us piecemeal but in a solid mass. The air rang with the shattering of wood and metal on metal. The points of their attack were the hearth weru of the jarl and the king but as we were so close, we had to endure the power of that first wall of steel. We jabbed forward as one while watching for the spearheads to come back at us. The housecarls were the best of the Saxon warriors and they struck where they aimed. These were not blindly jabbed spears. They sought eyes and weaknesses in our armour. Even when I had been a boy and practised with my father, I had known I had skills. At the time I did not see them as special for they came naturally but my brothers and fathers commented on them. My hands had often come up to protect myself without me even being aware I was doing so. So it was on that day in Cent as my shield came up to deflect the spearhead. My eyes did not leave the housecarl who saw a young warrior and an easy victim. When Saxon Slayer darted out, I put all the power I possessed into the blow and although his hand came up to block the strike with his shield, my right hand was quicker and drove into the housecarl's cheek. Saxon Slayer's head was narrow at the tip but a handspan down widened to be three fingers wide. The wound in the cheek grew wider and blood flowed. Saxon Slayer's head scraped off a cheekbone and along the hairline. It cut the strap on the helmet and the helmet flew backwards. Aksel was behind me and his spear saw the bare head and he rammed it into the centre of the Saxon's skull. The huge warrior fell backwards.

There was another warrior behind him, but he was not a housecarl and as the mailed man fell into him, he lost his balance. In his falling, the housecarl's shield smashed into the spear arm of the next housecarl and Sweyn Skull Taker did not spurn the opportunity to skewer the Saxon. Lodvir also possessed great skills and his strike had also taken out a housecarl. Alf's opponent was suddenly faced by four spears as those around him fell. He was a good warrior, but you cannot defend against four spears. One will find a gap and Alf's struck the mail in the man's chest and, tearing open the mail links ripped into the padded kyrtle and then his chest. With the weight of the clan behind us, we all took a step forward. We had no choice in the matter. The obstacle that was before us, the housecarls, were no longer there and as we stepped, we jabbed with our spears at men who did not anticipate their front-rank being shattered. Sweyn Skull Taker stabbed the warrior who had fallen, and I moved towards the Saxon who had been in the third rank. We were now a bump in the enemy line. Battle lines are rarely even for long, but we jutted prominently into theirs. With Griotard anchoring one end and Lodvir the other we were a danger to the integrity of the Saxons. It brought us closer to Eorledman Ordwulf.

I did not kill the man before me for I stumbled over the body of the man killed by the hersir but, in my stumbling Saxon Slayer found the man's thigh and it drove in the length of the spearhead. He tried to step back but his weakened leg would not take the weight. As he fell, backwards, the weight of his body tore Saxon Slayer from my grasp. Had we still been amongst the housecarls then I would have been a dead man, but these were farmers and landowners who had good weapons and trained but they were not the professionals that were the housecarls. I had time to draw Oathsword. Behind me, Aksel and Enwald were still jabbing their spears at any who came close to me but now that we were in the press Oathsword was a better weapon. I stepped into the gap, stamping on the face of the fallen Saxon. It was not cruelty. The stamping ensured that I did not slip, and it gave the man a merciful death. I was now the point of an improvised wedge. We had not practised this. All the training had been to protect the hersir and now Sweyn One Eye and Alf were guarding me.

Oathsword was better used as a slashing weapon and I slashed at Saxons who could not use their spears for there were too many men pressing behind. Had they used an overhand strike they might have succeeded in wounding but as it was the weak blows, even when they struck, made no impression. Oathsword, in contrast, found necks that were unprotected by shields which were slow to rise. I began to hack a passage through the Saxons. Sweyn and Alf had also dropped their spears to draw swords and the three of us were almost like a scythe taking wheat. We were all mailed and the men we fought were not. If I had been a hawk above the battlefield, I might have seen that the hole we had made had been enlarged and the left flank of the army was pushing back the Saxons. The main thrust of the Saxons was still against King Sweyn and so, unknowingly, we were swinging around.

When I looked up to view ahead, I realised this, and I saw, two ranks ahead, Eorledman Ordwulf swinging his sword above his head. King Sweyn's hearth weru were falling. The Eorledman's housecarls saw the chance to end the battle by killing King Sweyn. It was a bloody battle with quarter neither sought nor given. Our small wedge was approaching from the spear side of the housecarls as well as the minor nobles and thegns of Wessex. They turned to face us but that meant that they were fighting men on two sides. I saw Griotard had also shed his spear and was using his axe to great effect. It came down to shatter a shield and break the arm of a thegn and Griotard the Grim, after headbutting the thegn split the man's skull with his axe. Pieces of metal, brains, and skull splatted the thegn's bodyguards and Lars and Leif took advantage as they stabbed and slashed at unsighted Saxons. Our enclave in the Saxon lines grew and I saw that Dreng had now joined our front rank.

I heard a Saxon voice roar out, "Angle right!"

The whole Saxon line tried to readjust to compensate for the threat we posed. As the Saxons tried to do so then the Danes to our left, including the warband of Beorn Bear Killer stepped forward as one and the pressure was renewed, Some of the spears of the housecarls had also broken or been discarded and they drew swords and axes. Alf had improved over the last year but when I saw him face the housecarl with the plaited beard and battle bands on his arms I feared for my cousin for he would be outclassed. I could do little to help as I was exchanging blows with a housecarl who was equally skilled. We traded blows on our shields as we each tried to find a weakness in the other. I knew that it would be a matter of fitness. One of us would make a mistake or tiredness would slow our reactions and the battle would end. As Alf was to my left, I could not help but take in the combat. Alf's skill lay in quick hands, but the Saxon had strength. I saw Alf's arm droop and drop as a mighty blow numbed it. As he reeled the housecarl lifted his arm to end the combat, but Alf's right hand darted out like a dragon's tongue and his sword found the housecarl's throat. The blood sprayed and that helped me for the housecarl I fought could not help but glance to his right. His protection on that side had gone. It was a minor distraction, but I took advantage and swung Oathsword horizontally above his shield and towards his chest. His mail almost held but the blow was so hard that the breastbone was broken, and my sword sliced through to the flesh. It did not penetrate deeply but the broken bone made movement harder. I pulled my arm back and lunged at his chest. This time my sword found the broken mail and breastbone. I had not yet used the tip and it drove through into his body. The two housecarls fell and there before me stood Eorledman Ordwulf and the Sword of Aethelstan.

I did not plan on fighting the warrior who had far more experience than I did but the Norns had spun and the housecarls close to the Eorledman advanced towards Sweyn Skull Taker and Sweyn One Eye. On the other side, the two housecarls saw Lodvir as the greater threat and moved towards him and Alf. It would be Oathsword against the Sword of Aethelstan, youth against age. The eorledman was using the sword two handed and be brought it down to smash into my helmet. I raised my shield and put my left shoulder against the padded side as I swung Oathsword towards his exposed side. His twohanded strike made my shoulder numb but my shield held. The cover was torn and there was a dent in the boss, but his sword would be slightly dulled as a result. My sweep should have found flesh but the housecarl fighting the hersir adjusted his position at the last moment and my sword hacked through, not the Eorledman's side but the skirt of the housecarl's byrnie and into his leg. The Eorledman raised his sword again but this time I saw that he intended a diagonal sweep. I lunged with Oathsword to avoid the housecarl's leg. The sword found the gap in the skirt of the Eorledman's byrnie and found his right calf. The sword came out bloody.

"Pagan dog!"

"Old man, you wield the Sword of Aethelstan, but I have another sword made by Alfred! Mine is a dragon sword!"

I had spoken to him to make him angry, but it had a different effect. He stopped in his swing, his sword in mid-air and stared at the blade. As luck would have it the writing faced him. I did not know why he had paused but I was not foolish enough to spurn his unguarded moment. I hacked at his side and this time Sweyn had slain the housecarl who had blocked my earlier blow and my sword bit through mail and undershirt to score a wound along the eorledman's side. I do not think he was badly hurt but the wounds, his dead housecarls and, for some reason, my sword, meant that instead of continuing his swing he stepped back, and a thegn stepped forward to swing at my left side. His sword hit my already numbed arm and emboldened he swung again. I cursed myself for thinking my battle over and I swung my sword over to hit his head. He blocked it with the shield, and I stepped closer to him. My left arm was numb, but my feet, legs and knees were unhurt, and I brought my knee up hard between his legs. He was not expecting the blow and our faces were so close together that I saw the pain I had caused, and he doubled up. I smashed Oathsword's pommel into the side of his head. He wore a helmet, but it must have hurt. I continued to pummel his helmet with blow after blow and he began to sink to the ground. I inverted Oathsword and drove the blade into his neck. I was aware that there were no living Saxons before me and that the wounded Ordwulf was being led from the field. We had won but, as I looked down the line, I saw that we were in no position to continue the fight.

Lodvir had his wits about him, "This battle is over. Strip the dead and be prepared to march back to the drekar. Sven Saxon Sword has bought us time. As soon as the Saxons reform they will attack." He pointed his sword, "See, already King Sweyn and his men are gathering what they can!"

I slung my shield and, after kissing the hilt, sheathed Oathsword. The mail on the housecarls I had killed was damaged and not worth the carrying. The byrnie I wore would suffice. The thegn's sword was a good one and I took that, a seax and a housecarl's sword. The men I had killed all had full purses and I was laden as we headed from the field. I picked up Saxon Slayer and a seax from the place we had begun the battle and then, laden down, joined the rest of the army as we headed from the battle. We had lost men and others were wounded but we had not yielded one pace. We marched to Hrofecester with heads held high. Our drekar was loaded already and, as darkness fell, we clambered aboard. We were weary and we were hungry but the longphort meant we could not leave until the drekar on the outside were moved. As soon as the king returned then that movement would be accelerated.

We placed our shields on the side and put our treasures in our chests.

As usual, our helmsman only knew about the battles we fought from our accounts, "We won?"

The hersir shook his head, "No, Thorstein, but we did not lose either and the clan gained the greatest honour for Sven Saxon Sword wounded Eorledman Ordwulf and made them fall back. We bear the hero of the battle!"

Men began to cheer, and it was not just on our drekar. Those close to us joined in. I felt embarrassment more than anything. I had not chosen to fight the old man and given a choice I would rather that Sweyn Skull Taker had done so! As they came aboard the four new men paused to speak with me.

One grinned and said, "You are, indeed, lucky, Sven Saxon Sword and I would gladly stand beside you or even behind you." He held up a housecarl's helmet, spear, and sword. "We are all richer before any treasure is shared."

I nodded, "I am just happy that most of us are still alive."

Sweyn Skull Taker shook his head, "Do not tempt the Norns. They know we are here, and we must escape the Tamese. Speak when we see the open sea before us."

He was right for we were unable to leave the port until dawn. A combination of some tardy crews and a tide which would not cooperate meant that the Saxons reached Hrofecester before we had left. Had they had archers in numbers they could have made life difficult for us but, as it was, the odd arrow they sent did not harm. They carried the wounded Eorledman, the Sword of Aethelstan still in his hand and he waved it defiantly at us. I noticed that their ire was directed at *'Golgotha'*. They must have assumed I was one of the king's men!

It was dawn and we were in the middle of the mass of heavily laden ships when we slipped through the channel between the Isle of Greon and the Isle of Sheep. The sun had been up for an hour when the ships ahead reefed their sail, a sure indication that trouble lay ahead. The hersir came back from the prow and shouted, "Don your helmets and prepare for a sea battle."

Alf asked, "What is it, father?"

"There are the masts of Saxon ships ahead. I think they planned to catch us on the Medway, but they failed. We will have a sea battle to fight if we are to reach the sea."

I had yet to fight in such a battle and I was not looking forward to the prospect. Fighting in mail at sea meant that I could die without a wound. A drekar moved around so much that it was hard to keep your footing. I had already taken off my sealskin boots and now I contemplated taking off my mail. I remembered when I had been on the Norse drekar and it had sunk.

The jarl and the king held a conference in the Tamese as the Saxons approached. Both fleets were under reefed sails. It gave better visibility and more control over the ships. It meant that we were approaching each other slowly. We had the advantage of the current. If we rowed, we would have more speed. After the conference, Jarl Harald had his drekar brought close to us. "We attack in two columns. You will be to steerboard of my ship."

Sweyn looked at Thorstein who nodded, "It will be like a nautical wedge!"

Sweyn shouted, "We understand. And after?"

"We sail home."

First, we had to fight another battle and this time we would not see the enemy as they approached. We faced the stern and would have to trust to our hersir, who returned to the prow and Griotard who would direct Thorstein. Now was the time for the clan to make their voice known and it was Sweyn One Eye, my cousin who did so.

When the clan of Agerhøne sailed the Somme
When the warriors fierce were to Frankia come
When Sea Serpent bared her bloody teeth
Her crew were filled with blood-filled belief
The Sword of the Saxons is strong and true
With a dragon sheath bright and new
The Sword of the Saxons is strong and true
With a dragon sheath bright and new
Skull Taker went to find monk's gold
Hidden in a church, made of stone and old
The Franks could not face his bloody blade
All who came near were quickly slayed
The Sword of the Saxons is strong and true

The Dragon Sword

With a dragon sheath bright and new
The Sword of the Saxons is strong and true
With a dragon sheath bright and new
Sven Saxon Sword fought like a bear
Three men were killed in the farmhouse there
Then a jagged spear broke his skin
Baring the bones and all within
The Sword of the Saxons is strong and true
With a dragon sheath bright and new
The Sword of the Saxons is strong and true
With a dragon sheath bright and new
As the ship sailed home a trap was laid
But Agerhøne clan were not afraid,
They rowed and worked as a single man
Determined to thwart the Frankish plan
The Sword of the Saxons is strong and true
With a dragon sheath bright and new
The Sword of the Saxons is strong and true
With a dragon sheath bright and new
The Njörðr played a cruel joke
The tide was turned, and their hearts were broke
Then as Frankish ships loomed at their side
A hero rose the battle to decide
The Sword of the Saxons is strong and true
With a dragon sheath bright and new
The Sword of the Saxons is strong and true
With a dragon sheath bright and new
Sorely hurt with sword in hand
Sven Saxon Sword saved the band
He hacked and slashed at Frankish skin
Fuelled by the power which lay within
The Sword of the Saxons is strong and true
With a dragon sheath bright and new
The Sword of the Saxons is strong and true
With a dragon sheath bright and new
When Thorstein rammed the enemy boat
And Sea Serpent remained afloat,
Njörðr smiled and the clan had won
Saved by Sven, brave Bersi's son
The Sword of the Saxons is strong and true
With a dragon sheath bright and new
The Sword of the Saxons is strong and true

The Dragon Sword

With a dragon sheath bright and new

Thorstein was happy with the pace. He could see the banks of the river and the other ships. Knowing where the danger lay in a sea battle was all. We had enjoyed victory in minor sea skirmishes, but this would be a major battle. If we lost, we would die! I saw now that we had an advantage for there were no ships before us. The ones at the rear of this drekar wedge would have ships on either side to contend with. On the other hand, we would be the first to strike! It was Griotard who warned us of action. "The hersir comes back from the prow! The Saxons are just four lengths ahead! Larboard crew, you will cease rowing on Thorstein's command. Then you will arm yourselves!"

Dreng asked, "Will we need shields?"

Griotard laughed, "We may need them, but it will be better this day if we fight without them!"

I had already decided to fight with a seax as well as Oathsword. The deck of any ship would be crowded enough without trying to find space to hold a shield and a sword. This would be close in fighting.

Sweyn Skull Taker reached us and donned his helmet. He drew his sword and I saw that in his left hand he held a small hand axe. "There are a pair of large Saxon ships and they are going to grapple the jarl's ship. We will ram the one on the Jarl's right. Steerboard crew, wait until we strike before you stack your oars!" As he climbed up, he stuck the axe in his belt so that he had two hands free. My sword was in its sheath and my seax in my belt.

Just then Thorstein shouted, "Larboard oars in!"

Alf and I pulled in our oar and stood. We were close to the mastfish and we stacked it before flanking the hersir who stood on the gunwale and held on to the forestay. It was then I saw the Saxon. She was higher in the water than we were. Their larboard oars were still rowing but we were approaching rapidly and remained unseen. Thorstein won the race and he turned to strike the Saxon just as I heard the order shouted to take in the larboard oars. I had just grabbed a stay to pull me up to the gunwale when our bow began to shatter the oars on the Saxon. Some must have managed to withdraw them, but some did not, and I heard screams from those who were speared by shards of ash. Then the side of our bow struck the Saxon and had I not had good balance and grip then I would have been crushed between the colliding hulls. As it was, I barely kept my balance. Thorstein must have instructed his boys well for grappling hooks were thrown to secure us to the Saxon. The hulls ground together until the power of the three drekar heading downstream began to push back the two Saxon ships. All this could change in a moment for more Saxons were heading for us.

Sweyn Skull Taker used the roll of the drekar to leap up and grab the Saxon's gunwale. Sweyn and I emulated him. I clambered over the side and saw a mass of Saxons awaiting us. Axes and blades came down to try to take us as we struggled aboard. I used a stay on the Saxon ship to pull myself up. One of the Saxons hurled a spear at me, and I barely moved out of the way in time. I leapt in the air as though I was diving into the sea. It was a risk, but the packed Saxons below would cushion my fall and I was wearing mail. One sword laid open my cheek as I fell into them, but the other blades caught on my mail byrnie. I was indeed cushioned as I landed but even as I heard the air being driven from Saxons, I was drawing my seax. I pushed into the face of one Saxon with my right hand to help me gain my footing while I ripped the seax across the throat of a second. A spear came at me and I had to use my seax to deflect it. I saw that Sweyn Skull Taker had also leapt and he was kneeling to hack into the skull of a Saxon as his sons leapt to land feet first next to him. They distracted the Saxons enough for me to draw Oathsword. As I had seen in the battles I had fought thus far the sight of the blade inspired fear. Writing on a blade meant it was special. I brought it over to split the skull of the spear-wielding Saxon and then felt a blow to my back. I whirled around with my seax and sliced into the arm of the Saxon who had tried to slash my back with his sword. He had not timed it well and I guessed had struck with the flat of his blade.

The rest of our crew had now boarded, Sweyn Skull Taker's hearth weru in a circle around him. I saw Lodvir's new men had done the same. None of them wore mail and were more evenly matched with the Saxons. I watched Sweyn Skull Taker make his way back to the steering board. Men were guarding the helmsman and the priests who stood there chanting their curses. The crew knew that, as in all sea battles, they would either win or die. There would be no prisoners taken. I used both of my weapons as though they were one. I slashed stabbed and hacked at every Saxon no matter which way they faced. The deck of the ship was soon slippery with blood. Sweyn Skull Taker slew the helmsman as his son, Sweyn, hacked through the ropes which worked the steering board. It was then I noticed that the deck was not only slippery with blood, but there was also seawater and that told me the Saxon had sprung strakes. That was confirmed when I saw that we were level with *'Sea Serpent'*. That would not last for we were sinking.

"Hersir, we are sinking!"

"Back to *'Serpent'*! Cut the grappling hooks!" As the men began to leave, he cupped his hands and shouted, "Jarl Harald, the Saxon is sinking!"

Most of our crew had already managed to leave the doomed Saxon ship. There were just ten of us left and, as we slew any surviving Saxons, we made our way across a ship which was now considerably lower than our drekar. Lodvir's men helped him up the side and then we did the same for Sweyn. I was just about to follow him when a voice behind me shouted, "Dane, I beg you, save my life!"

I turned and saw, emerging from a sea of Saxon corpses, the priest from the church in Hrofecester. Alf and Sweyn One Eye had begun to climb, and I saw that the Saxon ship was about to slip beneath the waves. Now that the grappling lines had been cut there was nothing else to keep her afloat. After sheathing my seax and sword I was about to turn and follow Alf when Mary's voice came into my head. She just said, *'Sven!'* Nothing more but it was enough to make me hold out a hand. "Hurry!" He scrambled towards me.

Lodvir shouted, "Leave him!" I said nothing but I grabbed the rope which Alf threw to me and which snaked down.

Just then I heard the hersir shout, "To the steerboard side! Repel boarders!"

The priest had managed to reach me although the water was up to his waist. I held out my arm and he grasped it. I began to climb but as the rest of the crew were fighting yet another Saxon ship there was no one to help me. The kyrtle beneath my mail was now sodden and with the weight of the priest, I was in danger of falling to the sea and certain death. As the Saxon ship sank, I had the weight of the priest as well as my mail. "Either use your feet to climb or die!"

He nodded and grabbed the rope. His weight lessened a little and when he began to climb it became easier for me. As soon as he put two hands on the rope, I was able to climb and roll over our gunwale. I had done all that I could for him and the hersir needed me. Leaving him to save himself I drew my weapons and ran to the hersir's side. I was just in time for a Saxon had climbed over the bow of *'Serpent'* and was running towards his unguarded left side. I did not hesitate but rammed Oathsword so hard into the man's side that my blade stuck in the gunwale. I let go and grabbed his sword. I used it to hack through the grappling rope which tied us together. Then I picked up his body and hurled it over the side into the Saxon ship. It, too, must have sprung a strake for it was lower and there was water there.

Sweyn Skull Taker shouted, "Throw the bodies back! Let us sink her!

Others had also cut ropes and the last few who had boarded us were now being butchered. The bodies were dropped into the Saxon. That prevented more men from boarding us and their weight helped to damage the Saxon. I saw that some were so heavy that they smashed through the deck of the Saxon vessel. I could see water in the hold. She was sinking. Some Saxons tried to climb aboard us, but they were soaked and wet, and there was no friendly rope to hold them. Sweyn Skull Taker knew the battle was not over and he looked around to see if there was danger from any other Saxon ship. There was still fighting taking place but most of the Saxon vessels had either been sunk or were heading towards the southern shore. Our tactics and nautical wedge had worked. We kept reefed sails until the last of the Saxons were eliminated and then watched as first the king and then the jarl unfurled their sails and began to head east.

I could not help smiling but I saw that Sweyn Skull Taker was not happy, "You nearly lost your life for a priest of the White Christ! What possessed you?"

I could not say Mary's voice in my head for it sounded foolish even to me. I just shrugged and said, "I know not."

"And what will you do with him now?"

I had not thought of that. He was my responsibility, and I would have to feed him. Perhaps the hersir was right. Should I hurl him overboard? I knew I could not kill that way. "I could sell him."

"And where would you do that? King Forkbeard would not condone it and a priest with soft hands would make a useless thrall. You already have one Christian thrall who serves little purpose unless you decide to bed her. What do you want with a priest?"

I had no answer. I walked over to him. The man was still cowering close to the place I had first used to row. He could not have understood our words but the gestures and raised voices would have left him in no doubt that he was not welcome.

"Master, I will be your thrall! I can help you."

His voice was quiet and in Saxon. No other would be able to hear or understand him, "And what could you do for me? You have soft hands and I do not need a cleric."

His eyes went to Oathsword, "I know about the sword!"

I took it out and held it to his throat, "Do not lie! What does a priest know about weapons?"

His voice was calmer as though he was on firmer ground and his words had the ring of the truth about them, "When I was a novice, I worked in Wintan-Caestre and copied documents. When I saw the blade

207

in the church, I knew what it was for I had seen those words, *'Melchior made me'* on a parchment. The sword was Alfred's Gift."

I felt a chill run up my spine. How could he have known that?

"It is a Dragon Sword and was ordered to be made by King Alfred. He gave it as a christening gift to King Guthrum when he became a Christian."

It had belonged to the Dane who had almost conquered Englaland. The sword in my hand seemed to speak to me; it said, *'I am that sword'*! I now knew whence came the sword. I had its story and that completed the circle that had begun when the Saxon King had bestowed the sword on a defeated enemy who abandoned the old gods for the White Christ. For some reason, I knew not what, I felt that my father was now happy. His spirit was no longer tormented and he was content.

Epilogue

I did not immediately tell the others what he had said, and I do not know why. They accepted that I had saved the priest's life for no apparent reason and put it down to the Norns. I kept him by the prow where I fed him. He was not bound for where could he go? Aksel and the others watched over him. There were spare blankets from the men who had died.

I wanted Mary to question him as she knew priests and I did not. The man had seemed like he was speaking the truth but who knew if that was the case. The first day at sea I asked him more about the sword. It seemed that Guthrum had been christened as Æthelstan. *Wyrd* for that was the name of Alfred's grandson. He had ruled as the king of Danelaw for ten years and then died. The priest, Father Nicholas, said that the sword was buried with him. Upon further questioning he revealed that a Saxon, Æthelmaer, a thegn from Wessex had coveted the sword and stolen it, defacing it to hide its origin. I knew that the man I had killed was no thegn and was too young to be Æthelmaer. The sword had enjoyed an interesting journey thus far and I wondered how much more there was to learn.

We were halfway home when a storm came upon us so suddenly that we barely had time to reef the sail. We had to take to the oars, and we rowed for half a night while we fought the storm. We were in danger of losing all the treasure we had taken as well as the ship and our lives. When dawn broke it was to an almost empty sea save for **'Stormbird'** and wreckage. We were all set to repair the ship when Aksel came down to the mast fish, "Sven Saxon Sword your priest has gone."

"Gone? Left us? How?" It was a foolish thing to say for there was only one place he could have gone, overboard!

He shrugged, "We heard him crying and praying during the storm and then he stopped. When we woke, he was gone. Some of the waves were fierce and had we not held on to the oars then…"

Thorstein shook his head and said, "It is the Norns and was meant to be. The sea has taken him and that is all there is to it." He gave me a shrewd look. "I think that he has told you all that he can about the sword."

"How…?"

"I watched and saw that when you did speak the sword was always unsheathed. I knew enough Saxon to have worked out some of the words."

209

Sweyn One Eye and Alf said, "What did you learn?"

There was no getting around it and I could not lie to shield brothers. I told them.

They looked at the sword and Sweyn One Eye said, "Then it is truly magical, but I would not wear it. The sword was made by a Christian for a warrior who became a Christian. It is cursed. Better, cousin, that you throw it into the sea."

Lodvir shook his head, "Like Sweyn One Eye I would not wield it, but it has chosen you for a reason, Sven and you cannot rid yourself of it. The blade might well be cursed but the curse will only affect you. For the rest of us, it seems to bring good luck. You are the only one who can wield Oathsword, the last sword of King Guthrum the Dane!"

The End

Norse Calendar

Gormánuður October 14th - November 13th
Ýlir November 14th - December 13th
Mörsugur December 14th - January 12th
Þorri - January 13th - February 11th
Gói - February 12th - March 13th
Einmánuður - March 14th - April 13th
Harpa April 14th - May 13th
Skerpla - May 14th - June 12th
Sólmánuður - June 13th - July 12th
Heyannir - July 13th - August 14th
Tvímánuður - August 15th - September 14th
Haustmánuður September 15th-October 13th

Glossary

Beardestapol – Barnstaple
Beck- a stream
Blót – a blood sacrifice made by a jarl
Bondi- Viking farmers who fight
Bjorr – Beaver
Byrnie- a mail or leather shirt reaching down to the knees
Cantwareburh- Canterbury
Chape- the tip of a scabbard
Drekar- a Dragon ship (a Viking warship) pl. drekar
Dun Holm Durham
Dyflin- Old Norse for Dublin
Eoforwic- Saxon for York
Føroyar- Faroe Islands
Fey- having second sight
Firkin- a barrel containing eight gallons (usually beer)
Fret-a sea mist
Fyrd-the Saxon levy
Galdramenn- wizard
Gighesbore – Guisborough
Gippeswic- Ipswich
Heiða-býr – Hedeby in Schleswig- destroyed in 1066
Hersir- a Viking landowner and minor noble. It ranks below a jarl
Herterpol – Hartlepool
Hoggs or Hogging- when the pressure of the wind causes the stern
or the bow to droop
Hrofescester- Rochester, Kent
Hundred- Saxon military organization. (One hundred men from an
area-led by a thegn or gesith)
Isle of Greon- Isle of Grain (Thames Estuary)
Jarl- Norse earl or lord
Joro-goddess of the earth
kjerringa - Old Woman- the solid block in which the mast rested
Knarr- a merchant ship or a coastal vessel
Kyrtle-woven top
Mast fish- two large racks on a ship designed to store the mast
when not required
Midden- a place where they dumped human waste
Miklagård - Constantinople

Njörðr- God of the sea

Nithing- A man without honour (Saxon)

Ocmundtune- Oakhampton

Odin- The 'All Father' God of war, also associated with wisdom, poetry, and magic (The Ruler of the gods).

Østersøen – The Baltic Sea

Ran- Goddess of the sea

Roof rock- slate

Saami- the people who live in what is now Northern Norway/Sweden

Sabrina- The River Severn

Scree- loose rocks in a glacial valley

Seax – short sword

Sennight- seven nights- a week

Sheerstrake- the uppermost strake in the hull

Sheet- a rope fastened to the lower corner of a sail

Shroud- a rope from the masthead to the hull amidships

Skald- a Viking poet and singer of songs

Skeggox – an axe with a shorter beard on one side of the blade

Skreið- stockfish (any fish which is preserved)

Skjalborg- shield wall

Snekke- a small warship

Stad- Norse settlement

Stays- ropes running from the masthead to the bow

Strake- the wood on the side of a drekar

Tarn- small lake (Norse)

The Norns- The three sisters who weave webs of intrigue for men

Thing-Norse for a parliament or a debate (Tynwald in the Isle of Man)

Thor's day- Thursday

Threttanessa- a drekar with 13 oars on each side.

Thrall- slave

Trenail- a round wooden peg used to secure strakes

Úlfarrberg- Helvellyn

Ullr-Norse God of Hunting

Ulfheonar-an elite Norse warrior who wore a wolf skin over his armour

Verðandi -the Norn who sees the future

Volva- a witch or healing woman in Norse culture

Walhaz -Norse for the Welsh (foreigners)

Waite- a Viking word for farm

Withy- the mechanism connecting the steering board to the ship

The Dragon Sword

Wintan-ceastre -Winchester
Woden's day- Wednesday
Wyrd- Fate
Wyrme- Norse for Dragon
Yard- a timber from which the sail is suspended

Historical Notes

The dragon sword is a blade of my own imagination although King Alfred did give a sword to the illegitimate son of Prince Edward, the king's son. Aethelstan became the first king accorded the title King of Englaland. As readers of my books will know swords are always important. This series will reflect that.

The story of the hatred between Sigrid the Haughty and King Olaf was well known at the time. King Olaf's rejection of her would eventually lead to King Olaf's death at the Battle of Svolder. That is another tale! King Sweyn Forkbeard raided Somerset and fought Ordwulf. He raided and took Man as well as sacking Tavistock Abbey which, until the Danish raid was the largest abbey in Wessex. The raid on Hrofecester and the subsequent battle were historical events. King Forkbeard was, like his son, Cnut, a Christian but many Danes were not. This saga reflects that.

- King Cnut- WB Bartlett
- Vikings- Life and Legends -British Museum
- Saxon, Norman and Viking by Terence Wise (Osprey)
- The Vikings (Osprey) -Ian Heath
- Byzantine Armies 668-1118 (Osprey)-Ian Heath
- Romano-Byzantine Armies 4th- 9th Century (Osprey) -David Nicholle
- The Walls of Constantinople AD 324-1453 (Osprey) -Stephen Turnbull
- Viking Longship (Osprey) - Keith Durham
- The Vikings- David Wernick (Time-Life)
- The Vikings in England Anglo-Danish Project
- Anglo Saxon Thegn AD 449-1066- Mark Harrison (Osprey)
- Viking Hersir- 793-1066 AD - Mark Harrison (Osprey)
- National Geographic- March 2017
- British Kings and Queens- Mike Ashley

Other books by Griff Hosker

If you enjoyed reading this book, then why not read another one by
the author?

Ancient History

The Sword of Cartimandua Series
(Germania and Britannia 50 A.D. – 128 A.D.)
Ulpius Felix- Roman Warrior (prequel)
The Sword of Cartimandua
The Horse Warriors
Invasion Caledonia
Roman Retreat
Revolt of the Red Witch
Druid's Gold
Trajan's Hunters
The Last Frontier
Hero of Rome
Roman Hawk
Roman Treachery
Roman Wall
Roman Courage

The Wolf Warrior series
(Britain in the late 6th Century)
Saxon Dawn
Saxon Revenge
Saxon England
Saxon Blood
Saxon Slayer
Saxon Slaughter
Saxon Bane
Saxon Fall: Rise of the Warlord
Saxon Throne
Saxon Sword

Medieval History

The Dragon Heart Series
Viking Slave
Viking Warrior
Viking Jarl
Viking Kingdom
Viking Wolf
Viking War
Viking Sword
Viking Wrath
Viking Raid
Viking Legend
Viking Vengeance
Viking Dragon
Viking Treasure
Viking Enemy
Viking Witch
Viking Blood
Viking Weregeld
Viking Storm
Viking Warband
Viking Shadow
Viking Legacy
Viking Clan
Viking Bravery

The Norman Genesis Series
Hrolf the Viking
Horseman
The Battle for a Home
Revenge of the Franks
The Land of the Northmen
Ragnvald Hrolfsson
Brothers in Blood
Lord of Rouen
Drekar in the Seine
Duke of Normandy
The Duke and the King

New World Series

The Dragon Sword

Blood on the Blade
Across the Seas
The Savage Wilderness
The Bear and the Wolf

The Vengeance Trail

The Reconquista Chronicles
Castilian Knight
El Campeador
The Lord of Valencia

The Aelfraed Series
(Britain and Byzantium 1050 A.D. - 1085 A.D.)
Housecarl
Outlaw
Varangian

**The Anarchy Series England
1120-1180**
English Knight
Knight of the Empress
Northern Knight
Baron of the North
Earl
King Henry's Champion
The King is Dead
Warlord of the North
Enemy at the Gate
The Fallen Crown
Warlord's War
Kingmaker
Henry II
Crusader
The Welsh Marches
Irish War
Poisonous Plots
The Princes' Revolt
Earl Marshal

**Border Knight
1182-1300**

The Dragon Sword

Sword for Hire
Return of the Knight
Baron's War
Magna Carta
Welsh Wars
Henry III
The Bloody Border
Baron's Crusade
Sentinel of the North
War in the West

Sir John Hawkwood Series
France and Italy 1339- 1387
Crécy: The Age of the Archer
Man at Arms (February 2021)

Lord Edward's Archer
Lord Edward's Archer
King in Waiting
An Archer's Crusade

Struggle for a Crown
1360- 1485
Blood on the Crown
To Murder A King
The Throne
King Henry IV
The Road to Agincourt
St Crispin's Day

Tales from the Sword

Conquistador
England and America in the 16th Century
Conquistador (Coming in 2021)

Modern History

The Napoleonic Horseman Series
Chasseur à Cheval

The Dragon Sword

Napoleon's Guard
British Light Dragoon
Soldier Spy
1808: The Road to Coruña
Talavera
The Lines of Torres Vedras
Bloody Badajoz
The Road to France

The Lucky Jack American Civil War series
Rebel Raiders
Confederate Rangers
The Road to Gettysburg

The British Ace Series
1914
1915 Fokker Scourge
1916 Angels over the Somme
1917 Eagles Fall
1918 We will remember them
From Arctic Snow to Desert Sand
Wings over Persia

Combined Operations series
1940-1945
Commando
Raider
Behind Enemy Lines
Dieppe
Toehold in Europe
Sword Beach
Breakout
The Battle for Antwerp
King Tiger
Beyond the Rhine
Korea
Korean Winter

Other Books
Great Granny's Ghost (Aimed at 9-14-year-old young people)

For more information on all of the books then please visit the author's web site at www.griffhosker.com where there is a link to contact him or visit his Facebook page: GriffHosker at Sword Books

Printed in Great Britain
by Amazon